A BLACKBIRD I

From the celebrated author of A
BLACKBIRD IN DARKNESS and A
BLACKBIRD IN SILVER, comes a third
novel, A BLACKBIRD IN AMBER. It
can be read both as a sequel and on its
own, for it is a fascinating fantasy story in
its own right.

The serpent, M'gulfn, the supernatural
channel of all evil, had been dead for
twenty-five years. But its death has released
a great energy into the world – an energy
which makes sorcery possible.

Gorethria is now ruled by the wicked
Xaedrek who practises a false, warped
sorcery in order to restore Gorethria to its
former glory. Melkavesh, a natural
sorceress, aware of Xaedrek's evil brand of
sorcery, is also deeply in love with him.
When he will not renounce his 'evil', she
flees to a nearby kingdom, Kristillia. Her
task has only just begun. She is confident
and optimistic – even though her friend,
Kharan, points out that the culmination of
her plans may well be a terrible and bloody
war.

About the Author

Freda Warrington was born in Leicester in 1956 and studied graphic design at Loughborough College of Art and Design. She has worked as an in-house designer for a local building company in Hitchin. She is now a freelance designer and lives in Leicester. Her first two books, A BLACKBIRD IN SILVER and A BLACKBIRD IN DARKNESS have both been published to great acclaim.

'Enjoyable readable fantasy . . . many cuts above the average'

Anne McCaffrey

A Blackbird in Amber

FREDA WARRINGTON

NEW ENGLISH LIBRARY
Hodder and Stoughton

*The characters and situations in
this book are entirely imaginary
and bear no relation to any real
person or actual happening*

A New English Library Original
Publication, 1988

NEL Paperback edition, 1988

British Library C.I.P.

Warrington, Freda
  A blackbird in amber.
  I. Title
  823'.914 [F]   PR6073.A74/

  ISBN 0-450-41903-7

Printed and bound in Great
Britain for Hodder and Stoughton
Paperbacks, a division of Hodder
and Stoughton Limited, Mill
Road, Dunton Green, Sevenoaks,
Kent (Editorial Office: 47 Bedford
Square, London WC1B 3DP) by
Richard Clay Limited, Bungay,
Suffolk. Photoset by Rowland
Phototypesetting Limited, Bury St
Edmunds, Suffolk.

Dedicated with love to Julie, Cath, Caroline, Keren;
Annette and Richard; and with special thanks to Mum,
the sorceress of the typewriter.

Nothing is ever forgotten . . .

Contents

Vardrav

Introduction

'Now I am not saying that once the Serpent is dead, all the Earth will become sweet and fair for eternity; on the contrary, new evils may spring up in its place. There will be a wild, wild age in which sorcery, a bright magic and a dark one, will hold sway; an age of vigour, as opposed to this age of lethargy and decay. The change must take place, or your world is doomed.'

The Lady of H'tebhmella.

A Blackbird in Silver and *A Blackbird in Darkness* told of a malevolent creature, the Worm or Serpent M'gulfn, and the perilous journey of three people to destroy it. Estarinel set out to slay it because it had ravaged his peaceful land, Forluin, but Ashurek of Gorethria's reasons were more complex. His brother, the Emperor Meshurek, had fallen into the power of the Shana (or demons) who were the Worm's servants. Once Gorethria's most ruthless war leader, Ashurek came to see that the Empire was evil, and he became an outcast from his land. Then his love, the Sorceress Silvren, was imprisoned by the Shana, and he discovered that the only way to free her and destroy the Empire was to uproot the evil at its source – the Worm itself. The third traveller was Medrian of Alaak, a woman who understood even better than Ashurek that M'gulfn was the cause of the world's ills.

But in the course of their harrowing journey, Ashurek, Estarinel and Medrian discovered that their Quest was more than a personal one. They met an enchantress, Arlenmia, a fanatical idealist who believed that when the Worm's power became total, Earth would be transformed into a kind of

1

heaven. But she was wrong; unless M'gulfn died, Earth would become a living hell. Then the three found out that they were being manipulated by supernatural beings known as the Guardians or Grey Ones. They were neutral, concerned only with maintaining a balance of energies in the universe. To them the Worm was no mere creature, but a concentration of vast power which must be dispersed at all costs. Human suffering did not concern them. While appearing to help the three, the Guardians deliberately concealed the knowledge that when the Serpent died, the Earth itself would be destroyed.

Embittered by this knowledge, Ashurek became hell-bent on achieving this destruction. But the mystical bird, Miril, showed him at last that there was a gentler way for the Quest to be fulfilled, and after many dreadful revelations and a nightmarish ultimate journey, Ashurek, Estarinel and Medrian finally succeeded in slaying the Serpent M'gulfn, and the world was preserved.

Then Ashurek swore that he would never again wield a weapon, and he and Silvren went to live peacefully on another world, Ikonus. Estarinel returned to Forluin in sorrow, for although his land was now safe, he had lost Medrian, whom he loved; only a sacrifice on her part had made the Serpent's death possible. In time, though, he rediscovered his love for a childhood friend, Lilithea, and together she and Miril showed him that happiness was to be found after all.

Now the world was ready to realise the Lady of H'tebhmella's prophecy. As Silvren once told Ashurek, 'This world has a bright and vigorous future with sorcery, not the sick power of the Serpent, holding sway.' But the transition was inevitably going to be complex and painful, by no means resembling the gentle growth of a plant; rather it would be like a long and difficult childbirth.

About Gorethria

There are matters not recorded in the first two books which need some explanation: namely, what happened to Gorethria after Ashurek deserted his command and disappeared into Tearn.

While Ashurek possessed the evil Egg-Stone, its power flowed through him and into his soldiers, locking them together into one invincible force. This had enabled only half the Imperial Army to hold the Empire, while the other half sailed the Eastern Ocean to invade Tearn. When Ashurek fled, the Egg-Stone's power drained from his army and they were left leaderless, demoralised and confused. Driven back by Tearnian resistance, they finally abandoned Tearn altogether and fled back to their motherland, the once-proud fleet straggling home in tattered threes and fours.

In the Empire itself, the Vardravians took advantage of the sudden weakening of their oppressors. Although some of the more secure conquests, such as Patavria and An'raaga, were hardly affected, everywhere else rebel armies drove the Gorethrians further and further back. Soon Gorethria could no longer declare that she had an Empire.

At this time Meshurek was still Emperor, openly despised by his own people but impossible to depose, because he had the protection of the demon Meheg-Ba.

However, a day came when Meshurek departed for Terthria and never returned. As was told in *A Blackbird in Silver*, he went to meet Ashurek, who killed him. But the people of Gorethria did not know this. To them, the entire royal family – Ordek XIV, the Empress Melkish and their children Orkesh, Meshurek and Ashurek – had died or vanished inexplicably, leaving the Empire in ruins and Gorethria herself in chaos.

Those members of the Inner Council and Senate who had not succumbed to Meheg-Ba's evil rallied and tried to maintain order. Answers were demanded, but a search party dispatched to Terthria discovered nothing. (The demon Meheg-Ba had always been careful to conceal its presence by erasing people's memories, along with other aspects of intellect.) Although Ashurek was rumoured still to be alive, he could not be found.

The people of Shalekahh were furious, and a ban on

further research failed to quiet them. A violent struggle for power ensued. Neither Meshurek, Ashurek nor their sister Orkesh had left any children, and none of the many rival claimants could prove the absolute right to the throne demanded by Gorethrian tradition. For centuries, Gorethrians had all been of one mind, united by their mutual desire for supremacy over every other race in Vardrav, so the anarchy into which the country now descended was as disastrous to their pride as to their national security. The sorrow of those who remembered the glory of Ordek XIV's rule was very real, and so unbearable to some that suicide became epidemic.

In the midst of this turmoil, the powerful rebel nations were advancing vengefully on their oppressors. Divided, anarchic, barely able to defend herself, Gorethria's destruction seemed imminent.

What averted that fate was itself a horrific kind of miracle, even more mysterious than Meshurek's fate. It began with unnatural weather, horrendous dark storms which smothered the whole continent. Long-dormant volcanoes became active again, earthquakes shook Vardrav along its length, tidal waves crashed like granite against the coasts. Plagues broke out; deformed, savage beasts wandered the land; and a nightmare of bloodshed and fear descended. A terrible despair gripped Vardrav, all sense of purpose was lost, and the rebel armies disintegrated and fled.

Though few knew it, this time of darkness was the manifestation of the Serpent's growing power over the Earth. When M'gulfn was slain, the darkness ended very suddenly, and a sweet, liquid dawn brought normality back to the whole world. Even the least superstitious muttered of serpents and gods; and some of the rebels said bitterly that the Serpent had protected Gorethria, its favoured land.

In Gorethria itself, the shock of these strange events had a sobering effect. The internal warring ceased and people began to speak of the need for unity, to take advantage of the respite before the Vardravian forces mustered again.

It was a need glibly expressed, but hard to put into practice.

4

The harm done by Meshurek was not to be undone in a few months, even years. The reformed army was disillusioned and badly disciplined. The Inner Council hung onto a tentative regency, but the rivalry over the throne continued. For eleven years Gorethria stumbled on with no monarch; and Gorethria without an Emperor was, as everyone knew, like a body without a head.

Eventually an Emperor was crowned, but this caused no lightning reversal of Gorethria's fortunes. The populace were appeased for a time, but given no real cause to feel encouraged or inspired. Orhdrek I was a ten-year-old child; a figurehead, not a real leader. The Vardravian armies were pushing closer again, while the Imperial forces remained demoralised and purposeless.

Evidently Gorethria's fate had only been delayed, not averted. Those years passed like a slow-motion nightmare, the interminable winding down of a clock in a void. Shalekahh's intellectuals continued to ponder angrily on why this had happened to them, once the most brilliant and ruthless race on Earth. *Why?* And it was sometimes said that if ever a man appeared who could tell them why, he would be the one to lead them to a glorious future.

But this was a touch of black humour, because most had concluded that there was no answer, and that Gorethria had no future.

1

A Survivor of the Serpent

DUKE XAEDREK of Shalekahh struggled to wake from the dream, but it held him, a velvet trap.

He very rarely dreamed. The last time, some years previously, had been a long, detailed nightmare about his mother and father. On waking a messenger had arrived to inform him that they were dead, lost in war. Since then he had dreaded dreams. Despite that, even in the throes of subconscious vision, some part of his mind remained detached, watching the strange scenes with analytical coldness.

There was a ship, delicately built of pale wood, drifting with obscure purpose in a pearl-green ocean. On the ship was a child with red hair. No ordinary red, but the dark, iridescent plum of copper beech leaves, mingled with the rose and gold lights of sunset. This vision seemed to have no beginning, no end, and no meaning. Yet it persisted as a glimmering backdrop to the rest of the dream, which was startlingly vivid, yet equally devoid of sense.

Xaedrek found himself in the Emperor's palace, moving slowly between the marble pillars of a long, salt-white hall. The walls were lined with the portraits of all the Gorethrian rulers since the first Ordek; hawk-faced men and women, with dark brown-purple skin and luminous brooding eyes. The legendary Empress Melkavesh, her white hair the only sign of her great age. Ruby-eyed Surukish I, from whose female line Xaedrek himself was descended. Her son, Ordek XIII, and grandson Varancrek II, and Varancrek's son, the eagle-fierce Ordek XIV, who was father of the infamous Meshurek II, wrecker of the Empire.

In the dream Xaedrek had the strange impression that he was underwater. He was drifting down the hall, not walking, and everything was surrounded by an aureole of blurred light. A few feet ahead of him was a tall woman with long, golden hair, and he observed without any sense of surprise that she was translucent, as if formed of a liquid slightly denser than the water. He could see straight through her to the portraits beyond, yet he knew that she was real, and should not be in the palace. In slow motion he moved to her side, purposing to challenge her.

She was staring at the painting of Meshurek; the broad chiselled face with its cold half-smile and deep-set, disturbed eyes. Next to it, Meshurek's twin brother Ashurek was captured exactly by the artist. The brilliant green eyes in that dark, high-cheekboned face were lifelike in their intensity. Xaedrek felt an illogical need to stop the woman from looking at those portraits and attend to him instead. He shouted, and although his voice made no sound, she turned to him as if she had heard.

Then he saw that, despite the pale hair, she was Gorethrian. Dark-skinned, arrogant, a terrible cold passion burning in her face. The shock-wave of some unknown, unpleasant emotion shuddered through him so that he could neither move nor speak, but it was not her expression, nor the wrongness of her being there that distressed him. It was simply her hair. A superficial detail, yet in the dream it seemed all-important, shimmering with malevolent esoteric meaning. No Gorethrian had ever had blond hair.

Then she was no longer at his side, but walking up an endless white staircase, while he was helpless to do anything but stare after her. The water swirled and darkened around him. The darkness became total, he could not escape it, could not breathe – he flailed wildly, fighting to wake up. He was being crushed by an intolerable pressure, slow, heavy waves of power which emanated from two massive, opal-smooth globes of rock. At first he could only sense them in

8

the void; then, as if starlight had begun to glimmer round their edges, he could see them, perfect spheres from which a luminous energy flowed in deep, soul-annihilating pulses. This seemed of such vast, profound importance that the world itself was dwarfed, but the actual significance remained, agonisingly, just out of his grasp. Again he struggled, but the weight of the dream pinned him. A sensation of dread and awe and inexpressibly poignant weirdness filled him, something that he yearned to capture and escape at the same time – his mouth stretched in a silent cry as the two terrible spheres thrust him towards oblivion with their leaden sweetness.

Then the child on the ship was there again, and she released from her hand a little bird the exact red of her hair, and at this Xaedrek woke up violently, shaking and sweating.

Around him the air was as thick as musty black velvet. He could not get his breath, as if a malign power were still pressing down on him. In panic he pushed back the silk sheets which were clinging damply to him, and half-fell from the bed. He was across the chamber and groping for the door before he became awake enough for reason to reassert itself.

It had been no more than a stupid, childish nightmare, the cause of which was obvious. Recovering his composure, he walked steadily across the pitch-black room to the window, intending to let in some fresh air. He found the edge of the curtain, its jewelled fringe cold and heavy against his palm. Drawing it back, he was astonished to find that it was not night, but broad daylight. He had slept well into the morning. Around his mansion the city of Shalekahh shimmered like an opal under a perfect sky, her delicate white towers gleaming with flashes of colour.

Xaedrek turned back to the room to see the darkness bleeding from it, slowly, like ink. He stood for a few moments in thought. Then he crossed to a chair, put on a robe of dark green satin, and sat down at his onyx-and-silver desk to reflect.

'What manner of nightmare was it?' he asked himself. 'That of my parents was no mere dream, but foreknowledge

9

of their death. Yet this was different. Mental impressions induced by an actual – presence, whatever – in the room?'

Xaedrek had a scientific mind, not prone to flights of fancy. He knew that the intense darkness within his chamber had not been a product of his imagination. Rather, it had been a similar darkness to that which he had conjured by a certain experiment the previous day. The experiment had left him disturbed and exhausted, hence his long sleep.

'However,' he murmured, 'it was not disquiet that made me dream. It was an actual return of that darkness.'

He considered the effect that the dream had had upon him, and discovered that the lasting impression was not one of horror or dread, but of exhilaration. Promise. The experiment had not failed after all, and he was on the verge of discovering something, the existence of which Meshurek had never conceived.

Elated, eager to progress his work, he summoned a servant and asked for his breakfast to be prepared. He bathed and dressed in a robe of white silk, heavily embroidered with silver thread and jet beads. He paused briefly to look out of the window as a line of Imperial Cavalry passed along the street below. Xaedrek sneered. They were bedraggled, battle-dusty. War was imminent, and they were all Gorethria possessed to defend herself!

The anger he felt at this was no uncontrolled, impotent emotion, but a lifelong passion, the sole motivating force of his life. It centred on the questions, how had Gorethria come to this, and what could he, Duke Xaedrek, do to restore her to her former glory?

Xaedrek was a court official, protector and friend to the young Emperor Orhdrek. At Xaedrek's own suggestion, Orhdrek had given him the task of researching into the disastrous events of recent years, which so far had been a mystery even to the wisest in Shalekahh. Why Ashurek had deserted his post of High Commander, just as the Gorethrian army was poised to vanquish Tearn. What had possessed him to murder his own sister, Princess Orkesh. And above all, what had become of the hated Emperor Meshurek, who vanished without trace some four years later. For the sixteen chaotic years since these events, theories had abounded. But Xaedrek was sick of theories. He wanted the truth.

There was a longstanding ban by the Inner Council against such research, imposed to prevent people's ill will towards the royal household from becoming something more dangerous. However, it had been easy enough for Xaedrek to persuade Orhdrek that it was time for the mystery to be solved. He had obtained the Emperor's personal consent to do anything he deemed necessary to that end.

Xaedrek made his way to the dining hall, a simple, beautiful room of marble, polished agate and gold. He asked a servant to bring some fruit, and sat abstractedly chewing a piece of spiced bread as he continued to pursue his thoughts.

Xaedrek, in the true Gorethrian mould, was tall and slim and graceful. He had a languid way of moving and a quality of stillness which could seem menacing, although his arched brows and well-shaped mouth lacked the grim set that marked most of the Gorethrian nobility. In a way that made him seem more dangerous, for it made the expression on his handsome face impossible to interpret. His skin was of a deep, sheeny brown with the merest hint of violet in it, and his irises were blood-red, like firelight glittering through garnets. He was only twenty-five, having inherited the dukedom at his father's early death, but despite his youth his long, silky black hair had touches of white at the front.

Ten years older than the Emperor Orhdrek, he had made a point of befriending the boy from his birth. Even as a child, Xaedrek knew that such care must one day repay him richly.

Indeed, it had already borne fruit. He had been allowed access to Meshurek's private chambers – sealed since his disappearance – and had found there, concealed by various ingenious devices, a remarkable collection of private papers and books. He had spent some weeks studying them, translating and interpreting and discarding until he finally reached what he became convinced was the heart of the enigma.

Meshurek had practised the lost art of summoning those beings called the Shana, or demons.

11

His records of what the demon Meheg-Ba had done for him – or demanded of him – were fragmented, hard to understand; Xaedrek realised that Meshurek had gone mad, just as everyone said. The details of the actual ritual of summoning were contained within an ancient book, evidently found by Meshurek in some forgotten corner of the palace library. It was hard to read. The pages were yellow, their edges crumbling to dust, and the ink was almost gone. But Xaedrek had spent hours studying the tome, struggling with every obscurity – just as the equally clever but less perceptive Meshurek had once done – until he felt confident that he understood the ritual well enough to make it work.

Xaedrek was not a fool. It was clear enough to him that the summoning of such a being was dangerous, that the bargains they offered were false and that all they desired was to leech strength, sanity, everything from the summoner. But he possessed an insatiable desire for knowledge that sometimes undermined his better judgement. Understanding the danger, curiosity still compelled him to practise the ritual. His advantage was that he went into it open-eyed, viewing it as a particularly risky experiment; his mind was calm and scientific, not ravaged by fear and paranoia as Meshurek's had been. Once he had encountered a Shanin, whatever happened, he would understand what had destroyed Gorethria.

Yesterday he had locked himself within a subterranean marble chamber and performed the long, arduous ritual. Once, twice, three times before exhaustion forced him to desist. And he had failed, no demon had materialised, not even the faintest glimmer of argent light in the blackness.

Cold and sick, his mouth thick with the tang of brass and dust, he had eventually collapsed, thinking he was about to die. But his bitterest emotion was frustration, the single thought, 'What did that idiot Meshurek do that I have failed to do?' That refusal to be beaten had given him the strength to escape the marble room, gain his bed and fall into hag-ridden sleep.

He took a long draught of a honeyed drink from an

12

exquisite glass cup. Even in these times, the craftsmanship of Shalekahh was unsurpassed. Rest, refreshment, thought, and daylight . . . all were excellent for putting problems into perspective. But he still could not accept that he had performed the summoning incorrectly.

Perhaps there were no longer any demons.

And yet, there had been *something*. A darkness, more than lack of light; a thrumming of power, like someone in another dimension repeatedly plucking a low string. A pressure in the air, something that had manifested itself a second time within his bedchamber – something that he had *seen*, draining from the air like liquid.

A wave of excitement shook him, but he suppressed it. 'Scientifically,' he thought with deliberate calmness, 'it must be possible to capture and channel that power.'

'Is anything wrong, Your Grace?' said a voice at his shoulder. He looked round and saw a serving-maid, about sixteen or seventeen, holding a large dish of fruit. She was neatly attired in a full-sleeved dress of russet silk. He lived alone and had few slaves, so was mildly surprised to see a new face.

'No. I'm just tired,' he said. 'I don't know you. How long have you been in my household?'

She seemed startled that he should take a personal interest in her, but she answered without any trace of servility, 'Seven days, Your Grace. Your steward has been training me. My name is Kharan.'

'And where do you come from?'

'An'raaga, Your Grace.'

'Ah, An'raaga. The "quiescent" land. Are you quiescent, Kharan?' The question sounded ominous. Xaedrek had the quiet, imposing presence that was not uncommon to Gorethrian nobility, and an ability to inspire terror in his subordinates without really trying. But this maid seemed to realise he was only teasing her.

'I suppose I am a fairly typical example of my race, sir,' she replied with a smile.

'What's this, a sense of humour?'

13

'If you prefer your servants humourless, Your Grace, I will oblige at once,' she answered, looking unwaveringly at him as if she were his equal. She was dark-haired and fair-skinned, not pretty, but something more than that. Her large eyes gathered light, and her smiling mouth and rounded figure radiated a very feminine charisma. He felt idly fascinated by her, as though he needed some distraction from the grave matters that occupied him. He thought again of the power that he had stirred, and felt a wave of exhilaration. Ambition. Gorethria's rebirth.

Carried along by it, his mood suddenly light, he asked impulsively, 'How would you like to be servant to the Emperor, Kharan?'

'Your Grace?' She was puzzled.

'Oh, I don't mean that child, Orhdrek,' he said quietly, grinning. 'I want you to stay with me. Well?'

He saw that the implication was not lost on her. It had been a reckless thing to say, the girl might have been a spy – but he doubted it. She did not have that haunted, insomniac look.

She stood very still beside his chair. He looked round to observe her expression, and their eyes met, hers as brown as ripe chestnuts, his ruby-brilliant. With a deliberate, graceful movement she leaned across him and slid the silver dish of fruit onto the agate table. He was enthralled by her, and she seemed to know it.

'Actually, Your Grace,' she replied with guileless honesty, 'I would much rather not be a servant at all.'

Gorethria's climate, always unpredictable, had become one of violent extremes. The worsening had begun around the time of Meshurek's disappearance, although that, surely, was coincidence. On the morning of Xaedrek's dream the sky had been a rich, shimmering blue, heavy with heat. Now, five days later, storms chased each other across the heavens, and the population of Shalekahh emerged only to carry out the most essential errands, wrapped in thick cloaks and cursing as they hurried through the savage wind and rain.

Kharan rose from the bed and went to the window to look up at the mauve sky and the jagged clouds skimming across it, the red of watered blood. Curtains of scarlet rain lashed Shalekahh's towers, drumming onto the broad marble streets so that a waist-high, pinkish mist was formed. Incessant crimson and green lightning threw buildings into dazzling relief, burning a confusion of images onto her eyes.

'This weather,' she said, clutching an embroidered gown around herself, 'I'll never get used to it.'

'If it worries you, close the curtain,' Xaedrek replied from where he reclined among the pillows of pale gold silk.

'Oh, I couldn't. It's horrible, but I can't help watching it. I wonder what causes it?'

'The world is changing,' he said cryptically. 'Forget the storm and come here.'

As she turned round to go to him, there was a knock on the door. Xaedrek, irritated but expressionless, got up to open it and found the captain of his personal guard outside.

'I hope you have a good reason for disturbing me, Baramek,' he said mildly. The man was a Gorethrian, uniformed in black war gear of leather and metal which was embellished with Xaedrek's ducal colours, red and white. Seeing Kharan, he looked at her with a mixture of embarrassment and disdain, but she returned his gaze coolly and with remarkable composure for one so young, let alone of an 'inferior' race.

Quickly returning his attention to the Duke, Baramek said, 'Something strange, Your Grace. An old woman, Tearnian by the look of her, has come to the house demanding to see you. I would have dispatched her, but she insists that you sent for her, so I thought I had better check with you first.'

'I sent for no one,' Xaedrek said.

'I thought not, Your Grace. My apologies for disturbing you. I'll dispose of her at once.'

'No – no, don't do that. I want to see her first. Go down and tell her that I will be there shortly.' Grimacing, the guard saluted and obeyed. Xaedrek's curiosity was such that he would not let even the smallest item slip past uninvestigated.

15

'Kharan,' the Duke said, 'I don't want you to stay in the servants' quarters. I'm going to arrange for you to have a room near mine. So you might as well go down and collect your personal belongings.'

'Oh – I've hardly got anything, my lord,' she said, startled.

'That can easily be remedied.' He smiled. 'And don't call me "lord", I have a name.'

A few minutes later Kharan was alone in the bedchamber, but smiling broadly at the silver-filigreed door. She had never understood what quality she possessed that men found so fascinating, but perceived nevertheless the wisdom of using it to her own advantage. Thus she had persuaded a slave-manager to bring her from a miserable, jungle-fringed province to Gorethria's capital. Thus she had obtained a post in the household of an aristocrat. And there was no doubt in her mind that being a mistress was infinitely better than being a servant – materially, if not spiritually.

Xaedrek entered his main reception room, a large hall whose high ceiling was supported by a double row of marble columns. The floor was tiled in a simple geometric pattern of black and white. Tapestries and paintings hung on the walls. The furniture was sparse but exquisite, silver and gold inlaid with various semi-precious minerals.

The old woman was waiting in the centre of the room, with Baramek at her side. However, Xaedrek's steward, Varian, was inexplicably slumped in a chair, sobbing.

'What is the matter with him?' Xaedrek asked. Varian, a Patavrian, had been with Xaedrek's family for years. He was a sullen but reliable man, always – until now – perfectly level-headed.

'I don't know, Your Grace,' the captain replied. 'I left him here with the woman, and when I returned, he was on the floor in a state of hysteria.'

'You had better take him to his sleeping quarters. Go on, quickly,' Xaedrek said brusquely, waving at the door. He waited until Baramek had helped the small, black-skinned man out of the hall. Then he turned his attention to the woman.

16

She was perhaps seventy – old by Tearnian standards, if not by Gorethrian ones – but she was still upright and handsome. Her skin was fair, her eyes grey and her hair white. She wore a grey robe with a tabard of white wool over it. He had never actually seen a Tearnian, but presumed she must be one; she was certainly from nowhere in the Empire. She stood demure and expressionless before him, her hands clasped, waiting for him to speak first.

The morning was gloomy, illuminated only by bursts of lightning, so he moved to a table and unhurriedly lit a lamp. He looked up at her, his red eyes glittering in the lamp light, and said, 'Well? You wanted to see me. Have you nothing to say?'

The aged female replied, 'Duke Xaedrek, you sent for me. It is for you to tell me what you require.'

'Madam, you are mistaken. I did not send for you. I do not know you. If you can furnish me with no clear explanation of your presence here, I must conclude that you are suffering from some personal delusion, and ask you to leave.'

'Duke Xaedrek,' the woman almost hissed. 'This situation is very difficult for me. Please do not make it any worse.' Xaedrek noticed that the storm had lent a strange quality to the atmosphere, so that her voice, mild though it was, seemed to come from everywhere at once, almost as though it did not belong to her.

'Very well,' he said patiently. 'Let us assume that my memory is at fault. Please, help me to remember why you think I sent for you.'

'Duke Xaedrek,' the woman said a third time, her voice strangled with suppressed rage, 'I am the demon you summoned.'

His initial reaction was to laugh, but he constrained himself. He walked slowly away from the table, leaned on a marble pillar, and looked at her in a way that would have filled even Baramek with fear. Quietly, he said, 'You expect me to believe that?'

'You must believe it.'

'No. You must prove it.' The woman did not answer, but

17

stood staring at him, her grey eyes full of argent flecks, like silverfish moving beneath a dusty pane of glass. In one instant he had dismissed her as mad; in the next, he thought, no one knows that I tried to summon a Shanin. No one at all. And he remembered the curious state of distress in which he had found Varian. If she spoke truth, the reason for Varian's terror became obvious.

'No. It's impossible,' he said. 'A demon is a silver, asexual being which shines with its own light. It steps directly from its own dimension to this when summoned. It does not knock on the summoner's door after an interval of five days like a common trader. Someone at court must have had me spied on, and enlisted you to perform this charade. You may as well cease now. I assure you, you would not like me to become angry.'

'Nor you me,' the woman persisted. 'Listen to me, my dear Duke. Proof is hard, the situation being as it is. Some would imagine they recognised me, but I am not she whom they think they know.'

'These riddles are not merely time-wasting, they are boring,' Xaedrek said, moving towards the door.

The woman intercepted him and gripped his wrists, her fingers as cold and hard as bone, her eyes full of something worse than madness. He recoiled from her. She hissed, 'You must listen. Sit down.'

'For five minutes. No more,' Xaedrek said, sharply withdrawing his arms from her grasp. He walked to the far end of the hall and sat at an onyx desk, motioning the woman to take the chair opposite. To his annoyance he found himself shaking. 'Go on.'

'What do you know of the Serpent M'gulfn?' she asked abruptly.

'It was a mythical creature, said to inhabit the North Pole. I know there are one or two primitive races in the Empire who worship it; I suppose that is where the myth came from.'

'You are wrong. It was no myth. It was real. But now it is dead. The Shana were its servants. But I am the only one left. My name is – was – Ahag-Ga.'

'Not Meheg-Ba?'

'Meheg-Ba was destroyed!' the woman exclaimed savagely. 'All destroyed by Ashurek. All except me!'

Xaedrek leaned forward. Whatever the truth behind this strange situation, the mention of Ashurek's name was enough to captivate his interest.

'Would you care to tell me how this came to pass?'

The woman-demon obliged with a vivid description of how, fifteen or so years earlier, the despicable Ashurek had lured the Shana from the Dark Regions so that Miril could slay them with her fatal touch.

'But that does not explain how you were fortunate enough to survive,' the Duke said when she seemed to have finished. His tone was no longer sceptical. The impassioned nature of her narrative, the detail which surely no trickster could have invented, and above all the metallic timbre of the voice – which he now realised was no effect of the storm – all combined to lessen his incredulity, bit by bit.

'I had been sent to destroy the House of Rede. I was not with my fellow Shana. I had taken on a human body – this form, in which you see me. Ashurek and his loathsome companions went on to destroy the Serpent. No one ever returned to the House of Rede to look for me – not even Eldor – so even the Guardians must have assumed that no Shanin could live on after its creator, the Serpent. But they were wrong. I did not die.'

The room flashed red and pale green, while thunder rumbled faintly and continuously overhead, mingling with the roar of rain. Xaedrek lit another lamp, though it did little to compete with the storm. Almost pathetically, the woman-demon asked, 'Now do you believe me?'

'Not yet. There are still a number of unanswered questions. If you were, as you claim, on the far side of the Earth while the slaying of the Serpent and your comrades was taking place, how did you know about it?'

'How could I not know what was happening to my fellows? You must realise, I still had power then. I could far-see. I knew exactly what was occurring, everything up until the moment M'gulfn died and its power dispersed into the Earth.'

'Well, I will accept that for now. But why do you still appear to be human? Everything I have read of the Shana –'

'I told you, this body is not mine,' the woman retorted with disgust. 'It is that of Dritha, who was Eldor's wife. I merely "borrowed" it. But when the Serpent perished, my power was lost. To my eternal regret I was trapped in this leaden form, with no hope of ever returning to my natural state. Perhaps that was why I escaped annihilation – sometimes I think Miril's touch would have been preferable.'

'You sound bitter,' Xaedrek observed.

'I am. You cannot begin to imagine the suffering of such a creature as myself, made to be immortal and powerful, and then reduced to – this.' She pointed at her body as if at a particularly repulsive insect.

'And you have lived on Earth ever since?'

'Existed,' she spat. 'It is hell to me.'

'Well, this is indeed fascinating,' Xaedrek said, sitting back and gazing at her as if he meant to dissect her with his eyes. 'So, your source of power is gone, but your consciousness has survived. Evidently your nature has been changed: you can no longer perform supernatural feats, nor travel instantaneously through the dimensions . . . nor possess your summoner.'

'I do not know what you mean by "possess",' the woman-Shanin said sulkily.

'Don't play games with me,' Xaedrek said impatiently. 'A demon filled its summoner – or anyone who encountered it – with overwhelming awe, terror, and desire to bend to it and do its will. You have inspired no such feelings in me. Yes, I can understand how such impotence must gall you.'

'Nevertheless, I warn you not to underestimate me. I am weak, it is true. Yet your servant glimpsed what I used to be, and cowered before me. And remember – I was still able to hear and respond to a summoning.'

'In fact, you must have been grateful when someone thought to summon you at last. A respite from the dreariness of your existence?'

'More grateful than you can know.'

'Now, listen to me, demon. Although your powers have altered, I am not so naïve as to think that your character has improved. I am not going to repeat Meshurek's mistakes. He imagined he could control Meheg-Ba, but he misunderstood its nature. From the beginning it was using and destroying him, yet he never perceived it. However, I ask you not to make the mistake of assuming that I am like him.'

'Then why did you summon me?'

'I knew it was a risk, but I have an enquiring mind. And now that you are here, and willing to talk, you might be able to give me the answers to certain questions.'

'As you are such a clever man, Duke Xaedrek, I can hardly believe you need me to tell you anything. Still, if it is what you want of me, I will do my best.'

'Well, demon – should I call you Ahag-Ga or Dritha?' The being did not reply, just stared at him with eyes as indifferent as a shark's. 'Something of the two, then. Ah'garith,' he said lightly. 'You see, Ah'garith, something has destroyed Gorethria. We have hung on for fifteen or sixteen years, but invasion by our enemies is imminent. And there is no greater wish in our hearts than to know why this has happened. I know that it began with Meshurek's foolish summoning of Meheg-Ba. But I want to know the exact manner of it.'

The woman-demon obliged, explaining in detail about the corrupt power of the Egg-Stone, Ashurek's betrayals of his country, the Quest of the Serpent. Xaedrek quickly began to see how everything fell into place, every event, memory, rumour, a thread woven into a tapestry whose colourful, jumbled picture is seen from a distance for the first time, and suddenly becomes clear.

And what a grotesque picture. He rose and wandered round the room as Ah'garith's metallic voice echoed on, feeling physically sick. Unclean. He stared at a sword on the wall. If Meshurek or Ashurek had walked into the hall just then, he could have cheerfully cut them to pieces where they stood –

'Duke Xaedrek? I think you are not listening to me,' the

demon said peevishly. 'I said, is this information what you wanted?'

'Yes, precisely what I wanted. I am grateful.'

'Then please stop looking at that blade. There is no point in attempting violence upon me. Only Miril could free me from this unpleasant existence.'

Xaedrek walked back to the table and half-sat on the edge, folding his arms. 'In that case, I could almost pity you. But not quite. After all, Meheg-Ba deliberately, calculatedly brought this chaos to Gorethria, and you are one of the same species, undoubtedly with the same callous and perverse designs.'

'Oh, you wrong me!' Ah'garith hissed. 'Here I have obediently answered my summons, told you all you wanted to know, demanded nothing in return, no bargain. Laid bare all my misfortunes and weaknesses.'

'Thrown yourself on my mercy? Forgive me, I am not impressed. There must be *something* in it for you. Speak plainly, now. As I warned you, I find nothing more boring than cryptic riddles.'

'To be plain, my Duke, I need you. But even if you help me, still your own rewards will be far richer than mine. As you see, I have no power to force you to do anything, and the laws of my existence still prevent me from acting without the direction of my summoner. In other words, there are things that must be done, but unless you instruct me –'

'I see,' Xaedrek said, smiling. 'And what would you have me instruct you to do?'

Ah'garith clasped her hands. Lightning caught gleams on her thick white hair, cast shadows across the deceptively mild face. She said, 'Upon M'gulfn's death a great energy was released which now fills and surrounds the Earth. The potential for that which some call sorcery. The hyperphysical arts. But so far none have discovered its existence, let alone understood its use.'

'Like an untapped reservoir. Unmined gold. Or unharnessed lightning . . .'

22

'Just so. However, there will be those who discover ways to channel and use the energy. It cannot remain inviolate for ever. It is up to us to lay claim to it, wield it, safeguard it from misuse by fools . . .'

Xaedrek was silent, thinking on this. What the being said made perfect sense. He had known that the world was in a state of change; the weather, the chaos in the Empire, all proved it. Freed from the Serpent's oppression, new possibilities gleamed in the Earth like jewels. And he had actually tasted that power, so he knew the Shanin was not lying.

He had devoted his scientific life to discovering something such as this. Now here was the embryonic dream within his hand at last . . . the means to make Gorethria great once more.

'And this energy . . . you cannot wield it for yourself?'

'No. I can draw the power, as you've seen, but I cannot shape or use it. To be honest, my Duke, I do not know how. That is for you to discover – what is so amusing?'

Xaedrek was grinning. 'Only that I've just realised – that it is my intellect that you need! Evidently one quality M'gulfn failed to bestow on its creations was intelligence.'

'There is no need to insult me,' Ah'garish whispered metallically. 'Yes, I will be reliant on your cleverness. But I am not totally helpless – so tread carefully.'

'I always do, believe me. But if we succeed, what do you hope to gain from this power?'

'I do not know. Revenge. For the Serpent, for my poor siblings. Escape from this wretched body.'

'That won't do,' Xaedrek said so sharply that the woman started. 'Do you think, after Meheg-Ba's corruption of this country, I would let it happen again? Allow a creature with self-confessed motives of such petty, despicable selfishness even to touch a power that might be Gorethria's salvation?'

After a pause, the being said, 'So, you refuse to work with me.'

'I didn't say that.' The demon, as Xaedrek had surmised,

23

was not the brightest of creatures. Already his own mind had leapt ahead to a fully fleshed plan, and the first step was to fulfil the rash boast he had made to Kharan on the morning he had met her. But there was no need to let Ah'garith see his exhilaration, or bait her with more than the tiniest morsels of information. In a way, he would be having his own kind of revenge: he would be using the Shanin as thoroughly, as heartlessly as Meheg-Ba had used Meshurek. At this thought, he allowed himself a cold smile. 'I think we can work together. You said yourself that you can act only upon my instructions. Well, I now instruct you to act as my adviser. If this sorcery can be wielded, it shall be done by myself. Or others. But I must make it clear from the start that I will not risk the power in your hands until I know for certain I can trust you.'

The demon gave an exclamation of annoyance, but sullenly agreed. 'And when do you wish to begin, my Duke? This evening? Tomorrow?'

'I see no point in waiting. Come, Ah'garith,' Xaedrek said pleasantly, moving to the onyx-panelled double door and holding it open. 'We'll start now.'

Outside, the storm ceased abruptly.

Kharan made her way along a graceful white corridor, her few belongings tucked under her arm. The servants' quarters, as was normal in Gorethrian households, were a smaller, more modest version of the main house; it was a matter of pride for servants – as they euphemistically termed their slaves – to be kept in excellent conditions. She was heading for Steward Varian's room, but the door opened before she reached it and the small, ebony-skinned Patavrian emerged and stood looking at her.

'Steward Varian, I heard you had been taken ill,' she said cheerfully. 'I was just coming to see how you are. Are you feeling better?'

'Keep your concern!' he snapped. She was taken aback; he had always been patient and quietly spoken before, if

24

rather morose. 'If you had friends here before, you have none now. *My lady*.'

Her manner became guarded, though no less pleasant. 'What do you mean?'

'We have just been instructed to ready the suite of rooms next to His Grace's. For occupation by your good self. And to call you "lady".'

'Oh. I see,' she said quietly.

'Do you?' His black eyes held hers fiercely. 'Being a slave to the Gorethrians is one thing. Unavoidable, if one is to live. But to be a – what shall I call you? Mistress. Fraterniser. Traitor. That is something quite different.'

'Traitor? To whom?' she gasped. 'There is no one else of my race in this household.'

'Perhaps the Duke thinks one An'raagan crawling into his bed is enough. My lady.'

She almost hit him at that, but restrained herself with a great effort of willpower. 'My race is not warlike, Steward Varian. We have never been true enemies of the Gorethrians, not really.'

'Oh, history knows how An'raaga rolled over and played dead when she was invaded. That miserable cowardice betrayed every other brave race who shed their blood struggling against Gorethria's tyranny.'

'Well, I would not call it cowardice,' she replied coolly. 'It was pure common sense. What would have been the point of resisting? We'd have been massacred, like the poor Alaakians, and all for the sake of pride. Instead, we have made the best of our situation, and as a result we avoided bloodshed and retained some independence. Now I have to make the best of this situation. I suppose you think I am nothing but a cold-blooded opportunist, and I dare say you're right. But I have to look after myself, just as everyone else does. I am not betraying anyone.'

'Not cold-blooded,' Varian said quietly. 'But very young, and very stupid. They say that Gorethria will be invaded in a few weeks' time. Invaded, and conquered. Myself, I doubt it. But if it was true, do you think the Vardravians will treat fraternisers any more kindly than they treat the Gorethrians themselves? Try telling a Kristillian or a Kesfalian that you were "not betraying anyone".'

Kharan shuddered. 'There will be no invasion. I don't believe it.'

'Perhaps not. But there is still Xaedrek himself. You don't know him. You don't understand what you are involving yourself in.'

'But he is a good master. A kind man. You told me so yourself when I arrived here,' she said, deliberately keeping her voice light.

'But still a Gorethrian. You wondered what made me ill, I expect? Well, my lady, it was fear. A creature which I can only describe as a fiend came here this morning at the Duke's command. It had the guise of an old woman, but it was no such thing. Its eyes shone like mercury, poison. I always suspected that he communed with things of darkness; now I am certain of it.'

'I think the weather has affected your mind, Steward Varian. You're talking nonsense.'

'You think so? Then try asking him what he does in those cellar rooms which he allows no servant to enter.' His voice became suddenly concerned, urgent. 'Maid, it is not too late for you to leave here, find another post –'

'Oh, now I understand,' she broke in. Although she did not feel self-assured, she managed to sound it. 'I have found a way out of slavery, so you are trying to frighten me back into it. Young I may be, but I am not that naïve. I don't care what he does, it's not my concern. I can look after myself.'

'I hope you can,' Varian said unpleasantly. 'For you have not made a friend of him. You have only made an enemy of everyone else in this household. To be utterly friendless takes more strength than most of us possess. My lady.'

'What a very wise man you must be,' she said, smiling coldly through her anger. 'As it happens, I've never had any friends. You talk of betrayal as though there were comrades to betray, but the truth is, no one is anyone's friend in this

26

city. This continent. If there is a war, no one will be freed. All the Vardravians will bring is more suffering. We're all of us alone. I am only doing what I must to protect myself.'

If these words did not silence him, nothing would. Taking a deep breath, she strode on down the corridor, her head high. But she did not manage to get out of earshot before she heard him mutter sourly, 'All you're doing is exchanging one kind of slavery for another.'

The way Kharan's future shaped itself seemed to owe nothing to Varian's sour predictions. A few days later, there was a lightning change in Gorethria's situation which no one had foreseen; something which so stunned everyone that the silence over Shalekahh seemed almost palpable.

It could be summed up by saying that the next thing Kharan knew, Xaedrek was Emperor.

How he achieved it remained a marvel to her. She knew little of Gorethrian politics, but in this case, although there was, of course, an official version of events which everyone accepted, only Xaedrek himself knew what had really happened.

The day after the Shanin came, he went to Orhdrek and informed him in confidence that he had discovered the truth about Meshurek and Ashurek. He carefully altered the account to omit any mention of Ah'garith herself.

'A shameful story. Truly shameful,' was Orhdrek's reaction. He was a thin, very serious lad who was finding the burden of being Emperor far too much. In fact, it was only due to Xaedrek that he was Emperor at all. His parents had been rival claimants to the throne, and had inevitably become bitter adversaries. In the course of time, his mother had been poisoned, his father slain in a fight, leaving the insignificant child Orhdrek with no one. But Xaedrek became his protector, and set to work with almost incredible cleverness and foresight for one who was himself so young. Without force, without subterfuge, with only simple eloquence and logic, he convinced the Senate that Gorethria must have a ruler, and that Orhdrek's double claim to the throne was incontestable.

Orhdrek was ten years old at the time of his coronation, Xaedrek twenty. Five years had gone by since then, and people were restless again, knowing that the boy was proving an inept ruler. But Xaedrek had watched everything with quiet detachment, only biding his time until at last he made the discovery that would bring his plans to fruition.

'I must tell them, of course,' Orhdrek muttered unhappily. 'The whole story. It's what the people have thirsted to know for sixteen years or more . . .'

'No, Sire. I advise against it,' Xaedrek replied, putting a reassuring hand on the boy's shoulder. 'It would only demoralise them further, and with enemies at our borders and invasion imminent, that would be disastrous.'

'Of course, of course. You're quite right. The disgraceful story shall go no further than this room. Oh, what a friend you are to me, Xaedrek. Where would I be without your help and advice?'

Unfortunately, within a couple of days, a rumour was coursing like a plague of rats through Shalekahh: Orhdrek had found out the truth about Meshurek, but was refusing to reveal it. Presently a vast, angry, fully armed crowd had gathered outside the palace, and those inside became very apprehensive.

Orhdrek had no conception of what to do for the best, so he continued to trust implicitly in Xaedrek, his only true friend. And Xaedrek advised him to be strong, to behave like a true Gorethrian, and not to bow to this unseemly pressure.

When his intention of remaining silent was announced, it hardly had a pacifying effect on the crowd; the air seemed black with menace, and fights broke out with the palace guards. The Inner Council panicked, and arrested Orhdrek, which quietened things for a time. Then events took another strange turn.

After a few hours under house arrest, Orhdrek died suddenly. It was presumed that two or three members of the royal family who had been rival claimants had taken advantage of the chaos to poison him, and put the blame on the Inner Council. Those within the palace tried desperately to keep the matter quiet, but sure enough, within minutes the crowd had somehow found out.

The palace was now in a state of siege, the Senate and court in uproar. Only Xaedrek had the remarkable self-possession – or insane bravado – to step outside unarmed and speak to the raging crowd.

Perhaps only his audacity saved him from being seized and slain at once. He was not a member of the Inner Council and had maintained a quiet presence at court so few even knew who he was. Yet somehow – probably by self-assurance and personal magnetism alone – he commanded their attention, and made a compelling speech.

The young Emperor Orhdrek had died while in the custody of the Inner Council, he said. Perhaps Orhdrek had been wrong to conceal the story of Meshurek, but the Emperor's word had always been law absolute. However, certain persons appeared to have taken the law into their own hands, and there was no greater wrong than this gross, unconscionable act, the murder of Orhdrek.

Already the mob were roaring their agreement. He went on, 'You see, it is easy to forget that Orhdrek, in his dignity and solemnity, was still a child. And the enormity of Meshurek's and Ashurek's betrayal of Gorethria were such that he can hardly be blamed for not wanting to impart the knowledge.

'It was I who discovered the truth. And now that there is no one to order me to silence, I propose to tell you it in full. It is the least that you, my fellow Gorethrians, deserve.'

Xaedrek had certainly not underestimated how much the truth about Meshurek's reign had come to mean to everyone. His whole strategy had hinged upon it. He was, himself, the source of rumour and other incitements, which had caused the mob to gather in the first place. A few well-placed hints had given the Inner Council the idea of arresting Orhdrek. Subtle stage-management had spread the news of the Emperor's sudden death to the crowd. But no suspicion of responsibility for these matters ever touched the Duke – or anyone, for that matter. They were unimportant.

The important thing was that the story was known at last. It was disgraceful, chilling in its enormity; the crowd were openly furious. Yet in the fury was a kind of exhilaration, a new sense of purpose. And their feeling of unity centred on Xaedrek. The one man who had kept his head, who had had the wit to find out the truth, and above all the decency to tell them . . .

When Xaedrek called for volunteers to restore order to the palace, every soldier there was behind him. The fifty men he chose were mostly his own, led by Captain Baramek; they had been scattered among the crowd with the ducal insignia removed from their uniforms. They entered the palace, arrested certain people, and gained the wholehearted support of the remaining courtiers and senators.

No time was wasted in declaring and crowning a new emperor. Xaedrek behaved in a suitably reluctant, modest way that only made everyone the more enthusiastic about him. Perhaps there was a touch of hysteria in the adulation, but it was soon seen that Xaedrek was not just another false hope. Gorethria had put her faith in him, and he did not let her down.

Kharan was speechless for a day when the Duke's household removed to the Imperial Palace. She had walked past it often enough, but now that she was actually to live there, she looked at it as if she had never seen it before. Set in a vast square in the centre of Shalekahh, it was a structure of breathtaking beauty, all ice-white colonnades, sweeping stairs and gleaming towers. Its many spires and turrets were intricately figured and exquisitely enamelled in jewel-like blues, reds and greens. Guards in black, white and gold Imperial livery patrolled within the white railings, checking the identity of all who passed in and out. Around the palace stood great Gorethrian beeches, with black trunks and shimmering red leaves. Behind lay the glorious gardens, with their sparkling fountains, lifelike painted statues, nectar-heavy, garish flowers. And there were also extensive stable blocks, coach-houses and barracks, carefully designed to blend in with the palace itself.

Within, it was equally awesome. The starkness of vast marble halls was relieved by ornately panelled doors, carved arches and filigree screens. Great paintings and tapestries adorned the walls. In the living quarters of the nobility – including those allotted to Kharan – the furnishings were rich and brightly coloured, and everywhere seemed to shine with precious jewels: the fringes of curtains, the edges of chairs, the frames of mirrors. The public rooms where the courtiers and the Senate gathered, including the throne room itself, were plainer; alabaster-white columns were offset only by touches of platinum, opal and jet, in order to distract neither from the humming-bird-bright clothing of the courtiers, nor the severe black of soldiers and officers.

When Kharan attempted to express her amazement at the beauty of the palace, the luxury of her rooms and the richness of the clothing he had provided for her, Xaedrek only smiled. When she raised the courage to ask him, 'What is going to happen now?' he replied enigmatically, 'Watch and wait. You'll see.'

Xaedrek's first act was to reorganise the army completely and improve communications throughout Gorethria. When the threatened invasion came, it was swiftly and effectively repelled, sending the rebels scurrying back into the Empire. The Vardravians were stunned. Victory had been assured, they thought. Surely Gorethria had not grown strong again? It must be a fluke.

There followed a quiet period lasting many months, when Xaedrek spent much of his time closeted within the cellar rooms of his old mansion, in discussion with various scientifically minded colleagues. Then Kharan would sometimes sit for hours looking out at the palace garden, breathing the spiced heat, or watching the trees thrash in a black gale, or gazing at gelatinous rain dripping mournfully onto the leaves, weighing down the lush flowers. And she would wonder if Xaedrek had forgotten about her. When he did arrive, his mood would vary according to how well his research was progressing; usually he would be cheerful, but his occasional moroseness did not trouble her, for then she delighted in her ability to restore his good spirits. The fact that he did not love her – and she did not love him – was totally irrelevant. Kharan was a realist, light-heartedly cynical about the idea of love, so it meant nothing to her. Nevertheless, they found a great deal of pleasure in each other's company, and a certain cool affection developed between them. Cool, because Xaedrek never, ever confided in her, and she soon realised that she knew him no better now than the first time she had met him, and never would. But it did not really matter. The arrangement was to their mutual benefit, and he was unfailingly courteous and considerate towards her.

It was about a year after the attempted invasion that the Imperial armies marched from Gorethria again. From garrisons in all the major cities they assembled at Zhelkahh, the black city set almost invisibly amid Gorethria's sable mountains. Then, as in days of old, they began to advance through Omnuandria, that broad, green no-man's-land which some called the Vardrav Way, because it was the route by which Gorethria had first invaded the rest of the continent. The cavalry moved like a tide of fire across the emerald hills, the sun flashing from them in spears of amethyst and copper light. Behind them marched line upon line of tall warriors, heavy cloaks of blood-red, black or purple swinging from their shoulders, their hawk-shaped helms iridescent like black opal.

The nightmare was beginning again.

As the years passed, Cevandaris fell, as did Mangorad and most of Kesfaline. Provinces where the Gorethrians had never completely lost control were reunited with the motherland: An'raaga, Alaak, Bagreeah, parts of Ungrem and Malmanon. There was still much work ahead of them, but Xaedrek was well pleased with progress. The collapse of the

32

Empire had taken perhaps twenty years in all, so it could hardly be rebuilt in less.

Through these years, Kharan knew that Gorethria's tyranny was spreading again, and that it was Xaedrek's doing, and that he was using some strange means more scientific than military. But she did not allow her thoughts to dwell on the matter. What he does is not my concern, she would tell herself firmly. I was no one, and now I am an emperor's mistress. Who am I to shun such good fortune?

Certainly it was fortune, materially. She had fallen into the lifestyle of a princess as easily as if she had been born to it. She was no embarrassment to Xaedrek in court, and moved among the nobles as if she was one of them, all cool dignity and grace. She knew they despised her. She was not Gorethrian. Xaedrek would never marry her. But she refused to let them think that their despite could hurt or even touch her. However hard they tried to intimidate her with cutting glances and veiled threats, still she went determinedly among them, day after day, her head held high.

As Varian had warned, all the slaves hated her too. Some less than others: there were a few who were, or had been, in a similar position to herself, and with them she shared some tenuous comradeship. But no real trust, for although they could not condemn her motive, there seemed to be something about it that they reviled within themselves, and so could not forgive in others.

Night after night, she told herself that it was her only choice, that the benefits outweighed all the disadvantages. And when Xaedrek was actually with her, it was easy to forget her doubts.

In time it was seen that Xaedrek had no intention of casting Kharan aside. Her position was established. Her perseverance paid off, for she was sullenly accepted at court, called Lady Kharan without any trace of sarcasm, even treated with pleasant respect by the servants now that they had grown used to her unique situation. Eight or nine years drifted by, and she could honestly say that for most of that time, all things considered, she was happy.

Gorethria seemed to become more and more vigorous than ever before, her forces glowing with a strength that seemed extramundane. Malmanon fell; Alta-Nangra was infiltrated across the River Nanuandrix. Kristillia, that most difficult of conquests, Gorethria's moonstone, was surrounded and poised to collapse.

Only Xaedrek knew what the cost of this new glory was, and as he was not paying the price himself, it meant nothing to him. Few Gorethrians – Ashurek being a notable exception – had ever suffered from conscience about the means they employed to increase their country's power.

Of course, rumours of the source of Xaedrek's power inevitably began to circulate, but he ensured that they were rumours of the right sort. The power was something new, clean, scientific, the very opposite of that which had corrupted Meshurek and wrecked the army. It was good (for Gorethria), but it was also very dangerous, and Xaedrek alone was able to understand and practise it. Because he was so careful to base these rumours upon truth, he gained a reputation which, combined with his compelling presence, commanded a degree of respect extraordinary even for the Emperor.

He never carried a sword, and wore simple brocaded robes more usual for a scholar than an emperor. He would often walk through the streets without a single bodyguard; it gave him a perverse delight to see people falling out of his path as they would normally only have done for an Imperial cavalcade with all the trappings. It always gave Kharan a shock to realise how afraid people were of him. She felt almost proud that he did not frighten her. Although she knew that this was a particularly foolish kind of arrogance, still sometimes she allowed herself a self-deprecating smile about it.

And yet Xaedrek was not without his problems. Nothing stays the same, yet the change was so gradual that Kharan could not even pinpoint the year, let alone the moment, when he began to seem different. All she knew was that he had used to find escape from his many worries and responsibilities when he was with her. Now he seemed to bring the burdens with him, as though she had lost the power to make him forget. And she saw him less and less often.

'He is working too hard,' she told herself one day. 'Even the Emperor is human and must rest . . .' Jumping up in sudden anger – which was part concern for him, part fear for her own status – she determined to go and find him, suggest that to forget his duties for a time was essential to his well-being.

She took an ivory-coloured palfrey from the stable and rode to the ducal mansion, which he still used for his scientific work. As she arrived Xaedrek emerged, flanked by Baramek – who was now High Commander – and an old Tearnian woman with a shock of white hair. Xaedrek walked straight past her as if he had not seen her, but the old woman turned and fixed her with such a cold, silvery stare that she slid off the horse's back and stood hanging onto the saddle, her knees weak and her head swimming. As she stood there, a hand gripped her elbow, making her jump violently.

It was the black-skinned Patavrian, Varian. He had stayed at the mansion when most of the others had moved to the palace.

'Well, as you've taken the trouble to come here at long last, you might as well come inside and see what is happening, my lady Kharan,' he said acidly. Xaedrek and the others had gone.

'Oh, Varian, did you have to creep up on me like that?' she gasped, regaining her composure. 'What are you talking about?'

Shaking his head, he began to guide her inside the large entrance hall. There was a taint in the air that made her cough, like the burning of flesh and other, unidentifiable substances. 'As you seem to be the only person in the whole of Shalekahh who does not know what is going on, I feel it is my duty to show you at first hand.' He pushed open the double door into the reception room and drew her in.

Arranged down the long sides of the room were two rows of pallets. The original furniture had been removed. Two or three tall Gorethrian women, dressed in the simple, white and silver robes of nurses, were moving about the room; they glanced with icy indifference at Kharan and Varian, then went on with their work. The Patavrian pulled her into the centre of the columned aisle and said, 'Well, what think you, my lady?'

On every pallet lay a man or woman, each of a different Vardravian race. There were no Gorethrians. Each was grey-faced and obviously in great pain, gasping as if every shallow breath was a knife thrust. Many were burned, their foreheads blistered, their hands lying black and swollen on the covers. The severe-faced nurses moved among them, administering medicines and doing what little they could to make them more comfortable, but there was something implacable about their agony. Their eyes, too brilliant in the drawn faces, all swivelled to stare at Kharan like an accusation of genocide. She stared back, horrified, uncomprehending, knowing only that whatever this meant, it was something of appalling, unconscionable sickness and evil.

'These are the ones who survived,' said Varian hoarsely.

'Survived what? I don't understand,' she whispered.

'Xaedrek's experiments.'

'But what – what has he done to them?'

'You tell me,' was the harsh response. 'You're the one who knows him so well, my lady.'

Clenching herself against the desire to scream and run, she turned and walked stiffly out of the room, across the entrance hall, and to the marble court outside. Reaching the palfrey, she fumbled to gather up the reins, but found she had no strength to mount. As she leaned shaking against the horse's warm flank, Varian followed her out and stood looking at her without sympathy.

'I had thought you would make a dramatic gesture, my lady,' he sneered. 'Be sick, or faint.'

'I'm sorry to disappoint you,' she said tightly, but then her self-containment deserted her. 'By the gods, Varian, what am I going to do?' she gasped, scrubbing tears out of her eyes with violently shaking hands.

'Don't ask me,' was the pitiless reply. 'I warned you, eight or nine years ago, to flee. I expect it's too late now.'

'He'd never let me leave. I'd be a fugitive – with nothing.'

'That's your problem, my lady. Close your mind to it, my lady. Go back to your luxurious life. There were An'raagans in there, but don't worry – you're not betraying anyone.'

When Xaedrek went to see Kharan that evening, he found her pale and quiet, her smiles forced. It had been an exhausting day with Ah'garith, posing many questions from which he could divert his mind only with great difficulty. More and more these days the practice of hyperphysics was obsessing him to the exclusion of all else. Perhaps he had been neglecting Kharan of late. He asked her if anything was wrong.

'If you no longer –' she began hesitantly, 'Xaedrek, if you no longer want me, you would tell me, wouldn't you? I want you to be honest. I would go away discreetly. I don't want to "disappear" in the night.'

'What a thing to say,' he exclaimed, genuinely astonished. 'It's true I have been busier than usual recently – the Gorethrian Empire does not run itself, if you hadn't noticed. That doesn't mean that I no longer want you. Certainly there's no question of you leaving, even less of you being disposed of by poison or whatever you're thinking of. No question of it. Is that clear?'

'Yes,' she muttered. He put his arms round her and she tried not to wonder what esoteric tasks those long, elegant hands had been engaged in earlier.

'You mean a great deal to me, Kharan, and always will.'

'Do I? Then why is it that you can't confide in me? You never tell me anything.'

He was silent for a moment, thinking about this. He would not bore his worst enemy with the affairs of the Gorethrian Senate. As for the matters which interested him, only Ah'garith and his few scientific colleagues could understand and share in those. Outside, a bolt of golden lightning illuminated the palace garden; he went to close the curtains, then turned round and stood with his back to the window so that his tall figure became a black, flickering silhouette against the diffused storm flashes.

'Well, Kharan, I'll tell you something I've never told anyone. I never used to dream. Dreams frighten me a little. But now I have a recurring dream, always the same: a child with red hair on a ship. That seems to mean nothing to me, it just is. Then I find myself in the Hall of Portraits, and with me is a woman whom I do not know. She is Gorethrian, with very dark skin. But she has bright golden hair, which I find extremely disturbing. What do you think it means?'

Before she could stop herself, the words slipped out, 'Perhaps it is something to do with guilt.'

2

The Sorceress

ON ANOTHER world, which some call Ikonus, a small silver-blue sun shone down on a fantastical edifice, drawing all colours from its scintillating planes and angles. Around it lay a vast, lush garden. The grass and trees gleamed with different tints of the rich green peculiar to Ikonus. Near the glittering building was a lawn that had been landscaped into a kind of amphitheatre with a mound in the centre serving as a stage. All around it stood men and women in pale robes; the atmosphere was one of cheerful anticipation.

The building was the School of Sorcery, where the use of enchantment and other, less élite arts were taught. A ceremony was about to take place, the most important one of the year, at which those who had achieved the rank of full Sorcerer were to be given their white robes.

On the mound stood the High Master, a dour-faced man with blue-black hair drawn severely off his pale forehead. The tutors of sorcery and the other arts stood in a loose semi-circle behind him, waiting for him to address the assembly.

Above the proceedings a small, silver sphere hovered like an all-seeing eye.

'Most of us remember,' he began, 'the tragic day when this world was almost annihilated. A thaumaturge – I will not call her a Sorceress – named Arlenmia, thinking to steal power for herself, destroyed our sacred Sphere Ikonus. Those of you too young to recall the event, have nevertheless lived with the consequences all your lives. More than thirty years of death and darkness followed. But all of you were steadfast until at last, through your courage, this world was healed and restored to light.' Cheers of joyful concurrence greeted these words, and he held up his hands for silence. 'But only this year, for the first time, can we say that the world is once more as perfect as it was, all darkness gone, the Sphere restored to its sacred function. This year we give special thanks to the powers of light for our salvation. We welcome with joy these six young men and women to the position they have earned, that of Sorcerer–Sorceress.'

There were never more than six each year, sometimes less. The training took ten years, and only those who were potential Sorcerers from birth could embark upon it. Among the two men and four women who now stepped forward to climb the mound was Mellorn, the daughter of Silvren and Ashurek. Her golden hair was startling against her dark skin.

Silvren looked proudly at her daughter as the High Master began to speak. His words were traditional, though no less stirring for that, concerning the nature of sorcery and the Sphere Ikonus. 'Thousands of years ago this world was torn by inexplicable outbreaks of war, devastation and plague. The first Sorcerers were those who discovered the cause of these scourges. The energy from which we draw our power is part of the world, and flows round and through the world like a magnetic field. As storms bring gloom and depression, as spring winds bring lightness and hope, so the energy has its positive and negative aspects. Indeed, the weather itself is a part of it. And it was the dark aspect of the power, unchecked, which caused hatred and warfare.

'So these first Sorcerers set to creating a filter which would absorb the negative energy, letting through only the positive. And after centuries of work, the Sphere Ikonus was complete – no mere symbol, but an actual mechanism to capture and contain darkness. And the energy which we draw through ourselves and shape into that which we call sorcery became as pure diamond.

'But that is not to say that the power is not still dangerous. It must be handled with the utmost respect and restraint, and only in the service of good, as we have taught you in your ten years of study. This is the Oath you are about to take, and must never break.' After a pause he added, his voice very grave, 'Arlenmia was one who broke her vows, and this world nearly perished as a result.'

He said this every year, but the words still made Silvren shudder. The pain was dull now, momentary; it was all far in the past, but could never be quite forgotten.

As a girl of sixteen, Silvren had been sent to Ikonus by Eldor to learn how to wield the sorcerous power with which she had been born. Ten years later, as a full Sorceress, she had gone back to her own Earth and played her part in the eventual destruction of the Serpent. When that was over, she and Ashurek – both feeling alienated from Earth – had returned to this world, nicknamed Ikonus after the mystical Sphere.

They had lived here contentedly for nearly twenty-five years. Ashurek had striven to keep his word to the Lady of H'tebhmella never to touch another weapon, and had lived as a scholar and horse-trainer. Silvren had spent much time working at the School of Sorcery, doing what she could to help repair the harm done to the world by Arlenmia. But she was happiest when she and Ashurek could be alone at their home, secluded among the green Ikonian valleys. Their existence here had not always been peaceful, but mostly it had been happy.

In their first year on Ikonus, amid the joy of their new-found love and freedom, their daughter Mellorn had been born. In the instant of her birth, Silvren knew she was a latent Sorceress, as she herself had been. The child had needed no encouragement to attend the School of Sorcery; intelligent and serious, she had avidly studied not only the élite art of sorcery, but all the other skills as well – the Ways between Worlds, the care of animals, soldiery.

'What's she going to do with all that knowledge?' her younger brother, Callin, would ask. 'I could run a whole farm just as well without, and have more fun out of life.'

Callin was eight years younger than Mellorn, a cheerful

41

and easygoing lad much like Silvren in temperament. He had no latent power for magic within him, nor any interest in it. Two years ago he had gone away to work on a farm in the hills, the only life he desired. Silvren and Ashurek were happy for him. But Mellorn . . .

At least now she had that for which she had striven so hard. The six students were kneeling before the High Master, taking their Oath to use their powers only as they had been taught, and only for good. The Oath was sacred, the cornerstone of the School: the single most important moment in a Sorcerer's life.

Their vows taken, the six students rose from their knees. Then the High Master went to each of them in turn, solemnly embracing them, and bestowing on each a long-sleeved robe, the revered symbol of their hard-earned status. Mellorn's colouring was the more startling against the dazzling white of the garment. Silvren caught her eye, and they both smiled. Then the High Master raised his arms, and the six new Sorcerers turned to gaze triumphantly at the audience. The great burst of cheering that acclaimed them was wild and deafening, and it marked the end of the ceremony and the beginning of the celebrations.

It was many hours before Mellorn eventually wandered home; the festivities had lasted all night, and now it was sunrise. Her mother had gone home several hours earlier, but Mellorn found it pleasant, in the sweet early morning, to be alone with her thoughts.

Silvren and Ashurek's house was a delicate villa of polished red wood, perched on an improbable hill. It was steep and narrow, a stalk of rock thickly clad with grass and trees. Only those who knew the particular path could gain the house; Ashurek preferred to live in this inaccessible solitude.

Mellorn ran lightly up through the trees and let herself in quietly, pulling off the white mantle as she entered her room. She threw it across a chair and put on a pale gold shirt and

42

black breeches instead. Not feeling like sleep, she went into the large, light room which they used as a study.

The walls were lined with books and manuscripts; the only furniture was a large desk and three or four chairs of the same sheeny red wood as the house. From the large window the forested vales of Ikonus could be seen, all velvet green and dark blue shadows. In the distance sparkled the School of Sorcery.

But Mellorn did not look out of the window. She sat down at the desk and stared at a small model of her parents' Earth, a curious toy which had fascinated her since childhood. Her mother had made it, with Ashurek's help and not a little sorcery; an exquisitely crafted representation of their world, with its moons and strange planes. A sphere about the size of Mellorn's cupped hands was inlaid with jewel-like colours which showed the two great continents, Tearn and Vardrav, lying in a foaming blue sea. The small green island of Forluin, the Arctic ice-cap and the tiny southern continent had also been carefully worked.

The Planes were represented by tiny flat discs – each enamelled in the appropriate colour – arranged round the Earth in an equilateral triangle. The White and Black Planes were at the corners of the base, the Blue Plane at the apex. The model floated – or appeared to rest on air – four inches above the surface of the desk. A breath was enough to set it in motion so that the two ivory moons danced round the spinning Earth, while the coloured discs moved in an orbit of incredible complexity. Spirals of silver wire caught the light as they turned, so it seemed that curves of energy were circling round and round the globe. Mellorn could have contemplated it for hours, and often had; there was something about it that concentrated her thoughts. My parents' Earth, she thought. My Earth?

There were light footsteps behind her, and Silvren leaned on the back of her chair. 'The movement of the moons is quite accurate,' Silvren said over her daughter's shoulder.

'You're up early, Mother,' Mellorn said, smiling.

'I couldn't sleep. Too much celebrating, I suppose.' She

blew gently on the Sphere, making it dance faster, shining blue, green and silver in a shaft of sunlight. 'The Planes aren't really discs, nor can they be seen from Earth, they're infinite, and in separate dimensions. But I didn't know how else to represent them.'

'It's beautiful. It always was my favourite toy.'

'We made it for you.' Silvren moved to look out of the window, where the sun gleamed warmly on her honey-gold skin and hair. The practice of sorcery bestowed an ageless quality, so that she seemed hardly any older now than when Ashurek had first met her. 'I'm sorry Ashurek wouldn't go to the ceremony.'

'It doesn't matter, I didn't expect him to. I know how he feels about me learning the skills of soldiery . . . and the rest.'

Silvren bit her lip, but thought better of making any reply to this. 'So,' she said lightly, 'you are now a fully fledged Sorceress at last. And you'll be a better one than I ever was.'

'I doubt that.' Mellorn left the desk and came to her mother's side. Standing, she was a head taller than Silvren; in fact, she seemed to have almost nothing of Silvren about her. Unlike her brother Callin, with his coffee skin and brown hair and tawny eyes, she was no mediocre compromise between the two races. She was all contrasts: nearly as tall as Ashurek, lean and long-legged, with the same dark brown skin on which purple lights played. She had a high forehead and cheekbones, a long, chiselled nose, and the set of mouth and eyebrows that could look cruel unless she smiled. Her eyes were large, the irises a brilliant green-gold. She could have been taken for a pure Gorethrian – except that she had Athrainian-blonde hair, a long, shining banner of pale and deep gold mixed, which fell to her waist, catching the light like fluid.

They looked out at the sweet morning landscape for a while in silence, each with an arm about the other's waist. Presently Silvren asked quietly, 'And what will you do now? Have you any plans? Sometimes I wish you would confide in me more . . .'

'I don't know,' her daughter murmured. 'This world . . . what can I do? Be a healer, a cultivator, a teacher? Or I could remain a scholar, or take a position of authority – what would it matter? Nothing I do will make any difference to this world, for good or ill – it runs more mechanically than that toy.' She waved a hand at the model of Earth. 'Everything is perfect. What is there to improve?'

'There's still work to do. Things are changing all the time,' Silvren replied earnestly. 'We've rescued Ikonus from near-destruction. Isn't it worthwhile to work at maintaining "perfection"?'

'Of course it is,' Mellorn said without feeling.

'But not for you?'

She looked round at Silvren, her eyes burning just as Ashurek's sometimes did. 'Oh, Mother, this world is so small! Everything flows from the School of Sorcery, everything returns there. Clockwork. There are no threats to order, all is benevolent and just and – utterly dull. And I am not even a native of this world.'

'You were born here,' Silvren pointed out.

'But my blood and all my instincts are of Earth,' she answered intransigently. Silvren knew that her own words and beliefs, however eloquently expressed, would never quench the strange fire that burned in Mellorn's heart. Since childhood she had been fascinated by Earth, always begging her parents to tell her about it. There seemed no reason for her to be so haunted by it, and they had hoped that she would eventually lose interest, as Callin had. But in her heart, Silvren knew that her daughter would never settle on Ikonus. The knowledge was bitter.

'How can I stay here?' Mellorn went on. 'For ever subordinate to the High Master, no matter how strongly I disagree with him.'

'What do you mean, disagree?'

'I think he is wrong about the Sphere.' She half-smiled. 'I can say that with impunity, now I'm a full Sorceress.'

'But the Sphere is fundamental to the working of sorcery!' Silvren exclaimed. 'How can he be wrong about it?'

45

'Because, Mother, I think it is dangerous. Should magic be so pure, all the darkness taken from it? It's unnatural. And look what happened when Arlenmia interfered with the Sphere – all that accumulated darkness was released on the world in one fell cloud. I think they were mad to rebuild the Sphere. They should have learned, and left well alone.'

'It had to be rebuilt, to reabsorb the darkness.'

'They should have found another way. Don't you see? It is like a drug – the more you use it, the more you need it. They have trapped themselves in a circle of total dependence on the Sphere. What if another like Arlenmia comes and it happens again?'

'It won't. It's better safeguarded now.'

'Well, I hope it is. Oh, Mother, I'm not arguing with you, I just need to say what I feel.'

'I know,' Silvren said, smiling.

'Mother, you described to me what happened on Earth. How, when the Serpent died, a positive and negative energy were channelled through the Silver Staff to create a new force, a power which could be shaped for sorcery.'

'Yes.' Silvren lowered her eyes.

'You were once your world's only Sorceress, born out of your time. But now the Serpent is dead, Sorcerers can exist freely. Isn't that right?' Silvren nodded. 'Well, and are there Sorcerers on Earth? Don't you know? Because I don't see how there can be.' Mellorn turned and walked slowly round the room, but her mother remained staring out of the window, one hand clutching the frame. 'No one has come here from Earth as you did, asking to be instructed at the School. And how else could anyone become an enchanter?'

'They must learn from the beginning, as they did on this world, once,' Silvren muttered.

'Then they could waste centuries in trial and error. Would that be right, do you think? Mother, I remember, when I was little, you often used to say to father that you ought to go back. That you were born out of your time for a reason, which was that when M'gulfn died and sorcery became possible, it was your task to guide and instruct those who had the

46

latent gift of magic. And every time, father would dissuade you. Until eventually you stopped mentioning it.'

She had circled back to the window. Silvren looked at her, her golden eyes shadowed by a mixture of regret and guilt. 'You don't miss anything, do you, Mel? Yes, I felt I should have gone back. But it was so easy to be dissuaded, when all I really wanted was to stay here with Ashurek and my children. Here was tranquillity and order; on Earth, the unknown, long years of work and danger. After everything that had happened, I couldn't face any more. I just couldn't face it. So, I have reneged on my duty. Do you think a day goes by when I don't think of it?'

'Mother, Mother, I'm not trying to make you feel guilty.' She slid an arm round Silvren's shoulders and kissed her on the cheek. 'I understand. No one would blame you, no one. All I'm saying is that I think I should go instead.'

Silvren stared at her, astounded. Then she said, 'No.'

'No? Just like that?'

'Mel, if you think I would let you go to Earth,' Silvren cried in a rare burst of anger, 'send you *in my place*, my own daughter, to fulfil the duties which I could not face myself – then you are much mistaken. You don't understand what a huge task it is, how hard – I could not let you –'

'But, Mother, I'm young. It wouldn't be a duty to me, it would be a challenge. I want to go.'

'No. I won't hear of it.' There was a silence between them, almost a tension, the pulling of an unknown but irrefusable future. Below them, sunlight and shadow moved imperceptibly across the green vales. After a long time, Silvren said softly, 'I have known people who tried to be more than human. Arlenmia. Medrian. Your father. And myself. But none of us were. And neither are you, my daughter.'

'I might be leaving, Caydrith,' Mellorn announced off-handedly. She was seated against a tree trunk, her legs stretched out in front of her.

'What?' Caydrith, who had been reclining on the grass,

sat up and stared at her. He was a tall, fair-haired young Sorcerer who had received his white robe at the same time as Mellorn. 'Would you care to be more specific? Leaving the School? Home? Me?'

'Something rather more extreme than that,' she said, twisting a stalk of grass between her fingers. 'Leaving the world.'

'Oh.' He continued to look at her, but she did not meet his gaze. 'I won't say, "I see," because I don't. How long for?'

'I don't know. Probably for good.'

'Oh.' He suddenly leaned over and seized her arms. 'For the Sphere's sake, why, Mel? Where are you going?'

'I'm not telling anyone where. I wouldn't want you to entertain thoughts of trying to find me. As to why – it's something personal. A compulsion, something I have to do. I don't know why. I just have to.'

'I don't believe it. You'd just leave – You can't even trust me enough to tell me what you're doing. What makes you so certain I couldn't help? If you are really that set against marrying me, you don't have to flee to another planet. Just say, "No".'

'Caydrith, my love,' she said, leaning her head against his shoulder. 'The last thing I want to leave behind is you. You don't know how difficult it is.'

'Then let me come with you.'

'I can't. I don't know what to expect. I will be working so much on my instincts that anyone else – even you – would only be . . .'

'A hindrance? Well, I know you've always preferred to work alone,' he sighed. 'I suppose I always knew that you would do something like this, one day. But I hoped –'

'Caydrith, I doubt that I'll ever marry anyone. It wouldn't work. I'd drive you mad, I'd never settle down. And you know what I'm like for ordering people about.'

'I don't mind.'

'I know. And that sometimes drives me mad,' she smiled. 'If you must know, I'm going to my parents' Earth,' she began to explain softly. 'Where sorcery is like a new-born

48

child with no parent to nurture or teach it. It's my Earth too . . .'

'And this means more to you than any love ever will,' he said, as if he was resignedly accepting the fact. He put his arms round her and they held onto each other for a long time, faces hidden in each other's hair. Eventually he said quietly, desperately, 'Mellorn, please don't go.'

'It's my Earth,' she repeated. And he knew that the words came from some diamond-hard part of her soul that no pleas could ever touch.

Two horses emerged from the trees and cantered up the long green slope of a hill. Both were grey, one heavily dappled, the other almost white. Arching their muscular necks, they pulled eagerly against the bit until their riders let them gallop. Ashurek's mount, the darker one, began to pull ahead, but Mellorn quickly drew level, relentlessly pursuing the conversation that her father seemed eager to end.

Before she could speak, he said, 'I have told you everything I can about Gorethria. There isn't any more to know. I think you must find some perverse pleasure in tormenting me.' His black hair and silver-fawn cloak streamed back on the wind as he rode, and his eyes were fixed ahead. Like Silvren, he was not much changed; it was not unusual for Gorethrians to reach a hundred and twenty years in perfect health, and he was barely half that.

'And when you sat and wrote reams and reams of Gorethrian history, was that torment?' she called back. 'No one forced you to do that.'

'No, they didn't. It was far from pleasant, and I don't know why I felt compelled to do it. Perhaps I had some vague hope that it might serve as a warning to others.'

'Father, I had a dream,' Mellorn said. They crested the hill and pulled the horses to a snorting, prancing walk. 'I was in a long marble hall which I somehow knew to be in the palace in Shalekahh. The wall was covered with portraits of all the emperors of Gorethria. There was one of you and one

49

of Meshurek. As I was looking at them, I felt I wasn't alone, and I turned round and found a Gorethrian staring at me. His skin was less dark than ours, and he had brilliant red eyes. His hair looked light at the front, as if it had turned partly white, although he was young – perhaps around thirty.'

'And what happened in this dream?'

'Nothing. I walked away from him, and woke up. Do you know who it might have been?'

'No, I can think of no one of that description,' he replied sharply. 'I know I've described the Hall of Portraits to you, but there was never one of me there. So don't imagine it was more than a dream, Mellorn.'

'I don't. It just fascinated me, that's all. I really find it hard to believe, Father, that you've absolutely no interest at all in what happened to Gorethria after you left.'

'Your belief or lack of it makes no difference. It is true. I do not give a damn about Gorethria. If there is any justice, I most ardently hope that she has ceased to exist.'

'You don't mean that.'

Ashurek turned in the saddle, restraining the grey with one hand, and stared furiously at her. In a low voice, he said, 'But I do. I don't know what more I can say to convince you of it. My brother committed acts of incredible evil. So did my father and mother and all my ancestors. None so evil as my surrender to the Egg-Stone, and the murder of my brother and sister – because, alone among them, I *knew* what I was doing, yet I did it anyway. But conscious or unconscious, evil is evil. And Gorethria was beyond redemption.'

As if she were completely unmoved by the passion of this statement, she said, 'I think your view of Gorethria has been coloured by your own unfortunate experiences.'

'Do you? Well, that is a very cool and Gorethrian way of viewing it,' he replied acidly.

She looked down at her horse's neck, and tidied a few strands of the long white mane. 'Father,' she said after a pause. 'If you were still there, you'd be Emperor now, would you not?'

Ashurek rode close to her, seized her arm, and pulled his

50

horse to a halt so that she was forced to stop as well. The grimness of his dark face, the fire in his green eyes, would have filled anyone with terror. He frightened Mellorn at such times, but her pride prevented her from showing it. He said, 'I doubt it. Not if they knew I had murdered Meshurek.'

'That's nonsense,' she retorted, holding his steel-sharp gaze. 'You've told me often how strict the laws of succession are, strict enough to override murder. Or insanity, in Meshurek's case. So strict that it's an anathema to them to have to put a cousin on the throne rather than a line descendant of the ruling family. Besides, from what you've told me, your killing of Meshurek would have been acclaimed, not condemned.'

'Very well, Mellorn,' he replied, the fury in his voice tightly controlled. 'I'll admit you're right. If I was still there, no one could contest my claim to the throne. But –'

'You've answered my question,' she said wryly. 'Please don't give me another lecture.' He released her arm and gave a brief, self-mocking grin.

'I suggest we dismount and let the horses cool off for a while,' he said. They did so, and began to walk side by side through the widely spaced trees, leading the greys.

With thoughtful deliberation, Mellorn said, 'That makes me an emperor's daughter, doesn't it? In fact . . . if I were in Gorethria in your continued absence, that would make me Empress.'

At this, Ashurek turned on her with such fury in his face that she could not hide her shock. She had often angered him before, but never to this extent. Certain that he was going to strike her, she braced herself for the blow, ice-cold with apprehension. It was not the prospect of physical violence that filled her with dread, but something intangible, a terrifying menace that seemed to emanate from Ashurek's burning-cold eyes and fill the air between them with a darkness in which knives clashed. And she knew that he had never, ever turned such a look upon her mother; Silvren was the one human being whom he had treated with unfailing gentility and tenderness, as if in subconscious recompense

51

for the deaths of his brother and sister, whom he had loved but wronged. And surely he abhorred equally the idea of turning such malice upon his daughter. Yet there was something within Mellorn, as she knew, that provoked it against his will. He saw a quality in her that he had hoped never to see again in anyone, something he could not bear.

The blow did not come; in time, he checked himself. A voice was crying inside him, What am I doing? This is my daughter. Silvren's daughter. How many times have I sworn that this was in the past, this compulsion to destroy those I love? Sick with himself, but still angered, he put his hands on Mellorn's shoulders, firmly but without hurting her.

His voice rough with emotion, he said, 'Do not ever let me hear you say such a thing again. Do not even think it.'

Unable to stop herself, she closed her eyes. When she opened them he had gone, and she had not even felt him relax his grasp upon her. He was several yards down the hill, leading the dappled horse back towards their home. Pulling the light grey's head up from the grass, she ran after him, her pride gone.

'Father, Father,' she called, holding onto his arm and then hanging on his neck until she compelled him to stop and face her. 'I'm sorry,' she said. 'I've always tested myself against you. Sometimes I can't stop. Even though I know I'm hurting you –' His anger gone, he shook his head, and suddenly hugged her fiercely. 'Father, I love you so much,' she said, her voice muffled against his shoulder.

'You're not hurting *me*,' Ashurek said. 'Not in the way you think, by reminding me of the past. That doesn't matter at all. How can I make you understand?'

'Try,' she said softly. 'I'm stubborn, but not stupid.'

'What distresses me is the feeling that you are drifting away from us. It's as though you are going back to everything that Silvren and I fought to escape, maybe to make the same mistakes, suffer the same anguish. I find that impossible to accept. I thought that with the Serpent dead and Silvren safe, nothing could ever go wrong again. But time and again I have had to stop her from going back to Earth.'

'I know. She still feels guilty about it.'

'But why should she?' Ashurek exclaimed. 'After what she suffered at the Shana's hands, I could not let her face anything else. She is not *that* strong. Everyone has a limit, and the Serpent was enough to make even the strongest surpass theirs. But once I was certain that I had persuaded her to stay here, I thought my family were safe, that my children would grow up in perfect peace and never know anything of Gorethria. Now a cold wind is blowing from there, tearing my daughter from me and drawing her back into the darkness. Well, Mellorn, can you look me in the eye and say it is not so?'

She met his gaze and whispered, 'No. No, Father, I cannot.'

'Then I have no choice but to say this.' His tone was stern, his face utterly compelling. 'I forbid you to go. I absolutely forbid it.'

'Forbidden her?' Silvren gulped, half-way between laughing and crying. 'Oh, Ashurek, so have I. Poor Caydrith came up to me in the School, distraught, saying that he had begged her not to go, but she wouldn't listen to him. What use is any of it?'

'Silvren, she is not going back to Earth!' Ashurek said fiercely, striding over to where she was standing by the study window. 'And I'll go to any lengths to stop her.'

'Such as what? Bind her hand and foot and lock her away? And even if you could bring yourself to imprison your own daughter, it would be pointless. She's a Sorceress, if you remember, and would be gone in minutes – if you managed to capture her at all –'

'There are invisible bonds, stronger ones. Those of love.'

'I know.' Silvren looked up at him, a shining film in her golden eyes. 'And if they no longer hold her, what will?'

'It's intolerable,' Ashurek muttered. 'I thought I'd broken the chain of evil. Now Mellorn wants to go back and continue it. Will it never end? She's just like my mother.

Just like me.' He reached out and clasped Silvren's hand. 'I always thought, beloved, that any child we had would be the image of you. Callin is, in character. But she – the problem with her is that she is a damned Gorethrian, heart and soul.'

'You'll have to face it. If she is determined to go, there's nothing anyone can do to prevent it. Neither of us must think of going after her. She is an adult. You can't hold yourself responsible for her actions any longer. Do you think your father was responsible for yours? No. We can't chase her like a runaway child. She's a woman, a Sorceress. Credit her with the ability to make her own decisions.'

Ashurek could not reply to this, but stood shaking his head bitterly. Mellorn came into the room, and Silvren turned and went to her, but her father stayed by the window, not looking at her.

Her head high, her tone matter-of-fact and calm, she said, 'Mother, Father, I wish you'd stop arguing about me. I can't tell you how sorry I am to cause you this pain.'

'Not sorry enough not to go, however,' Ashurek said.

'I can't change my mind. I decided years ago – I think I've always known that I have to go to Earth. It's a compulsion . . . do you understand me? Something I have to do, whatever the cost.'

'The cost will be higher than you know,' Silvren said, her voice tight because she was fighting not to cry. 'I used to be so thankful that you would never be as alone as Ashurek and I once were. Now I fear you will be.'

'Don't worry about that, I've always been alone. Inside.'

At this Silvren stared at her, and swallowed, and shook her head as if at a sudden, bitter realisation. Eventually she said sombrely, 'Then, if you must take on this task, you must do it in the right way. You must discover or create something like the Sphere, which will purify the energy –'

'Mother,' Mellorn interrupted. 'You think that the Earth will one day be the same as Ikonus, with the Sphere, and everything perfectly ordered?'

'Without restraint, the power is too dangerous. It must be like this.'

54

'No. It will never be the same. It will be totally different.' Then something broke within Silvren – the pain of losing Mellorn, or regret that she would never see Earth's future – and she began to weep.

Ashurek came forward and embraced her, and looking over her bowed head he said gravely to his daughter, 'I think from the moment you were born I knew that something like this was destined to happen. I never wanted you to become a Sorceress, because of what Silvren was forced to endure, thanks to her sorcery. Yet I could not prevent it. I also remember that I forbade you to learn the use of weapons, yet you disobeyed me. So I suppose I must accept that it is futile to try to control you at this late stage.'

'Father, I was never anyone's to control,' she said, looking levelly at him. 'I suppose you are right. I am a damned Gorethrian.'

He replied quietly, 'There is something pitiless in you, Mellorn. A core of iron which no gentle feelings can ever touch. It's not strength, it's a kind of blindness. I don't know how to explain it. You'll never understand, and the coldness will never warm, unless you see Miril's eyes. But Miril is dead.'

'Gone?' Mellorn's brother, Callin, exclaimed. 'Gone where?'

Silvren tried to explain.

'But when is she coming back?'

'Didn't you hear me? It's very unlikely that she will ever come back, my love.'

'Gone for good – and she never even came to say goodbye to me?' Callin gasped. After a few moments of stunned silence, he put his arms round Silvren and said cheerfully, 'What have I done to deserve a sister like that? Never mind, Mother, you've still got me. If that's any consolation.'

'Oh, it is. You don't know how much.'

It was not until Callin was alone, some hours later, that he allowed himself to give way to tears. Maddening as his sister was, he loved her; for him to have left *her* without a farewell was beyond contemplation.

The ocean was a plane of indigo glass, flat and calm beneath a clear, blue-black sky. Occasionally a stray breeze roughened the water so that an expanse would shimmer like a reflection of the stars, each tiny wave tipped with silver. Against the arch of night, the twin moons gleamed like perfect orbs of porcelain, their aureole blending with the light of countless frosty stars.

A ship moved across this ocean, almost noiseless save for the lap of water against its sides. It was a vessel of cobweb beauty, silvery-pale, its slender masts and ice-delicate spars blanched by the moonlight. The sails were furled and the crew were rowing in silence, as if that which stole colour also had some intangible, subduing effect on their spirits.

Before them, the coast of Forluin drew nearer.

The ship, *The Silver Staff*, had been sighted before night-fall, and many people stood waiting for her. Some were on the soft, pearl-white beach, some atop the cliffs and some round the natural harbour for which the vessel was heading. These folk were unmistakably Forluinish, possessing an aura of graceful beauty that was unique to their race. They waited serenely in twos or threes or groups, their long hair mingling and their cloaks billowing like clouds whenever the night breeze touched them.

Among them stood a brown-haired man, Falin, and his silver-fair wife, Arlena, sharing the silent anticipation. *The Silver Staff* had been feared lost, but now she was home.

As the pale ship drifted nearer, everyone began to converge on the harbour, a mass of ghostly, moon-splashed figures. The vessel had anchored before Falin and Arlena reached the quay, and already the first of the crew were disembarking. They were slender men and women, clad in sea-bleached tunics and leggings. Voices filled the air as people called out and waved to their loved ones, yet the crew's joy at being home seemed strangely half-hearted, uneasy.

At once a whisper went through the crowd, 'They've lost someone.'

Arlena gripped her husband's arm, but he said, 'Don't worry. It couldn't be our son.'

'It's got to be someone's,' she replied.

All round them, the sailors were mingling, seeking and finding parents, children, lovers and friends. Falin and Arlena began to push their way urgently through the crowd, craning their necks in vain for a glimpse of their son.

The Silver Staff had been on a trading voyage to An'raaga, the nearest tip of the Vardravian continent. These voyages were rare, for the Forluinish were loath to leave their land, but once every few years, a crew of the more adventurous would make the long sea-trip to Port Raag, and bring back goods and tales from the outside world. *The Silver Staff* had been away for three years – over half a year longer than was usual – and the families of the crew had been fearful for their safety.

Now the crowd on the quay were beside themselves with relief, but the shadow over their happiness was tangible. The loss of even one crew member was cause for grief.

Arlena fought her way to the end of the gangplank, the strain of three years' waiting culminating in sudden panic. The last two seafarers were stepping onto the quay, and neither of them was her son, Falmeryn. He was not there.

The two were Edrien and Luatha, a man and woman who had been close friends of Falin and Arlena for years. The four of them had gone to the House of Rede with Estarinel, and the bond between them was unbreakable. But there was no joy in their faces as they disembarked and approached their anxious friends; their eyes were grave and their mouths were sad.

'Falin, no . . .' Arlena whispered as Luatha slid a comforting arm through hers and Edrien placed a heavy hand on Falin's shoulder. And before they spoke she knew exactly what they were going to say and the gentle, terrible tone they would use.

'We've some bad news. About Falmeryn . . .'

It took them ten days to ride from the coast back to Trevilith, the central area of Forluin where they lived. The countryside shimmered all shades of green and gold and russet, and the fair woodlands around them echoed with birdsong. But for once Falin and Arlena did not appreciate it. They rode home swiftly, with bowed heads and heavy hearts.

'Do you want to tell your mother first?' Falin asked.

'No. Estarinel,' she replied.

So they came to a small valley fringed by trees, about half a mile from the Bowl Valley where she and Estarinel had once lived with their family. No one lived there now, it was farmland; memories of the Serpent had been too strong for them to rebuild the house. Those terrible events had happened twenty-six years ago; long over, though never forgotten. No trace of defilement remained, and Forluin had become richer and lovelier than ever as if in compensation, but for a nightmare second, induced by her grief, Arlena experienced a vivid recollection of that time, the same strangulating fear.

'Falin, will you tell them?' she asked. 'I don't think I can.'

'Of course, beloved.'

In the centre of the valley was a cottage of softly coloured stone, half-concealed by golden beeches, surrounded by orchards and herb gardens. Oblique shafts of sunlight hung in the air like silver-gold gauze, outlining every leaf, flower and insect with light, iridescent on the coats of the great brown horses who grazed round the edges of the valley. In the nearest herb garden a dark-haired girl of about twenty was hoeing a bed of camomile. She was Filmorwyn, Estarinel's youngest daughter.

Seeing them, she waved merrily and called out, 'Mother! Father! Falin and Arlena are here!'

Tethering their horses, they walked slowly towards the cottage, hand in hand. Filmorwyn ran over to them and

58

hugged them both, asking excitedly, 'Well, Aunt Arlena, has *The Silver Staff* come back yet?'

Estarinel and Lilithea came out to meet them, smiling, but before any greetings were exchanged, before Falin could even begin to explain, Arlena was in her brother's arms, weeping.

'Falin?' said Lilithea anxiously. 'Didn't the ship come back? What's wrong?'

'*The Silver Staff* returned safely,' he replied, 'but Falmeryn was not aboard.'

'Oh, dear gods,' Filmorwyn cried.

'What do you mean?' Estarinel asked quietly, stroking Arlena's long silver hair. 'That he is dead?'

'I don't know. I suppose so. He disappeared in An'raaga,' Falin answered shortly.

'I could bear waiting for the ship to return, even when it was months late, but now there's no hope of anything. E'rinel, I felt as if the Serpent came back,' Arlena sobbed against Estarinel's shoulder. 'Just for me, personally, as if –'

'Hush. Don't say that,' he whispered into her ear, rocking her. 'Don't ever say that. Come into the house, and we'll talk about it. Have you told mother and Lothwyn yet?'

'No. E'rinel, would you tell them for me? I don't think I could bear to.'

'Yes. It's all right. Come on.'

Within the cottage, they talked for hours, although no amount of talking could change the situation. When it grew dark, Estarinel lit lamps whose light danced on the creamy walls and the soft-hued, woven rugs. Lilithea and Filmorwyn brought them food and wine.

'Falmeryn left the ship on his own while they were in Port Raag. There was nothing strange in that, Edrien said, because they'd never considered it a risk to go about alone in An'raaga. Obviously they were wrong,' Falin said. 'He didn't come back, and they couldn't find him.'

Estarinel and Lilithea's two older children were with them now. Arviel was a quiet, graceful young woman with shining, russet hair. Her brother, Farinel, resembled Estarinel closely, except that he was brown-haired, like Lilithea. Both were deeply upset at the news; their cousin Falmeryn was very dear to them.

'I didn't hold Edrien and Luatha responsible for his welfare, and I don't blame them for an instant,' Falin continued. 'But I think they blame themselves. They were more distraught than us, if that's possible. The ship was late because they stayed in An'raaga for six months, looking for him. *Six months*. There was no more they could have done. At last they decided that they must come back, before everyone at home thought the ship had gone down.'

Estarinel leaned forward, his face half-shadowed by his long, dark hair. 'But they found no proof that he was dead? Then he may well still be alive.'

'That might be worse,' Arlena said, her voice unsteady. 'Edrien said – he said they heard a rumour of slave-traders in Port Raag. Men who take people to serve the Gorethrians. Oh, gods.'

Falin put his arm round her and said in a low voice, 'I've been thinking of going to An'raaga myself, with anyone who'd come with me, and –'

'Oh, Falin, no!' Lilithea broke in. 'What good would it do? Vardrav is vast, you'd never find him. It would be terribly dangerous. One person missing is bad enough. How would it help to risk the lives of others?'

'Lili is right,' Estarinel added. 'Imagine how we'd feel if you went away, how my family would feel if I went with you – the chain has no end. Please promise me you won't, Falin.'

Falin looked into his friend's gentle eyes, recalling all they had been through together, and he nodded, saying quietly, 'You'd think after surviving the Serpent, nothing else could hurt us, wouldn't you? But it still can.'

'Oh, why did he have to go?' Arlena exclaimed wretchedly.

'You used to say you'd like to go yourself. Remember?' Estarinel said, gripping her hand. 'He has your adventurous spirit.'

'That was a long time ago. One sea voyage to the House

of Rede was enough to last me a lifetime, and the Serpent cured me of being adventurous for good.'

'Don't worry, Aunt Arlena,' Filmorwyn said consolingly, and Arviel added, 'I'm sure he's still alive, convinced of it. You mustn't give up hope.'

'Oh, Estarinel is lucky,' Arlena said with feeling. 'He has the three of you. I have only one son.'

'Who is a grown man, and quite capable of looking after himself,' Farinel put in. 'He'll find his own way home.'

Falin and Arlena looked at each other, somehow strengthened by this statement. Estarinel said, 'He's the same age as I was at the beginning of the Quest, and I've always considered him more courageous and level-headed than I was then. Arlena,' he met his sister's tear-lucent eyes, 'Hoping is easy, but you must do the hardest thing of all now.'

'Which is to wait. I know it will be unbearable.'

'More than that. It is to go on living. We've done it before and we can do it again, as often as is necessary.' As Estarinel spoke, Lilithea came to sit beside him and slid her arm through his, her rich bronze-brown hair half-concealing her face, as if she were moved by memories and the poignancy of their happiness. 'And you will bear it, because we are with you.'

3

'We will Escape'

You are not betraying anyone, my lady.

Kharan rode blindly, her hands in their jewelled gloves locked on the reins. She was beyond the outskirts of Shalekahh now, but still she could not escape the presence of Gorethrians. There were army encampments all around the city, rows of tents like brilliant beetles plated in red, gold and blue. Soldiers strode to and fro between them, their cloaks hanging like the folded wings of vultures. Officers rode by on fire-gold horses, which danced along with their heads high, trailing fire from their manes and tails. The very air seemed to swell with the easy confidence of these conquerors whom no resistance, no plea for pity could turn aside.

For the first time, Kharan hated them. Yet she knew that her hatred was a tiny, ineffectual thing that could neither help anyone nor change anything.

Close your mind to it, my lady.

Sensing his rider's tension, the palfrey began to gallop. She was normally a diffident rider, but now she urged it on recklessly, as if in an impotent bid for escape. She thought that if she saw any more Gorethrian faces, she would go mad. The horse's hooves thudded on the lush grass, and the fire-red, weeping trees flashed past her in a blur, but she rode with her head down, paying no heed to her direction. Gorethria had a unique, feverishly coloured loveliness, but to her the surroundings held no beauty at all; the grass seemed carved from malachite, the trees made of metal, the milky-blue sky as cold as quartz. There was no softness, no comfort in this alien landscape; and no escape from the blackened, agonised faces which haunted her inner vision.

These are the ones who survived.

She was in Shalekahh again, riding slowly between the opal-white spires like a runaway child returning shamefacedly home. What a coward I am, she thought. I could have ridden away into the mountains. No one would have taken any notice, Xaedrek would not have realised until it was too late. I still could turn round and flee . . . With this thought burning in her skull, she let the ivory-white palfrey plod steadily back towards the palace, knowing that she could not do it.

'What a fool I was, what a despicable, arrogant, damned fool to imagine that I was not frightened of Xaedrek,' she thought bitterly. 'Admit it, Kharan, you are terrified of him. Terrified, terrified.'

There is no question of you leaving.

She rode under an arch into the mews where the horses for the personal use of the Emperor and his household were kept. A marble square with an elaborate fountain in the centre was enclosed by four rows of stables as symmetrical and graceful as the palace itself; they were built of pure white stone, intricately carved and embellished with pastel colours, and they had rows of glittering, arched windows and gilded turrets. Two small stable-lads worked non-stop to keep the square impeccably clean, the Gorethrians being a highly fastidious race.

No groom came out to meet Kharan and she was relieved at this, although it meant she had to dismount from the side-saddle somewhat awkwardly without assistance. She quickly led the palfrey into the mews and stabled him herself, deliberately taking an age to untack and groom him, careless of soiling the pale dress she wore, and praying that none of the stable-hands would come in and see her. More than anything she wanted to be on her own.

All too soon the task was ended. She stood stroking the horse's warm neck with a visibly trembling hand; now there

63

was no reason to stay in the stable, and someone was bound to come in at any moment, yet she still could not gather courage to return to the palace. She had been out riding for hours, but the temporary escape had only made things seem worse. She felt she would rather die here, now, than go back and face Xaedrek again.

Not that he would miss me anyway, she thought with mixed feelings.

On an impulse she ran along the length of the stalls and climbed a ladder into the hayloft. A pointless action, for it solved nothing and she could not stay there indefinitely; but it gave her a welcome illusion of refuge, at least for a few minutes. Here the air was warm and sweet with hay, here were the mellow hues which Gorethrians so despised; the muted tones of bare wood and straw.

She crossed the floorboards, ignoring the dust gathering on her silken skirts, and stared out of the arched, leaded window. It was several weeks since Varian had shown her what was inside the mansion. Weeks! And she had done nothing in that time except struggle with her conscience, agonise over her impossible situation. The few times she had seen Xaedrek – for he was more preoccupied than ever now – she had chanced only the mildest, most oblique questions about what he was doing; and he had parried them with such cool levity that she had immediately lost her nerve. There was something behind his light manner that filled her with dread. While loathing her own cowardice, she knew in her heart that confronting him was utterly futile. She knew he was evil. How would inducing him to admit it change anything? It would only made him realise that she was turning against him. And those who opposed Xaedrek tended to vanish into the mansion, presumably to make some fatal contribution to his research.

She shuddered. She was trapped in this nightmare. En-slaved by her own conscience and faint-heartedness.

'You were right, Varian, damn you!' she cried aloud, her voice tight with anger and pain.

To her horror, she heard a voice behind her say hesitantly,

64

'Oh – you startled me – I wasn't expecting anyone to be here.'

She swung round violently and saw a young man climbing up through the hatch into the hayloft. He was slim and long-legged, clad in the cream-and-gold livery of the Imperial mews, and he had long, glossy, red-brown hair. She had never seen him before. But what stunned her most was the unmistakable beauty of his fair-skinned face, the clearness of the dark grey, almost violet eyes. He was Forluinish.

Had she but known it, he was even more surprised than she. It took him several seconds to realise who she was. He saw a woman of moderate height, shapely rather than slim, clad in such clothes as – usually – only the Gorethrian aristocracy wore: a close-fitting, full-sleeved jacket and a long skirt of ivory silk, quilted and figured with complex designs that were thickly sewn with pearls, silver thread and tiny crystals. Her luxuriant dark brown hair was trimmed to jaw level, as was the current fashion at court, and her fair skin had a rosy, dusky sheen which almost seemed to change with the light. She could not be described as beautiful – her face was too square, her chin too pointed, her nose a touch too long – and yet there was something more than usually attractive about her. Even in her obvious state of distress, there was warmth and softness in her large, brown eyes, humour in the curve of her mouth. As she stood staring at the Forluinishman, twisting her gloves nervously in her hands, he realised, incredulously, that she was the Emperor's esteemed mistress.

'I – I didn't think anyone would come up here,' she stammered at length, desperately embarrassed.

'I didn't mean to startle you,' the man said, equally bemused and at a loss. 'But these are my living quarters.'

'Oh,' she gasped. 'I'm sorry. I didn't know.'

'It's all right. I was just surprised, that's all.' There was an awkward silence. Then he asked cautiously, 'You are the Lady Kharan, aren't you?'

'Yes,' she muttered, looking at the floor, obviously upset at being recognised.

'My name is Falmeryn. I have charge of the grooms in this section of the mews . . .'

'And you have to live in a hayloft?' she exclaimed, looking at him in surprise.

'By choice. I prefer it to the grooms' quarters. It means there's always someone near the horses.'

'You're Forluinish, aren't you?' she asked hesitantly. 'What on Earth are you doing in Gorethria?'

His face became troubled. 'I was on a trading voyage to An'raaga. I stupidly left the ship on my own and was seized by some men whose occupation was providing slaves for the Gorethrians. I tried pointing out that Forluin was nothing to do with Gorethria, therefore they had no right to abduct me. They laughed. I was dragged across Vardrav, which took months – over a year, I think – and brought to Shalekahh.'

'That's terrible,' she said with feeling.

'Not so much for me. I've not been badly treated. I was given this job because I knew about horses, and when I'm with the horses I forget everything else, and I'm happy. But my friends on the ship . . . and my family.' He shook his head. 'Heaven knows what they think has happened to me.'

'I'd better go,' she said, but she did not move.

'You don't have to.' They looked at each other, the awkwardness still there, but fading. Then Falmeryn said, 'There's something wrong, isn't there?'

She turned away and looked out of the window, biting her lip. Like a physical jolt it struck her that he was the first person who had spoken to her with any genuine concern since – in fact, she could not remember a time.

'Would it help to talk to me about it?' he asked.

'I couldn't. I mean – no, it's nothing.'

'Then – if you just want to stay here, on your own, for a while – I'll go. I've got a few things to see to, anyway –'

'No, don't go!' she exclaimed before she could stop herself. She turned round and he came to her side, somewhat hesitant because he was conscious of who she was. She said, 'You must think I'm mad, lurking in here like this – but I just needed some time to think.' She put a hand to her forehead, suddenly dizzy.

'There's only hay to sit on,' Falmeryn said apologetically. 'But you might feel better if you sat down.' She nodded, and let herself be guided to a truss of hay, knowing that her self-possession was sliding away, but unable to prevent it. She was shaking. This sudden, unlooked-for kindness in the midst of her distress was devastating her. The one defence she had against breaking down, the only thing that enabled her to behave day after day as if nothing had changed, was that her dilemma was known only to herself. Once she told Falmeryn, it would no longer be her secret; and she did not even know if he was to be trusted.

But at this particular moment, she no longer cared.

'If I tell you, you'll despise me,' she said hoarsely.

'I doubt that,' he said, sitting beside her. 'Lady Kharan, I don't even pass judgement on the Gorethrians. Why should I condemn you?'

'Don't call me "lady", please. I don't know where to start.'

After a moment, he prompted her gently, 'You're from An'raaga, aren't you?'

'Yes, but I only spent my childhood there. I don't remember my parents – I suppose they must have died. I was brought up with about thirty others, all of us orphans, until I was twelve. Then the slave-traders came – not Gorethrians, but villains from Bagreeah – and took us all back there. No one tried to stop them. I think they must have bought us.' She frowned, then continued, 'It was when the Empire was weaker, but there were still Gorethrians in Bagreeah, and they'd come and go from Shalekahh along some secret route which the rebels didn't know. Well, after three years I was sick of the jungle, so I persuaded a slave-manager to take me to Shalekahh.' She was determined to be honest, to leave Falmeryn with no illusions about her. 'When I say "persuaded", I mean I used the only talents I had at my disposal. And I contrived a post in a nobleman's house by the same means. That of Duke Xaedrek as he was then.

'Shalekahh seemed like paradise to me, so beautiful, so

clean, so graceful. Different from everything I'd known. But I wanted . . . I didn't want to be a *slave* in it. I wanted to be part of it. And I craved riches and status, almost as a way to take revenge on the Gorethrians for making a slave of me.

'And it was so easy. So easy. Five days after I met Xaedrek, I was no longer his serving maid, but his mistress. I was utterly calculating about the whole thing, because when I want to charm a man, I can, and it meant a lot to me to prove that I could "conquer" a Gorethrian aristocrat who made the rest of his household fall over themselves with fear. I thought I was so clever. I was just seventeen.'

'Was this long ago?' Falmeryn asked.

'Nine years. Don't ask me what Xaedrek sees in me. I don't think he'd ever look at a woman at all if I wasn't there – in fact, he hardly even looks at me lately.' Her shoulders sagged, her hair fell forward and hid her face. 'I've always been so hard-headed, totally unsentimental and cynical about everything. But this has got the better of me. Xaedrek is involved with something terribly evil, obsessed by it. Not just renewing the Empire, something even worse. I suppose I've always known it in my heart, but it was so easy not to think about it . . . until I was shown proof so horrible that . . .' She trailed off, shuddering. 'Falmeryn, I'm frightened. I thought I was strong. Now I find out how weak I am, how utterly helpless.'

'They talk about him having some dark power. I try not to take any notice. What was this proof?'

Haltingly, she tried to explain what she had seen in the mansion. 'I don't know what he's doing, I don't want to,' she concluded, 'but it's something I can't – here I've been gaily living the life of a courtier, playing all those petty games of despite with the Gorethrian nobility, laughing at them, thinking I'd "defeated" them in some way, and all the time, Xaedrek has been –'

She broke off, white-faced and shivering. Falmeryn, stunned to see how genuinely, deeply horror-stricken she was, hurried to fetch her a goblet of wine which she drank gratefully.

When she was calmer, he asked unexpectedly, 'Do you love him?'

Kharan stared at him as if he had said something incredible. 'I've never loved anybody. And no one, I swear it, has ever loved me. To put it at its most basic, I used him for material gain, and to escape slavery. And he used me as a pleasant distraction from his duties. You look shocked.'

'I am, a bit. It's only that things are not like that in Forluin,' he said quietly.

'Well, aren't you lucky?' she retorted.

'I don't see how you can live with someone for nine years and feel nothing for them.'

She looked at the goblet cupped in her hands. 'Perhaps I did once. Not now. All I know is that I've been deceiving myself for nine years. I thought I was in control, that I'd made myself the equal of Gorethrians. What an idiot! All I've been doing is condoning that evil. I can't stand it any longer, and I don't know what to do.'

'Why don't you leave him?'

'Because I'm a miserable coward!' she exclaimed angrily. 'I used to imagine I wasn't frightened of him. The truth is, I'm terrified.'

'Is he cruel to you?'

'No – oh no, it's more subtle than that. He is kindness itself. That makes it worse. But he'd never let me leave. It's not that he needs me, or would miss me, it's just the principle of it. Everything he has, he must keep. I'm more a slave than you, Falmeryn. Now, aren't you going to tell me I'm unprincipled and wicked and deserve everything I get?'

'No. I think you're being very hard on yourself, Kharan.'

'Damn.' She scrubbed tears out of her eyes. 'I refuse to cry. It can't solve anything.'

'It might make you feel better.'

'I don't want to feel better! If I did, I might think this situation was not so bad after all, and let it drift on. Closing my mind to it.'

In a low voice, he said, 'I feel the same as you. I can't bear to think of what the Gorethrians are doing to the rest of this

69

continent. Every day I think, today I will take a horse and ride to the coast and escape. But I never do. It's not that easy. I know I'd be pursued and killed, and I don't much like the idea. I'm frightened, too.'

'You are?' she looked up at him in surprise.

'But by not making the attempt, I'm also condoning evil. Living comfortably at the Emperor's expense, happily looking after his horses. Does that make me any better than you?'

'I don't know,' she said, and broke into silent, convulsive sobs which shook her whole body. For a childish moment she wished he would put his arms round her and comfort her, but, still aware of who she was, he did not.

'I wish I knew what to say to you, Kharan,' he said. 'I can't see any solution.'

'I can,' she cried, drying her eyes on a glove. 'But I'm too much of a coward for that, too.'

'Don't,' he said gently. 'Don't even think of such a thing. Look, all I can see at the moment is that you need a friend. So do I. Will you come and see me again? Whenever you like . . .'

'I shouldn't . . .'

'But you will?'

She nodded, and stood up unsteadily, brushing strands of hay from her clothes. 'Now I really must go.'

'Are you sure you're all right?' he asked concernedly.

'Yes.' She took a deep breath and tidied her hair; suddenly, she felt just strong enough to return to the palace, if not to face Xaedrek. 'I don't know why you've been so kind, but I'm grateful.' She climbed over the lip of the hatch, but just before she descended, he reached out and took her hand.

'We're both prisoners, Kharan. It's not something either of us can solve alone.' For a long moment they looked at each other, and she felt the last of her embarrassment swept away by a fellow-feeling so intense that her heart leaped. Almost in a panic at the strangeness of this sensation, she half-fell down the ladder and hurried away.

Xaedrek walked slowly across the subterranean marble chamber, his arms folded, his ruby eyes thoughtful. He was wearing a dark red robe with loose sleeves and a deep border of gryphons and hawks worked in black pearls round the hem.

'No, I don't want you to do anything, Varian,' he said. 'Just sit in that chair and talk to me.' The small Patavrian obeyed, the tendons on his hands standing out as he clutched the carved arms of the chair. The light in the chamber was even and white and apparently sourceless. It made the four marble columns look flat, almost unreal.

On one side of the room, between two columns, was an arrangement of greenish glass rods and gold metal tubing, some twelve feet wide and reaching to the ceiling. It shimmered as if a liquid light, immune to external laws, was oozing continually along the tubes. It had a weird kind of beauty, but its purpose was obscure. Varian had often seen it in use and still did not understand what it did, but the sight of it always caused a cold, nauseous perspiration to spring from his pores.

'Well, Steward Varian, tiresome though this is, I'm afraid I have to take you to task. Don't look so dismayed, it won't take long. Just a few words.' The Emperor stood at the side of the chair and looked down at the dark-skinned man.

'Your Majesty?'

'We both know the unfortunate event to which I refer, of course.' Varian was silent. 'Come now. Must I remind you? For reasons best known to yourself, you took the Lady Kharan into the rooms above and showed her things which you must have known would disturb her. She has not been well since. Can you provide some sort of explanation for this aberration of yours?'

'It was – it was an impulse, Sire. Foolish, I know,' Varian grunted almost inaudibly.

'Foolish? To call it wickedly irresponsible would be an understatement. How could she be expected to comprehend the necessity of my work? I do not discuss it with anyone except a particular few. You know that.'

71

'Yes, Sire.'

'Then you do understand how stupidly you've behaved?'

Varian longed to shout out what was in his heart, as if the very passion of it was a venom that could strike Xaedrek dead. But dread cleaved him to the chair, clogged the words in his throat. He muttered, 'Yes, Sire, I do.'

'Excellent.' Xaedrek smiled. 'The lecture is over.' He walked over to the esoteric apparatus and began to make adjustments to it. Slowly, Varian's hands relaxed on the chair arms. No punishment. He shivered with relief, and slumped in the seat, too weak to stand up.

The door opened and the woman-demon Ah'garith entered, clad in a long mantle of a sickly green hue.

'Ah'garith, good, you're just in time to give me some assistance,' Xaedrek said. He was paying no attention to Varian, but as the steward rose furtively and made to edge towards the door, he said, 'Come here, Varian, I need your help as well.'

Varian went to his side, still nervous, but unsuspecting. Ah'garith was at the far end of the apparatus, sliding back a marble slab to reveal a triangular area of a substance which scintillated with shifting greens and blues. As she stood on it, it bounced slightly, like living muscle. She raised her hands to grasp the ends of two glass rods, touching her forehead to a third, and her whole form began to vibrate as if shaken by an invisible hand. Varian felt sick. Now they would bring in some wretched prisoner. He had witnessed it many times.

Xaedrek, meanwhile, was checking a large spiral of clear glass that ran down from the top of the apparatus, and terminated in a huge transparent sphere. Into this he sifted a quantity of a dark green powder. That done, he said, 'Step up, would you, Varian?'

The Patavrian gaped at him, praying desperately that he had misunderstood.

Patiently, Xaedrek took his arm and guided him to the place where the unfortunate victim usually stood. 'Yes, I

72

want your energies today. You know how the subject is attached to the equipment, don't you? Well, in you go.'

'Your Majesty –' Varian's legs buckled and Xaedrek had to hold him up. 'No. No. Why me?'

Nothing but kindness in his voice, Xaedrek said, 'I did tell you that you'd done something misguided in the extreme. To be honest, Varian, I've begun to doubt your loyalty. Torture is so old-fashioned, such a waste of everyone's energy, don't you agree? Whereas you can be happy in the knowledge that this, though it may be uncomfortable, is done without malice and solely to make a positive contribution to Gorethria's welfare. Thus your end will expiate your folly.'

Varian screamed.

'I am sorry, Varian,' the Emperor said, easing him into position amid the glass and metal tubes so that his body was held fast by them. 'You won't necessarily die, you know. If you don't, there'll be no further retribution.'

A deep buzzing noise filled the chamber as Ah'garith drew power through herself, fed it into the rods. The white light became intense, tinged with green. The rods vibrated, cold and hard against Varian's skin, pressing into his back, stomach, shoulders, head. He felt them becoming warmer, now hot, now burning, and through his blurred, half-conscious vision he saw light dancing dizzily along the tubes like some wild, fluorescent liquid.

The light and heat began to enter him, accumulating in his body as if it were a battery cell. For a few seconds he felt a mad exhilaration; the discomfort of the rods was gone, and he seemed to be suspended in a lake of diamond light, his arms outstretched, filled with a power that could rend Shalekahh and bring the black mountains crashing down on the ruins. Then the pain began. The light became white heat, searing his nerves, burning his lungs raw, and he had no more control over it than over a gale, rushing into him and through him and onwards down a white tunnel that spiralled into infinity.

And with it he felt his being, both flesh and soul, slowly shredding away. He was the accumulator for an energy as fierce as lightning, which, while itself of dazzling brightness, devastated and blackened whatever it struck. But Varian's agony was more than fire on flesh: it was a profound disruption of mind, a cauterisation that could never heal. If he survived, the unique taint of that vast and terrible power would stay with him for ever, an insanity haunted by the stench of scorched bone.

The chamber swam with light, energy flashed round and round the glass spiral and entered the sphere, which now shone like a miniature sun. Xaedrek watched the whole thing carefully, judging the precise moment at which to terminate it. After about ten minutes, he saw the power begin to fluctuate and lose its intensity, and he called, 'Enough.'

Ah'garith stepped away from the apparatus and the brilliance faded. Xaedrek went to inspect the contents of the sphere and nodded with satisfaction as he saw that the powder had turned from dark green to a delicate, pale gold.

'Very good,' he muttered. 'I'll have them administer this to the men of Legion VIII. Ah'garith, would you send in a servant to dispose of –' He waved a hand at Varian, whose swollen, blistered body was now hanging limply within the cage of rods. Ah'garith, infuriated at being ordered about, gave Xaedrek a venomous look and obeyed. Presently two men entered the chamber and bore Varian away, but Xaedrek was now busy with the powder, and took no notice.

Varian had been very lucky. He was dead.

Two days later, Kharan went to see Falmeryn again. To her relief, she found him alone in the mews, feeding the horses.

'I thought you weren't coming back,' he said, giving her a hand into the hayloft and pulling up the ladder after them.

'I almost didn't,' she murmured, looking through the window at the white square below. Four members of the Inner Council rode under the arch, talking and laughing, and she stepped back quickly in case they looked up and saw her.

'Because of Xaedrek?'

'No. I haven't seen him,' she replied, but volunteered no further information.

'Well, you look more cheerful today.' He smiled at her and she half-smiled back, seeming composed but somehow unsure of herself.

'I feel better. It helped a lot, talking to you.' Her face became thoughtful. 'I used to live in Port Raag, when I was a child in An'raaga. I remember a ship coming from Forluin once, many years ago. It was lovely, all silvery wood, so delicate. Everyone ran down to the quay, talking excitedly as if – as if people from another Plane were visiting us. When the Forluinish came ashore, I stared at them and thought how beautiful they were, unearthly in a way . . . not as Gorethrians were alien to us, but the exact opposite, something gentle and golden . . . yet distant. Something we could never hope to capture or understand. The Forluinish ships meant such a lot to us. They were infrequent and unpredictable, but that only made them more mystical. The people around me had always spoken of the Forluinish with love, and when I saw them come from the ship that day – although I never met any of them – I knew why. I've never forgotten that feeling.'

Somewhat taken aback by this, Falmeryn said inadequately, 'That's how you knew I was Forluinish . . .'

'Yes. How long have you been here?'

He came to her side and replied sadly, 'About three months, in Xaedrek's stables. Before this I was in Zhelkahh for a few months; that was after crossing Vardrav, as I told you. It's about three years since I left Forluin.' In a low voice, he added, 'But I'm not spending the rest of my life here. I'm going back to Forluin. I don't know when or how – but I am.'

'You really hate it here, don't you?' she said, putting a sympathetic hand on his arm. 'I didn't realise.'

'I don't hate it. But it's not my home . . . Seeing Gorethrians every day, I could just about tolerate their arrogance while the knowledge of their wrongdoings remained abstract. But since you told me about Xaedrek's mansion –' he closed

75

his hand on hers. 'I feel I ought to do something to stop it, but I don't know what.'

'I don't think there's anything anyone can do to stop him,' Kharan whispered.

'You're not at all like I would have expected,' Falmeryn remarked after a moment. 'I have seen you often – even if you've never noticed me – and you looked as you described yourself.'

'A cynical opportunist? Thank you.' She grinned in spite of herself.

'That's not quite what I meant. You seemed proud, uncaring . . . but in your heart you are not like that at all.'

'Don't be too sure of that, Falmeryn.'

'But I am.' She found she could not avoid his intense, gentle gaze. 'Otherwise you wouldn't be here now. You would have made excuses for Xaedrek and forgotten what you saw.'

'Well, don't you make excuses for me,' she muttered, detaching her hand from his arm in a desperate attempt to resist the growing attraction between them. 'I swear to you, Falmeryn, I'm not trying to charm you for some ulterior motive. I like you too much.'

'I never thought you were,' he said, still looking intently at her. 'And can't you believe that I like you too?'

'That's the problem,' she confessed. 'No one has ever shown me genuine kindness and concern before. No one at all. I'm just not used to it.'

'Not Xaedrek?'

'Oh, it's not the same thing at all!' she exclaimed. 'Don't you know how civilised cruel people can be? There was no love or warmth in it. Of course, I was well aware of that, and thought it didn't matter . . .'

'But friendship does matter.' Falmeryn put his hands on her shoulders and she wondered if he could feel how fast her heart was beating. She had long thought that her childhood impression of the Forluinish was an idealised one; now she realised that it was not.

76

'I know,' she whispered. 'But I've only known it since I met you. Two days.'

'It's a terrible thing to be deprived of love as you have been. And as I've been, as well. I know what this continent's like – I haven't seen a friendly face since I left An'raaga.' He gently brushed a few strands of hair from her cheek. His grey-violet eyes seemed to contain all the tenderness and hope that she was feeling, but none of the confusion. 'I want you and I need you, Kharan. If you don't feel the same, tell me now and we'll forget we ever met.'

She was lost. Her arms were round him and they were kissing, long and passionately.

'This is why I wasn't going to come and see you again,' she said into his hair, trying to recover her breath. 'Because I knew if I did, this would happen. It makes everything so much more complicated.'

'I'm so glad you came back,' he replied warmly. 'But you're wrong. It makes everything perfectly simple.'

And now something had happened which Kharan would previously have dismissed as a laughable impossibility: she had fallen instantly, desperately in love, and that realisation changed everything. Her life at the palace suddenly seemed a colourful nightmare in which Xaedrek was a looming shadow-figure; only Falmeryn was real, and he was all that mattered to her.

In the days that followed she visited him as often as she possibly could without arousing the suspicions of servants or courtiers. It was impossible to tell how closely she was watched, if at all; but she knew there were many who would have relished an opportunity to disgrace her in Xaedrek's eyes. Yet her need to escape the cold brilliance of the Imperial court and find refuge in Falmeryn's arms swept away her terror of discovery.

Xaedrek, however, was the one person who certainly did not notice anything. While not closeted with the Inner Council or going about the affairs of state, he was almost continually at the mansion. When Kharan did not see him, she somehow found the self-possession to speak lightly to him, as if nothing had happened. And far from appearing in any way suspicious of her, he was more preoccupied and distant than ever, and would only talk to her for a short time before retiring to his own chambers – or returning to the mansion.

She did not know whether to feel glad or unnerved.

Weeks went by, and all the time she knew the situation could not continue. She felt she was living in a dream, a strange haze of incredible happiness which was tainted with dread and guilt. She and Falmeryn were risking their lives every time they saw each other and yet from the beginning their passion was a complete and obsessive one that took no heed of danger. Kharan could only wonder at how she had managed to exist before she met him.

As for Falmeryn, he was equally fascinated by Kharan. It was an aura that he could not define: a sweetness in the dark gleam of her eyes or a certain tilt of her head, a spirit that shone when they were together and everything else ceased to exist. He could see why Xaedrek had kept her by him to the exclusion of all others; but if Xaedrek was incapable of love, Falmeryn was not, and with Forluinish open-heartedness he adored her.

So they would cling to each other in the heart-rending joy of love, made more poignant for being edged with fear; and they would talk for hours, drifting in a golden lake of suspended time, not wanting to believe that this feeling of warmth and safety was illusory.

'You make Forluin sound so beautiful,' Kharan said. They were lying in each other's arms on a cover of faded mauve silk – a cast-off from the palace – wrapped round a straw mattress – a contrast from the opulence of her rooms, but luxury had ceased to mean anything to her. 'I would so love to see it.'

'You will, one day,' Falmeryn replied softly.

'You'd take me back with you?'

'Of course. I'm not going back without you.'

She leaned on his chest and looked at him with a half-smile. 'Are you sure? Perhaps there's someone waiting for you there, a wife, a lover . . .'

78

'There are many people I love, but I am not "spoken for",' he answered teasingly.

'I can hardly believe that. I don't want you to break anyone's heart. Especially,' she tangled her fingers in his long, red-brown hair, 'not mine.'

'There is only you, Kharan, I swear it. How do you think I feel when you go back to the palace every night?' He suddenly held her so tight that she could hardly breathe. 'I want to go back to Forluin, and I want you to come with me. That's all there is to it.'

'You make it sound so straightforward. I just don't see how it's possible.' Her eyes serious, she lay back, gently trailing her fingers along the smooth, fair skin of his arm. 'Perhaps we could get out of Shalekahh – I can, because I have the usual freedom of a courtier. But any further . . . you know that unaccompanied "slaves" outside the city are killed on sight. And the countryside is swarming with soldiery.'

'I know it will be difficult. But not impossible,' he said reassuringly. 'We're going to plan it very carefully and we are going to escape. But it must be soon, Kharan. How much longer can we go on like this? We should be able to walk outside together in the sunlight and the trees, not have to meet in secret as if we were doing something wrong.'

'Oh, I agree. But it's not just that. Shalekahh seems like an empty shell to me now, cold, soulless stone, while this hayloft is paradise. But it's just another escape from reality, a way to turn my back on Xaedrek's evil.' She sat up, her brown eyes shining with sudden defiance. 'Oh, Falmeryn, I'm sick of living in fear! I refuse to be frightened any longer.' He gripped her hand and they gazed at each other with love and determination. 'We will escape. And it will be very, very soon.'

A shimmering tunnel stretched before Mellorn, its smooth, pale grey walls as insubstantial as smoke caught in moonlight. Her mouth was dry with apprehension, but that only made her step more resolutely through the threshold. At once the green woods of Ikonus began to elongate and fragment in the periphery of her vision, presently vanishing altogether. That world was now behind for ever, and all she could see was the flat greyness of the infinite corridor.

Silvren had informed her that she could not go to Earth without passing through the Blue Plane, but Mellorn had no wish to discuss her intentions with the H'tebhmellians or anyone else. Using all her instinct, skill and knowledge of the Ways between Worlds, she had created this path directly to Earth. Calorn had been a good teacher.

Now she was drifting down the tunnel, and zigzags of light began to flicker in the translucent walls: white and palest lemon, rust and magenta and dark blue, pearl-green turning to lilac. The stress of moving from one dimension to another manifested itself as physical discomfort; she felt that a roof of rock was pressing down on her head, that invisible, bony fingers were driving into her collarbone and ribs. She resisted an urge to squirm and close her eyes.

She lost her sense of time, but did not allow her mind to dwell on the danger of what she was doing. Withstanding disorientation that might have driven others mad, she fixed her thoughts relentlessly on her destination. The odd colours began to dance wildly, tearing at the fabric of the tunnel so that it frayed and streamed out into the ground, or the sky . . . Like someone emerging from a drugged sleep, Mellorn had no idea of where she was or what she was looking at.

She was in a blackness that was repeatedly slashed by blinding lights, fire-orange, blue, and venomous green. She was sprawled on a rough, wet surface while water roared down on her, and a cacophony of violent detonations deafened her. Gasping, she pressed her hands to her ears and struggled to sit up. What hellish dimension had she landed in?

She closed her eyes, using her sorcerous knowledge to seek the reality behind the external confusion of impressions. Within a second she understood, and laughed out loud at herself. A storm! Ashurek had described Gorethria's eccentric weather to her. In the same moment she knew that she was exactly where she had planned to arrive, a dense forest some twenty miles south-west of Shalekahh. Another flash of searing lightning illuminated the black shapes of trees towering around her, and she took a deep breath of triumphant relief.

She rose to her knees and remained there for a few seconds, bending forward to press her hands onto the wet ground, touching for the first time the leaves and stones and soil of her own Earth. Then she felt something run over her hand. She shook it off and stood up, wiping her fingers on her cloak and pushing back her long, dripping hair.

'Gorethria,' she whispered, elated. She stared up at the storm-torn sky, the luminous clouds fleeing tormentedly between whips of lightning. Bitter rain ran into her eyes and mouth. 'Gorethria.'

She got her bearings, and began to walk towards Shalekahh. Many practical problems faced her, the first of which was the question of shelter; she could have created an aura about herself which would have dried her wet clothes, protected her from the rain, given her some light by which to see her way. But she was wary of using her power so soon after her arrival. As yet she knew nothing of this world; what her parents had told her, however detailed, could never compare with first-hand experience, and things might have changed drastically in the past twenty-five years. It was just possible that any use of sorcery might draw attention to her and to begin with she needed to be unnoticed and anonymous. Ironically, even the means of making herself as good as 'invisible' to ordinary humans might make her shine like a beacon to those with sorcerous skills – if any such existed. Until she knew more, she could not take the risk.

Presently she realised that whatever had run across her hand was now clinging to her left foot. She stopped, and a long burst of white lightning revealed a huge, crimson spider, its armoured body the size of her fist. From the way it was carefully injecting a substance into the leather of her boot, she decided it was safest to assume that it was poisonous.

She shook her leg, but it clung on with claw-like pincers. Kicking at it with her other foot also failed to dislodge it, but it now seemed to realise that its venom had not entered her flesh. It swiftly ascended towards her knee, where it could get a purchase through the soft fabric of her breeches.

Galvanised, she had released a burst of energy at it before she had consciously decided to do so, an instinctive self-protection. The arachnid curled up and thudded onto the ground. But Mellorn also found herself lying on the moist earth, gasping and in agony as if she had been kicked in the stomach.

'What the hell –' she muttered, staggering to her feet. Suddenly her head and limbs felt as if they were weighted with lead, while a cold, sickening ache throbbed down the length of her spine.

For a moment she wondered if the spider's poison had entered her bloodstream after all, but she knew it had not. Tentatively, she summoned a little power, cupping her hands around a sphere of golden light, then letting it disperse; and at once the discomfort and heaviness grew worse.

Sorcery had never caused her pain before.

'Well, Mother, this world is different, isn't it?' she said to herself grimly. Questions and speculation thronged into her mind, but in her heart it was as if a great, black iron gate had slammed shut between her and her previous easy, golden life on Ikonus. She had known that things would be difficult, but never in her worst dreams had she foreseen this crippling restriction on her sorcery.

There was now no question of seeking even conventional shelter from the storm; she would not risk further venomous creatures finding her in the night. Grinning defiance at the thunder, darkness and rain, she pulled up her hood, wrapped her cloak round her and strode on towards Shalekahh.

As the night wore on, a dry wind sprang up and swept away the storm. Thunder was replaced by the soothing rustle of leaves, and now Mellorn could see the shapes of trees waving against a blue-grey sky. But dawn brought another surprise; all the trees were red. Some were massive and black-trunked with plum-coloured foliage that shone scarlet when disturbed by the breeze; others were slender, shaped like tall flames of glittering copper. Brilliantly hued birds sat in their branches, uttering a slow series of mournful, haunting notes, and sharp-toothed, striped mammals scattered across the forest floor as Mellorn approached.

Soon the nature of the forest changed, and she knew she was nearing its edge. Here the trees were younger, and they were mostly a kind of maple with bronze bark and lobed, blood-red leaves. A thrill of anticipation shook her; if her wayfinding skill had not led her astray, she was about to set eyes on Shalekahh for the first time. And if Ashurek had been right, perhaps there would be nothing to see but a fire-destroyed ruin with crows nesting in the skeletal towers.

She stepped from the trees onto a hillside. She was on high ground, and the view that stretched for perhaps thirty miles to the skyline took her breath away. From where she stood, folded hills ran down towards a vast, flat valley. The slopes were clad in grass of a particularly rich, delicate green. Here and there, outcrops of black rock jutted out, softened by drifts of russet and purple heather. Everywhere were clumps and copses of trees in many exquisite shades of red; and all these vivid colours did not clash but blended to make a landscape of such melting beauty that Mellorn almost exclaimed aloud. A glassy-silver river wound across the valley floor, and on the far bank the rubescent forests began again, running like fingers of flame into the foothills of towering, jet-black mountains. Brooding and uncompromising, those mountains dominated the horizon, touched by only a few streaks of white as if even snow dared not brave the sable peaks. As she stared at them, an unknown emotion caught in her chest. Curls of white cloud sailed along just above them like swans, but the rest of the sky was a cloudless, sultry blue. The sun, a golden-yellow globe much larger and richer than that of Ikonus, was already warming the air.

And gleaming in its oblique rays, spread out across the lush valley, lay the city of Shalekahh. Perfect, undamaged, lovelier than any of Ashurek's descriptions could ever have made it sound, it glistened like a crown of opals and diamonds.

'You were wrong, Father,' Mellorn breathed. 'Gorethria has not ceased to exist.'

She stood there for a long time, taking in every detail of the city she considered her true home, following the shape of every tower and minaret, noting the flashes of jewel-bright colour amid the ice-whiteness. She was too far away to see people, but it looked as though there were extensive army camps all around the outskirts – what else could those lines of bright tents and silken banners be? Practical considerations began to intrude on her awe-filled reverie, for she was not one to remain lost in wonder for very long, even at the miraculous sight of Shalekahh.

She had no set plan in mind. Her father's foray against the Serpent had been a quest, a converging of energies upon a very specific goal. Hers too was a kind of quest, but one whose end she could not see, fanning out from a central point into any number of unpredictable possibilities. She knew that Silvren would have begun the task upon the more neutral, safer continent of Tearn, but it was not mere impetuosity that had brought Mellorn straight to Shalekahh. Where else would her obviously Gorethrian face go unremarked?

She smiled to herself, then started, knowing with cold certainty that there was someone behind her. She *had* been in a dream, or she would have known much sooner; cursing her inattention, she swung round.

Confronting her was a Gorethrian officer mounted on a fire-coloured horse. The dark face beneath the black helmet gave her a shock: it was so like her own and her father's and yet so different, the first strange Gorethrian visage she had seen. The man was tall and clad all in black, with a leather breastplate and a heavy cloak of gold-trimmed purple flung over his shoulders. And he was aiming a particularly lethal-looking crossbow at her heart.

A second after she turned, however, he lowered it.

'My apologies, my lady,' he exclaimed. 'By the gods, I almost killed you. It was your grey cloak – I thought you were a stray slave.'

She breathed a secret sigh of relief that she had left her hood up, hiding her un-Gorethrian fair hair. She had to strain to understand what the man was saying, for although Ashurek had taught her to speak his language, they had rarely used it in conversation. And she had no clear idea of what was considered 'ordinary' behaviour in this situation. Still, she had to start learning some time. One thing she knew for certain was that to appear in any degree unsure of herself would be fatal.

'Haven't you ever seen mourning?' she snapped.

'Never quite such a cloak as that, my lady,' the officer replied, politely but without deference. She had chosen grey on purpose, for Ashurek had once told her that those in mourning were, as a rule, respectfully left alone; but not, apparently, when they were several miles outside the city. 'You are somewhat wet and muddy,' he observed.

'My horse threw me,' she lied, immediately wondering if it was usual for those 'in mourning' to ride.

'Then perhaps I can offer you assistance in returning to the city,' he said smoothly. His eyebrows were raised, but whatever his thoughts were, he did not speak them. She accepted, and he gave her a hand to sit behind him on the saddle; at once she regretted it, for now she would have to give an excuse for not going to any specific address within Shalekahh. Yet perhaps it would be an easy way to enter the city without being challenged. 'Might I enquire your name?'

She paused, then said firmly, 'Melkavesh.' It was the Gorethrian name she had decided to use; and henceforth, she thought determinedly, she would be known by no other.

'You are not from Shalekahh, are you, Lady Melkavesh?'

'No.'

'I thought not. I can't place your accent at all.'

If this was an oblique request for information, she ignored it. She would equally have liked to question the officer, but was wary of asking something obvious or foolish enough to rouse his suspicions even further. So they continued in silence as the horse cantered skittishly down the hill towards the pearl-delicate spires of the city. The grass crackled under its hooves, for the heat of the sun had already dried last night's rain; with every hoof-beat, a fragrant, heavy scent was released into the warm air. Soldiers turned and watched as they wove between the bright, silken tents.

Presently she ventured, 'It was quite a storm last night.'

'Yes.' The broad shoulders in front of her shrugged. 'But who isn't used to it by now, my lady?'

'Indeed.'

They rode through a line of ornamental, weeping trees whose scarlet leaves also gave off a spicy aroma in the sun's heat. The city had no wall; a marble road led directly between the first of the pale, graceful buildings. To her relief, the officer said, 'You'll forgive me, I hope, if I leave you here, but I have to continue my patrol.'

'Oh, very well,' she said, shamming irritation. She dismounted, seizing the edge of her hood before it fell back and revealed her hair.

'If I might offer a word of advice, my lady, don't ride alone beyond the edge of the city. At least, not whilst wearing the grey.' He saluted her with sardonic courtesy, turned his horse and rode away.

Mellorn-Melkavesh stood in the edge of Shalekahh, almost laughing with relief. Perhaps he had been suspicious of her, but thought she was most likely just an eccentric aristocrat. She began to walk towards the centre of the city. The street on which she found herself was a broad avenue lined by graceful purple-red beeches and white mansions of elegant symmetry. Shalekahh was no less beautiful at close quarters. The intricately cut marble slabs beneath her feet shimmered with iridescent veins, and further along the avenue she saw a team of slaves working hard to keep it spotlessly clean. Two women, elegant in dark green and gold, gave her a curious glance as they passed.

It did not take her long to discern that the population of Shalekahh were, without exception, richly and immaculately dressed. Crossing an open area of fountains, statues and red-bronze trees, she observed three people in genuine Gorethrian mourning: pearly, silken garments which bore no resemblance to her stout, mud-spattered cloak. Now more than ever she realised how shabby she must look – even the servants who passed her were clad as neatly as their masters, if less elaborately. No wonder she was attracting so many suspicious looks.

Shalekahh was, as Ashurek had hinted, a very strange city in certain respects. It was so designed that there was literally nowhere to hide or be anonymous; no slums, no winding alleys, no taverns or dens of thieves. All was clean-lined, elegant and open. Neither was there a market or any shops; only the private premises of craftsmen and traders, which could not be entered freely, certainly not dressed as she was and with no genuine identity. It was a society at once too open for anonymity, yet totally closed against the stranger.

Now my problems have begun in earnest, she thought, sitting on the edge of a fountain which was reasonably secluded by trees. She could do nothing until she had obtained suitable clothing, and she could not obtain clothing whilst looking like this . . . this was apart from the fact that she had no money anyway. She was also desperately hungry, and as for finding lodgings . . .

It seemed she would have to resort to sorcery at some stage, but she was still reluctant to do so. As well as the other considerations, she was bound by her Oath to the School of Sorcery, never to use her powers for corrupt reasons, stealing and deception among them.

Presently she found her way to the palace and walked slowly past, gazing at the gleaming colonnades, the cold-eyed statues of past emperors, the intimidating guards in Imperial black, gold and white. So, she thought, there is still an emperor. It seemed bizarre and ironic that she did not even know who it was; she could hardly walk up and ask one of the guards . . . she grinned at this, then felt a strange thrill of mixed anger and excitement. That is my family's home, she thought. Ashurek's birthplace . . . my birthright!

A guard passed close by and stared hard at her. The day was very hot, but she still had her cloak on as it was the only way she could keep her hair hidden; she swiftly walked on, suddenly feeling an acute sense of danger. For a time, she wondered whether to leave the city altogether; then she decided it would solve nothing. When evening came she returned to the open area, hoping to find somewhere among the trees secluded enough to sleep. But she found herself constantly dodging Gorethrian nobles strolling in twos and threes in the cool, fragrant twilight, and as it grew darker, there seemed to be soldiers patrolling everywhere. She found no rest.

By morning, she had torn the lining from her cloak and fashioned a kind of turban which she hoped resembled ones she had seen some Gorethrian women wearing. She discarded the rest of the garment. Her tunic and breeches were dark, almost black, and although they were not even vaguely Gorethrian in style, she hoped that she now looked somewhat less conspicuous.

As she began to wander through the streets again, a light-skinned slave passed her, carrying a basket of red fruit. With arrogant coolness she reached out and took one, realising that the poor boy could hardly protest. She was right; he scurried on his way with lowered eyes as if terrified of her. Then she felt a strange coldness in her throat; her ancestors had lived by enslaving the rest of the continent, but everything Ashurek and Silvren had taught her, everything she had come to believe in at the School of Sorcery, made slavery an anathema to her, something she could not stomach.

Eating the stolen fruit, Melkavesh walked on and soon witnessed further evidence of Gorethria's continuing dominance over Vardrav. About twenty men and women of various races were lined up outside a white mansion, flanked by several guards with red and white insignia on their ebony uniforms. The guards looked bored, but the prisoners – for that was what they were, she was certain, not just servants – looked sick with fear.

She went past as slowly as she could without attracting

attention, and saw a Gorethrian in a long, dark blue robe come out of the mansion, choose a tall Vardravian from the line, and lead him inside. Then she heard one of the guards say to another, 'Apparently Kristillians give the best results.'

The second soldier replied, 'Aye, well, we'd better hurry up and conquer Kristillia, hadn't we? Then he'll have an unlimited supply!' They both laughed, their teeth white against their purple-brown faces. At this, a woman broke from the line and began shouting at them, angry and incoherent. The first guard stepped up to her and, with an absent flick of his black-gauntleted hand, knocked her senseless. Then he drew his sword and turned to the rest of the prisoners, who were shifting and murmuring uneasily. 'Might I remind you all that we have orders to disable and not kill. So don't think you're going to escape that –' he pointed his blade at the mansion, 'by finding a swift death on a sword. You'll receive a wound all right, not fatal but exceedingly painful. Now, let's have no repetition of such stupidity, or you'll make things that much more unpleasant for yourselves.'

The prisoners subsided into abject resignation to whatever awaited them, and the guards shook their heads and grinned at each other.

Melkavesh, however, in her amazement at witnessing this scene, had forgotten her need to saunter by unnoticed. A mixture of horror, outrage and curiosity had rooted her to the spot. 'If this is typical behaviour of the Gorethrians,' she thought wildly, 'then my father was right. By the Sphere, he was right!'

Too late, she heard the first guard say, 'D'you see that woman over there, staring at us? She looks like a refugee from the far side of Alta-Nangra. Fetch her over here, will you?'

'Are you sure, sir?' said the second. 'She's an aristocrat, from her face.'

'I don't care if she's the Emperor's bloody sister. He won't tolerate anyone loitering around here. Go and arrest her.'

4

In Mourning Grey

FALMERYN HELD the reins of the pale golden stallion while Xaedrek dismounted, then turned to lead the horse into the stables. The Emperor was deep in conversation with his companion, a thin-faced scientist, and did not even glance at the Forluinish groom, but Falmeryn waited on the pretext of allowing the lad with the second horse through the door first, and stared fixedly at Xaedrek's red-cloaked back until he and the scientist were out of sight under the arch.

'I do not believe in hatred,' Falmeryn thought. 'And yet, in a way, I hate him.' It was partly disbelief that one man could have – or even want – such power over others, partly frustration at the impossibility of defying him. Sighing, he stabled the horse and began to remove its tack. Of course it was possible to escape. He thought of Estarinel, who had undergone many more terrible experiences and braved far worse situations than this for Forluin's sake. In comparison, the mere fleeing of two people from Shalekahh was nothing. And his love for Kharan had given him real hope that they would succeed. More than hope: belief.

'I wouldn't look at him like that if I were you,' the stable-lad commented wryly from the adjoining stall. 'Eyes in the back of his head, they say. See straight into your mind.'

'Have you finished there?' said Falmeryn without inflexion. 'Well, go to the grain store and measure out the feeds, will you?'

The boy obeyed, and Falmeryn climbed to the loft to pitch down some hay. To his astonishment he found Kharan there, standing by the window. She was wearing a bodice and full skirt of cloth-of-gold such as she would usually only wear within the palace, and she was blanched and trembling.

'Kharan, is something wrong?' he asked concernedly. 'Don't you know Xaedrek was here a few minutes ago –'

She ran into his arms. 'He didn't see me. Falmeryn, I'm afraid I've just done something incredibly stupid.'

'Calm down. It can't be that bad,' he said, hugging her. 'Tell me what it was.'

'There's a suite of rooms in the palace that used to be Meshurek's. No one goes in there, except Xaedrek, but I have to walk past them to my rooms. The door's usually locked, but today it was ajar, and I could hear a terrible groaning from inside, like someone in pain – or some*thing* – it was only a faint sound, but horrible, not quite human.' She was hanging onto his arms, speaking rapidly and continually glancing out of the window. 'So I went in. There was no one there – I mean, not Xaedrek or anyone – but strapped to a kind of sloping couch there was this creature. I – I don't know what it was. It was human, but very tall, and it had four arms – two pairs, one below the other. And its skin was absolutely black, darker than a Patavrian's, and its eyes were like coal, with no whites.'

'A creature from one of the Planes, I would think,' Falmeryn said dubiously.

'I don't know. All I knew was that it was in terrible distress. There were bandages on its chest and stomach.' A spasm of revulsion shook her as she whispered, 'Xaedrek must have been experimenting on it, and left it there, suffering. It was intelligent and fully conscious, and it seemed to be arguing with itself – I don't know how to describe it. Although it *looked* frightening, its speech was gentle. It was in pain, maybe dying, yet it lay there speaking calmly of the nature of life and death. When it could catch its breath between groans.' There were tears in her eyes. 'I didn't stop to think, I undid all the straps restraining it, and asked if there was anything I could do to help it. It said it needed to find a little black stone. We looked together and found the stone on a

91

side table. Then it said it could make its own escape now, and it thanked me and told me to go. So I hurried out of the room, and a few yards along the corridor I almost went headlong into Baramek. Do you see?'

'I think so. Go on,' he murmured, stroking her hair.

'Baramek saw me coming from Meshurek's chamber. Within a few seconds he would have been in there himself, found the creature loose, and known that I'd freed it. Baramek's always despised me, and as for Xaedrek – he won't look kindly upon me interfering with his – his "work".' She looked anxiously out at the square again. 'So I fled straight here, before Baramek came after me. And now I've put us both in danger. I'm so, so sorry.'

'Did anyone see you come in here?'

'I don't know. Probably.'

'Kharan – beloved, look at me,' he said gently. 'There's nothing to be sorry about. I'd have done the same – freed that poor creature. You did the right thing. Now, come on.' He clasped her hand and pulled her towards the hatch. 'We're going.'

'Now?' she gasped.

'Yes. From what you've said, Baramek will have men searching for you by now, and I doubt that it'll take them long to trace you here. We have perhaps five or ten minutes.'

'Falmeryn – I can go back now, apologise to Xaedrek, say it was an impulse – there's no need for you to be involved, it's not too late. But if we flee now, we'd be caught and that would be the end.'

'You want to go back and apologise?' he said, pausing half-way down the ladder and gazing up at her. His eyes were so intense, so clear that they seemed to wash all the confusion from her soul.

'No!' she exclaimed. 'No, I don't want to go back and lie and grovel to a – to a torturer. But I want to protect you.'

'That's protection I don't need,' he replied without rancour. 'What's more, how can I be sure he'd "forgive" you? It's too late. Come on, quickly.' Numb, she followed him down the ladder and along the line of stalls. 'You know as well as I do, if we don't go now, we never will.'

A rush of dread went through her at these words, because she knew he was right, and she realised that here and now she was facing the moment she had tried to put off for months, the point of no return. In a daze, she found herself fumbling with the straps of the pale golden stallion's bridle, while Falmeryn saddled a black horse in the next stall. The release of the creature she could smooth over, but a blatant attempt to escape was inexcusable; and she still doubted that she had the courage to risk everything in this way. They'll have sealed the palace grounds, she thought wildly. This is insane . . .

Everything looked white and unreal to her as they led the horses into the square and mounted. Her heart seemed to be driving all the blood out of her body and she felt sure she was about to faint. But she did not. In the midst of her fear, a deeper instinct rose to the surface and took over, enabling her to cope. It was partly resignation to the fact that this had become inevitable, partly determination to end the lie she had been living.

Falmeryn also felt apprehensive, although his feelings were not complicated by the doubts that plagued Kharan, and he was rather more confident of success. He gave her a reassuring smile and asked, 'Are you ready?'

'Yes,' she said, almost fiercely. She was sitting astride, and the delicate cloth-of-gold dress was torn. She added, 'We'll ride slowly, so as not to attract attention. I know the shortest way to the edge, then we can gallop, and we'll be past the army and into the forests before they know it.'

Suddenly three stable-lads emerged from the far side of the mews and stared curiously at them. 'Ignore them,' said Falmeryn. 'Come on.'

They passed under the arch and started down the long tree-shaded avenue towards the outer walls of the palace grounds. The horses jogged and pulled against the bit, infected by their riders' nervousness. Two sentries were on duty at the tall, golden gate. Usually they saluted the Lady

Kharan as she rode through, and she could see that the gate was open and that they were standing one on either side as normal; but the avenue suddenly seemed ten miles long. She dared not look round at Falmeryn. It was like a dream she had once had of drowning, struggling helplessly in the clear, calm, lethal waters of a lake, and as if in a dream she saw one of the sentries look at them and point, and she saw them both move into the gateway, their long pikes crossed to bar the way.

'Damn!' she exclaimed, in that instant more angry than afraid.

She heard Falmeryn cry, 'Charge them, it's our only chance!' and as his horse passed hers, a streak of black, she spurred the stallion after him, reckless with defiance.

Taken by surprise, the sentries were knocked out of the way. The two horses burst out into the wide mall beyond, their hooves clattering on the marble slabs. For two long, glorious minutes they galloped in wild freedom, no soldiers anywhere in sight, only a few startled faces here and there along the way.

Then, hard behind them, there was a line of fire-gold horses with dark Imperial guards bent low over their necks. Kharan glanced round, and wished she had not, but Falmeryn cried, 'We can outrun them. Don't give up!'

What followed was no dream, but excruciatingly, vividly real. Ever afterwards Kharan remembered every detail of the next ten seconds: the saddle chafing her legs through the thin cloth of the skirt, the heat of the stallion's neck under her hands, the heaving of its sweat-dampened sides, and her own raw struggle for breath. Then there was the thud of a weapon on the horse's back, not an arrow, but something unseen, a burst of preternatural power. And the horse went down under her. The fall winded her, jarred her whole body. The stallion was unhurt and immediately struggled to its feet, slithering on the marble surface. Her stomach filled with sickening pain as one of its hooves crunched into her hip. As she lay there, stunned and gagging, she saw Falmeryn haul the black horse to a halt, leap off and run back to her.

Desperately, she tried to tell him to go on without her, but she could not even draw breath to whisper.

He was beside her, helping her sit up, his arms round her – and then he was gone, torn away from her, struggling and protesting.

There were guards in black uniforms all round them, some cloaked in gold and white and some in red. Two of them were holding Falmeryn, another two bent down and lifted Kharan to her feet. There was something macabre in the way the others – perhaps eight in all – held their swords, a kind of malicious humour, as if the blades were only symbols of the dark power which Xaedrek had instilled in their wielders.

Kharan sobbed, but only for air. She was too angry to weep. To her dismay she saw that Baramek himself led the party, and was walking forward to confront her. He was unhelmeted, his curly hair brushed back from a face that was as dark and harsh as obsidian. Gorethrian beauty was absent from those severe features, and his eyes were a malevolent ochre-yellow. It seemed that he was going to gloat over her downfall, but she still possessed enough pride to make an icy riposte. Better still, to speak first.

'Is something wrong, Commander Baramek?' she said so sarcastically that Falmeryn forgot their predicament and stared at her.

'Yes. It is my regrettable duty to arrest you, Lady Kharan,' he said flatly.

'Twelve armed guards to detain two unarmed riders is certainly regrettable,' she snapped. 'What is the meaning of this? The Emperor will have something to say –'

'My lady, I have to inform you that the Emperor is fully cognisant of the reasons for your arrest, and himself dispatched me to escort you back to the palace.' Far from gloating, Baramek was so matter-of-fact, even indifferent, that her rage and defiance began to fade into a horrible, cold sense of panic.

'What are these reasons?'

'I think you know well enough what they are, my lady,'

Baramek answered, turning away almost wearily. 'And I do not have to tell you what the penalty for treason is.'

'Treason?' she tried to say, but no sound came out.

'Bring the man separately,' Baramek instructed the two Gorethrians holding Falmeryn. 'They are not to see or speak to each other again.'

'Let him go!' Kharan almost screamed. 'He has nothing to do with this – for heaven's sake, he's only a groom, he was merely escorting me –'

'Please, my lady,' Baramek said. 'He can plead his own case before Xaedrek. And that particular privilege will only be awarded him, as I'm sure you appreciate, because of your own singularly delicate position.' He raised a hand, and the two guards began to march her back towards the palace. She struggled to turn and look back at Falmeryn, but suddenly there were mounted men round her, and she caught only the merest glimpse of him. He was standing rigid in the grasp of two Gorethrians, his beautiful face pale with shock, his mouth soundlessly framing her name. Then the horses closed in, the guards jerked her arms painfully every time she tried to turn her head.

'Falmeryn,' she gasped, realisation hitting her like a wall of ice water as the black tide bore her away. She would never see him again. She remembered nothing of the return to the palace except a grey daze of shock and weakness and unbearable knowledge. Her fears had been well founded, and this was only the beginning – but like a litany to ward off surrender to hysterical grief and terror, only one thought echoed ceaselessly round her pain-fogged mind.

I will never, ever see him again.

'I could delegate more of this work,' Xaedrek said conversationally, making a fine adjustment to a glass rod as Kharan was led into his presence. 'But I prefer to remain in personal control . . . Sit down.'

Kharan remained standing. From the palace she had been brought to the mansion, and left waiting for hours in what had once been her room in the days before Xaedrek was Emperor. Now two female guards had brought her to an underground chamber that she had never seen before. It was dominated by a weird construction of gold and glass tubes. Other than that the only furniture was a marble work bench at one end of the room, faced by a white, carved chair at the other. The tang of metal and burning that pervaded the whole house was choking here, but Xaedrek seemed oblivious to it.

He detached a large sphere from the apparatus and carried it over to the bench. He sifted its contents – a pale gold stuff like fine sugar – onto a flat tray, then began to make notes on a piece of parchment. Without looking up, he waved the guards out of the room. The door closed behind them, and now he and Kharan were alone. But it was several seconds before he put the quill down, leaned forward on the bench, and looked at her. She was standing rigidly by the chair, managing to meet his gaze despite her enervating fear.

'You won't sit down?' he said. 'As you wish. Well, Kharan, you will be gratified to learn that the Hrunneshian you released made a successful escape to the Black Plane. I should've concealed the lodestone, and locked the door, I suppose. My research upon the neman was not complete, and its untimely termination is extremely inconvenient to me.' He looked down at the tray, picked up a small glass scoop and filled it with a quantity of the powder. 'I never thought that you, of all people, would do something . . .' for almost a minute he was silent as he divided the powder between several crystal phials. Kharan waited in agony, resisting an urge to hang onto the chair for support. Then his ruby-red eyes met hers again. 'Something which could result in you being accused of treason. Sabotaging Imperial research.'

'Xaedrek, I –'

'Let me finish.' His tone was cool, completely emotionless. 'To be honest, I could not care less about the wretched Hrunneshian. Consider it forgotten. The other matter, however, concerns me very deeply. Baramek tells me that he has

97

suspected you for a long time of conducting a clandestine affair with one of my grooms, a man called Falmeryn, but he did not wish to trouble me with the matter until he had proof positive. Well, is it true?'

Struggling to find a voice in her dry, convulsed throat, she said, 'If I denied it . . .'

'I'd know you were lying.' He left the bench and came towards her. The sleeves of his blood-red robe were turned back, revealing the dark forearms and long, fine hands; the hands of a scholar or an artist, not a warrior – not a torturer, she thought irrelevantly. 'But I want to hear the truth from your own lips, as they say.'

'Yes, it's true,' she muttered inaudibly.

He was as close as was possible without actually touching her; paradoxically the very familiarity of his presence lessened rather than increased her fear. Softly, he said, 'Why, Kharan? I thought we had an understanding. What's changed? Perhaps it is my fault. I have had little time to spare for you of late, it's true, but you must know that it was of necessity, not by choice. You wanted to remind me that you existed?'

'It's not that.'

'What, then?'

Her mouth thick with conflicting emotions, she whispered, 'I've come to realise that the nature of what you do is evil.'

'I'm afraid I don't see the connection.' He walked back to the bench and lifted the glass sphere. 'Surely you never thought a Gorethrian noble – let alone the Emperor – was likely to be what you'd consider "good"? Empires are not won by being kind and merciful.'

'I realised that. At least I thought I did. I closed my mind, made sure I never thought of it.'

He took the sphere back to the apparatus and reconnected it. Returning to her side, he put his hand on her shoulder and said, 'And I made sure I never spoke to you about this work, never tried to explain or show you the reality.'

'Why?' she exclaimed, surprised and suddenly angry. 'Because you think I'm stupid?'

'No. The opposite. You're perceptive and intelligent and I knew what your reaction would be.'

'Then you admit that what you're doing here is evil?' she gasped.

Xaedrek shrugged. 'It may be. I regard it as essential scientific work. I really do not have time to worry about what is evil and what is not.'

'Well, to me it is,' she said fiercely, shocked at her own boldness.

Unexpectedly, he asked, 'Kharan, are you afraid of me?'

'Yes,' she said through gritted teeth.

'I don't think you are. I still see the lovely young girl who looked at me quite fearlessly and said what she felt. An openness and lack of awe that made you totally different from anyone I'd ever known, Gorethrian or otherwise. My feelings for you have not lessened; it is only that the Empire has intruded relentlessly on my time.' He turned away from her and went slowly back to the workbench. 'I can't tell you how much I regret that this has happened. That you have found it necessary to turn away from me to another man. And then to flee as if you thought yourself a prisoner here.'

'Am I not?' she muttered, desperately confused. Was he saying what he really felt, or were his words coldly calculated to distress her? He turned and gazed at her, but she could not read those brilliant red eyes at all.

'Why have you done this, Kharan? Why? You think me so iniquitous, but have I ever said an unkind word to you?'

'No.' She could not tell whether the edge of passion in his level tone was real or feigned.

'Have I ever treated you with cruelty or contempt or anything but consideration and care?'

'No. You don't understand. You make it sound as if I planned it, but I met Falmeryn by accident.' Bitterly, she added, 'You have never loved me, but Falmeryn loved me, and I him. You've no right – I am not your wife –'

'And I tell you, Kharan, if I ever take a wife she will never mean a fraction of what you have meant to me.' He went

99

behind the bench and absently picked up a phial. 'You misjudge the strength of my feelings for you.'

'I don't think so.'

'That saddens me. So, you stumbled in horror at my evil, and he was conveniently there to catch you? And you fled to him not to make me jealous, but because you were desperately in love and could not help yourselves? I suppose you think that this talk of love will move me to pity. Well, my lady Kharan, whatever you intended, you *have* made me jealous – unlikely as that may seem – and I am inclined neither to be understanding nor forgiving about this.' He drew a piece of parchment towards him and began to make notes again. Kharan, watching him, felt suddenly sick and cold. 'I realise that it began when my steward, Varian, took you into the rooms above.'

Trembling violently, her throat full of ice, she nodded. 'I would've found out anyway, sooner or later. I don't blame him.'

'Don't you? I did.'

There was a silence. Eventually she choked out, 'What do you mean . . . you *did*?'

Like flames, his eyes met hers. 'Steward Varian, my lady, is dead.'

Then Kharan did sit down, heavily, as if she had been shoved into the chair. With horrified culpability, she stammered out, 'You killed him. Because of me.'

'I am not vengeful,' Xaedrek replied evenly. 'But when something displeases me, I sweep it from my path swiftly and without malice. He died a useful death –' he waved a hand at the sinister apparatus '– contributing his life energies to the advancement of Gorethrian hyperphysics.'

Kharan's dusky-rose skin blanched as white as the marble floor; she sat stricken, shaking her head like a mechanical doll and mouthing soundlessly over and over again, 'Ye gods. Ye gods.'

Xaedrek calmly went on working, measuring and examining the gold powder, making careful notes. Perhaps four or five minutes went by before he said, 'You are silent, my lady, but I am sure your mind is not. Tell me what you are thinking.'

Unclenching her jaw, she tasted blood. 'I am thinking, my lord, now I know why I have been brought here.'

'What – you think I am going to execute you in the same way?'

She shook her head woodenly and croaked, 'I think you are going to bring Falmeryn in here and execute him in front of me.'

Xaedrek put down the glass tube he was holding and stared at her, seeming genuinely shocked. At length he said quietly, almost sadly, 'Kharan, you seem to think I am a sadist. I am not. I thought you knew me better than that by now, but evidently I was wrong. I have no such intention. Nor would I wish to take your energies in such a way – oh no, Kharan. Not yours . . . aside from that, it is neither quick nor clean nor inevitably fatal.'

'I know. I've seen.'

'For you, Kharan,' he went on, staring intently at something glittering on a piece of glass, 'a conventional execution. Beheading. There is a nobility in it . . . which befits what you have been to me.'

So violently was she trembling already that there was nothing for her body to do except convulse into ice-cold stillness. If it was possible to die of shock, she wished it would happen here and now, but her heart, a traitor, continued to beat leadenly. Of all the things she had dreaded, she had never, ever dreamed that he would actually kill her. She might have said it; but she had never truly believed it until this moment. Anyone else – but not *her*.

'Execution?' That she was still sitting on a chair was an illusion; in reality she had stumbled off a cliff, and was falling.

'Have I tried to deny that I am what you think me? I am quite pitiless, as you should know.' He was still bent over his phials and papers, and it suddenly struck her why he had brought her to this room. She almost laughed – or screamed, or cried – aloud. It was not that he was about to slay or

101

torment her, it was simply that he was too busy to interrupt his work even for the time it took to speak to her. If this was not the worst realisation, it was the most degrading, the one which brought her to total despair.

'And Falmeryn?' she said, her voice weak but clear.

'I have already spoken to him. We had a most interesting conversation. He was very angry and spoke eloquently of Forluinish values, love and mercy and so on. I was impressed by his spirit, but unmoved. I could find no mitigating reason for him not to perish.'

'Must I beg?' she cried. 'Do what you will with me, but please, please let him go, he's done nothing wrong –'

'Desist, my lady. It ill becomes you and it can change nothing.'

Overcome by her own helplessness, she subsided. She did not even have the anger left to curse Xaedrek, call him a monster, a bastard, anything that might have given her feelings some release. She had not even the strength to hate him. How can you hate something that has no soul? she wondered. Everything seemed futile, hollow, unreal, and around her the room was growing paler and paler. She heard herself ask, 'What will happen to him?'

'Alas, my lady, that is something you will never know. I would not cause you pain by telling you.'

'But death?'

'Yes. He will be dead before you.' She had thought Xaedrek was at the bench, but now he was drifting towards her through a white sea, his voice echoing with sudden, incongruous concern, 'You are unwell.'

'Help me,' Kharan murmured faintly, and passed out.

After the guards had taken Kharan back to her room, Xaedrek remained alone in the chamber for some time, leaning on the marble bench with his head in his hands. Presently he recovered himself and stood upright, saying aloud, 'It is over. In the past. There is only the future . . .' With perfectly steady hands and eyes as cold as fireless garnets, he took one of the phials of powder (which he called 'amulin'), tipped it into a goblet of water, and drank it.

102

Almost at once he felt the power begin to pulse into his body, like yellow light curling and dancing along his arteries. He paused for a while, judging the strength of its effect. Then he opened the door and shouted for Ah'garith.

The woman-demon came swiftly from another room, a half-smile on her face, her hands primly clasped. 'When is it to be, Sire?'

'The hunt tomorrow. The execution the day after.'

'It is well, Sire. She was unimportant, a mere nuisance. Best –'

'Ah'garith, be quiet,' Xaedrek said with self-restraint. 'We've work to do. I have been testing the amulin produced by the few Kristillian prisoners we have. The results are excellent, far better than any other race we have tried.'

'Why is that, Sire?'

'I don't know. Neither do I know why they've resisted conquest for so long. They are a tenacious people. Most of them have survived, so can be used again. Commander Baramek and I have outlined a plan for the invasion of Kristillia, but producing enough amulin to supply the troops for that venture is still a problem.'

Ah'garith seemed to take this as a personal affront. 'I work for you day and night, Sire, drawing the power. What more can I do?' she said peevishly.

'I don't know, Ah'garith. I wish I did.' Xaedrek gave her a cold, searching look. 'Nine years have gone by since we started our research. Yet we have progressed no further than this crude method.'

'It works,' the demon pointed out.

'Yes, to a certain extent. Temporary hyperphysical powers bestowed by consuming a powder; an extraordinary discovery, I'll admit. But it's not enough. For example, have you any idea how long it takes for messages to cross the Empire, even using swift relays, beacons, and signalling mirrors? How hard it is to monitor the movement of enemy troops? And yet, Ah'garith, you have made frequent mention of a talent which you used to possess, known as far-seeing.'

'Yes, but I possess it no longer,' the woman-demon spat. 'Why do you not believe me?'

'Oh, I believe you.' Xaedrek walked slowly across the room, and leaned on the chair. Kharan's warmth was still in it. 'Though I have often suspected that you have not told me as much as you might have done. Perhaps out of fear that I'd learn something which would enable me to dispose of you?'

'That is nonsense, Sire. I've contributed everything I know, all my power, to your cause. You wrong me. I am as frustrated as you at our lack of progress. What is more,' she hissed passionately, 'the loss of my far-sight is like being blinded. Blinded!'

'I'm not interested in your personal feelings about the matter,' Xaedrek answered unsympathetically. 'I am simply telling you, Ah'garith, I must find a way to far-see. It is essential to Gorethria's advancement.'

The Shanin moved to the workbench and gazed avariciously at the pale gold substance in the glass phials. In a low, intense voice she said, 'Sire, if only you would let me taste a little of the amulin which you give so freely to your armies. I feel sure it would restore my lost skills and enable us to make the progress you desire.'

'It's out of the question,' Xaedrek said flatly. 'And I am in no mood for yet another discussion of the matter. Finish preparing the machine for the next subject, will you. As you have nothing constructive to offer, we'd best devote our time to producing as much amulin as possible.' The demon obeyed grudgingly, muttering to herself.

Ah'garith had expressed the desire to take amulin too often for Xaedrek's liking. It bestowed temporary sorcerous powers on humans. What it might do to the demon was another matter, and however curious Xaedrek was to find out, he still had no intention of allowing it. He suspected strongly that it would restore Ah'garith to her former powers, make her able to disobey him, even enslave him as Meheg-Ba had enslaved Meshurek. The risk was too great, even for him.

All his life, Xaedrek had trusted no one except himself. Even his close colleagues in the Inner Council, whose absolute loyalty was unquestioned, he treated with caution and detachment. So it seemed a humourless irony that he was forced to work in close co-operation with the demon, when there was no one he trusted less.

In the nine years since Ah'garith had answered his summons, they had worked uneasily together. She blatantly resented the bond that forced her to obey him, and he could not be certain how strongly it held her. She had not defied him yet, but he knew she was biding her time. Continually having to watch her imposed a strain on him which he could ill afford. Sometimes she seemed like a devil crouched on his shoulder and he sensed waves of darkness flowing from her, a void of malice and ill-intent that was redolent of a past age, Meshurek's insanity and the Serpent's gross evil. Her true intent had nothing to do with Gorethria's well-being. Sometimes Xaedrek had an icy suspicion that her presence was slowly grinding down his spirit, and, however careful he was, in the end he would be destroyed as Meshurek had been. The thought angered him.

'The day after tomorrow for the Lady Kharan's execution?' Ah'garith's voice intruded on his thoughts. 'Not much time for her to brood upon her folly. If only you would allow me a few hours alone with her, I would teach her the meaning of suffering . . .'

In two strides Xaedrek was across the room, and a blow from the back of his hand sent Ah'garith reeling against the marble wall. Normally he could not have assailed her in such a way, but amulin gave him, temporarily, equal power. Her physical shell jarred and bruised, Ah'garith lay crumpled on the floor, regarding the Emperor with scorpion-sharp eyes.

'If you were dispensable, demon, I would dispense with you,' Xaedrek said in a low voice, his vermilion irises shedding flame. 'If I lived a thousand years I could not find the words to express how deeply I despise you. You're a thorn in my side which I will not suffer a moment longer than I need to. You'd do well to recall that.'

105

Infuriated, the demon dragged herself to her feet. 'Ungrateful,' she hissed. 'Without me, you'd have none of this. No power, no throne, no hyperphysics. No Empire. And what do I receive in return? Hatred. Insults, both to my person and to my intelligence. No trust, no responsibility. The meanest cur in Shalekahh would receive better treatment at your hands than I do. But do I complain?'

'Often,' Xaedrek said, rubbing the back of his neck tiredly.

'You use me. Use me!' the demon spat. 'I offer you my help, and you ruthlessly take advantage of my misfortune, my powerlessness – nine years is long enough to teach me that I will get no reward from you, my master.'

'Oh, you've learned something, have you? Remarkable. Now answer me this, demon: how can I give trust and responsibility to a being whose first response to the Lady Kharan's unfortunate situation is to ask if you might go and torture –' he broke off. 'The simple fact is, I do not trust you, Ah'garith, and unless your thoughts take a more worthy turn, I never will.'

'The human race,' she muttered. 'If I'd known the Serpent would die and this would happen . . .'

'What, Ah'garith?' Xaedrek prompted, folding his arms. 'What would content you? I've told you my feelings. So tell me the truth in return.'

Ah'garith looked up at him and murmured, 'Destruction. Yes, utter destruction of all life. That would avenge my siblings. That would content me.'

Xaedrek gave an exasperated laugh. 'But you're immortal. What would you do when everyone and everything is dead? Is it worth an eternity of boredom?'

'Yes,' the demon answered with unhesitating malevolence. 'It doesn't matter, I don't care what happens afterwards. It would be a long, enjoyable process. I could kill every human individually, using an infinity of tortures, diseases, humiliations –'

'Enough,' Xaedrek interrupted sharply. He felt intense disgust, but restrained himself from expressing it any further. He had always put his feelings second to what was exigent for Gorethria's benefit. He knew Ah'garith hated him because she could not dominate him. Without him she had nothing, but likewise he depended wholly on her for his power. So however much they loathed each other, they were condemned to remain locked together by mutual need. Until Xaedrek could find a way to rid himself of the demon – by discovering an alternative source of power – there was no more to be said.

'Your goal and mine are so different as to be utterly incompatible,' he stated wearily. 'But my goal is attainable. Yours is not. So get on with your work, Ah'garith, and let us speak no more of this.'

And the woman-demon obeyed, with a poisonous, sidelong glance. But after a moment she whispered metallically, 'Incompatible? I don't think so, Sire.'

Kharan sat staring out of a window without really seeing the salt-white towers or the hot arch of the sky beyond. The view had lost its reality for her and become just a flat image, or a series of images, false Shalekahhs, each lasting exactly one second before the next flashed imperceptibly into its place.

Her life was made up of seconds; no other measurement of time had any meaning for her. She had not been told how long she would remain here before the end came; nor had she any idea of how long she had sat here already, motionless, her hands folded in her lap, her eyes fixed on the window. Despite the heat, her hands and feet were freezing cold.

She thought of many things, but they all came back to Falmeryn. In this second, she wondered, is he still alive? In this one – dead? Or this one? Or this?

He will be dead before you.

Darkness came, and a terrible storm, but any power such weather had to disturb her was gone. She gazed blankly at the thrashing sky until a female guard came and led her to the bed. Then she dozed fitfully, but found herself seated in the chair again before dawn, as if she had returned to it in her sleep. Several times the guard brought her food which

107

she did not touch, and enquired politely if there was anything she required. Kharan did not know if she had replied or not, because none of it had any meaning.

She was in a tunnel, travelling swiftly and inexorably towards a blank, solid wall. Her sick dread of dying was unbearable, yet it had become a mere background to far worse emotions, like a cold, pale plain out of which her thoughts rose like serpents to torment her. She did not feel sorry for herself; perhaps she would have done, if Falmeryn had not been involved. But as it was, it seemed only just that she should die, and all her sorrow was for him.

My fault, all of this is my fault, she thought. First poor Varian. And now Falmeryn, Falmeryn. If not for me he would have lived. If only we had never met.

And if only . . . if only she was with him now, safe in the refuge of the hayloft, where all was warm and golden and he was with her, his arms wrapped round her, his smooth skin pressed against hers, their hair, dark brown and red-brown, mingled together. And there was so much she had wanted to say to him, and now she would never have the chance . . . perhaps this was the worst, this almost physical ache to see him and hold him . . . Tears ran from her glazed eyes, but she did not move even to brush them away. She felt she would have bartered her soul, killed, anything, just to have one last chance to hug him and tell him how much she loved him before Xaedrek's men tore them apart.

Is this the price of my arrogance? she wondered. I deluded myself that I could jump into the fire, consort with a man like Xaedrek, and not be burned. Destroyed. I was wrong and I must pay – oh, but why not alone? Why poor Varian – and why, why Falmeryn?

Because, a voice answered inside her, *because it is the only way you can be made to understand your guilt and responsibility*.

There was something she could have done, an escape that might have worked, if only she had thought of it. Now the plan went through her mind with crystal clarity, over and over again, as if acted out by puppets who grinned with relish at her misery.

And even when it had seemed too late, in Xaedrek's underground room, her pride had betrayed her again. My determination not to be afraid, to tell him the truth! she thought bitterly. It had seemed important at the time; now it seemed trivial, ludicrous in the face of the consequences. If only I had lied. Been penitent. I was so convinced he was merciless, but what if I was wrong? I could have charmed him, convinced him, everything would have been all right . . . but I was too proud. Falmeryn is being punished for my pride . . .

However deluded these thoughts were, however much pain they were causing her, she could do nothing to stem their manic repetition. Fear and wretchedness had paralysed her, destroyed any capacity she had for objectivity. Again and again she passed through anger, bitterness, terror, resignation, disbelief that this could be happening, certainty that at any second Xaedrek would walk through the door and tell her that she and Falmeryn were forgiven, wild hope followed by despair – but every emotion she suffered came back to the same cold sense of bereavement, while time carried her relentlessly towards the unseen, pitiless wall.

Will I be brave? she thought. Then: Falmeryn will.

Another night passed, another fragrant, cloudless morning came. She felt calmer, and moved mechanically round the room, washing, dressing and combing her hair. They had provided a dress of pale grey silk – heavily sewn with pearls and silvery opals, but grey all the same. Did they always put condemned prisoners in mourning? she wondered. It seemed appropriate. She looked at herself in a mirror and noted with a certain bitter amusement that her face was almost exactly the same colour as the material.

The door opened and the saturnine female guard entered with a tray of food.

'I don't want anything,' Kharan said. Previously the

woman had shrugged and left, but now she balanced the tray on one hand, took a goblet of wine from it with the other, and held it out to her.

'If you can manage nothing else, my lady, drink this,' she said.

'Why?'

'Later, you will be glad that you did.'

Kharan understood at once. 'It's today, isn't it?' she said hoarsely. 'There's some drug in the wine that will make me . . . not care. How considerate of Xaedrek. He always was so considerate.'

'I will leave it on this table,' said the guard indifferently.

As she turned to the door, Kharan asked urgently, 'How long?'

'Not long, my lady.' The woman's cloak flared out in a draught, then the door slammed, and she was gone.

Kharan stood in the centre of the room, giddy with the fear that only those who are about to be put to death can imagine. Will it hurt? she thought. Will I make a fool of myself, struggle and beg to be spared?

Then she thought: This means that by now, Falmeryn is gone. She hugged herself against the sudden lurch of her stomach. No, impossible, not him. She shook her head, compulsively, as if a strong enough denial could alter things. Then she looked up blankly and thought, If he is dead, I do not want to live.

She had no gods to pray to, but she half-prayed to Falmeryn's memory, 'I don't want to be forgiven, I don't ask for anything except to be strong. Please, my love, help me to be strong.

'I will not take Xaedrek's drug. I want him to know that I did not take it, that I was brave.'

But she was not brave or strong. If she had been, none of this would have happened. If, if, if. She paced the room, feeling her terror increasing moment by moment, stealing the blood from her limbs so that they became heavy and ice-cold. Whenever she moved, a spasm of trembling shook her, and she knew that she would soon have no control over

110

herself at all, that panic would possess her and she would be unable to feign bravery however much she wanted to.

She walked slowly to the table and lifted the goblet, muttering, 'Your health, Xaedrek. You have won.' Then she drank the wine.

An hour later, they came for her. Four guards, two men and two women, cloaked in red. And she did not make a fool of herself, but smiled coldly at them and held her head high and followed them as if in a dream.

When Melkavesh saw the tall soldier staring at her and heard him say to his subordinate, 'Go and arrest her,' a sure instinct told her that any attempt at diplomacy would be wasted. Even before the guard took one step towards her, she was running, and above the sound of her own swift footsteps on the slabs, she heard several voices exclaiming, cursing and arguing. The sound receded. She glanced back, and saw that one of the soldiers was now pursuing her. But Melkavesh could run very fast indeed, and she was not hampered by cloak or sword.

There were few people about, but those that were looked at her in surprise, and she knew that it would not be long before others joined the chase. Recognising the avenue along which she was fleeing as one that led directly to the palace, she swerved off to the left and found the sun glaring into her eyes, mirrored by the whiteness of the tall buildings around her.

Squinting, she ran on. For a few seconds the street was empty, and she gained the vague impression that she was in some kind of administrative area: there were fewer trees, no gardens such as surrounded the premises of craftsmen, and the buildings had a stately, grave aspect.

The street gave onto a square, and she saw guards on the far side. Retracing her steps she found a side turning, but she was rapidly giving up hope of finding anywhere to hide. How could any city be so devoid of alleys or hidden corners? There was another square ahead, but this one had a strange edifice in the centre, a small, square fort whose walls were windowless. It could only be a prison. From a plain turret on one corner, a grey banner rippled in the sluggish, hot breeze.

No one about. Melkavesh drank in several ragged breaths and wiped sweat from her forehead. Crossing to the fort she ran on, a sheer wall towering above her on her left.

But as she rounded the corner of the prison, her luck expired. There were four guards marching towards her, their cloaks glowing like red coals over their iron-black uniforms. Unable to slow down in time, she virtually ran into their arms.

'What's this?' one said, and she felt a powerful grip on her elbow. She wrenched backwards and with eerie co-ordination, all four drew their swords at once, like dancers in a macabre ballet.

'Now, my lady,' said another. There were two men and two women, barely distinguishable as such in their black helms. Between them was a fifth, paler figure whom Melkavesh did not really take in. She stepped back, poised for combat. As she was unarmed, this must have looked ridiculous to the guards. But she knew that if she turned to run, she would have a sword in her back at once, and she was not about to surrender. 'Don't cause trouble. We're busy. You'd better come in with us –' And he indicated an almost invisible door fitted flush with the wall.

Now Melkavesh knew that however suspiciously she behaved, while it was believed that she was Gorethrian, she was unlikely to be slain on sight. But at that moment the makeshift turban slid from her head, and a mass of vivid golden hair tumbled with the slowness of honey onto her shoulders, startling in the sunlight. She cursed, and the man said flatly, 'Disguised slave. I knew it. Let's finish her, quickly, and get on.'

Melkavesh found a steel blade swooping towards her neck, and she ducked, summoning power. She had no choice but to use sorcery now. Yet the energy came reluctantly into her body. It was no longer the dancing, star-soft light that she

112

had possessed on Ikonus, hers to command like a responsive, exuberant horse; instead it felt like a heavy ichor, oozing along her limbs like molten glass, making her nerves sing with pain. She ignored the pain, and brought up her arm to meet the second sword.

Just as the weapon made contact with her flesh, her forearm was suddenly enveloped in a cloud of golden stars, and the blade shattered. The guard's expression became one of astonishment. Two more swords swung at her and she leapt back agilely so that they only nicked her tunic. The ground seemed to tip beneath her as a terrible sense of shock and disorientation flashed through her. It was not alarm at the danger she was in but something deeper – a sudden awareness that hers was not the only preternatural power being wielded in this fight. It was invisible to her sight but vivid in her mind: the swords threatening her were encrusted with a black energy that dripped from them, splashing darkness onto the marble slabs. If this was sorcery, it was of no kind she recognised, but something alien and corrupt which offended her like the blood of a slaughterhouse.

Sickened, she fought on. The guard she had disarmed, a woman, seized her from behind and she felt that dark energy burning on her neck like a bear's breath. But her own power, disabled as it was, was still stronger. Struggling as if oblivious to the steel points pressing on her throat and stomach, she dragged more energy into herself. Silver-gold light flared from nowhere, and one blade vaporised even as it began to cut into her neck. The man jumped back, dropping the hilt in shock, and in the same moment she managed to produce a shield of radiance that forced her attackers back as if they were like poles of a magnet. Safe within it, she raised her arms and delivered, with perfect accuracy, four tiny, dazzling comets. Each of the guards felt something strike his or her forehead that was without substance, yet as cold and hard as a hailstone, spreading blank unconsciousness into their brains.

One by one they fell, their imposing figures sprawling into an awkward tangle of black and blood-red leather. They would not die, but when they recovered consciousness they would have lost their memory of Melkavesh.

And it meant she had broken her Oath, but there was no time to think of that now. She gritted her teeth against pain and nausea and looked around.

Standing amidst the prostrate guards was a startled-looking woman clad in a bejewelled, pale grey dress. She said nothing, only stared at Melkavesh as if she did not comprehend what had just happened, and did not really care, either. She was not Gorethrian; evidently a prisoner, Melkavesh thought, and on an impulse decided to rescue her.

'Well, come on!' she exclaimed, swiftly removing a helmet and cloak from one of the guards and putting them on. Surprisingly, they felt cold; she had expected them to make her unbearably hot, but they seemed to afford protection from the heat of the day. The woman did not move. Exasperated, Melkavesh pushed a black helm onto her head, threw a red cloak round her shoulders and seized her arm. 'Keep the cloak pulled round you to hide the dress,' she snapped. 'Don't run. Walk fast.'

The woman shrugged and obeyed. Her pupils were very dilated, and her face had the slack tranquillity of one who was drugged – or simple . . . Holding her by the elbow, Melkavesh hurried her away from the fort, cursing her bad luck in rescuing someone so singularly unhelpful.

'Now, listen, do you know this city well?' she said in the way that someone who loathes children might address a child.

'Oh, yes,' the woman replied vaguely.

'So, you can speak after all?' Two tall officials in robes of dark blue went past, ignoring them; Melkavesh sighed with relief. The disguise was at least superficially effective. 'I need to find somewhere to hide. So do you, don't you?'

'You can't hide here,' she said, and laughed.

'For heaven's sake,' Melkavesh grated. 'There must be somewhere. Think!' Exhaustion had made her edgy; she had not slept for two nights, nor eaten anything apart from a single fruit, and her bones ached from the strain of using

114

sorcery. 'Haven't you a friend who could take us in? Somewhere to eat and sleep, and be safe?'

'I was safe once, but they slew him,' the woman said. 'It takes more strength than most of us possess.'

By the gods, she's completely mad, Melkavesh thought. Impulses to help others should be strongly resisted. As she was wondering how best to abandon her, the woman suddenly took her arm and said, 'This is what I would've done, if I'd lived.' And she led Melkavesh with swift, decisive steps along a street which presently took them between the elegant premises of craftsmen.

Here the houses were smaller, built of milk-white stone with pointed silver windows. Each was surrounded by a walled garden. Most had a plaque on the filigree gate, indicating what craft or trade was practised within; there were jewellers, shoemakers, swordsmiths, glass makers. There were many Gorethrians about now, servants too, coming and going from the houses on various errands. Fortunately the sight of two guards – even one smaller than normal with the cloak wrapped round herself rather than pushed back – seemed to attract no attention.

'Her name is Anixa, and she's Kesfalian,' the woman was saying, with a semblance of lucidity. 'She was my dressmaker, you see, one of the court dressmakers. The thing is, she has her own premises – no Gorethrian overseer. She's answerable to her Guild, of course, but they only visit her once every few weeks. Here it is –' She pushed open a finely wrought silver gate, and Melkavesh found herself in a formal garden of fountains and lush, plum-red trees. The woman went on, 'This is what I should have done, brought Falmeryn here, only I didn't think. I didn't think, so he is dead and it's my fault. Does that make sense? Is that fair?' And she laughed again, a hollow desolate laugh that made Melkavesh feel very uncomfortable.

They reached the house and the woman knocked lightly on the white-and-silver panelled door. After a moment it opened and a slender, dark female stood on the threshold, staring guardedly at them.

The woman pulled her helm off and smiled. 'Anixa, it's me, Kharan. Don't you recognise me? Can we come in?'

The dressmaker, Anixa, stepped back and allowed them over the threshold. Within was a large, light room, with bolts of brilliantly coloured cloth stacked against the walls, and half-finished garments lying across a long table. 'How can I help you, my lady?' she asked.

'I suppose you've heard about my execution?'

'My lady?'

'Didn't you wonder why they asked you to supply this dress?' She flung the red cloak onto the floor, held out the grey silk skirts and pirouetted unsteadily. She came to a standstill, swaying slightly. 'Listen, Anixa, you would do anything for me, wouldn't you?'

'Of course –'

'If I said to you, "I am going to be killed unless you hide me here," you would hide me? My lover, too?'

Anixa, obviously perplexed, glanced uncomfortably at Melkavesh. 'Lady Kharan, are you all right?'

'Yes, darling Anixa, what makes you think I am not?' Kharan leaned forward and stroked the dressmaker's face. Anixa was looking almost pleadingly at Melkavesh, who shrugged. 'You would have done, wouldn't you? Let me stay here, I mean?'

Obviously thinking that Melkavesh was a genuine guard, and that she and Kharan were trying to extract some kind of confession from her, Anixa remained silent. So Melkavesh mouthed, 'Humour her,' and eventually the dressmaker nodded and said, 'Yes.'

'I knew it! What a bloody fool I am! Did you know, in Shalekahh the punishment for being stupid is death? Not just your own, but that of the person you love most. I was just trying to explain this to –' she turned to Melkavesh and frowned, as if she had only just noticed her. 'Who are you?' she demanded in a low voice. 'This is some trick of Xaedrek's, isn't it? Some horrible joke.'

'No, it's not,' said Melkavesh firmly.

'Madam, please tell me what is going on,' the dressmaker implored.

'I wish I knew,' Melkavesh muttered. She took Kharan's arm gently and said, 'I rescued you, but I don't know who you are. Come and sit down, and we'll talk –'

But there was a hazy fire glittering in the woman's eyes, and she staggered out of Melkavesh's grasp and hissed, 'Rescued? How could you be so cruel? I should have been dead by now, and perhaps I'd have been with Falmeryn. How much more must I be punished?' She fell heavily to the floor, striking her head. 'All I wanted was to die. Just to die.' Her eyes rolled upwards under the lids, and she passed out.

5

Anixa

WHEN KHARAN came round, she was lying in a comfortable bed, enveloped in cool, white sheets. For a long time she was unable to think where she was, or how she had come to be there; it seemed she had been having a terrible dream which had gone on and on . . . then she saw the strange Gorethrian woman seated by her bed, and a wave of black depression crushed her.

'How do you feel?' Melkavesh asked. She had carefully hidden her hair in a strip of silk given to her by Anixa.

'Dreadful,' Kharan said. 'How do you expect me to feel? I've such a headache. Is there any water?'

Melkavesh got up and brought her a glass. 'You've been unconscious nearly all day. It's evening. Your dressmaker has been very helpful, lending us this room. I think we're safe here. There were soldiers in the street earlier, but none have come to this house.'

Kharan looked unimpressed. She finished the water and lay back, staring at the ceiling. Melkavesh went on, 'I wish you would tell me about yourself.'

'What?' she exclaimed, turning her head to glare at the Gorethrian. 'You want to know about *me*? You're the one who should be explaining herself! I would like to know why Xaedrek has done this . . . although I can guess. They call him a psychomancer: he must have read my mind, and decided it would be more of a punishment to keep me alive.'

Shocked by the bitterness of this speech, Melkavesh de-

118

cided she could achieve nothing by trying to conceal her ignorance. Softly, she asked, 'Who is Xaedrek?'

Kharan sat up violently, her chestnut eyes glittering. 'I don't believe this. The plan is to drive me mad, is it? Well, I will tell you something. I'm not frightened of you, and there is nothing you can do to hurt me. Xaedrek has done his worst already.'

'Why do you think I'd want to –'

'You're Gorethrian, aren't you?'

'Kharan, listen to me,' Melkavesh said gently, pulling the material from her hair and shaking it loose. 'I don't know how to make you believe this, but I'm going to try. I have to trust someone. I'm a stranger to Shalekahh. More than that – I'm a stranger to this Earth.'

'By the gods, your hair,' Kharan breathed. 'I'd forgotten about it.'

'I'm half-Athrainian. It's a long story – will you listen?'

Kharan lay back, hesitant, guarded, yet indifferent. 'If you like.'

Melkavesh began to explain who she was and why she had come to Earth. As she listened, Kharan's apathy turned to amazement, and by the time the story was finished, she had temporarily forgotten her own troubles.

'Ashurek's daughter? You are Ashurek's daughter?' she exclaimed.

'Yes. But I don't want anyone to know, not yet.'

'It's unbelievable,' she murmured, shaking her head.

'But you understand that I have come here without the faintest idea of what has happened in the last twenty-five years. That's why I genuinely do not know who Xaedrek is.'

'The Emperor,' Kharan replied with a dry laugh.

'Where were those guards taking you when I intervened?'

'To be executed. Beheaded.'

'Ah. So that square building is a place of execution?'

She nodded and murmured, 'How strange. Another ten minutes and I would have been dead.'

Hesitantly, Melkavesh asked, 'Did you mean it when you said you would rather not have been rescued?'

119

'I don't know yet. Don't ask me that.' Kharan frowned, then said, 'You must have thought I was insane. I'd been given this drug, you see, to make me calm, and I just didn't know what was happening. I thought it was a dream. Was I talking nonsense?'

'A little, but you retained sense enough to come here.'

'Not really. That was part of the dream.'

'Will you tell me why you were going to be put to death?'

Kharan was beyond caring whether Melkavesh was a genuine friend or not; all at once she craved the childish comfort of telling the sorry tale to an outsider. But as she began, it suddenly seemed much harder than she had expected. When she came to explain about Falmeryn, she found herself weeping uncontrollably, her face hidden against Melkavesh's shoulder.

'And I do – I do wish I was dead,' she sobbed. 'I loved him so much, and I'll never see him again. And I've no one to hate except myself. It was my fault.'

'From what you've said, it was Xaedrek's fault.'

'No, because I knew all along what Xaedrek was like, and what I was risking. But the worst thing is that I was convinced that there was nowhere Falmeryn and I could flee to and hide. But while I was waiting to be executed, the idea jumped out at me, like a horrible, grinning imp in a child's nightmare. We could have come here and Anixa would have hidden us. It went through my mind over and over again, the image of us coming here and hiding, everything being all right. As if I was trying to turn back time, or torment myself into madness.

'And then there you were beside me, in what I thought was a dream, saying "There must be somewhere we can hide." So it was purely automatic to come here. It was as if it was happening to someone else, not me, and that other person was mocking me. "This is what you should have done, fool."'

'Is Anixa a special friend of yours?'

'Not really. It's just the way she is. I knew she would do it, without questions, without betraying us to the Gorethri-

120

ans. She has no love for them – or for me – but she belongs to herself.'

'Well, you were right, Kharan. She *has* hidden us, and been extremely helpful.'

'I wish I'd been wrong,' Kharan whispered. Then she looked up, her eyes wide. 'We are both in trouble, aren't we? Xaedrek will want to know how I escaped. And you killed four of his guards.'

'I didn't kill them. They'll recover.'

'And be able to describe you.'

'No. I . . .' Melkavesh's dark face became introspective. 'I took their memories. They won't be able to tell him anything.'

'Is something wrong?' Kharan reached out and touched her arm.

'Yes. I'm hungry. Aren't you? I'll go and find Anixa, and see if she minds feeding us . . .'

'Oh, poor Anixa!' Kharan exclaimed. 'Oh, will you ask her to come in here? I should apologise, and explain.'

Melkavesh rose, smiling. Looking down at Kharan, ill and pale though she was, she saw a buoyant spirit that was most definitely not ready for death.

'You can stay here as long as you wish,' the dressmaker said, ladling a thick grain soup into their bowls. Kharan had recovered sufficiently to get up, and they were seated round a table in Anixa's dining room. As the whole of her ground floor was given over to her trade, the living quarters were in the first and second storeys. This gave a sense of security that Melkavesh hoped was not false. The rooms were white-walled, clean and simply furnished.

'You're so kind, Anixa,' Kharan said. 'I'm sorry about this morning.'

'It's forgotten, my lady.' She lit a large candle in the centre of the table. 'You know, of course, that many courtiers visit my premises. However, there should be little risk. There has never been any reason for them to come upstairs.'

'In fact, if this is the haunt of courtiers, Xaedrek would certainly not expect us to be hiding here,' Melkavesh said, breaking a piece of bread.

'If they come to question me, you can be sure that I'll say nothing to them. I do not much like Gorethrians –' she looked sideways at Melkavesh, 'but they do not intimidate me, either. Would you like some cheese, my lady?'

Anixa was a woman of middle years, with an elfin, enigmatic quality. Her skin was bronze in colour, but dappled with lighter patches that had a bluish sheen in some lights, pale gold in others. This was no defect of birth, but the normal appearance of a Kesfalian. Her hair was black, long and straight, her eyes pale amber. In manner she was direct and respectful without being servile, but she never smiled. Melkavesh was not sure what to make of her, and as they had told her almost everything that they had told each other, she could only hope that the dressmaker was as trustworthy as Kharan believed.

'I don't know how we can repay you,' Kharan said. 'You can have that awful grey dress – take the opals and pearls off it, they are worth a fortune.'

'Thank you, my lady,' Anixa responded practically. 'I think I can trade them without detection.'

There was silence for a time while Kharan and Melkavesh ate hungrily. Although Kharan had felt she never wanted to eat again, some survival instinct took over and she discovered that she was famished.

Presently Melkavesh asked, 'Does anyone else come here, apart from your customers?'

'Only the head of my Guild – who is Gorethrian, of course – every twenty or thirty days. There are not many like me, craftsmen who work without Gorethrian supervision. It is only because my work is favoured by the court that I am allowed this privilege. The trust I am now abusing,' she added without a glimmer of humour.

Kharan said, 'Melkavesh, unless you'd found someone like Anixa very quickly, you would never have got anywhere. Everyone in Gorethria is identified by their membership of a noble family, the army, or a Guild. Without proof of identity you cannot go anywhere, not even to buy a loaf of bread.'

'Wouldn't I send a servant to do that?' She raised an eyebrow.

'Well, yes. That's another difficulty. There are so many things that no self-respecting Gorethrian would dream of doing for themselves. With your face you could not even have passed yourself off as a slave, but as for your hair –'

'I had come to the conclusion that matters were going to be rather difficult,' Melkavesh said drily.

'You'd have been under arrest by now.'

'I almost was, twice.'

Anixa excused herself and went downstairs to finish some work, leaving them alone.

'Look, Melkavesh,' Kharan said, staring down at her plate, 'I am not the brightest of people. A lot of what you told me earlier, I didn't really follow. What is it exactly that you want to do to the Earth?'

'I don't want to do anything *to* it,' she said, her green-gold eyes luminous in the candlelight. 'The Earth is full of energy, released when the Serpent M'gulfn died. I suppose my ultimate aim is to found a School of Sorcery, where people with the latent gift can come and learn to wield the power . . . This must sound mad to you. Does it?'

'No, it doesn't, actually,' Kharan replied flatly. 'Falmeryn's parents were involved in the Quest of the Serpent. His mother is Estarinel's sister. He told me all about it. I'm not saying I understand it all, but I believe you.'

'Oh,' said Melkavesh, taken aback. 'Good. That helps. The thing is, I can do nothing until I understand the power myself. It's different from my own world. There's so much I need to find out – the exact nature of it, whether anyone wields it already – I hardly know how to start. I thought I could do it completely alone, but now . . . the truth is, I would like some help. Will you help me, Kharan?'

Kharan ran a hand nervously through her hair and avoided the question. 'We need to escape from Shalekahh as soon as possible. It needn't be so hard now. You can easily pass for a Gorethrian, and I can pretend to be your servant. I don't know where we shall go, though.'

'I wasn't planning to leave Shalekahh immediately,' Melkavesh replied, toying with an exquisite wine glass, which was the exact colour of her eyes. 'I've only just arrived. There's nowhere else I can learn as much as I can here. You know Xaedrek well, don't you?'

I should have known – she wants to use me, Kharan thought. 'What of it?' she snapped.

'When I was fighting those guards, I was aware that they had some kind of sorcerous power. Like mine, but . . . wrong, artificial and tainted somehow.' She shivered slightly at the memory. 'Do you know anything about this dark power that Xaedrek has?'

'No. He wouldn't tell me, and I didn't ask.'

'Well, I've got to find out. I could do it by "far-seeing"; spying from a distance, as it were. But if he is a true Sorcerer, he might find me out, so it must be done by normal means. I want to meet Xaedrek.' She saw Kharan freeze, saw the colour leaving her face and her eyes becoming glassy. But she went on, 'I can only do it with your help, your knowledge of the court . . .'

At this, Kharan jumped to her feet as if someone had struck her. Her expression was one of blank misery. Melkavesh realised she had misjudged her state of mind; a degree of delayed shock was inevitable after what she had undergone. Knocking her chair over, she turned and rushed from the room, making the candle flame dance wildly. Melkavesh made to follow her, then decided against it. Perhaps it was better for Kharan to be left alone until morning.

What am I doing here? Kharan wondered, lying on the bed in darkness. One moment I am almost dead . . . the next, being told some fantastical tale by a woman who claims to be a Sorceress and Ashurek's daughter, and wants to meet

Xaedrek . . . whoever she is, I don't want to be used by her. I don't want to know.

But she felt numb, confused, unable to judge right from wrong. Melkavesh appeared well intentioned, and she seemed to be against Xaedrek's methods. From what Falmeryn had told her (in those long, drowsy afternoons when she could have listened to his voice for ever . . .) Ashurek had not been evil at heart, and Silvren had been wholly good. And they had destroyed a great evil, and Melkavesh only wanted to continue that noble work . . .

But she was Gorethrian.

And then there was fear. Xaedrek was bound to find her. Anything can be gone through once, but now she was intimate with every aspect of that terror, she was certain she could not face it again.

I don't want to be unhappy, and I don't want to die, she thought. How have others coped with this misery? A part of her spirit longed to be resilient and decisive, to make bold choices and take responsibility for her own destiny, like Melkavesh. Like Xaedrek. But a grey, leaden mass had settled in her soul, and she could only be herself, and that self was numb and apathetic and cynical.

She decided to help Melkavesh. It was a coward's decision, she knew, made because she could not resist Melkavesh's will any more than she could resist Xaedrek's.

And because she knew of no alternative, and because she could not care less anyway.

The next morning, she helped Anixa in the small kitchen, and carried bread, fruit and milk into the dining room for their breakfast. When the dressmaker had gone down to open her premises, Kharan said to Melkavesh, 'You wanted my advice?'

'Very much,' Melkavesh answered gently.

'All right, here it is: Xaedrek will destroy you.'

There was a pause. 'Is that all you have to tell me?'

'I'll tell you whatever you need to know. But I never want you to say you weren't warned.'

'Well, I'll bear it in mind,' Melkavesh said, and her tone

was thoughtful, not condescending. She walked over to a window and looked out at the garden, where a Patavrian boy was diligently sweeping the paths. 'I don't wish Xaedrek to know who I am, or anything about me. I want to assume a false identity, so that I can infiltrate the court quietly, make my investigations without attracting any notice.'

'It was lucky, wasn't it, that you happened to rescue someone who has intimate knowledge of the ways of the Imperial court . . .' Kharan said drily, coming to her side.

'Very. If it was luck,' Melkavesh said thoughtfully. 'I was trying to remember something that the Guardian, Eldor, once said to my father. "There is no such thing as pre-ordination . . . it is only that certain things become inevitable."' She looked round at Kharan, who was still pale, her eyes red-rimmed and glittering. 'Anyway, don't think I don't appreciate your help. I do, very much.'

Not responding to this, Kharan folded her arms and said, 'Identity will be a problem. To try to gain a post at the palace, as an official or a guard, would be pointless. They are vetted very thoroughly, and even if you did, it would be thought very strange if you tried to speak to the Emperor without an official reason. Your only hope is to pose as an aristocrat. But all the noble families are known at court.'

'Every single member?'

'Well, not by sight, but they're all in the records . . . of course, there are many who are spread throughout the Empire, and have been there for years, even through the time when Gorethria was weak.' An idea came to Kharan, and as she pursued it, she temporarily forgot her grief. Colour returned to her cheeks and her face became lively. 'There was a large family who ruled in Bagreeah, the House of Calmek. I was one of their slaves, a long time ago. It's a terrible country, all jungle, very remote from here. A few of the family would travel to and from Gorethria occasionally, but most of them would not be known in Shalekahh. There was a Lady Melkavesh . . .'

'Whom I could impersonate?'

'I don't see why not. You can say you've travelled alone

126

from Bagreeah. It's very unlikely you'd meet anyone who knew the real Lady Melkavesh. And I can tell you everything you need to know about the family and the country itself.'

So it was agreed. Kharan would give Melkavesh the background information; Anixa was to provide her with suitable clothes and false insignia. On a set day each month, the Emperor held court for visiting nobles and army leaders who were normally out in the Empire; the next one was in seven days' time. 'Xaedrek is not always there in person,' Kharan said. 'You'll have to take that chance. But it's the only way that you can enter the palace without an official reason.'

Gorethria was still run on traditional lines, Kharan explained. The Senate consisted of three hundred nobles, Guild masters, administrators and war leaders. From that body the twelve members of the Inner Council were elected – in theory, at least; in practice, those chosen always included the High Commander and eleven other men and women who held specific high offices. And each had originally been selected for his or her post by the Emperor himself.

The three most powerful Councillors at present were High Commander Baramek, a man called Amnek, and his wife, Shavarish. The latter two were close scientific colleagues of Xaedrek.

The rest of the court consisted of aristocrats, officials, valets and handmaidens – most of whom were themselves of noble birth – and their various children and retainers. Then there were the Imperial guards, but the only ones who lived in the palace were Xaedrek's personal guard. Non-Gorethrian slaves within the palace were kept to a minimum, all supervised closely by Gorethrian overseers. They were well treated, but fear of the dreadful penalties for insubordination kept them under control.

Gorethria was hierarchical, yet classless; all Gorethrians, noble or otherwise, found status by joining the army, a Guild, or some other authoritative body. All menial work was allocated to the Vardravian slaves.

'It sounds just as my father described,' Melkavesh commented. 'Nothing has really changed after all.'

'Except that there's no royal family as such. Xaedrek has no close relations. I suppose he'll have to marry, for the sake of succession . . .' Kharan trailed off, because Melkavesh was looking at her in a way that made her suddenly uncomfortable. After a pause she said, 'Being who you are, you must consider him a usurper. Do you?'

'I told you, my only concern is sorcery,' Melkavesh answered evenly. 'Tell me something about my "family" in Bagreeah.'

In the days that followed, they spent many hours talking, both determined not to overlook any detail over which Melkavesh might be caught out. Meanwhile, Anixa made her a costume suitable for wear at court; a robe of lustrous black silk sewn with an intricate pattern of scarlet jewels, and a sleeveless overgarment in quilted satin, of a deep violet that was almost luminous.

'It's beautiful, I'm impressed,' Melkavesh said, turning slowly as she admired the clothes in a mirror.

Anixa grunted non-committally, as if to say it was not one of her best, but it would do. Then she said, 'You will have to do something about your hair.'

'Yes, I know. I thought some sort of covering, a turban –'

Kharan shook her head. 'No. It's no longer the fashion at court, you'd be laughed at. We'll have to dye it.'

'I don't want it dyed,' she answered so vehemently that Kharan started laughing.

'I'd never have thought you were vain.'

'It's not vanity. It's because –' Melkavesh found the reasons too complex to explain. 'I'll tell you one day.'

'Well, I have some cloth dye that will wash out,' the dressmaker said. 'It only becomes permanent if you boil it.'

'You are certainly not boiling my hair! Very well, if you insist. Cloth dye it is,' Melkavesh acceded.

'And you'll have to cut it. Like mine,' Kharan said. But Melkavesh drew the line at that, so between them Kharan and Anixa contrived a way of arranging her newly dyed black tresses in a way that would not look too unfashionable.

Adjusting a jewelled pin, Kharan paused, resting her hand

on Melkavesh's shoulder. 'I've been wondering if I should tell you this. It's very strange. Xaedrek once told me that he had had a recurring dream for years of a Gorethrian woman with bright golden hair. Do you think –'

Melkavesh looked up, her eyes wide with astonishment. She gripped Kharan's wrist and almost gasped, 'I was going to ask you to describe Xaedrek to me, but I don't think I need to. His skin is a few shades lighter than mine, and there are some white strands in his hair, and he has arched eyebrows and ruby-red irises. Well, is that Xaedrek or not?'

'It is,' Kharan whispered, a strange sensation in her stomach. 'How did you know?'

'I've had a recurring dream as well.'

The palace at night was like a great iceberg against the night sky, eerily lit from within. Light and shadow had changed places, and recesses that were dark during the day now shone with a glassy white light. The portals were open, and figures moved towards them with stately poise, silhouetted for a moment before vanishing into the light.

Melkavesh moved with them, one of them, sensing all around her the rustle of satin, the faint clicking of jewelled hems, the warm essences of sandalwood and amber on silken-dark skins. As she entered the palace she felt no trace of fear, only an electric excitement. From the murmur of voices around her, she knew that despite their cool poise, the other visitors shared her anticipation.

They were now in a lofty marble hall, as cold and beautiful as ice, filled with a soft, clear light. Imperial guards stood at intervals along the wide curve of a staircase. There were palace officials welcoming the guests, guiding them one by one to a desk where a Gorethrian clerk sat over a large book, checking the identity of each visitor. With most of them, Melkavesh observed, this was a mere formality, swift and courteous. When her own turn came, as she had anticipated, the check was more thorough.

'I am Lady Melkavesh of the House of Calmek in

Bagreeah,' she stated. The clerk gave her a searching look with his cold green eyes and turned the pages of the thick volume until he found Calmek's page and located a Lady Melkavesh, and compared the intricate heraldic symbol on her sleeve with the illumination in the book. Now she would find out that the real lady was dead, or had entered the palace five minutes earlier, or that Kharan had forgotten some vital detail of the insignia . . . the clerk made a note in a separate book, nodded and said, 'Thank you, my lady.'

The deception had worked! She was free to ascend the stairs and pass through the echoing halls to the Imperial court with the other Gorethrians.

The throne room was more breathtaking than the entrance hall, all crystal whiteness. There were about five hundred people there, yet the vast room did not seem crowded. All were dressed in brilliant colours, kingfisher blue and fiery orange, viridian and scarlet and purple-red, black and topaz-yellow. The effect was as startling as the luminous colours of tropical fish, and stirred odd emotions in Melkavesh. Such scenes had been part of her father's life . . . The outrage she had felt in her two encounters with Xaedrek's soldiers was forgotten as she moved forward to blend with the aristocrats.

And strangely, she did not feel like an outsider. Like a fish thrown into water, a hawk on the wing, she was in her element. Effortlessly reflecting the easy confidence of those around her, she began to exchange greetings and small talk as if she had been at court all her life. She knew that she could not have carried it off anywhere else, but she was Gorethrian, and she belonged here.

As yet there was no sign of Xaedrek. To one side of the throne-dais, a Cevandrian quartet played softly on pearl-white, spiral wind instruments. In contrast to the hall, the throne itself was iron-black, ornate yet almost grotesque.

A goblet of rich red wine was thrust into Melkavesh's hand and a voice said, 'My lady, I always make a point of greeting newcomers.' Facing her was a woman even taller than herself, extremely lean, with a long, narrow face and hair cropped to jaw-level, like Kharan's. Although the signs of ageing in

Gorethrians were few, Melkavesh estimated her to be about sixty. Her eyes, a brilliant sapphire blue, were accentuated by a robe of the same colour. 'May I enquire your name?'

'Lady Melkavesh.' The woman clasped her hand briefly, and again Melkavesh sensed the taint of wrongness that she had felt in her battle with the four guards. She wondered if the woman could likewise sense her sorcerous powers; but there was no sign of recognition on the long, dark face. Melkavesh said, 'I am afraid your name escapes me.'

Now the woman did look surprised. 'I am Shavarish,' she said, as if stating the obvious. Of course. Kharan had spoken of Shavarish, a senior member of the Inner Council and one of Xaedrek's scientific colleagues.

'My Lady Shavarish, you must forgive me. I am only a peasant, you see, newly arrived from Bagreeah. I have a lot to learn.' This seemed to strike the right note of dry self-mockery, and the lady smiled.

'Evidently. You have my sympathy, living in that wretched province, I mean. What brings you to Shalekahh?'

'Do I need a better reason than escaping Bagreeah?' Shavarish laughed at this. Melkavesh continued, 'I've been so looking forward to seeing the Emperor for the first time.'

'Well, you may be disappointed. He dislikes these affairs because they keep him from his work. He may not come, and if he does he won't stay long.'

Melkavesh looked rueful. 'A shame. I would so like to meet him . . .'

'Oh, so would they all.' She waved an elegant hand at the groups of visiting nobles. 'Particularly those with marriage-able daughters, little realising that *they* are the ones he takes the greatest pains to avoid.'

'I don't blame him. I suppose it would be very predictable of me to ask if there's likely to be an empress soon?'

Shavarish laughed. 'Very, but excusable. We'd all like to know. Personally I doubt that he will ever marry. He's the sort of man to whom the idea of a child to rule after him means nothing. But state pressure . . . who knows.'

131

'I thought he did not marry because he was devoted to a mistress,' Melkavesh said, carefully offhand.

'Oh, you haven't heard.' There was the ghost of a smirk on Lady Shavarish's mouth. 'It ended in the most extraordinary scandal. She was unfaithful to him, so he had her put to death. The only wonder of it was that it hadn't happened sooner. Imagine, an An'raagan at court!' She sipped her wine with studied thoughtfulness, as if she was trying not to smile.

'That must have been an uncomfortable situation . . .'

'Utterly appalling,' Shavarish agreed in a low, confidential voice. 'Don't get me wrong, Xaedrek is respected and loved. But no one likes the Emperor to have a weak spot. Her demise has been the cause of rejoicing at court for days – oh, all very discreet, of course. No one would wish to risk upsetting Xaedrek.'

'Of course not,' Melkavesh said, raising her eyebrows. 'So she is dead?'

'As far as I know.'

Melkavesh, somewhat stunned by this, did not reply. Her mind worked briskly through possibilities until she came to the most logical explanation: only the four guards taking Kharan to be executed knew she was not dead. Their own memories of the rescue would be vague. What could they have told Xaedrek? Evidently they had decided to tell him nothing, for fear of punishment – and Xaedrek, wishing to forget the matter, had not asked. Melkavesh grinned to herself.

'Lady Melkavesh, I could grow to like you,' Shavarish laughed, misinterpreting the grin. 'I think I will introduce you to Xaedrek myself. Why have you been hiding in Bagreeah?'

A tall, thin man approached and Shavarish introduced him to Melkavesh as her husband, Lord Amnek. 'Is the Emperor going to make an appearance?' she asked him.

'Yes, I persuaded him that it would be diplomatic. But it will only be for a few minutes.' He regarded Melkavesh with a kind of glowering indifference and moved on.

An hour or so went by, with still no sign of the Emperor.

One or two speeches were made by palace officials, welcoming visitors from far parts of the Empire. Melkavesh circulated discreetly, listening to conversations about the current state of various countries, military strategy, the continuing difficulty of invading Kristillia. She learned a great deal. Eventually she found her way back to Shavarish's side. Kharan had described her as a 'scientific colleague' of Xaedrek. So she must share his knowledge . . . Perhaps Melkavesh should concentrate upon her rather than the elusive Emperor, but she did not know how to broach the subject without arousing suspicion. As she was pondering this, a door opened at the far end of the throne room and Xaedrek entered.

He came in flanked only by two guards, but the effect on the assembly was electrifying. All conversation stopped, every eye turned to watch him as he ascended the steps to the throne. Melkavesh stared at him in astonishment. It was not just his compelling presence, which was not pomp or majesty but something less tangible and more affecting; it was that he looked exactly as he had in her dream. It was no vague resemblance, no coincidence; she had dreamt specifically of *him*, and now she doubted that it had been a mere dream.

The Emperor seated himself and looked expressionlessly at his court. He was wearing a garment of rich red silk held in by a wide silver belt, and his dark, white-touched hair fell softly to his shoulders. He wore no crown and was more simply dressed than anyone else there, yet the quiet power of his personality filled the hall like a dark fire. Melkavesh, some thirty feet from him, could clearly see the intense, beautiful ruby-red of his eyes.

As one, the court bowed. There was genuine, deep respect and reverence in the gesture, and Melkavesh felt moved: like a sudden blaze of light, it came to her that Xaedrek had saved Gorethria. For a moment there were tears in her throat, as images of Meshurek, Ashurek and Xaedrek stirred a mixture of emotions in her chest. Yes, she loved Gorethria as if she had been born here, and yet . . .

133

Now the Emperor began to speak, welcoming his visitors, thanking them for their tireless work in maintaining and extending the Empire. The speech was short, almost understated, but the words were heartfelt and brought a mood of exhilaration to the court. Some began discreetly to work their way to the front; they were too well mannered to jostle one another, but all were hoping desperately that Xaedrek would notice and speak to them personally. Shavarish, half-smiling, took Melkavesh's arm and led her towards the foot of the dais.

The speech over, it was Xaedrek's way to descend from the throne and move among his court at will. It was not permitted for anyone to address the Emperor, so all the visiting nobles depended upon him to approach them. And the more eager they looked, the more likely he was to pass them by. Essential meetings took place at smaller, official functions; this was a purely social event, so he was not obliged to notice anyone.

Melkavesh watched him speaking to this group and that, and she saw how brief and courteous each exchange was, how Xaedrek's eyes would be intent on the person he was talking to, then drift beyond them, as if he had discovered all he needed and lost interest within a few seconds.

Then she realised with a sinking feeling that she had one chance only to engage his attention, and that would not be the easy matter she had envisaged. To his eyes, she was no different from the others here, a loyal subject, but only one of the hundreds, thousands he had to deal with. There was no reason on Earth why he should indulge her wish for a lengthy conversation. Shavarish's introduction would be all but useless; he would give her the merest glance and be gone.

He was approaching now, heedless of the tall aristocrats bowing as he walked past them. His eyes were on Shavarish and he did not seem to have noticed Melkavesh.

'Lady Shavarish, I can't spend any longer away from the mansion,' he said in a low voice. 'I'm sorry to interrupt your own enjoyment of the evening, but I need both you and Lord Amnek to assist me.'

'Of course, Your Majesty. At once,' the lady replied. 'Just allow me to introduce my guest. I did promise her I would. The Lady Melkavesh of the House of Calmek, in Bagreeah.'

Melkavesh bowed. As she raised her head, Xaedrek took her hand in a cool, impersonal clasp, murmuring the correct greeting, but his gaze was already drifting beyond her. He was looking for Amnek in the crowd, and his thoughts were wholly elsewhere.

Melkavesh had an aptitude for thinking very quickly, which others might call impulsiveness. She had told Kharan that her plan was to infiltrate the court quietly, without attracting attention, but at this moment it seemed that if she did not command Xaedrek's interest at once, her chance would be gone for ever. Rather than let it pass, she decided to take a risk, one which might cost everything.

In her experience, one Sorcerer always recognised another. To her, Xaedrek's power was palpable – if dark and distorted. Yet he showed no sign of realising what she was. So in the brief second while he clasped her hand – whether it was quick thinking or sheer recklessness – she allowed a faint golden current of sorcery to pass from her palm into his.

His reaction, invisible to Shavarish's eyes, was to Melkavesh one of violent shock. His expression barely changed, but he seemed to freeze, and instead of dropping her hand, tightened his grip on it. And now his eyes were fixed intensely on hers.

'Your Majesty, it is a great honour to meet you,' Melkavesh said, looking steadily, innocently back at him.

Then he released her hand, but continued to stare at her. In the same even tone, he said, 'Lady Shavarish, there is a slight change of plan. I am going to my private office. Wait five minutes, then bring the Lady Melkavesh to me.'

The Emperor turned and strode from the throne room without a backward glance at anyone. All around her Melkavesh sensed sighs of disappointment. The level of conversation rose, and the musicians began to play again. She

135

looked round and found Shavarish staring at her, stony-faced but wide-eyed.

'What can the Emperor want with me?' Melkavesh exclaimed with a suitable mixture of fear and wonder. She did not have to feign it, for she was feeling fierce exhilaration at the success of her ruse, combined with a nervous thrill of anticipation. What had she done?

'My lady, I am as puzzled as you,' Shavarish answered. 'However, I will be frank with you. You are either exceedingly privileged, or in extreme danger. It depends upon what it is about you that has aroused his curiosity.'

'You are the first member of the House of Calmek I have met, although I know they have ruled admirably in Bagreeah for centuries,' said Xaedrek pleasantly. Shavarish had been sent on to the mansion, and Melkavesh was now alone with him. They were in a small room which was all shades of silver, restful to the eye. The walls were painted with scenes from Gorethrian history. There was a polished agate desk and several chairs, but Xaedrek did not sit down or invite her to.

'Thank you, Your Majesty,' she replied. So far the Emperor had asked only a few neutral questions about her background, and she was continuing to impersonate a naïve young woman from the unsophisticated far side of the Empire.

'Why have you come to Shalekahh? It can have been no easy journey, especially alone.'

'It was tolerable. I've never understood how my family can bear to stay in Bagreeah. I have longed to see Gorethria all my life, Your Majesty.'

'And how do you like your motherland?' he asked, moving to the curtained windows and turning to look at her.

'Gorethria's beauty, Your Majesty, is beyond description. My only regret is that I did not come sooner –'

'Lady Melkavesh,' he interrupted, obviously impatient to discover something more concrete. 'I will come to the point.

136

Do you know anything of that which we call hyperphysics?'

'Your Majesty?'

'The power that is more than physical. The superstitious might call it magic, but it is greater than that. It is real, and it can be called from the Earth to our aid. Give me your hand.'

He moved to the front of the desk and half-sat on the edge, so she was obliged to walk over to him. They joined right hands as if in a formal greeting, but this time she released no sorcerous power from her fingers. His grip was light, his eyes glowing but unreadable. Standing close to him, she realised with a jolt that his presence was more than pure power: he was also extremely attractive.

He continued, 'When I touched your hand before, I felt a similar power in you. I want to know whether or not you are aware that you have it. Do you know what I am talking about? You must be honest. There's nothing to fear.' Kharan had been right – he seemed both gently spoken and charming.

She swallowed, and replied carefully, 'Your Majesty, I'm not sure. I have been aware of some strange – force, I don't know what to call it, within me, for a long time.'

'Can you control it?'

'Sometimes.'

'Show me.' Again she released a trickle of golden electricity into his hand, aware that she could probably have killed him if she had wanted to. He looked with interest at the faint cloud of stars coalescing round their fingers, but after a minute he pulled his hand from hers and said, 'Enough. And you are sure you do not know where this power comes from?'

'Your Majesty, I – to be honest,' she lied, 'I came to Shalekahh in the hope that someone might be able to tell me.'

Xaedrek smiled and shook his head as if in wonder, and his expression, far from being threatening, was open and friendly. Melkavesh wondered who was deceiving whom.

'Well, my lady, all I can tell you is that I have studied the power for years, and in all that time I have come across only one other who can draw it directly into herself as you can.

But she cannot control it, and it is of a different nature.' This excited her curiosity at once, but she did not allow her wide-eyed expression to alter.

'I've heard that you are a great scientist –' she began, but he broke in, 'I don't require flattery, or anything except that you address me as you would a friend. Now, I hardly need to question your loyalty to Gorethria and myself.'

'Of course not, Your Majesty,' she affirmed vehemently.

'Then – how would you feel if I told you that this power you possess is going to make a great contribution to Gorethria's future? Greater than you can imagine.'

'I would not know what to say,' she replied truthfully.

'I am asking you for your help, my lady. I will not compel you. If you refuse, no more will be said.'

'The Emperor needs my help? How could I refuse?'

He smiled again. 'I want you to work with me. As a colleague. In return for all I learn from you, you shall receive all my knowledge. And a salaried post as a member of my personal staff, of course. Is this acceptable to you?'

Melkavesh was completely taken aback. She had thought it would take months of subterfuge to discover what she needed; and here she was being freely offered the knowledge. But so much else besides. She perceived how easy it would be to be drawn into Xaedrek's dark spiral, how hard to escape. But again, if she did not take the risk, she would achieve nothing.

She parted her lips to reply, but the words stayed in her throat. As she met his gaze she felt her pretence falling away; not because he intimidated her, but because it was suddenly as though they were two equal souls in a void, stripped of everything except truth. *Called from the Earth to our aid* . . . she had heard the exact same phrase from the High Master of the School of Sorcery many times, and the words touched her in a way she did not understand.

Xaedrek took her hand again and lightly kissed it. 'Believe me, this meeting is as startling for me as it is for you. Perhaps more so. But fortuitous. And for Gorethria herself, utterly invaluable.'

'I'm not sure I understand,' she smiled.

'But you will. It will all be explained.'

And Melkavesh bowed, and said, 'Your Majesty, without flattery, I am honoured to accept the post. My only desire is to serve Gorethria as best I can.'

'Excellent. I am a notoriously bad host, but on this occasion . . .' He crossed the room, filled two goblets with a diamond-clear wine, and handed one to her. 'We should celebrate. I warn you, my colleagues are often expected to work through the night, but I won't demand that of you at such short notice. Meet me in the palace library tomorrow morning, one hour after sunrise.'

And they drank to each other in silence, their true thoughts hidden behind smiles. As for Xaedrek, Melkavesh had deceived him almost completely. He sensed that she was not as innocent as she seemed, but that did not really matter to him. The important thing was that she was a new source of power, hopefully one that would enable him to dispose of Ah'garith. And she had appeared as if from nowhere, like a miracle. If he had believed in gods, he would have fallen to his knees in thanks.

He had recognised her face from his dreams, but those visions now had a different interpretation, and no longer seemed threatening. Her hair was black, of course. The golden hair of the dream had been a symbol of the power she would bring, its strength and purity. A banner to show that the breakthrough he had been seeking was imminent. Nothing sinister.

For the first time since Kharan had died, Xaedrek laughed.

While Melkavesh was away, Kharan tried to sleep, but failed. Every time she closed her eyes, images and memories of Falmeryn began to torment her towards madness. While she had been occupied helping Melkavesh and Anixa, life had taken on a semblance of normality, and she had almost returned to her old self, but alone in the darkness, grief rose up to meet her like a wave. And as the reality of what had happened began to settle in her soul, her private misery grew worse. Every time she thought she was beginning to bear it, the pitiless black river would drag her under its surface once again.

She rose from her bed and sat looking out of the window, numb and cold, half-heartedly wondering how long Melkavesh was going to be. The moons were half-full, and they imparted a ghostly light to Shalekahh, so that the delicate buildings resembled transparent shells of wax lit from within by dying candle flames. Kharan bowed her head onto her hands and began to weep with quiet abandonment. She had no reason to suppose she was not alone, so when she felt a hand on her shoulder, she jumped so violently that she thought her heart would fail.

'I'm so sorry, my lady,' said Anixa, 'I didn't mean to startle you.'

'How long have you been standing there?' Kharan gasped, shaking. 'I didn't hear you come in.'

'I have a light step. I thought I heard you crying, and came to talk to you.'

'Well, that's kind, Anixa, but I don't think there's much to be said,' Kharan replied, drying her eyes and trying to sound cheerful. But Anixa remained with her hand resting on Kharan's shoulder, looking out at the night, as still and dark as a statue carved from shadow. And Kharan began to find her presence comforting, and because any kind of comfort tore at her, reminding her of Falmeryn, she wept again. Presently she said, softly, 'It was all right while I was helping Melkavesh . . . something to think about. But when there's nothing else, the abyss is still there. One moment someone is with you; the next they've gone, and you can't see them or touch them, and however hard you search you'll never find them. Never. I don't know how anyone can bear it.'

'Nor I, my lady,' said the dressmaker. Her hands were cool against Kharan's skin, and she smelled sweetly of the fine velvets and silks with which she worked all day. 'I have also lost loved ones at the Gorethrians' hands. I was a girl

140

in Kesfaline, in the days of Meshurek. I never knew anything but life under a Gorethrian governor. They had ruled us for centuries. They took our crops, mined our hills, seized the young and strong as slaves . . . and because we could not accept their rule, they caused us to live in perpetual fear. The threat of death, slavery or torture hung over every family, and we thought it would last for ever.

'Then suddenly, unlooked for, we had our freedom. The Kristillian army came over the mountains, and we joined them, and drove the Gorethrians from our land. We did not know why they had become weak, but neither did we care. For the first time in a thousand years, Kesfaline was free. And our joyful independence lasted all of – what? Fifteen or sixteen years. Then Xaedrek came.' One side of Anixa's face caught the moonlight, one eye gleamed pale amber while the other remained in shadow. Her voice was quiet and sombre. 'In those few years of freedom I had married and had a son. We thought the time of darkness was over. Never once did we dream that Gorethria would grow strong again, but one day, as I returned home from buying cloth, I saw flames leaping from the roof of our house. The whole village was afire, and the Gorethrians were back. My husband and child were slain as they tried to escape the fire, and I was captured and brought to Shalekahh.'

'Anixa – I'm sorry,' Kharan stammered. 'And I was with Xaedrek then, trying not to think of such things.'

'My lady, I am not telling you this to make you feel guilty,' Anixa said. 'Not even to point out that you are not the only one who has such grief to bear. I mention it because it has to do with Melkavesh.'

Outside, leaves were stirring in silhouette across the half-faces of the moons. Kharan asked quietly, 'What about her?'

'Well, my lady, do you think we are right to be helping her?'

Kharan stared at her and exclaimed, 'Gods, I don't know! I think she's – well intentioned. Not like Xaedrek. But I've given up trying to judge right from wrong.'

141

'Well intentioned, indeed. But the best of intentions may lead to disaster.'

'What exactly do you mean?'

'I find myself in the centre of a paradox,' Anixa replied. 'As one who hates Gorethria's tyranny, I hope that she will stop Xaedrek.'

Anixa had never spoken so openly before, and Kharan began to feel disturbed for no reason she could pinpoint. 'You're thinking that even if she does, she is still a Gorethrian herself?'

'More than that. The sages of Kesfaline have always prophesied that someone would save us from Gorethria, only to bring something worse upon us. Not just to Kesfaline, but to the whole world. We have a belief that we are the protectors of the secrets of the Earth, and if those secrets are violated, disaster will follow.'

'What sort of disaster?' Kharan asked anxiously.

'I do not know, my lady. You see, the Gorethrians strove for centuries to suppress our belief, which was somewhere between a religion and a philosophy. They only succeeded in driving it underground. Now the knowledge is safeguarded by a handful of sages in Kesfaline, so the rest of us know *of* the belief, but we do not know the truth which lies behind it. Alas, I am no sage. But when Melkavesh came and spoke of sorcery, I had a premonition that that which my race has long dreaded will come to pass.' As the dressmaker spoke, Kharan felt for one dislocating, terrifying moment that she was sharing the vision; and it seemed to her that Anixa was not bounded by human flesh, but part of the night, stretching out into darkness, linked to Earth, sky and moons in some incomprehensible, mystical way. The silence was like velvet constricting her throat, and into it, Anixa stated, 'Perhaps it is Xaedrek who should stop her.'

The words gave Kharan a jolt of fear, like the hand falling on her shoulder when she had thought herself alone. She jumped to her feet and cried, 'Don't talk like that, Anixa. You're frightening me. It's not making any sense. Who are you, really?'

142

'I'm Kesfalian, my lady,' Anixa said, as if that explained everything. 'No doubt if you spoke to a Kristillian, they would tell you something quite different. The Kesfalians and the Kristillians are sibling races, and we love each other and share many beliefs. But on certain matters we cannot agree. It's as though they look outwards while we look inwards. Theirs is an overt religion, but they fail to see the truth of the secrets that lie behind it. Their priests will not heed the warnings of our sages, and they will not see the danger until it is too late.'

'What danger?' Kharan demanded, irritated by unreasoning fear.

'I don't know. Would that I did. It is known only by the sages of Kesfaline.' She raised her dark, slender hands to grasp Kharan's arms. 'My lady, all I know is that something is happening, and you are caught up in it, even more than I. Can you not feel it?'

'Yes. Yes, damn it!' Kharan exclaimed, her jaw clenched. 'These are not random events. Melkavesh is heading for some great or appalling destiny, and we are not helping her of our own accord, but being swept along with her. Is this what you mean? Yes, I feel it, Anixa. It's what is waiting for me in the abyss. Oh, gods –' She bit her lip and gazed out at the garden. 'If Falmeryn was with me, I could face it. But not alone. Not alone.'

'What are you frightened of?' Anixa asked softly.

'Everything. Having to be brave, make decisions . . . others putting trust in me. I'm a dreadful coward, Anixa, that's all there is to it. What have these mystical things to do with me? I don't understand, and I don't want to get involved.'

'But you already are. And, my lady, there is no need just to be "swept along". You have the power to change things. When Melkavesh is taking the wrong course, you can correct it.'

'How will I know whether what she's doing is right or wrong?' Kharan cried, exasperated. 'And even if I do, do you think she'll listen to me? I've less influence over her than I had over Xaedrek!'

'But you must make her listen. *You must*,' Anixa persisted, and Kharan, through incomprehension and fear, lost her temper.

'How can you put this responsibility onto me?' she snapped. 'You can't expect me to judge her behaviour according to a few vague warnings of "disaster" which even you can't explain clearly. There's something you don't understand, Anixa. If I don't find something to believe in, I'll go mad. So if I must make a decision, I here and now decide to trust Melkavesh implicitly,' she concluded flatly, her eyes glittering.

'You'd do better to put faith in yourself,' the Kesfalian responded.

'Oh, I used to, in the days when I believed that I could use the Gorethrians for my own gain and thus have revenge on them. Then I found evil staring me in the face and I realised it had all been self-delusion. So I put my faith in Falmeryn instead – and now there's nothing. Nothing except Melkavesh. I believe she's good, and that if anyone can stop Xaedrek, she can . . . and I don't think anything else matters.'

Anixa released her arms and said gently, 'Perhaps you are right. Xaedrek must be destroyed, and all else is secondary. Whatever else she may do, I believe that she will oppose him.' The dressmaker turned her head as a movement outside caught her eye. 'Look, she's coming back.'

Below the window, a tall figure was crossing the garden, just visible in the faint, pearly light. Anixa ran down to open the door, and a few seconds later, Melkavesh was entering the room in a swathe of brilliant lamplight. She was smiling broadly and did not notice how subdued Kharan was.

'Well, you were right!' she said, flopping into a chair and pulling the jewelled pins from her hair.

'What about?' Kharan said guardedly. She sat near her on the edge of the bed, but Anixa remained in the doorway, her arms folded and her face expressionless.

'Xaedrek. He is utterly charming.' She shook her hair loose and yawned. 'And I have some very good news for

144

you. He thinks you are dead. So he won't be looking for you!'

'How do you know?' As Melkavesh explained, Kharan felt a pang at knowing Xaedrek believed the execution had gone ahead. Had he really felt nothing at all? she wondered. She swallowed, and asked lightly, 'And you met him?'

'It all went better than we could have hoped!' Melkavesh began to relate the evening's events animatedly, oblivious to Kharan's increasingly stony expression. 'I don't know how to thank you for your help,' she concluded. 'Without you – and Anixa – I could never have –'

'You're going to work with him!' Kharan interrupted, so bitterly that Melkavesh stopped short and stared at her. Kharan looked across at Anixa, but the dressmaker said nothing, only shook her head resignedly. 'I don't believe it. After everything I told you, everything you said –'

'Kharan, please calm down.' Melkavesh reached out and took her arm, but she pulled away. 'Appearing to co-operate with him is the only way I can find out what I need. I'm not betraying you. I won't really be helping him.'

'No?' Kharan took a deep breath and walked over to the window. Mastering herself, she turned and looked steadily at Melkavesh. 'If you believe that, you're a bigger fool than I am. You cannot deceive Xaedrek. No one can. Don't delude yourself, you *will* be helping him. He'll see straight through you and if you don't do his will, he'll use you and crush you. You must know it in your heart – if you don't, then you are –' she paused, and aimed her words like knives '– more arrogant, and worse, than he is.'

6

An Imperial Pastime

IT WAS a perfect day for hunting.

While Kharan sat imprisoned in Xaedrek's mansion, the
day before her intended execution, the weather outside was
calm and sweet. The previous night's storm had exhausted
itself, leaving the sky washed clean, a newborn dome of cyan.
Later, it would become too hot to ride, but now, in the early
morning, the coolness of the air filled both the horses and
their riders with eagerness, while hounds ran in circles,
yelping their excitement. A fresh breeze was moving through
the forests beyond Shalekahh, shaking rain from the foliage
in showers of jewels. And where sunlight caught the moisture
it evaporated, filling the air with the fragrant scents of earth,
grass, and the essential oils of plants. The hunt were in high
spirits; the ideal weather alone would make this a chase to
remember.

Falmeryn watched them approaching from a distance. He
was outside Shalekahh, far beyond the army camps, on the
edge of a forest. With him were six guards; he was chained
to two and stood between them, but the others sat on rocks
or leaned against trees, exchanging idle comments to relieve
their obvious boredom. None of them paid him any attention.

As the hunt drew closer, he could identify individual
horses, even recognising several of those which he had had
in his charge. There were many fire-gold war-horses, dancing
along with heads in the air, manes and tails flying out like
flames. There were strongly built crossbreds, pale gold in
colour; creamy-grey palfreys; tall, long-legged hunters, some

black and some dark brown. Their riders, all members of the Imperial court, were dressed in breeches, tunics and short cloaks of various rich colours and designs, and their mounts' trappings were no less ornate. Leading them were five Hound Masters, identified by white capes with broad blue stripes that gleamed like lapis lazuli. There were even young children among them, mounted on red chestnut ponies and wearing gold helmets to protect their heads should they fall.

In front of the horses trotted the hounds, twenty couple in all. They were lean and graceful beasts standing four feet high at the shoulder. The silky fur on their legs and bellies was a mixture of red and gold, shading to white on the back, giving the curious impression from a distance that they were covered with snow. Their long, fine heads were white, with red stripes running from nostrils to ear flaps, indented over the eye to give them a frowning look. Their eyes were an incongruous, intense blue. Their jaws grinned and their feathery tails waved with canine delight at serving their Masters.

Falmeryn had never had any connection with the hounds; they were tended only by their Gorethrian Masters, for they had been trained to kill any human they did not know.

'Is Xaedrek riding today?' one of the guards said.

'Anybody's guess,' replied another, shrugging.

He should have felt afraid, and yet he did not. The fresh morning and the invigorating scents of the countryside recalled Forluin, made fear seem out of place and his situation unreal. But thinking of Kharan, he was filled with angry despair. Just as she blamed herself for his fate, so he blamed himself for hers. *She* had known – had warned him – what a risk they were taking, and he had not listened, had not believed Xaedrek could possibly be as bad as she said.

He knew better now.

But too late. He had not protected Kharan; he had failed her.

After the guards had arrested him, and he had helplessly watched Kharan being borne out of his reach for ever, he too had been taken to the mansion and brought before

147

Xaedrek. The treatment he received was not what he had expected. He had not been locked in a cell, tortured or interrogated; Xaedrek had been unexpectedly civil, giving him hope that he would listen to a plea for humanity and mercy after all.

'I am to blame,' Falmeryn had said, leaning on the bench as Xaedrek continued to work, not looking at him. 'She was frightened and had no one to turn to and I took advantage of her. I am the one who should be punished. Not her.'

'That is not what she told me. She said you were in love.' The Emperor sounded faintly scornful.

'I do love her. That's not her fault, is it?'

'Isn't it? She's well enough aware of her own attractiveness. And she told me the exact opposite of what you have just said – that it was all her fault, and *you* were the wronged innocent. Your defence of each other is quite touching.'

'Then you'll spare her, you must –' Falmeryn cried.

'Touching, but also pathetic. Childlike. Putting me in the role of a monster from whom you must flee, hanging onto each other like infants. I dislike the implications. The truth is far simpler, quite straightforward. The Lady Kharan was mine, and she is no longer, and I am displeased, angered, resentful – add any bitter emotion to that list you like.' His voice was offhand, but with a chilling edge to it. 'The past cannot be undone, but it is in my power to end the situation, and so I will.'

'But gently. Humanely,' Falmeryn said with a firmness that surprised himself. 'How will shedding our blood help anyone?' Xaedrek raised his eyes to meet Falmeryn's, but did not answer. 'Banish us. Send us back to Forluin.'

'Forluin,' Xaedrek echoed thoughtfully. He was silent for a moment, pausing in his work. 'You are wonderfully selfless, Forluinishman. I expect you will offer your life in exchange for hers next.'

'I would, if you'd accept it,' he replied quietly.

'Are all your race so noble?'

'We do our best,' Falmeryn said with a touch of sarcasm.

'Have you ever wondered,' Xaedrek said lightly, as if he

148

were talking to a friend, 'why Gorethria has never taken an interest in Forluin?'

'I know why.'

'It is because Forluin is of absolutely no strategic importance. However, if it were – if, for example, the west coast of Tearn launched an attack upon the eastern seaboard of the Empire – highly improbable though that is – then we would seriously consider making it an outpost.'

'Are you trying to intimidate me by threatening Forluin?'

'Just the opposite. I am saying that I would not threaten your country merely for the sake of revenge. Vengeance is the most uneconomical of motives, illogical and wasteful. But I thought you'd be interested to know the reason for your island's apparent security.'

'Well, you're wrong,' Falmeryn retorted. He moved round the bench to face Xaedrek, unafraid of him. He feared what the man could do, but his actual personal aura – which others so dreaded – made no real impression on Falmeryn. Something within his own personality gave him detachment. Perhaps it was that the Forluinish had never taken the idea of emperors seriously. 'Forluin is protected. It is no secret – I'm surprised you don't know.'

'Well, I am ever eager to learn. Please explain.'

'Thousands of years ago – the date isn't precise – ships began arriving on our coasts from Tearn and Vardrav. They had heard that Forluin was a rich and fruitful land where diseases could be cured, so they had left their own countries to live in ours. At first there were only a few, and they were accepted. But more and more came until Forluin was in danger of being overrun. The Forluinish are gentle, unwarlike, but many of the visitors were not so peaceable. What were we to do? We were in danger of losing our land. If we tried to drive them out, there would be war; if we let them stay, our freedom and everything precious in our land would be eroded and finally destroyed.'

'An interesting dilemma.' Xaedrek had never really given Forluin any thought before; he shared the usual Gorethrian misconception that they were unsophisticated peasants, cowardly ones at that. Scornfully, he added, 'If you are truly such a generous and unselfish people, in theory you should have given your land to the invaders and accepted the consequences. Evidently you learned that self-sacrifice has its disadvantages.'

'We had been willing to share our good fortune,' Falmeryn said in a low voice. 'We learned that it was impossible. Others did not share our love and respect for the land. If we gave it away, it would cease to exist. No one would have gained anything in the end, so you could say that when put to the test we proved as selfish and territorial as any other race. As a mother fights to protect her young, so we fought to protect Forluin. Instinctively and single-mindedly.'

'A war?' said Xaedrek, surprised.

'We were ready to take up arms. Probably we'd have lost a conventional battle, being unused to fighting. But the H'tebhmellians intervened and gave us their help. Forluin was unlike the rest of the Earth, they said, and must be preserved, and in the end, the visitors left of their own volition, without bloodshed.'

'How?'

'I don't know whether I can explain, because I don't really understand myself. It was partly an aura bestowed on the island by the H'tebhmellians, which compels those with ill intentions towards Forluin to return home. And partly a power within ourselves.'

'Which is what?'

Falmeryn shrugged and answered, 'To be strong without using force I suppose.' Xaedrek stared at him expressionlessly. 'It is possible, you know,' Falmeryn went on with sudden fervency. 'You don't have to prove your strength by executing Kharan just for – for displeasing you. What's the use of it? If you ever loved her, felt anything for her at all, how can you be so merciless? How –'

And Xaedrek suddenly smiled, turned, and put his hands on Falmeryn's shoulders. 'Such passion,' he said. 'Such passion. I really like you, Falmeryn, and I respect you, which is something I can say for almost no one else. Now I understand what she saw in you, I could almost forgive her.'

'Then forgive her. Please,' Falmeryn whispered.

Xaedrek turned away and leaned on the bench, shaking his head. For a few heart-stopping seconds Falmeryn believed he had changed the Emperor's mind. 'It's not a question of proving anything. Nor even of blame, which may be partly mine. It is simply the cleanest end to a regrettable situation.'

'For the Lady's sake –' Falmeryn gasped, the room reeling around him. Only Xaedrek was still, the immovable centre. Suddenly there were guards on either side of him, as if Xaedrek had sensed that he was about to forsake his belief in non-violence.

'Her death will be swift and painless, she'll hardly know anything about it,' the Emperor explained, like a kindly physician. 'A noble, Gorethrian death, because – whatever you think – she did mean a lot to me. And your own will be a perfectly traditional one for a non-Gorethrian servant.'

Now Falmeryn was afraid, and could not speak.

'You know, of course, that one of the favourite pastimes of the Imperial court is hunting. Sometimes, the quarry is human, when a slave is to be put to death, and is young and strong enough to give a good chase. Unfortunately, it will most decidedly not be swift or painless, but that is the nature of the hunt, and it is no dishonour to you. Nor any pleasure to me,' he added. 'I will not be there.'

How often had Falmeryn himself readied horses for such hunts? Sick with himself, with fear, with everything that happened, he could find nothing else to say to Xaedrek, and was dragged mutely from the room. And now it was the following morning, and he stood chained to the Emperor's guards, watching the glorious spectacle of the hunt trotting towards him, so colourful in the early sunshine.

How hard it was to face death with so much unsaid, unresolved. What would Estarinel have done? he wondered. Found some vulnerable spot in Xaedrek's character, or overpowered him and rescued Kharan? But the reality of a situation was never clear-cut, nor the means of escape obvious – if they existed at all. The hounds were only thirty yards from him now, milling around each other, their tails thrashing cheerfully as they snuffed idly at the ground and air.

The six guards stood to attention and began to walk Falmeryn towards a great copper-red tree, a traditional starting point of the hunt. The five Masters were shouting sharp commands to the hounds, holding them in check until the right time. One of the guards pulled Falmeryn's cream-and-gold jacket from his back, leaving him bare-chested, in breeches and boots which were the remains of his Imperial groom's uniform. The jacket was taken to the Hound Masters.

The riders had halted, and were looking intently at Falmeryn. They liked to have a good sight of their prey, even though he might not be recognisable when they saw him again. The hunt was that much more enjoyable if they knew whom they were chasing. The horses fidgeted, jangling their bridles and trappings, while their riders talked and laughed. Falmeryn recognised Shavarish and other court notables; even High Commander Baramek was there. But Xaedrek was not; he had spoken the truth when he said he did not relish such spectacles.

One of the Masters had dismounted and was surrounded by his eager canines. He was holding out the jacket for each of them to sniff in turn. Having got the scent, they waited obediently for his next command, their great, eager eyes fixed on him. Finally he remounted his horse and threw the jacket to them, and they perfunctorily savaged it until he called them off. A ragged cheer arose from the riders. Then the Master raised his whip and signalled to the guards, who began to unlock Falmeryn's chains.

'You will have about half an hour's start,' one of the guards told him. Servants who had followed the hunt on foot were now going among the riders with drinks and sweetmeats, nervously trying to avoid the attentions of hounds. 'It doesn't matter where you go, they'll still scent you out. But here's one bit of advice: don't try to hide in a tree. It makes for a poor chase, and a worse end. The dogs can jump and climb.'

'*Hounds*. Don't call them "dogs",' another guard corrected.

And now Falmeryn was free. 'Go on!' shouted the first guard, giving him a violent shove. And Falmeryn ran.

A vague, rebellious idea passed through his mind; he would hide only a few yards away, thus getting it over with quickly, and frustrating their hopes of a long, exciting chase. But this heady illusion of freedom, this apparent chance to escape, were too strong for him. His instinct was to survive, and he plunged wildly into the red undergrowth of the forest.

They were south-west of Shalekahh. His only hope might have been to cross the River Kahh, which ran from north to south on the far side of the city, but that was at least an hour and a half's run from here, and he knew he stood no chance of reaching it. In fact, he could not think clearly to make any kind of plan at all, and as soon as he entered the forest his sense of direction deserted him. He ran in wild panic, adrenaline coursing through his body, his skin prickling hot and cold as if he could already feel a hound's breath on his back. The floor of the forest was soft with fallen leaves and treacherous with roots and stones. He was running downhill; above the insistent, rhythmic crunching of his feet, he could hear the bell-like calls of birds, the roar of their wings as his passing alarmed them. Tree trunks, black and maroon and bronze, went past him in a jerky blur and he found himself continually turning and twisting to avoid collision.

A pain in his shoulder, as if someone had stabbed him with a needle, subdued his panic like a blow. It was only an insect, a non-venomous one; there was a cloud of them dancing about him like magenta fireflies. Swatting at them, he forced himself to slow down and get his breath. He looked around at the emerald green ferns, the bright fungi protruding from moist hollows in tree trunks. Above, delicate, crystal light filtered down through layers of lush foliage, dappling the forest floor with all shades of pale red, crimson and amber. In every direction the forest looked the same. He had a feeling of unreality, yet his situation was only too real.

He ran on steadily, trying to pace himself. The insects followed him, feasting on his arms and back, until he gave up trying to brush them away. He was beginning to feel thirsty and stopped to drink from a small pool, but the water was foul. He went on, knowing that thirst would soon become a torment.

He wondered if the hunt had set off yet; he could not judge whether an hour had passed, or five minutes. At the moment, he felt that he was out-distancing them, approaching safety, yet he knew this to be an illusion. This chance of escape was no chance at all: the hounds would pursue his scent as easily as if the forest had been torn away and they were loping after him in clear sight. But the illusion was strong, and the instinct to survive an absolute compulsion.

He made for thicker undergrowth which would hamper the hounds, and halt the horses completely. But he soon realised it had not been a good idea. Thorns tore at his flesh and unseen creatures clung to his boots, trying to inject poison through the leather. He was struggling uphill. Bushes tugged at him and he flailed through them as if fighting the current of a river. At last he gained the crest of the hill with relief. The ground here was clearer. His mouth was thick with thirst and he had to slow down to a walk to recover his breath.

As he did so, he heard in the distance the faint, clear music of hounds on a scent.

A wave of renewed fear swept sickly through his stomach. He broke into a run and headed deeper into the forest, his feet sliding on hidden stones and twigs. The trees here were huge and ancient, looming darkly around him, and the air was clammy with the wet scent of fungus. Liver-coloured flowers lay in the shadow of rotten tree trunks, waiting for small creatures to wander into them unawares.

Sweat stung the insect bites and tears in his flesh; his shoulders ached and his throat was raw. But he dared not slacken his pace now. Falmeryn heeded the guard's advice not to climb a tree; the idea was not even tempting. Silent birds sat broodingly in the branches, snakes twined among the leaves. He passed clefts in knolls of earth and rock which would have concealed him from human eyes – but how terrible it would be to be cornered by those fell hounds . . . he stumbled on, suffering the first pangs of exhaustion. As he began to tire, his anxiety seemed to increase in proportion, as if an invisible hand were hanging lead weights on his limbs, one by one.

He never knew how far he ran before they started to catch up. It seemed no time at all. Somewhere behind him a couple of hounds were working through the dense belt of undergrowth, while the Masters took the others round by a clearer path to rejoin the trail at the top of the hill. A line of riders cantered easily after them, exhilarated by one good gallop and anticipating another. Presently one of the Masters began to lead them eastwards where the trees were well spaced and the ground firm. No point in going deeper into the forest where it would be hard for the horses, he said; hounds would do the work there.

But Falmeryn knew nothing of the manoeuvring behind him. He was only aware of his nightmare flight, blurred yet agonisingly vivid. Time and again a rock would twist his foot, an unseen drop jar his bones in a stomach-sinking lurch. His tendons felt like torn wire. His shoulders and back were in a spasm of tension, burning. His throat was thick and bitter with thirst, and an iron spike stabbed his lungs with every short, desperate breath. Branches whipped him as he crashed through them, unable to control his tired muscles to avoid them. Exhaustion was becoming agony, and the voices of hounds were much nearer now. They were gaining on him swiftly. The urge to flee swept through him like madness and he stretched out his tortured legs to run faster, faster . . . but he could not increase his pace. His limbs would no longer obey him. He could only struggle on mechanically, an automaton made of wood and lead.

There was a flash of white to his right, and running beside him was the first hound. It loped along easily, as if mocking his pace. Panic churned in his stomach, and he veered to the left. Fear and instinct, not thought, now ruled him totally.

155

He could hear the other hounds behind him, their great paws thudding on the forest floor, and he could hear the glassy notes of a hunting horn. The huge canines were at his heels, their musical yelps shrilling through his head. He could almost sense their hot breath on his skin. Sweat was pouring off him, yet he shivered, and the wet air of the forest seemed to be choking, drowning him.

Why did they not overtake him and pull him down?

They were running closer now, bunched on his right side. Of course, they were driving him. The forest was too close for the horses. They wanted him where it was more open.

He slowed down, involuntarily, for his body was desperate for oxygen. The hounds bounded playfully along behind him as he stumbled along, sucking air into his raw lungs. Now the trees were widely spaced, the undergrowth sparse. Crystal light splashed through the red foliage, the forest floor was a russet blanket of peat and fallen leaves. The atmosphere became dry and warm, and Falmeryn, despite the cramp knifing through his ribs, suddenly found he could breathe.

He was running downhill again, a gentle slope, but enough to help him recover partially. But what was the use of that? They would run him into the ground anyway; it would only make the chase longer and more interesting for the hunters. Which was what they wanted.

But still he fled compulsively. For a few minutes, he had the illusion that he was leaving the pursuers behind; the forest was silent, filled only with the sound of his own harsh breathing and rhythmic footfalls. Then he heard the sound, distant at first, but growing nearer, like the slow onrushing of a wave. The soft thunder of horses' hooves.

He glanced round. The hounds were a hundred yards behind him. Perhaps a quarter of a mile further back, but swiftly catching up, the hunt followers were galloping steadily through the trees. They were bent forward on their horses' necks, their dark faces eager and intent. The Hound Masters led them, resplendent in white and blue. Sunlight flashed on them; they must have been a glorious and noble sight to an onlooker. But they filled Falmeryn with blind terror and

156

despair. He cried out hoarsely; then, above his own voice, he heard the clear, thin, pitiless note of the horn, the note that said to the hounds, *kill*.

Their spasmodic yelping built to a crescendo of baying, exquisite music in their Masters' ears, and they ran in a tight pack, one wide, undulating, creamy-white fleece. They were a proud sight to anyone – except their quarry.

Now Falmeryn ran as if he had only been ambling before. He ran until his lungs were bursting and the air felt like sand scraping in and out of his dry, swollen mouth. His ribs were a barbed cage in which his heart lurched wildly like a huge rock. He could no longer see where he was going. Red and green halos burst across his vision, his eyes stung with sweat. His whole body was lanced by pain, and his legs were dull and heavy with exhaustion, as though they did not belong to him. But somehow his mind transcended his body's agony and forced him on at a wild pace. He had no idea of his direction and did not know that he was leading the pack towards the edge of a steep drop. The Hound Masters had failed to divert him onto flatter ground, but it did not really matter to them, for he was almost spent and the hounds would soon be upon him.

And now he could not even hear the hounds' voices. His arteries were pounding, blood roared in his ears. His head swam with pain and blackness and wild terror. But however desperate he was to avoid his fate, there came a point where his exhausted muscles could no longer obey. His mind was still screaming at him to flee, flee, but his body was stumbling and falling.

He collapsed onto a bush, which sprang back and flung him onto the ground. For a moment he was stunned, oblivious to everything except the hot spears of agony in his chest as he fought for breath. Then he opened his eyes, and through a cloud of black stars, saw the hounds coming to him.

Oh, they were beautiful creatures, with their soft russet and white fur, their lean, striped heads. They were snuffing at his boots, then at his legs, then his whole body – He struggled to sit up, almost out of his mind with fear. Their

157

noses were ice-cold against his hot skin, but their breath was warm and smelled of the bloody meat on which they were fed. He flung an arm out above his head, seized a limb of the bush, and pulled himself backwards a few inches. Leaves and grass stuck to his skin and one of the hounds began to lick at his chest as if to cleanse him. Its tongue was rough and wet, and its hard white teeth scratched at his flesh.

His initial, agonising breathlessness subsided, but his limbs were trembling with weakness. He could hardly move. He wished only for it to be over, and yet they seemed to be hesitating. He wondered . . . he had always had an empathy with animals, as did many of the Forluinish. Did they sense this, and not wish to harm him?

Cautiously, he stretched out a hand to the nearest, looking into its fierce blue eyes. He spoke softly to it, the words emerging hoarsely from his clogged throat. It stared at him. It seemed to grin, and saliva dripped from its lolling tongue onto his hand. Its companions were yelping deafeningly and running around him in excitement.

He sat up, hope growing in him. Slowly and painfully he pulled himself into a crouching position, his own head on a level with the hounds', so that he did not seem to threaten them. Again he held out his hand and whispered gently to them.

And then he looked up, and saw the horses pulling up in a ragged line behind the hounds, snorting and prancing, their coats damp with sweat. He saw a Hound Master raise the white glass horn to his lips, and heard the single thin, falling note. The riders' anticipation was almost palpable. He saw Baramek's harsh face set in an expression of grim satisfaction, Shavarish smiling, Amnek glowering . . . Falmeryn froze, one hand touching the hound's head.

In the same instant, he felt its teeth in his arm.

The hounds were well trained. They had waited for the riders to catch up before killing.

He tried to stand up, failed, and staggered backwards. The hound's teeth were locked in his flesh and his whole arm went numb. Now the others were on him, and he felt their soft fur brushing his skin and their paws pressing down on him before they bit. He was pinioned against the bushes by four or five of the creatures, and their ivory fangs were in his legs and side. Another snapped at his throat, before fastening on his shoulder. The pain was excruciating. A hallucination darkened his mind: he seemed to be caught in a weird metal cage, with vices of freezing cold iron clamped on his body and limbs. Then, mercifully, the combined fear, pain and shock sent him dizzily into oblivion.

He did not feel the bushes give way beneath him, nor did he know there was a twenty-foot drop beyond them. The hounds bore up his body for a few seconds, shaking and tearing at it, but they could not hold it. The flesh ripped between their teeth, and they lost their purchase. The body rolled down the drop, bouncing loosely against rocks on its way, until it came to rest at the bottom of the little cliff. The canines hung over the edge, whimpering, but it was too steep even for them to follow. Presently the Hound Masters called them off, and the whole hunt moved to the edge to look down.

The Forluinishman's body lay in an awkward tangle, slicked with blood. There were murmurs of satisfaction; hounds had done their job well. It was usual to leave the corpse where it had fallen; the countryside around Shalekahh was littered with the skeletons of those who had suffered a similar fate. Now the excitement was over, there was no particular reason for them to find a way down to the body. It was considered bad taste to take trophies.

So the hunt wheeled away from the drop and began to jog-trot back towards Shalekahh. The hound-pack ran gaily in front, licking their bloodied lips. Some of the nobles rode alongside the Hound Masters, congratulating them on the excellence of the hounds; finest pack in Gorethria. Baramek smiled indulgently at his ten-year-old daughter, who was talking enthusiastically to a friend about how well the man had run and how bravely he had died. Everyone agreed that he had given a good chase.

Human hunts were, by their nature, sadly short-lived; but

159

for the aristocracy of Shalekahh, the unique satisfaction of them more than made up for that. And it would not be long until the next.

Melkavesh, wearing a cloth-of-gold robe and an azure cloak, went to the palace library in the morning as arranged. It was closed to the public while the Emperor was using it, but she was expected, and was let in by a female librarian. Xaedrek was already there, seated at a wide marble table covered with books and manuscripts.

He stood up and greeted her pleasantly, then dismissed the librarian. Melkavesh was left alone with him in the echoing, columned halls. If he had guards on hand, she could not imagine where they were; but Kharan had said that people feared him more because he did not need a body-guard.

'Sit down, Lady Melkavesh,' he said, indicating the chair next to him. 'I propose to take you fully into my confidence, in order that you understand exactly how you are going to help me.' She sat down gracefully, looking enquiringly at him. She wondered if he instinctively trusted her because she was Gorethrian – or was it that he could simply kill her on a thought, if she proved untrustworthy? On both counts, his confidence in himself might – for once – betray him.

'In the course of my initial research,' he went on, 'I found this. The library yields remarkable treasures, if you have the patience to search.' He slid a book towards her. It was about twenty-five or so years old, hand-copied in small, neat writing and bound in soft calf-skin. It was titled, *In my Workshop* and the author was Setrel, of Morthemcote in the Retherny Valley, Excarith.

Melkavesh had heard a lot about Setrel from Ashurek. She leafed through the pages, realising it had been written after her father's meeting with the village Elder. There was mention of Excarith's war with Gastada, but most of it was devoted to Setrel's scientific experiments with both the natural and the supernatural.

160

'How was this book brought here from Tearn?' she asked.

'Oh, we have many Tearnian books. Scholars have always sailed between Gorethria and Tearn, regardless of war or politics – it's nothing remarkable. What intrigued me was that the author makes mention of a Sorceress called Silvren of Athrainy.'

'Who?' said Melkavesh, as much out of surprise as anything.

'Silvren,' the Emperor repeated. 'I have heard of her from another source, but I'll come to that later. It appears that she possessed extramundane power in a time when that was theoretically impossible. Only the Serpent commanded such power. No human did – with the singular exception of Silvren. However, the point is this: the author, Setrel, also seemed to have found a way of capturing a similar power artificially.'

Melkavesh looked up from the book and held his eyes, absolutely intrigued. 'How?' If Ashurek had spoken of this, she had not really taken it in.

'He produced a salt from certain plant substances, acids and minerals. Somehow this powder drew into itself what little sorcerous power was free in the Earth. It had very little strength in itself, and yet he claims that demons and other creatures of the Serpent were terrified of it.'

'I think I have heard of the Serpent . . .' she said vaguely. Xaedrek proceeded to explain what she already knew – and in greater detail – about the slaying of the Serpent and rebirth of the world. Yet it was fascinating to hear the story from someone new.

'In theory,' Xaedrek continued, 'Now that M'gulfn is dead, many Sorcerers such as Silvren should now exist. But it does not seem to be so. To be honest, I still do not know why, and perhaps I never will. But I have always been fascinated by the idea of such power, and determined to find a way to harness it for Gorethria's use.'

'Evidently you have succeeded,' she said softly. 'How was it done?'

'Firstly, I attempted the summoning of a demon, which had a rather strange result.' He described Ah'garith's arrival.

'The Shanin told me what I have just told you, about the Serpent, Silvren, and so on. It – she – had no explanation of why Sorcerers do not exist. However, she has a certain ability to draw power into herself, though not to control it – rather like yourself.

'The question was, how to make the power usable. I studied Setrel's book and practised his methods. At first the results were disappointing. Perhaps Setrel's success was a fluke: the substance I made had no energy within it, nor could it be made to absorb and hold Ah'garith's. But after months of work, I developed a modified compound, a dark green crystalline salt, using various acids combined with a mixture of living and inert materials. Now this could hold Ah'garith's power, but the results were poor. What was missing was a human element.

'When human energies are added to the demon's – rather, when her power is passed through a human – it becomes magnified, stabilised, infinitely more potent. I constructed a special machine for the purpose. It channels the energy from Ah'garith, through the human, and thence into the powder.' From the folds of his robe he took a glass phial, half-full of honey-gold crystals. He placed it on the table before Melkavesh. 'The dark green salt changes colour, as you see. In this form it is called amulin.'

'How is it used?' she asked, staring at it.

'Its administration is extremely simple. It is put into water and swallowed.'

'Swallowed?' she said incredulously. He smiled at her expression.

'Yes, Lady Melkavesh. And it gives those who take it temporary hyperphysical powers. Greater strength, the ability to move or destroy things without touching them, to stun and even to kill opponents likewise. Swords, arrows and spears, from being haphazard weapons, become lethal in the hands of those who have taken amulin. It can sometimes give a certain, rather limited degree of foreknowledge. Intuition.'

'And who –' she hardly knew what to ask first, 'who is permitted to take it?'

162

'Not everyone, obviously. We can barely produce adequate quantities for our needs at present. Soldiers receive it before they go into battle. So do some of the palace guards, while they are on duty. And certain members of the Inner Council, for experimental purposes.'

'Isn't it harmful?'

'No. Why should it be? It is pure energy, and the salt which holds it is inert. The effects last perhaps a day. The doses given are tiny, and the powers bestowed on an individual are limited, obviously. No one is transformed into a god by it.'

'Or even a true Sorcerer.'

'Quite,' he said, giving her a disturbingly intent look.

'So you do not fear that anyone will attempt to harm you whilst under its influence?'

Xaedrek half-smiled, shaking his head. 'It is not a drug, my lady. It does not affect the minds or loyalties of those who take it. If anyone offered me harm, I would know it, and it would hardly matter whether they had taken the power or not.'

'Of course, Your Majesty,' Melkavesh answered evenly.

'If you are wondering, there is an optimum quantity which only I know and take. Imbibing more is no advantage, but if it is taken every day, there is a gradual increase of the effect. So it is quite easy to ensure that no one gains greater strength from it than myself. However, I rarely have cause to wield the power.'

'It is a safeguard.'

'Yes. Well, my lady, have you anything else to ask me?'

'Your Majesty – I hardly know what to say. I had no idea that the renewed strength of the Empire was due to so remarkable a discovery.'

'It's not so remarkable,' Xaedrek sighed, as if he were suddenly tired. He leaned forward and put his hand over hers. 'But you, my lady Melkavesh – *you* are a remarkable discovery.'

'In what way?'

Quietly, watching her face for her reaction, he said, 'I

163

think you are a Sorceress born. Like Silvren. The first since her. You don't need amulin, the power is in you.'

Melkavesh managed to look suitably amazed.

'I'm sure you will agree, your personal interest in this phenomenon must take second place to Gorethria's requirements of you,' Xaedrek went on. 'I warn you, you may find it more of a burden than a blessing.'

She gazed at him for several seconds before replying, 'Serving Gorethria could never be a burden to me. What do you want me to do?'

'Initially, we will study the strength of your power. If that proves successful, I want you to help me produce more amulin. As I told you, we can't make enough. We need a great deal for the invasion of Kristillia to be successful. As to what else your power can do, I hope to discover that in due course. It will be a delight to work with you, my lady, particularly after Ah'garith.'

'Is she . . . uncooperative?'

'Sometimes. It's not that. She is a demon, inherently ill intentioned and destructive. I despise her, yet I have had no choice but to work with her.' He suddenly smiled and kissed her hand. 'Until now.'

They had been talking all morning. Xaedrek stood up and said, 'I hope you will excuse me, my lady, but I must go back to the mansion. Please stay and read Setrel's book, and these others.' He pushed some manuscripts towards her. 'I will have a servant bring you some refreshment. The only reason I won't take you to the mansion this afternoon is that Ah'garith is there. I do not want her to know of your existence. However, tomorrow I will send her away, and I will show you my work in more detail.'

Melkavesh sat alone in the library, for several hours, lost in thought. She was quite shocked by what Xaedrek had told her. She had never dream' it was possible to create a pseudo-sorcery by such strange means; such a thing was unknown on Ikonus. It seemed totally wrong to her. And the part played by the Shanin Ah'garith made it much worse. As yet she did not know what Xaedrek meant when he spoke of human energies, but she remembered what Kharan had told her of the tormented, burned Vardravians in the mansion. And she had seen for herself the line of prisoners waiting to go in, wretched with terror. Well, tomorrow she would find out what it meant.

She shuddered at the thought. She tried to read Setrel's book, but after a while her thoughts wandered back to Xaedrek. By the end of their conversation he had seemed markedly less formal, relaxed, almost confiding. She was convinced that he genuinely trusted her, and in a way she hated to deceive him. It was against both her nature and her Oath to the School of Sorcery.

Not to deceive others. Not to steal memory, however exigent it was. Not to abet evil . . . In the space of nine days she had already broken her Oath at least three times.

'I am not on Ikonus now. I will do what I must,' she told herself firmly. Putting it from her mind, she forced herself to concentrate on the manuscripts. There was so much she needed to find out; it was obvious that Xaedrek had unlocked only a superficial secret, and in reality knew less than she did. All she had discovered so far were enigmas. There were no Sorcerers; her own power was reduced, even maimed; and a creature of the Serpent still walked on the Earth.

The next day she went to the palace again, and a court official guided her to the mansion. Xaedrek met her in the entrance hall and led her directly down to the underground rooms where he worked; she saw nothing of the injured Vardravians, only closed doors. But the miasma of burnt flesh made her gag.

'I apologise for the stench in here,' the Emperor said. 'I am used to it, and no longer notice. I forget that it upsets newcomers. It is an unfortunate side effect of the crude process we are forced to use.'

Melkavesh coughed, and tried to look unconcerned. They were entering a small marble chamber lined by workbenches. Shavarish, Amnek, and two assistants were there adjusting a complicated set-up of glass tubes and vessels. They looked up from their work, and Shavarish gave Melkavesh a brilliant, almost conspiratorial smile. Amnek nodded to the Emperor, but ignored her.

'I believe you have both met the Lady Melkavesh,' Xaedrek said. 'She is to work with us, so I hope you'll make her welcome . . .'

'You are more than welcome, my lady,' Shavarish said warmly, adding with levity, 'Your Majesty, I hope you have not forgotten that she was *my* discovery.'

'Of course not. Everyone plays their part,' Xaedrek answered, smiling. 'Here we make the green crystal. Shavarish and Amnek supervise the process, which is a complex one . . .' He went on to describe it to her, indicating various parts of the glass equipment, and showing her the different liquids and substances used. Melkavesh listened, but also watched Amnek and Shavarish out of the corner of her eye. It was not only Xaedrek she must get to know, but those close to him as well.

After they had talked for a long time in the laboratory, he showed her several other rooms where various aspects of research took place. Finally he took her into the largest of the subterranean rooms, the one containing the contraption of metal and glass rods.

Melkavesh walked into the centre of the room and stared at the apparatus. Unearthly light was sliding ceaselessly along the tubes. It was beautiful, yet it gave her a feeling of coldness and sickness so intense that she almost turned and ran out of the room. But Xaedrek was closing the doors behind them. She made herself remain still and expressionless, trying to perceive the machine's nature. It was alien to her, offending her external senses and violating her deeper, sorcerous ones. It emanated deadly evil, and the smell here was so bad that her nose and mouth seemed full of blood.

Xaedrek touched her arm and she jumped. She had been using sorcery to investigate the apparatus; she stopped abruptly, still not knowing how aware he was of her power.

'Lady Melkavesh, you seem awed by it. There's no need to be.'

'I – I can almost feel the emanation of energy, Your Majesty,' she stammered.

'I also sensed your own power just then – as if the machine was calling it from you,' he said softly. Melkavesh felt ill, claustrophobic, but she mastered the feeling. Although the School of Sorcery had taught her much about evil, this was her first real taste of it; if she was to fight it, she must be able to withstand it.

'Yes . . . it comes and goes,' she said vaguely.

'Let me show you how the apparatus works,' he suggested, leading her closer to the machine. 'Tell you, rather. I would give you a practical demonstration, but I can't do that without Ah'garith. Incidentally, no one but myself knows of your power, not even Amnek and Shavarish. They believe you are simply a promising scientist. I think it safer if they are not told until the demon is finally disposed of.'

Melkavesh had a sudden, odd intuition. 'You don't think that Ah'garith would be – jealous of me?'

'It's very likely,' Xaedrek replied, sliding back a marble slab on the floor at one end of the apparatus. 'Her psyche is primitive, almost childlike. I never know exactly what she is thinking, but you can be sure it is something unpleasant. Now, this is where Ah'garith stands.'

He showed Melkavesh a triangular area which shimmered with pale blues and greens. It had a sentient look to it. 'What is it?' she asked.

'A sort of lens, I suppose. It is made of the muscles of certain reptiles, impregnated with amulin. And some human tissue. It enables the Shanin to focus the power through herself. Perhaps you will not need it, my lady; we shall experiment.'

Melkavesh suppressed a violent shudder and hoped he had not noticed. He continued, 'The demon's power then enters these rods, and passes through them to here . . .' He thrust a hand into the centre of the apparatus. 'This is where the human subject stands. This is the crux of the process. When the energy enters the subject's body, it does not pass straight through. It accumulates and increases, becoming far greater

167

than the power which the demon originally put in. When it builds to a critical point within the subject, it begins to travel along these extraction rods –' he traced them with his dark fingers, 'and is carried along the spiral into this sphere. It's empty at present, but normally it would be filled with the green salt, which turns gold as the energy transforms it.'

'And it has to be a human?' Melkavesh asked, her tone utterly cool, one of scientific curiosity. To voice her horror would be so un-Gorethrian as to arouse suspicion – not to mention scorn.

'Yes. No animal – nothing else at all – gives the same result. Human energy is the essential catalyst.'

'And what is the effect on the – er – subject?'

'About two-thirds of them die. The energy at that stage is something like lightning, lethal. The ones that survive are badly burned, but can be used a second time – after which they also die.'

'None recover?'

'Oh, some do. Those whose first results are poor aren't used again. But there's not much point in bringing them back to health. The process seems to destroy their sanity, so they are no longer any use as servants. Unfortunate, but the method leaves much to be desired, as I said.'

'It seems – somewhat wasteful.'

'Aye. Well.' Xaedrek shrugged. 'There is no shortage of Vardravians these days, so it is not really a problem.'

'How many – subjects are used?'

'Between six and ten each day,' he answered offhandedly. 'I'd like to double that. It's a question of time. I can leave Amnek to supervise the process, but I like to check each batch of amulin personally – added to my Imperial duties, it is a difficulty.' He walked over to his workbench and began to show her how the powder was examined and divided into phials. 'The interesting thing is that some races give noticeably better results than others. Kesfalians are good, but Kristillians surpass everyone else. I have often wondered why.'

168

'Some intrinsic spiritual strength?' she hazarded.

'It must be something of that sort. Kristillia has always been the hardest of countries to conquer. It is proving impossible at present. Strange, for they certainly have no hyperphysical power. It seems to be sheer determination. Anyway, I wish we had one Kristillian for every ten Patavrians.'

'Have you never discovered what sort of results are given by Gorethrians?'

'Of course not, my lady.' Xaedrek raised his eyebrows and stared at her. 'That would be murder.'

For three days, Xaedrek was wholly occupied with state duties. He instructed Melkavesh to go and assist Shavarish for that time. Reluctantly, she did so; it was simply not done to disobey the Emperor, however plausible an excuse she might invent. Meanwhile, Amnek supervised the use of the machine, under strict instructions not to let Ah'garith even glimpse Melkavesh. So, mercifully, she still did not see the machine in use, but even through closed doors, she could hear muffled screams as she worked.

In the evenings she returned to Anixa's house, drained to the point of exhaustion by horror.

'I warned you,' Kharan said coldly. 'Do you know, you are the first squeamish Gorethrian I have ever met? Obviously I haven't instructed you well enough. Attend: you are supposed to cry out with disgust at a speck of dirt in the street, and smile joyfully at a river of blood.'

'Kharan, will you be quiet?' Melkavesh snapped. 'You're being ridiculous. I agree that it's evil. But I can't even begin to fight it until I understand it. And I can't find anything out without appearing to co-operate. You must see that.'

'But how long is it going on for? How much help are you going to give him before you decide it's enough?'

'I don't know,' Melkavesh retorted acidly. 'But it won't be nine years.' Kharan's expression became stony with inward pain, and Melkavesh immediately regretted her words. 'Oh, Kharan, I shouldn't have said that. I'm sorry. I know this is hard for you. Please try to be patient. And have some faith in me.'

'I'm trying. I really am,' Kharan replied quietly. 'When are you seeing him again?'

'Tomorrow. At the palace this time.'

Kharan sighed and sat back listlessly in her chair. 'And you're looking forward to it. Fascinating, isn't he? And such good company.'

'I'm under no illusions about him,' Melkavesh stated. 'I know he only wants to use me. And I don't much look forward to an interrogation about my supposed unknown "powers".'

Xaedrek, however, proved unpredictable. When she was shown to his private office the next afternoon, he was not there. She waited two hours, and started to get angry. She had made up her mind to leave, when Xaedrek suddenly arrived and was so apologetic that he disarmed her completely. He had been delayed by state matters, he said, adding, 'My lady, you are a refreshing sight after almost four days of Senate and army business. For once I feel disinclined to work. Our investigation of the extent of your powers can wait. Let us talk instead. I'll have a servant bring us some food and wine.'

'That will be very pleasant, Your Majesty,' said Melkavesh, surprised.

'I hope it will make up in some degree for my discourtesy. By the way, there's no need for you to call me "Your Majesty".'

As they ate and drank, she was at first very much on her guard, but she soon sensed that Xaedrek, for once, did not have an ulterior motive. He asked no awkward questions, and demanded no personal information of her. Presently she began to relax, and they talked in the easy, general way that friends with a mutual interest would. Thanks to Ashurek, she felt she knew Gorethria as well as anyone who had been born there, and had no difficulty in conversing about it with genuine enthusiasm.

'I believe you know more of Gorethrian history than I do,'

Xaedrek smiled. 'Why didn't you tell me that you are a scholar?'

'Oh, to me it is not scholarly to study something one loves,' she answered honestly.

She did not know it, but she all but won Xaedrek's heart with this remark. She was right in believing he took her honesty and loyalty for granted, but it went deeper than that. He had no family, and had never had a true confidante – nor felt the need for one until he met Melkavesh. Baramek was the nearest he had to a friend, but he was a soldier, not an intellectual. And he had never talked deeply to Kharan, for the simple reason that only another Gorethrian could share Gorethrian sensibilities.

There were several factors that made Melkavesh seem different from his other countrymen. Firstly, he saw her as an innocent, someone who had not been made corrupt and cynical by Shalekahh society. And her supernatural power made him feel that she somehow belonged to him: she was his protégée, the one he had been seeking all his life. In addition, he found her easy to talk to. Under her cool and guarded manner, he knew there was a like mind. And although the way she addressed him was correctly deferential, her eyes betrayed that she had no fear of him but saw him as an equal. He always respected that.

She was also the first woman since Kharan to whom he had felt attracted.

Melkavesh sensed this, and every instinct told her to discourage him. Yet she did not. For days she had been haunted by thoughts of Xaedrek's atrocities, but here, warmed by his friendliness and at ease with him, the knowledge seemed distant and irrelevant. Despite what she had said to Kharan, she found him more intriguing than she dared admit. Kharan was right; he was good company, impossible not to like if you could forget what he was guilty of.

'There is a freshness in your love of Gorethria,' he remarked, 'almost as if it's something you have discovered for yourself, rather than being taught it by your parents.'

That is more true than you can know, Melkavesh thought, and smiled. They had left the office and were now walking through the ice-white, columned halls of the palace, arm in arm. She said, 'It's so hard to believe Gorethria almost ceased to exist. That one man such as Meshurek could destroy it.'

'Two men, really,' Xaedrek said drily. 'Ashurek played his part. But then, it only took one to understand what had gone wrong and put matters right . . .'

'I think what you have done is quite incredible, Your Majesty,' Melkavesh replied, fervently but ambiguously. 'Not only to bring order back here, but to restore the Empire.'

'It was simply a question of doing what had to be done,' he said dismissively.

In a way, the palace was a living museum, rich with wonders of breathtaking beauty that transformed the bloody history of the Empire to one of transcendent glory. Melkavesh could not help but be affected by it. She had never seen anything lovelier than the paintings, statues and works of art that drifted past her dazed eyes. Every room had its own unique splendour, its own story to tell. But beneath the surface beauty of Shalekahh's unsurpassed art and architecture ran an even more powerful current. It was the sense of Gorethria's free, fighting spirit, their belief in their absolute superiority over every other race, which was not mere arrogance but a kind of unquenchable joy in their own being. She had always had that exhilaration within herself, and channelled it into her sorcery, but now she felt the blood of her father's ancestors claiming her spirit. However much she might condemn Gorethria's urge to oppress other nations, it was not something alien to her, but something she understood. Even shared. Was she not a Gorethrian of the royal house?

'My lady, here is the Hall of Portraits,' Xaedrek interrupted her thoughts. 'Would you like to go in?'

'Oh yes,' she exclaimed. 'Of all the palace's wonders, this is one I've most longed to see.'

They passed through the ornate doors and entered the long, salt-white hall where the likeness of all Gorethria's rulers hung. At once Melkavesh felt she had stepped into a dream: it looked exactly as it had in her sleeping visions. Was it possible that she had actually walked here before in some kind of involuntary astral projection? The thought was frightening. Suddenly oblivious to Xaedrek, she left his side and wandered very slowly along the line of paintings, stricken by feelings of awe and unreality.

The first portraits were ancient, well over a thousand years old, and so dark that they were only just recognisable. Yet in all the grim, brooding faces of her ancestors, even the oldest, the eyes seemed alive, following her, demanding that her strength and loyalty match theirs, threatening some unspeakable fate if she failed . . . She felt her confidence shredding away under their gaze, all her convictions swirling and streaming away from her on a cold, pitiless wind. What did they want? That she seize her birthright? The conflict that had always burned quietly within her began to grow intense, and it seemed that the palace was hemmed in by stormy black mountains, and the floor was tilting under her feet. Her mind told her that Gorethria's tyranny was utterly wrong, and that she should not be suffering a moment's doubt about the need to end it. But her heart was drawing her into darkness, whispering that Xaedrek was a usurper, and it was she who belonged in the palace, on the Imperial throne – not him.

'Empress Melkavesh,' said Xaedrek into the silence. She started violently and turned round to stare at him. He was walking towards one of the paintings, the hem of his indigo robe brushing the marble tiles. 'Your namesake, my lady. One of the Empire's greatest ever rulers.'

Melkavesh recovered herself; of course, he had been referring to the portrait, not addressing her. Moving calmly to his side, she studied the dark, vulture-harsh face, contrasted by milk-white hair and intense green-gold irises. 'No beauty, was she?' she commented.

'Except for her eyes. They are just like yours.'

173

'The double moonstone on the shoulder of her robe symbolises her conquest of Kristillia, does it not?'

'That's right. I'm impressed by your knowledge of such an obscure fact.' Xaedrek sounded pleased. Then, as if echoing her thoughts, he continued, 'It was the Empress Melkavesh who said that the soul of Gorethria was one of absolute beauty and absolute horror. You cannot love one aspect and hate the other. Either you embrace it all or you reject it totally. Gorethria tolerates no half-measures.' *Don't go on, please don't go on*, she begged silently, but he added, 'The three of us have much in common. The Empress Melkavesh's secret was simply that she would do anything, anything at all for Gorethria. And so will I. And I believe, my lady, that you share this single-mindedness.'

Melkavesh gave him an inscrutable sideways look, and he watched her as she turned from him and drifted onwards along the line of portraits. Yes, he was certain that his strange dream had been of her. Prescience. She did not look quite the same, of course; she was wearing a sleeveless cloth-of-gold robe, rather than a white mantle, and naturally her hair was black, not golden. But the eyes were the same, as was every graceful, elegant line of her form. Suddenly he experienced an exhilaration that had not been so intense since the morning, long ago, when he had met Kharan and informed her with absolute conviction that he was going to be Emperor.

Now he felt with equal conviction that despite what the court cynics believed, there was going to be an empress. Indeed, he had already instructed a court official to investigate Lady Melkavesh of Bagreeah's background, but that was a mere formality. Smiling to himself, he strolled along the Hall to catch her up.

But Melkavesh's thoughts were not on Xaedrek. She was thinking of her father, his insis nce that Meshurek's portrait had been the last, that there had never been one of himself in the Hall, and therefore her dream had not been a genuine vision. She had reached Meshurek's portrait now, and it was exactly as she had dreamt it, only more vivid. The face had a bland, cold look of insanity that chilled her. But beyond it were three more paintings. The last was of Xaedrek, of course, recently painted and jewel-bright. The one before was Orhdrek, the boy-Emperor who had preceded Xaedrek. But between Orhdrek and Meshurek, the beloved, familiar face of Ashurek stared uncompromisingly at her.

She stood still in astonishment. *There never was a portrait of me there* . . . But her father had been wrong, and her vision had been a true one.

She felt Xaedrek's hands on her shoulders, cool and firm, the silk of his sleeves brushing her bare arms. Trying to keep her voice steady, she said, 'Why is Ashurek here? He never claimed the throne . . .'

'No, but he was declared Emperor in his absence,' Xaedrek replied over her shoulder. 'Didn't you know? I suppose it wasn't common knowledge outside Gorethria. Communications across the Empire were in chaos in those days. It was a vain attempt to maintain stability. Pointless really; everyone knew he would not return. But there it is. In theory he was Emperor, so here is his portrait.'

Outwardly Melkavesh was calm, but a storm was gathering within her. *No half-measures.* She felt that Silvren's gentle teachings and all her father's dire warnings were being borne away from her on a whirlwind, leaving only the grim, irrefusable call of her birthright. And she did not want to face the storm. Suddenly, desperately, she needed to turn away, escape, seek refuge in any distraction that would save her from having to think about it.

Xaedrek was innocent of her turmoil. His thoughts were elsewhere. 'Lady Melkavesh . . .' he said softly into her ear, then kissed her neck.

It took a lot to surprise Xaedrek, but he was absolutely taken aback by the passion of her response. One moment she was as still and quiet as stone; the next she spun to face him, and was kissing him on the mouth, hanging tightly onto him as if she feared she was about to drown.

7

Shadow on Satin

MELKAVESH WOKE, disoriented for a minute. The light had a silver-blue, underwater quality, glinting softly on filigree panels, exquisitely made furniture, a bejewelled bedcover. It was dawn, and it was raining outside. Xaedrek was still asleep beside her. She propped herself up with one elbow on the pearly satin pillow, and looked down at him, waiting for him to wake. She felt calm and clear-minded now, the previous day's conflicts soothed by sleep. Perhaps they would return later; but not yet.

Presently Xaedrek woke up, and smiled at her gazing sleepily down at him. '*Now* will you stop calling me "Your Majesty"?' he said, pulling her towards him and kissing her. For the present, it seemed that Gorethria, sorcery, politics, everything had ceased to exist; there was only the light and the rain cradling two guileless souls. But the feeling could not last for ever. Eventually Xaedrek sat up and sighed, 'Unpleasant as it is, I'm afraid that we must get up and face the world. We have a lot of work to do.'

'Not without breakfast, I hope,' she said.

'Of course not. Don't hurry, I'll have a servant bring us something.' He put on a robe and went out into the antechamber, leaving her alone in the room.

She bathed and dressed, then went to the window and opened the velvet curtains. The palace garden gleamed and rippled in the wet air, and gelatinous blue rain clung to every leaf, flower and twig. Statues dripped mournfully in the avenues of shimmering trees. Melkavesh rested her forehead

176

against the glass, thinking of Caydrith, the lover she had left behind on Ikonus. She had loved him – still did – and yet she had left him without hesitation to pursue her future. Just as Xaedrek had disposed of Kharan. Without pity or regret. Xaedrek would approve, she thought with acid humour.

She moved across to the bed and began searching among the sheets for her jewelled hairpins. As she did so, she noticed that what she had taken for a shadow on her pillow was in fact a grey-black smudge. 'Anixa's wretched hair dye,' she muttered, cursing. An attempt to brush it off failed, so she turned the pillow over and hoped Xaedrek would not notice.

As she and Xaedrek went to the mansion on horseback, accompanied by two red-cloaked guards, she was aware that she was still too much at ease with him, even complacent. She knew it was dangerous, but could not seem to shake herself out of it – until they entered the mansion. Then the sickening tang of burning metal and flesh hit her like a wave of cold water, breaking her trance.

A door to her left stood ajar, and although she could see nothing, she could hear tormented groans – more of mental than physical pain – from within. She clenched her hands, set her jaw against showing her revulsion; but Xaedrek was not watching her for these signs. He took it for granted she would be unmoved.

I must tolerate it, she told herself severely. Only by tolerating it for the time being do I stand a chance of ending it.

She was in no doubt at all that this genocide must be stopped, yet she was still having difficulty in connecting Xaedrek personally with the horror. It was so hard to be objective. She was on her way to both loving and hating him with equal passion, but regarding him with cool detachment was impossible. And she envied him, envied his single-mindedness, lack of conscience, and absolute belief in Gorethria's superiority. Is he never tortured by doubt? she wondered. By duality?

177

The marble room where the machine stood smelled strangely clean this morning, a smooth aroma of metal that made her feel ill.

'I have sent Ah'garith to do some research for me,' Xaedrek told her as they entered the chamber. 'We have all day. Sit down.' She sat in the white, carved chair where, in the past, Varian and Kharan had sat frozen in fear of the Emperor. By contrast Melkavesh was on her guard, but quite unafraid.

He stood in front of her and took her hands, saying, 'Now, Melkavesh, I want you to try and summon your power. As strongly and for as long as you can. Don't rush, though, gently at first.'

If she had summoned her energy as strongly as she could, she would probably have destroyed the mansion. So she called only a little sorcery into herself, letting it dance like silver-gold fireflies round her fingers. Xaedrek hurriedly released his hands from hers.

'Good. Go on,' he said, absently rubbing his hands together as if to ease the pain of a static shock. She drew more power, until she appeared to be covered by a cloud of golden electricity. She maintained it for several minutes with ease, but then she suddenly slumped forward, coughing, filled with heavy pain.

'Are you all right?' Xaedrek asked anxiously.

'It hurts,' she gasped, and she was not acting. The difficulty she had had using sorcery when she first came to Earth had not diminished. The same leaden ache filled her spine, dragged on her bones, constricted her skull with a band of iron.

Xaedrek held her hand, stroked her cheek, kissed her; to her surprise, he seemed genuinely concerned. After a minute or so the severity of it eased, and she drew a deep breath and said, 'The pain's faded. It was unpleasant, but not intolerable. Like a brief attack of a severe fever.'

'I see. Perhaps the power causes a raising of the temperature, or a shock to the system.'

'No. It feels as if something is blocking the power –' she

stopped abruptly, realising she was about to tell him too much. 'I don't know.'

'Well, perhaps practice is needed. Are you ready to try again?'

Melkavesh drew the energy again, and this time it was longer before the pain seized her, and it seemed less severe. Xaedrek sent a guard to bring her a hot, spiced drink, which she found reviving; then he made her try a third time, and a fourth. All the time she was inwardly cursing the pain; she who had been one of the strongest natural Sorcerers on Ikonus, now felt like a cripple. But while Xaedrek was observing her scientifically from the outside, inwardly she was conducting her own private experiments.

There were different ways of calling the power: from the ground, from the air, from the sky, and it could be drawn through the legs, arms, heart, brain, any combination of those according to the purpose for which it was to be used. Normally this was an instinctive process, but now Melkavesh began to ponder it more deeply, drawing the sorcery in a slightly different way each time, giving it different nuances and observing her physical and mental reaction. Xaedrek was right. Practice was required; after all, this was another world, and the nature of the power was inevitably different. It was wilder and rougher, unrefined and hard to control . . . As the day passed she began to appreciate that she was by no means crippled, but needed time to acclimatise.

But she also learned that adapting to this Earth was going to be a longer and harder process that she had envisaged. She could learn to cope with the pain; nevertheless, the pain was still there. Something was wrong, and if Silvren, for example, had asked her what it was, she could hardly have put it into words. In her mind, it was an image something like looking at the sun, and finding that despite the dazzling brilliance of it, the centre is dark.

By the middle of the afternoon she was exhausted. 'I don't want to overtax you,' Xaedrek said. 'To continue now might do more harm than good. Go home, and rest. Tonight and tomorrow I must produce more amulin with the demon, but

179

the day after . . .' He moved close to her and kissed her until she again began to forget sorcery, the mansion and everything else. Then he stepped back and seemed about to say something – but apparently changed his mind. He escorted her to the entrance hall, saying, 'Melkavesh, you have never told me where you live.'

'I have lodgings . . .'

'In the visitors' quarter?'

'Yes, thereabouts,' she muttered.

'Well, I will see about that,' he said ominously. 'Now, wait here, and I will have a horse and escort brought to accompany you home.'

. But by the time Xaedrek returned with a guard, Melkavesh had already gone. He dismissed the puzzled soldier and smiled to himself. He could not help but admire her independence.

'Where have you been?' Kharan exclaimed as Melkavesh arrived. She dropped the bodice she had been embroidering, scattering beads everywhere, and ran across the room. Visibly restraining herself from embracing Melkavesh, she cried, 'I was desperately worried. You've been gone all night!'

'Yes, I noticed it got dark, then light again,' Melkavesh said sardonically. Anixa came into the doorway and stood there unspeaking, a dark, elfin figure in a close-fitting black dress.

'Anixa was concerned, too,' said Kharan lamely, turning away from Melkavesh as if she felt drained and defeated in some deep, personal way that she was trying to keep hidden.

Suddenly Melkavesh's heart went out to her, and she said contritely, 'You really were worried, weren't you? I'm sorry. But I was quite all right.'

'Oh. I see,' was the short response. Melkavesh wondered if Kharan guessed that she had been with Xaedrek all night. If so, was there any point in trying to lie about it? It would just be adding insult to injury. Kharan had been cold and withdrawn ever since Melkavesh had first met Xaedrek, and she could not really blame her. From escaping Xaedrek she was now trapped again, and still in a state of shock over Falmeryn's death. Melkavesh had no wish to make things harder for her.

'It's going well. Xaedrek trusts me,' she began gently.

'Melkavesh, I really don't want to hear about it!' Kharan broke in. She folded her arms and said in a flat tone, 'You say you were safe. Perhaps you were. I was, until I crossed him. But I've been thinking about the past, and there's something I must tell you. Remember the young Emperor Orhdrek? He thought Xaedrek was his best friend. But Xaedrek murdered him.'

Melkavesh was astonished. 'Surely not – other claimants to the throne were blamed –'

'No. I'm certain of it. It was Xaedrek,' Kharan repeated adamantly. 'All I'm saying is that you are not necessarily safer with him because you are Gorethrian. Or because he appears fond of you. Be careful, that's all.'

'I will be. Don't worry, Kharan. I'm aware of the danger, and I'm not helpless. I have my sorcerous powers . . .'

'Of course,' Kharan said with a forced smile. 'Well, in that case I won't issue any more dire warnings – you must be sick of hearing them by now. You can obviously look after yourself, and I'm sure you know what you're doing, Mel.'

'I wish you sounded as if you meant that.'

'I wish I meant it,' Kharan said, and began to laugh, her sense of humour briefly dissolving her bitterness. They laughed together, and there was a transient warmth between them, but Melkavesh was uncomfortably aware of Anixa in the doorway, unsmiling, observing them shrewdly but keeping her thoughts to herself.

Several days went by. Xaedrek continued to observe the strength and constancy of her power, and Melkavesh continued to keep up the charade while using the experiments for her own purposes, namely to acclimatise herself to the Earth. She spent some nights with him; on others, he was working with Ah'garith, so she went back to Anixa's house. Thankfully, he never demanded that she take part in the

181

amulin work, beyond helping Shavarish make the green crystal. But she was growing more and more apprehensive, because she knew he was eager to put her power to practical use.

Meanwhile she used every opportunity to learn as much as she could about him, his colleagues, the working of the Gorethrian state. She became something of an enigmatic figure at court, because everyone had heard rumours that the Emperor had a new favourite – mercifully, an eligible Gorethrian aristocrat this time – but she was rarely glimpsed, and no one seemed to know anything about her. *Who is Melkavesh?* the whisper went round, inevitably reaching even Ah'garith's ears after a time. The woman-demon grew suspicious, and ever more bitter and petulant. But being under Xaedrek's orders, she was forbidden to make her own investigations, so she remained in enforced ignorance.

Meanwhile, Melkavesh discovered one vital fact that she had longed to know ever since she first stepped onto the Earth. Xaedrek could not far-see. There were several methods by which she could do so herself: calling distant images into water, or sending a projection of her mind outside her body. But she had not dared practise these methods to spy on Xaedrek. If he had been a true Sorcerer, he would have sensed them, and found her out. Now she came to realise that he could only sense her power when she was actually in the same room as him, but more importantly it meant that he was unable to spy on her. He genuinely knew nothing of who she really was, nor of Anixa and Kharan. But she still would not watch him by supernatural means: even if he did not notice, the demon might. Besides, it seemed almost unfair, especially as she had had such success with conventional subterfuge.

Xaedrek often spoke of his desire to far-see; to be able to watch any part of the Empire from Shalekahh, to command armies from a distance, to pass messages instantaneously rather than wait weeks for them to be carried. It was one of his greatest hopes of Melkavesh's potential, so she was careful to keep him hoping while giving him no concrete evidence that far-seeing was possible.

Obviously Ah'garith had been of no help in this. Xaedrek believed her prescient ability had been damaged by the trauma of the Serpent's death and her imprisonment in a human body. However, she had shown skills in other areas. He told Melkavesh of how, some months earlier, Ah'garith had sensed the passing of an Entrance Point to the Black Plane close to Shalekahh. His curiosity outweighing his sense of danger, he and the demon had found the Point, and passed through to the Black Plane Hrunnesh. There they had encountered a race of philosophical nemen, tall, four-armed beings with coal-black skin. Having induced one to find them an Exit Point back to Earth, they had captured it and brought it with them.

'An intriguing creature,' Xaedrek told Melkavesh, as they lay enfolded in satin sheets one early morning. 'I wish you could have seen it, spoken with it. It had a pure intellect, unclouded by human emotions. I was carrying out some experiments on its anatomy, which I'm sure no one has ever dreamed of doing before. I don't see why not – surely the Planes are not supposed to be outside Earthly science?'

'What did you find out?' she asked.

'It was certainly not human. Its flesh had a plastic quality, almost like pliable crystal. The internal organs differed radically: there was a huge, slow-beating heart, and the lungs almost filled the whole trunk. There were no organs of digestion, and its blood was so thick as to be almost solid. It seemed ill adapted to survive on Earth. As it was dying anyway, I intended to see how it reacted in place of a human in the amulin process. Unfortunately, someone took pity on it and set it free; it found the lodestone with which it had brought Aligarith and myself to Earth, and fled back to Hrunnesh. Since then I've had no time for such diverting experiments, but it was most interesting while it lasted.'

'Yes, it must have been,' Melkavesh agreed dubiously. She sympathised both with Xaedrek's thirst for knowledge and Kharan's compassion.

But no true Gorethrian would let pity interfere with progress. All of them seemed just as single-minded as Xaedrek: Shavarish, Amnek, Baramek, all the others she encountered. And it was the Emperor who had reunited them with this fierce strength of purpose. His own passionate belief in Gorethria rekindled the racial pride that, in Meshurek's time, had almost been lost.

Melkavesh got on unexpectedly well with Shavarish, who despite her forbidding appearance, was friendly, humorous and enthusiastically loyal to the Emperor. To Xaedrek she embodied all that was good about Gorethria; the pride, lack of conscience, vigour and love of life. She plainly adored her husband Amnek, although Melkavesh could not personally see the attraction. Amnek's presence was glowering, hawk-like, and his unnatural height and leanness added to his sinister quality. He was habitually quiet, and never spoke to Melkavesh at all unless it was absolutely unavoidable. She sensed that he disliked her, and she soon realised why. Amnek was a pure scientist. He put nothing before the pursuit of scientific knowledge, not even his family or Gorethria itself. He respected Xaedrek – whom he had encouraged and taught since the Emperor was a boy – because there was no weakness in him. But he sensed that in Melkavesh, if there was a battle between science and compassion, compassion would ultimately win, and for that reason he despised her.

High Commander Baramek was a different matter. He was a soldier, a traditionalist with an instinctive distrust of supernatural methods. Kharan had described him heatedly as, 'A vile man who loathes anyone not Gorethrian. It was his happiest hour when he arrested me.' But Melkavesh found him down-to-earth, open, almost fatherly towards her. There was nothing devious in his character; his love for the Emperor, Gorethria, and his own family were of the same straightforward, unswerving quality. He was well loved by the army, and of all the Gorethrians she met, she found him the most honest and likeable.

The other members of the Inner Council were people of like mind, who shared Xaedrek's dreams and goals. Xaedrek

184

was a perceptive judge of character, and would have no one around him who fawned on him while keeping their true thoughts secret. Melkavesh observed that his close advisers would often disagree and argue with him (which the rest of the Senate would not dare to do) while remaining unquestionably loyal. But even though he had chosen a completely trustworthy Inner Council she noticed that he still did not fully rely on them. He remained detached and trusted only himself.

And, to some extent, Melkavesh. She soon found out that only she, Amnek and Shavarish knew that Ah'garith was an actual Shanin. The other Inner Councillors, and those who worked in the mansion, believed she was merely an old woman with some strange power. After what had happened to Meshurek, Xaedrek knew that many would be alarmed and angered if they knew the truth. He had long since purged the court of the few who opposed him when he took the throne, but he was always alert to the slightest undercurrent of dissidence. If there were any who were still secretly dubious about his reign, he had no wish to give them a weapon to use against him.

Which made Melkavesh wonder: what would the reaction of the populace be if they understood the wrongness of Xaedrek's extramundane power – and if they knew that she was the true heir to Gorethria's throne?

Twenty or so days went by, and she managed to stall Xaedrek's use of her power. When he first proposed that she was now ready to create amulin, she panicked inwardly, horrified at the idea of using the machine to murder some poor Vardravian. She thought quickly, and suddenly discovered a remarkable ability to transform the green crystal to amulin directly. She placed her hands on the salt, and it absorbed her power and turned to pale, hyperphysical gold.

At first Xaedrek was excited by this, and began to talk of disposing of Ah'garith. But there were problems. She found the production of amulin a deep, enervating drain on her strength. It seemed to suck her dry, as salt greedily draws up all available moisture. She could make only one or two batches before collapsing with exhaustion, racked with pain. And Xaedrek soon found out that the powder produced was not as powerful as that made through the machine. The reason was obvious to Melkavesh: to divide her personal power between, say, a hundred individuals was simply not feasible.

Xaedrek became concerned for her health, and made her rest for four days. She stayed at the palace for that time, genuinely touched by his kindness, although she knew in her heart he was only worried about losing his alternative source of power.

Presently Xaedrek suggested that she move to the palace permanently; not on the basis that Kharan had been there, he took pains to make clear, but as a noblewoman in her own right, a senior member of the Emperor's personal staff. She refused at first, then changed her mind. After all, Kharan and Anixa would undoubtedly be safer if she did not go there so often. Soon she had her own suite of rooms, and as much freedom as any other courtier – when she was not with Xaedrek.

Kharan, meanwhile, grew more and more depressed. She had been at Anixa's house for over a month. Being 'in hiding', she had not been out of doors once in that time. She had kept herself as busy as possible, helping the dressmaker, but however hard she tried she could not keep her mind from grief and dark thoughts of the future. Often she wished she had died at the appointed time – this was scarcely living at all. She felt like – and indeed was – a prisoner, chained and confined and bereft of hope. She liked Anixa well enough, but did not understand her. Part of her depression stemmed from the Kesfalian's strange aura, her moroseness, and the incomprehensible warnings she had issued about Melkavesh. Only when Melkavesh came home was there any life in the house; at least then she heard something of the outside world, even if they did nothing but argue.

When Melkavesh announced that she was moving to the palace, Kharan hardly realised the implications at first. Only when she had gone, and Kharan had sat staring at the same square inch of embroidery for an hour, did it hit her. She went to find Anixa and said harshly, 'She's not coming back.'

'What do you mean, my lady?' Anixa still addressed her deferentially out of habit.

'Don't you realise? She doesn't need us any more. Why should she come back? She's got where she wanted to be. You and I are on our own.' She sighed, walked slowly to a window and stared out at the garden. 'I should go, Anixa. I can't stay here for ever. It's putting you in danger.'

'That doesn't concern me. My lady, you must stay. She will come back. Your destiny and hers are linked.'

'Are they?' Kharan longed for some down-to-earth advice, and was sick of hearing only vague, enigmatic prophecies. But she felt too weary to lose her temper about it. She turned to Anixa and put a hand on her arm, a silent plea for her to be ordinary, not mystical. 'No. She's gone. I know that she and Xaedrek are lovers . . . and the odd thing is, I don't even care. Good luck to her. She's achieved what I tried to, but never could, never in a thousand years: to become his equal.'

'For the sole reason that she is Gorethrian, and you are not. Does this knowledge not . . .' Anixa touched her own heart, 'offend you? Seem fundamentally wrong?'

'I suppose so. Are you trying to turn me into a rebel?'

'I am trying to make you care about something.'

'I cared about Falmeryn. There is nothing else.'

'Nothing else. People being murdered, and killed in battle, and enslaved is nothing. Is that so?'

Kharan was silent. After a minute she said quietly, 'I should never have listened to her. "Trust me," she said. Anixa, I must leave Shalekahh.'

'Where will you go?' Anixa asked, and Kharan had no answer, and she knew she would not leave, because she had no courage, either.

Melkavesh would have been concerned about Kharan's state of mind, except that she was too involved with Xaedrek to give it any thought. She was on a knife-edge of exhilaration, passionately enthralled by him, yet coldly deceiving him at the same time. She knew it could not last; that it had gone on for thirty days was a miracle. And she still had no fixed plan – at least not one that she would admit to herself. She lived in the palace for seven days, appearing to co-operate with Xaedrek while actually doing her best to stall progress. She knew he was growing dangerously impatient. By night, however, they eagerly sought each other's arms, and all else was forgotten. Perhaps she was too ready to put the dilemma from her mind, for in the darkness, the faces of Ashurek and Silvren would haunt her – beloved faces she would certainly never see again – and then she would turn to Xaedrek and cling to him until the torment eased.

Her sorcery was growing stronger, and she was learning to cope with the physical pain it caused. She would have welcomed a chance to use it properly, not realising how soon – and unwelcomely – the chance would come.

It had to happen.

On her eighth morning at the palace, she went to the mansion with Xaedrek as usual and entered the subterranean chamber. She sat in the white chair, alert yet at ease, thinking that if he required her to make amulin, she would try to put more strength into it. If she let him believe they were making progress, it would lessen his impatience. But Xaedrek did not begin at once; he seemed to be waiting for something. After a minute he went to the door and opened it; then she heard him say, 'Ah, at last,' and two white-clad Gorethrian nurses entered, escorting a tall man with reddish-bronze hair and a long red beard. He was wearing only a pair of loose white breeches, and his skin was a curious mixture of colours, gold and brown and ivory swirling together. But it was not his odd colouring that made Melkavesh stand up and stare at him, horrified.

His hands and face were burned as if from within, black and swollen and cracked, shining redly with blood. His eyes were half-closed, but she could see the glassy, trance-like gleam of agony in them. He was young and strongly built, but he could only just stand with the aid of the nurses.

'This is a Kristillian,' Xaedrek was saying. Melkavesh barely registered the words through her shock. 'As you can see, he survived a first session in the machine very well. He's not badly burned, and still strong. Help him into the apparatus,' he instructed the nurses. Melkavesh helplessly watched the Kristillian being forced into the cage of rods, which held him securely in a standing position. The nurses left, and she still could not find her tongue to object. 'Melkavesh, you'll agree it's time we tried this,' Xaedrek went on. He took her arm and led her to the spot where Ah'garith usually stood to summon power. 'Although you can create amulin without this process, you must agree it's not been totally successful, and a terrible drain on your strength. But I'm convinced this will produce infinitely better results than the demon ever could – and without tiring you.'

He slid back the marble slab, revealing the triangular, green-blue patch. 'I'm not sure whether you'll need the lens or not. Try it.' Melkavesh stepped onto the substance, which bounced under her feet like muscle. An unpleasant sensation, like the return of feeling to numb limbs, went through her, but she hardly noticed. All her attention was focused on the wretched man in front of her, hanging limply within the glass and metal rods, his muscular shoulders moist with sweat. A talisman hung round his neck like an unheeded prayer.

Xaedrek said something she did not hear. In her mind, she could visualise what would happen. The lens would flood her with power of a debased sort, as if it were a filter with an opposite function to the Sphere Ikonus; one which let through only evil. Electricity would pour from her with such force that the Kristillian's body would be consumed; silver-white lightning would fill the room and in the end . . . the amulin produced would be pure and potent beyond Xaedrek's wildest hopes.

And nothing, nothing would induce her to do it. Xaedrek was instructing her to summon power and feed it gently into the rods. She turned to him and said, 'I can draw no power.'

'What do you mean?'

'Just that. The energy will not be summoned.'

'Step away from the lens,' Xaedrek said. He slid the marble slab over it. 'Perhaps that's the problem. Stand on the slab instead, and try again.'

'It's no good,' Melkavesh said. 'There's nothing there. Perhaps it's the machine itself . . .'

'Keep trying,' Xaedrek insisted. She pretended to do so for several minutes, while the Emperor paced the room, his expression growing very cold. The Kristillian's groans filled the room with terrible sound.

Finally Xaedrek said, 'Enough.' He went to the door, summoned the nurses, and – to Melkavesh's relief – had the Kristillian removed. 'Come and sit down, Melkavesh. I'm going to understand this if it's the last thing –' There was a knock at the door, and he strode to answer it, cursing quietly.

A guard was there. 'Your Majesty, High Commander Baramek needs to see you at once.'

'Very well. Tell him I'm on my way.' He turned to Melkavesh and said, 'Baramek is not in the habit of interrupting my work for no good reason, so I had better see him. I may be some time. Go back to the palace, and meet me in the garden at noon.'

When Xaedrek had gone, Melkavesh paced slowly round the room, thinking. What conflicts there had been within her were gone, driven out by a pure shaft of conscience. The sight of that Kristillian's pain, Xaedrek's offhand assumption that she was prepared to add to it, and finally kill him, had shaken her fundamentally. No secondhand knowledge of Xaedrek's wickedness could ever have touched her like the anguish in that man's once-proud eyes. Kharan was right, this had gone on long enough. Too long.

She flew out of the room, slamming the door behind her. Ascending the stairs two at a time, she arrived in the entrance hall, trembling with outrage. There was no sign of Xaedrek and Baramek; they had probably gone back to the palace together. Before her were the double doors leading to the reception room which was now used as a hospital for the unfortunate survivors of the amulin process.

190

She grasped the cold, jewel-studded doorknob and entered.

The two nurses looked up at her, and she strode unhesitatingly over to them and said, 'Would you both please leave. I have to examine one of the subjects in privacy.' Calm self-assurance came naturally to her, and the nurses did not dream of objecting; after all, she was Xaedrek's close colleague. They left the room, and Melkavesh, having made sure the door was firmly closed, began to walk slowly between the pallets.

Pity and anger tore at her heart as she looked at each Vardravian in turn. They were just as Kharan had described. Their shallow, agonised breathing; the red flesh shining through splits in the blackened skin; and worst of all, the almost palpable wave of madness and torment that flowed from their gleaming eyes.

Grim with purpose, she looked among them until she saw the red-bearded Kristillian. He looked stronger than the others, as if he still had his reason. She quickly went to his bedside, knelt beside him, and whispered, 'Don't fear. I'm going to heal you.' The glistening crescents of darkness between his half-closed lids swivelled to meet her gaze, and she almost cried out at the agony in them. She laid her hands on his forehead, and summoned healing energies into her body. Presently faint silver-blue flames began to stream from her hands and lick over the Kristillian's skin until his whole body was enveloped in soothing power. Healing was an exhausting process, and this time she found it more draining than usual, for as she eased his pain, she perceived the nature of the damage. It was an insanity induced by contact with a wild and terrible power. The mere touch of it made her want to writhe and recoil, struggling against the metallic taint of blood in her mouth, the dark pressure on her eyeballs. Xaedrek's hideous machine . . .

It was wrong, wrong, wrong. Sorcery was not to be used in this corrupt way, and it was her duty, her purpose on Earth, to stop it.

After a few minutes, she felt the man's mental torture

ease. His eyes fell shut and he uttered a great, soul-weary sigh which shook his whole body. To her relief, she felt the darkness being driven out by true sorcery, like a harsh cry lost on the wind. Almost at once, she could not even recall what it had felt like. She let herself relax, her hands falling from the man's face, her head dropping forward with exhaustion, and for a moment she remained there, drinking in great gulps of air.

Then she recovered herself, and examined the Kristillian's face and hands in a businesslike manner. The skin was still blackened, but the swelling was going down, and soon the damaged surface would slough off and reveal the whole, perfect flesh beneath. Most importantly, the man was no longer in mental or physical pain.

'You will sleep for a long time,' she said into his ear. 'When you wake, you will feel much better.' She made to stand up, but the man's eyes suddenly opened fully, transfixing her.

'I feel better now,' he whispered in a puzzled tone. 'Who are you? Why have you healed me?'

'I would heal everyone here if I could, but I don't have the time or the strength. Hush. Go to sleep.'

But the man determinedly struggled to sit up, exclaiming, 'It's so I can be used again, isn't it? For a moment I thought – ah, by the moons, I should have guessed. The machine again.' She saw him shudder.

'No. No!' she whispered fervently. But he was right: if she left him here, he would be used again. She felt in a pocket of her robe and found the phial of amulin, the same one that Xaedrek had given her in the library some weeks ago. She slipped it under his pillow, saying, 'If you want to escape, take this powder. It will give you a chance of getting past the guards. Only a chance – it's up to you to take the risk.'

The man obviously knew what the powder was. He stared at her, utterly astonished that a Gorethrian should give him what appeared to be genuine help. Then he abruptly seized her arm and hissed, 'You're not Gorethrian. You look it, but you are not. Please tell me who you are.'

'I am Melkavesh. I want to stop the use of the machine. I can't tell you any more,' she said. But she was intrigued by the man, and he seemed willing to talk to her. 'What is your name?'

'I am Irem Ol Thangiol, of Kristillia.'

'But Kristillia is still independent of Gorethria. How did you come to be here?'

'Prisoner of war, of course, my lady.' He lay back on his pillow, looking away from her. 'How do you think we've remained free? By fighting without cease for the last seven years. I was with a scouting party; we were ambushed and brought here to be used in Xaedrek's unspeakable necromancy. My comrades are all gone. Murdered, one by one, in the contraption. I am the last. But they will capture more of us, no doubt.' His voice was heavy with grief, and Melkavesh raised a sympathetic hand to tidy his tangled red-bronze hair.

'I know little of Kristillia,' she said. 'Please tell me something about your country.'

'Kristillia is beautiful. There is no finer, nobler land,' Irem Ol Thangiol answered simply. 'And we are strong. We have survived centuries of Gorethria's tyranny. In that time we have tasted freedom only since the Empire collapsed.'

'And you drove out Meshurek's armies, and freed Kesfaline . . .'

He nodded slowly. 'It grieves me to recall the joy of that time. Our freedom was so sweet, sweeter than we had dreamed possible.'

'And it must have seemed like a bad dream when Gorethria grew strong again, and Xaedrek's armies attacked you,' she whispered.

'A bad dream!' A fierce passion burned in his face, knotted the muscles in his shoulders. His fists clenched like rocks. 'The Worm asleep on its bed of ice could have had no worse nightmare. But, my lady, we still have our freedom, and having once found it, we will never let it go again. Never, not until they slaughter every last one of us.' And suddenly, to Melkavesh's distress, Irem Ol Thangiol broke into great, deep sobs which convulsed his whole body. His grief was too distant, too deep for her to comfort; she could only watch, and swallow her own emotion. 'Damn Gorethria. Damn their arrogance,' he said hoarsely. 'They think themselves so civilised, so far above us that we are mere barbarians by comparison. But they don't even understand what they're destroying. Their time is over! They'll bring disaster if they don't accept it.' He rubbed tears away with the back of his hand. She waited for him to continue; but then he turned his head to look at her, and as she met his gaze, she did not need to be told any more.

Afterwards, she could never remember whether he had used words, or whether it had been a touching of minds; all she recalled was the vision. It seemed to her that Ol Thangiol's massive frame, prostrate on the bed, was somehow symbolic of Kristillia's threatened freedom, like a newly felled tree. She saw in his eyes the pride and beauty of a country which was unknown to her, yet achingly familiar, like a half-remembered dream. A vista of beauty and tragedy passed across her inner vision; sweeping pastel hills, graceful men and women seized by dark warriors and dragged, chained and humiliated, to Shalekahh. It was only then that Melkavesh understood for the first time: Kristillia was not a jewel for Gorethria to pluck and place in her crown. It was a civilisation in its own right, a land with its own spirit, philosophy and dreams which owed nothing to Gorethria. It was as ancient, and had once been stronger. And there was something in Kristillia's soul that the world needed, and it would be everyone's loss if Xaedrek succeeded in the conquest.

The vision faded. Melkavesh could see moisture gleaming on her own eyelashes, like multiple blurred moons, and she felt a falling sensation catch at her throat. A poignant sense of destiny took flight within her, but she did not yet understand what it meant.

Whatever had touched her soul had affected Irem Ol Thangiol equally. He was staring at her with a dark look of wonder in his eyes. 'You are a true enchantress, a daughter of the moons, Jaed and Fliya,' he said. 'Our priests have always said that one such as you would come. What are you doing here? You should be in Kristillia, we need you . . .'

'I must go. The nurses will wonder what I'm doing,' she said, standing up. 'I would like to talk to you at length, Irem Ol Thangiol, but there isn't time. I'll remember what you've said.'

'Wait,' he whispered. 'A gift for a gift.' He removed from his neck a silver chain on which two small ivory orbs hung, one joined below the other by a single link. He pressed it into Melkavesh's hand, and some instinct told her not to refuse it. 'It means much to me that you safeguard it.' She nodded and fastened the chain round her own neck, which, judging by his gratified expression, was the most courteous and correct thing she could have done.

She put one finger lightly on the Kristillian's lips, half-smiled at him, and turned to leave – only to see the doors opening, and an ominous figure standing there.

It was an old woman, fair-skinned and white-haired, dressed in a shapeless green mantle. An unimposing creature, outwardly – but Melkavesh's witch-sight pierced the disguise instantly, and she recognised the being as a Shanin, a demon. Revulsion filled her, a deep, heartfelt loathing born partly of Silvren's and Ashurek's long battles with the Shana, partly of her own instinct.

The demon's stare was like viscid grey ice, pure malice. Melkavesh was certain that Ah'garith recognised her as a Sorceress. Somewhere in the back of her mind, ghastly memories of their persecution of Silvren chilled her. For a full minute they confronted each other, and the air between them grew thick with their mutual contempt and hatred. Then Melkavesh strode forward, pushed past Ah'garith, and ran out of the mansion.

Ironic, she thought, that Xaedrek had taken such pains to conceal her from the woman-demon. If he had not, Ah'garith would have exposed her for a charlatan weeks ago.

It seemed her charade was almost at an end. She had never lacked self-confidence, but the thought of what Xaedrek would do when he found out still gave her a pang of dread. The sensible thing would have been to flee Shalekahh at once, but some dogged perversity impelled her to return to the palace as arranged. Somehow the Kristillian had changed everything, and she had no clear idea of where events were leading. Whatever happened, she must see Xaedrek.

A heat haze rippled over the palace garden. Later there would be a storm, perhaps, but now the sky was a heavy, deep blue, drawing all the richest hues from bushes and flowers. Red, violet and plum, emerald and amber – it seemed that she and Xaedrek walked in a living tapestry.

'Baramek is going to Kristillia,' he told her. 'Another setback with the invasion, so he wants to supervise it personally.' Xaedrek seemed quite his usual self; she was certain that he had not spoken to Ah'garith yet, nor found out that she had healed the Kristillian. They were strolling along a grassy path in the shade of red trees, arm in arm. The air was warm with the scent of flowers, busy with bright insects.

'Will you go too?' she asked, trying to sound casual.

'I don't know. I might.' They walked on in silence for a few minutes. Presently Xaedrek said, 'Lady Melkavesh of Bagreeah . . .' he paused, and she thought he was addressing her, but just as she parted her lips to reply, he continued, '. . . is married, and still lives in Bagreeah with her husband and their two children. She is about four inches smaller than yourself, and her eyes are dark, not bright green. She has never been to Shalekahh, and I doubt that she ever will. She also –' he raised a hand to touch her head – 'does not need to dye her hair black.'

He stood still and faced her, his hands on her arms. 'If you must do so, my love, you should choose a better dye. One which does not rub off on pillows. Who are you, Melkavesh?'

'How did you find out I was not . . .'

'I had a court official investigate your background, that's all. With the result that I learned a lot about someone else . . . but not you.' He put an arm round her waist, inducing

196

her to walk with him. 'It turned your stomach, being asked to kill that Kristillian. You think I did not notice, but I did. Yet I sense no weakness in you. I would like an explanation.'

'I dislike killing people. Is there something strange about that?'

'No. So do I. But I have had to do many things I dislike, in Gorethria's service. I did not think it too much to ask the same of you. Still, here is an easier request: go and wash that stuff out of your hair.'

'What? Where?' Melkavesh exclaimed.

'I don't care. In that fountain,' Xaedrek said, pointing to a marble basin filled with dancing streams of light. Melkavesh shrugged and obeyed. If the pretence was to be dropped, it might as well be dropped spectacularly. She found the situation at once frightening, and faintly amusing.

She pulled the pins out of her hair, bent over the edge of the fountain, and let her long hair flow out into the water. Whorls of black dye spun on the surface, quickly carried away by the cascade of droplets. Water alone could not remove it all, so she assisted the process with a touch of sorcery. Soon her hair was perfectly clean. She stood up and ran her fingers through the long, damp tresses, creating an aura of warmth to dry it as swiftly as possible. After a few minutes her hair was a cloud of bright gold round her head, brilliantly haloed by sunlight.

And Xaedrek stared at her, his ruby eyes very cold, and muttered, 'By the gods. It's true.'

'What is?'

'I've dreamed about you. I thought it was just a nightmare,' he said acidly, 'but I was wrong. I have to admit it is very beautiful, and suits you.'

She said nothing, but his next words – spoken in the same level tone – shook her. 'Ah'garith came to me in a state of agitation a short time ago, saying that she had encountered you in the mansion, and recognised you as . . . how did she put it? "The same kind as that filthy witch Silvren." She informed me that I was mad to work with you, and that if only I had trusted her, she would have told me weeks ago that you are . . . well, what are you?' He came up to her and gripped her shoulders. 'I don't like being lied to. I trusted you.' There was emotion in his voice now. 'I have never trusted anyone as I trusted you. And all that talk of your love for Gorethria – that was the worst lie of all.'

'I wasn't lying!' she cried indignantly. 'I do love Gorethria.'

He looked intently at her, and now she felt no amusement, only a wintry touch of fear. 'I do believe you mean it,' he said. 'I'm not normally obtuse, but I fail to understand this. Is it true that you are a Sorceress, like Silvren?'

She set her jaw and faced him squarely, refusing to be intimidated. 'Yes. I was deceiving you when I pretended ignorance about my powers.'

Xaedrek was angry, as much with himself as with her. Something had not rung true about her, yet in his eagerness to find a way to get rid of Ah'garith, he had let himself be blinded to it. He was unused to making mistakes, and harshly self-critical when he did. 'What was the aim of this deception?'

'I wanted to investigate these false powers you have.'

He considered this. 'Because you, as a natural Sorceress, are jealous of others finding ways to wield the power?'

'It's not a matter of jealousy. Your methods are intrinsically wrong, barbaric and unnatural.'

'Perhaps they are. But power is power, and unfortunately, as I was not blessed with the gift of natural theurgy as you appear to be, I have no choice. I'm not interested in a moral debate. I want to know who you are.' His red eyes lanced into her. 'Well?'

Melkavesh did not know how much to tell him. They had shared much in the past few weeks, and it was impossible to switch from lover and confidante to adversary in the space of minutes. 'I haven't prepared a lie to extricate me from this,' she sighed. 'I can't see any reason not to tell you the truth. You know who Silvren is. Well, I am her daughter.'

Xaedrek seemed to freeze, as he had when he had first sensed her powers. 'But Silvren is dead. Ah'garith told me

198

she was killed when the Serpent was slain. And so was Ashurek.'

'Ah'garith was wrong.'

'From Silvren, your power and the colour of your hair,' he said slowly. 'But your father must have been Gorethrian . . .'

'Yes,' she answered, quietly and evenly. 'My father is Ashurek.'

It was the first time she had ever known Xaedrek lost for words. He stepped back from her as if to see her more clearly, his expression uncharacteristically introspective. She sensed the many thoughts that must be flashing through his mind, but his eyes remained unreadable, and his silence was ominous.

Eventually she said, 'Don't you believe me? Ashurek and Silvren did not die. They went to another world, where they remain. But I have come back.'

'So I see,' he replied drily. 'Yes, I believe you. So fantastical a tale could only be true. And I can see Ashurek in you – you strongly resemble his sister, Orkesh. Well, at least the prescient dreams now make more sense. But why have you come back?'

'Because I always felt I belonged here. I wanted to see Shalekahh, my ancestors' home. And I wanted to know if there was sorcery on Earth and what form it took.'

'Is that all?' he asked sharply.

'That's all,' she responded, but he did not look convinced.

'No. If you are truly Ashurek's daughter, there must be more.' He turned and walked away from her, a tall, slim figure in blood-red silk, and she stared at his back and thought, *It would not be hard simply to kill him.* As she struggled to suppress the idea, he turned to face her, his arms folded. 'I admire your cleverness, Princess Melkavesh,' he said thoughtfully. 'No one has ever deceived me before, never mind with such success. You have undoubtedly proved worthy of your royal blood.'

She was growing impatient with his imperturbable poise, and felt an urge to shake him out of it. 'Well, what do you intend to do about me?' she challenged him, her tone

199

vitriolic. 'Execute me? Put me in the machine? Or perhaps it will be poison, like poor Orhdrek.'

She expected him to deny his predecessor's murder, but his silence was as good as a confession of guilt; worse than that, it was a dismissal of the matter as something long over and quite irrelevant. He only shook his head and half-smiled. 'Oh, Melkavesh, no. What reason have you given me to do something so drastic – beyond wounding my pride?' His tone was gently self-mocking; he chose the most unexpected moments to be charming, and she could never tell whether it was calculated or natural. 'Perhaps I'm being hasty in assuming that because you've misled me, you are automatically my enemy. You say you love Gorethria. So tell me, armed with your knowledge of my hyperphysics, what do you wish to do? I'm interested to hear your views, even if they do conflict with mine.'

The gentle tone of his voice gave her sudden, wild hope that he was not as intransigent as he seemed. Melkavesh walked hesitantly up to him and touched his arm. 'You'll listen to me?' she asked.

'I'm always prepared to listen. It's the best way to avoid subterfuge.'

'Very well.' Determined to speak her mind, she began, 'Your method is wrong. Sorcery has its own laws. It should only be wielded by those with the latent ability to draw the power. To do otherwise is to break the natural law, and the result is corruption of the power and of those who wield it. Look, you're using a demon, a creature which, by rights, should be dead, and whose aims are purely evil. You have to maim and murder to gain the power, and then what is it used for? Nothing constructive. More killing, warfare, domination over others. Can't you see that it's wrong? I want you to stop.'

'You're asking me to stop,' Xaedrek echoed. 'And the power will remain the privilege of the lucky few, and Gorethria will sink into oblivion?'

'There's more to it than that,' she retorted.

'Of course. You want an ideal world – there's always

something refreshing in that.' He put his hand on her shoulder. 'I don't want to argue with you, Melkavesh. I see now that you are an idealist. So am I, of course. The difference is that my aims are realistic, while yours are totally naïve. Still, you are young, and cannot be blamed for the misguided notions implanted by your mother. Your Gorethrian side is very strong and I have no doubt that it must eventually triumph. I am not one to bow to state pressure, but on this occasion it would please me to do their will.'

'What on earth are you talking about?' she exclaimed.

'Marriage,' said Xaedrek. 'I am asking you to become my Empress.'

Now it was Melkavesh's turn to be shocked into silence. She had expected wrath, interrogation, even to have been placed under arrest by now. This turn in the conversation was so unexpected that it took her breath away. Xaedrek smiled at her expression and went on, 'I never thought I would meet anyone whom I would wish to marry. There was once someone I cared for – alas, she was not Gorethrian, and she suddenly developed a conscience about consorting with me. It seemed unfortunate at the time, but perhaps it was meant to be. It is you I have been waiting for.'

'Xaedrek, wait – you mean that in spite of everything, you want to –'

'I had already decided, and this does not change things totally. Being objective, you have done me no harm, nor do I think you ever intended to. On the contrary, you've shown every sign of being quite fond of me.'

She glared at him, hardly able to find the words to express her feelings. '*You* had decided – Was I to have been consulted?'

'Of course, but surely you don't object? I am offering you Gorethria's throne.'

'As your wife,' she murmured. 'And what would the price of this marriage be?'

'Why so cynical? All I require of you is your absolute loyalty, to Gorethria and to myself. No more than any emperor demands of his spouse. The point is, now there's no need for deceit, you can work with me openly, and we can begin to make real progress at last.'

She moved into the cool shade of a tree and leaned against the trunk, trying to think. Huge insects of brilliant metallic hues droned around her. Of course, there was nothing extraordinary in Xaedrek's proposal; his reasoning was swift and clever, but quite transparent. She grinned bitterly. 'Well, I am not such a fool as to believe you have fallen violently in love with me. You offer marriage as a way to control me. I shall put aside these "misguided notions" of humanity and become a true Gorethrian. I shall devote my powers wholly to Gorethria's service. And especially,' she added softly, 'I shall be content with being Empress through you. Not in my own right. No safer way to remove my threat to your position than by marrying me, is there?'

'Only one,' Xaedrek replied, walking slowly to her side. 'And I've no wish for that, because I need you. It's pure common sense. You are powerful, so I want you on my side. But more than that, you and I are very alike in some ways. I have felt closer to you than to anyone else in my life, and I don't want to lose you. Some believe me as inhuman as Ah'garith, but it is not so.'

'Then you must prove it,' she said, and he made to kiss her, but she slid out of his arms. 'That's not what I mean. If I accept these conditions of marriage, it's only fair that I ask something in return, isn't it?'

'Naturally.'

'Then I ask you to give up your horrific method of hyperphysics, and destroy that loathsome Shanin, Ah'garith.'

'That would be a pleasure, my lady, and I will do so – the moment you are able to provide my armies with equal power,' Xaedrek answered smoothly.

'No. I mean at once. Your armies will no longer need the power, because my second condition is that you withdraw all troops from Vardrav.'

The change in Xaedrek's expression put her tentative hopes to flight. His eyes, no longer unreadable, burned with anger, menace, even scorn, as if she had stirred a viper within his

202

soul. He said in a low voice, 'We had both best forget you said that.'

'No,' she said adamantly, forcing herself to hold his terrible gaze. 'I am serious. I love Gorethria, but I hate the methods you use. Murder and war and bloodshed. It must stop. Only then can I marry you.'

'That is ridiculous.' Xaedrek turned away and strode down an avenue of lush scarlet flowers. She followed him. 'You don't even understand what you're asking, Melkavesh. It's impossible. Gorethria can exist in no other way. I thought you understood that, shared my beliefs.'

'In a way, I do. But I believe equally strongly that Gorethria can survive, her pride intact, without subjugating the rest of Vardrav, without –'

'Noble sentiments, my lady, but utterly naïve.' She felt his dark fingers closing on her arm, forcing her to halt and face him. 'Gorethria tolerates no half-measures. Either you accept it all or you reject it all. You know this, so if you hate the means we use, you are Gorethria's enemy. Such dissent is unpleasant enough in a Vardravian; in you it is an abomination.'

Now Melkavesh had made him openly angry, and she knew for certain that her first instinct about him had been correct. His attitude was immovable: Gorethria's strength came before all else, and the wrongness of it meant nothing to him. To imagine he would even consider her conditions had been – as he said – too naïve for words. But at least she had touched him, and that gave her courage.

'I've no wish to harm you,' he went on. 'So I am going to ask you again to marry me. This time, be more careful how you answer. If you refuse, you have no future. I will regard it as a declaration that you oppose me, and I will be compelled to imprison you and possibly have you slain. I hope I have now made myself clear.'

'There's nothing clearer than a threat.' She tried to speak lightly, but her heart was in her throat. Xaedrek was drawing her to him like a dark whirlpool; if she agreed to the marriage on his terms, her destiny would be entwined with his, her own beliefs lost in darkness. There would be no defying him, no hiding her thoughts from him. Yet if she refused . . . she dreaded him as an enemy. His aura of menace had never seemed stronger than at this moment, and his ruby eyes paralysed her.

But she was also strong, with a powerful Gorethrian pride that would not allow her to bend to another's will. Folding her arms, she looked coolly at him and said, 'I will marry you gladly, but only on the conditions I have stated. You neglect the fact that I am being more than magnanimous in disregarding my own claim to the throne. However, if *you* refuse . . . you force me to recall who is the rightful ruler of this country, and I will stop at nothing to overthrow you.'

'Ah,' said Xaedrek quietly. 'Now we have the truth. This talk of humane reform, beneficent sorcery and the rest, was all to conceal your real intent. Your plan all along has been to usurp me.'

'You talk of usurping!' Melkavesh cried. 'I am the legal heir to Gorethria's throne! You may be descended from emperors, but no more closely than any other noble in the Senate. You got poor Orhdrek onto the throne by clever words and trickery, and then you murdered him. If that's not usurping, I don't know what is!'

'You may be right,' said Xaedrek in a low voice. 'But I tell you I did not do it for personal gain, but for Gorethria's sake. It had to be done to save her from ruin, and it was the only way. No one else could have done what I've done for my country, and the people know it. Why should they want to replace me with you, for the sake of a few outmoded laws of succession? They don't know you. You've proved nothing. All you are is the daughter of Ashurek, the man who wrecked the Empire then fled, abandoning us to our fate.'

Melkavesh was now furious. 'Abandoned? Don't you understand? I thought you knew the story – Ashurek slew the Serpent itself. If he hadn't, the whole world would have perished. If not for him, Gorethria would not exist. Nothing would!'

'Then he should have come back after. Not sent his

204

daughter twenty-five years later. It's too late,' the Emperor replied intransigently.

'He did not send me. It was my own decision to return.'

'It makes no difference. I have offered you everything, the throne, a share in what I thought you loved, Gorethria's glory, yet you are so proud that you prefer death. Well, you are truly an emperor's daughter in that.' His voice was bitter, his eyes dark and cold, like garnets.

'Much as I regret it, I cannot compromise,' she said. 'I have come here to fight evil, not abet it.'

It was only then that Xaedrek seemed to accept that she was just as single-minded and obdurate as he. He shook his head and sighed, 'Oh, Melkavesh, I had hoped . . .' and suddenly he looked so weary and sorrowful that she was taken aback, and almost went to him, but the moment passed. The hardness returned to his face and he stated ominously, 'You must understand, however, that I can permit you no chance to fight me. I still need your power, so if you will not help me of your own free will, I am forced to compel you.' Then Melkavesh felt a cold prickling between her shoulder blades, and she turned and saw Ah'garith standing a few yards away, grinning.

She froze. For a moment she felt her own power was an illusion, and she was utterly helpless, drowning in the dark vortex of Xaedrek's necromancy. And it came to her in a lightning burst that there was only one solution to the situation, which was to kill Xaedrek. As long as he lived, the evil would continue, and no amount of argument would change his course. But if he died, a fresh start could be made. Inwardly, her spirit cried out against this terrible decision; he meant more to her than she dared admit. But in the Gorethrian depths of her soul, she could be as pitiless as Xaedrek himself.

'You are not going to force me to do anything, demon or no,' she said grimly, stretching out one arm towards him. 'Nor are you going to kill me. I have my own destiny.'

Power flooded her, a shroud of pale radiance, and she focused it into one dazzling sword of light. But Xaedrek was not taken by surprise. Even as she flung it at his heart, his own hyperphysical strength emanated from him to form a dark translucent shield. Dark met light, and the violent concussion of energy flung them both onto the ground.

Melkavesh scrambled to her feet, gathering strength for another blow. She projected a stream of fatal lightning towards him, but this time, he was faster. A hammer of greenish-black energy fell onto her skull, and her own sorcery shredded and burst into a cloud of stars which only just saved her life.

Her legs buckled but she kept her feet and drew herself upright, dizzy and shaken. Xaedrek was facing her, his eyes blazing blood-red with a fury she had never seen in him before. The grass and trees around them were singed, and all the birds and insects had fled. Ah'garith, meanwhile, did nothing. She just stood watching them, laughing.

Melkavesh saw a spear of coppery energy leave Xaedrek's hand and rush towards her head, and she cast out a shawl of light to intercept it. There was a detonation, a swirling of red and silver sparks. This time neither fell: they stood with legs braced, staring angrily at each other through the fading clouds of sorcery. Melkavesh was stunned to discover how adept Xaedrek was at using the power. He was equally astonished to realise that she was going to be harder to capture than he had imagined.

The battle could go on until one of them weakened, and Melkavesh, already struggling against the familiar, heavy cramp in her limbs, knew that she would weaken first. She could not kill him after all. Her only option was to flee while she still had the strength.

'Enough. This is pointless,' said the Emperor. She watched him through a shield of lambency, but he did not attack her again.

'Why? Because you can't win?'

'You're stronger than I realised, I'll grant you that. I admire your strength of will, but this attempt at assassination has sickened me.' There was no sorrow in his eyes now, only ice-cold despite. 'I see that your false beliefs are too deeply ingrained to be excised. Whatever you would have me believe, you are no friend of Gorethria, and if you ever seized the throne you would destroy everything.'

'That's nonsense,' she spat. She felt as furious and determined as he looked.

'Desist. You are deluding yourself. Even if I could force you to help me – which I doubt – I now realise that you are too dangerous to be left alive. However, before you die I want you to understand that your death is not for my benefit, not for the sake of revenge, but for Gorethria's protection.'

'Gods, you mean it,' she whispered. For several seconds they gazed at each other, and it seemed the garden and everything had ceased to exist; they were two disembodied spirits drifting across space, and somewhere in the darkness two massive, unseen spheres of rock awaited them . . . The feeling passed and she added coolly, 'As we both seem to have made our positions quite clear, there's no more to be said.'

'No. No more, my lady,' Xaedrek murmured, and he lifted his hand and beckoned to the Shanin. 'Come, Ah'garith.'

Melkavesh swallowed with revulsion as the leering woman-demon began to shuffle towards her, eyes glistening like poison-smeared razors. But she did not plan to wait and see what the demon was going to do. Armouring herself with silver-gold light, she sprang forward and ran straight at Xaedrek. He stepped aside in surprise, and aimed a violent blow at her protective shield. But she had been braced for it, and sprinted on without stumbling or looking back. 'Ah'garith!' she heard Xaedrek shout, then, furiously, 'Help me, damn you!'

She raced between trees, past statues and lush flowers and fountains, making for the outer wall. She was an eerie figure, her golden robe and golden hair flowing out behind her like liquid, swathed from head to foot in an aureole of light motes. She sensed Xaedrek following her, felt bursts of power disintegrating against her shield. One blow would have killed her, if her sorcery had weakened, but despite her pain, it held. By the time she was in sight of the twelve-foot high white wall, he had given up the pursuit. No doubt he had gone to summon guards. Briefly she wondered why the demon had not joined the chase; whatever the reason, she was grateful. Then the wall confronted her, and she made a prodigious, sorcerous leap, scrambled over the top, and let herself down lightly on the other side. To the protective shield she now added a cloak against being seen. This did not make her truly invisible; but it affected the minds of those she passed, so that they did not register her presence. Now no guards, not even Xaedrek himself, could pursue her.

Thus safeguarded – and exhilarated at her escape – she ran on through the streets of Shalekahh, heading for Anixa's house.

'I just cannot believe it,' said the Lady Shavarish, shaking her head in astonishment. 'She seemed so genuine. Don't blame yourself, Sire, she took all of us in, no one more than I.'

Xaedrek glared at her, not wanting her judgement on whether he was to blame or not. He had assembled Shavarish, Amnek and Baramek in his private office to explain about Melkavesh; Ah'garith stood motionless and blank-faced in the corner, like an automated doll at rest.

'I have to agree, Sire,' said Baramek. He placed his black helm on the desk and smoothed his hair. 'She seemed a true daughter of Gorethria, open, true and loyal. This revelation is . . .' he trailed off as if he could not find strong enough words to express his shock and sense of betrayal. 'Unspeakable,' he concluded inadequately.

'Sire, if I might speak my mind,' began the thin, grim Lord Amnek.

'You always do, my friend. I value you for it,' Xaedrek replied.

'Unlike Commander Baramek, I never thought that your fondness for the Lady Kharan showed any weakness in you.' The High Commander gave him an angry look, but Amnek – seated at the desk – ignored it. 'But this Melkavesh is a different matter. From the start I saw that her mind was tainted with concerns other than science and Gorethria's welfare. Yet you seemed blind to it, freely involving her in our work, trusting her on every level. It concerns me the more deeply because you are the last person I would have expected to make such a mistake.'

'I freely admit it was a misjudgement,' Xaedrek replied tightly. Even his three closest colleagues did not guess how hard he was battling to conceal his emotions beneath a sheet of icy calmness. He found himself in an extremely delicate situation, and it was essential that he remained in control. 'Her power seemed to answer Gorethria's needs. We all wanted to believe it.' A faint sneer was heard from Ah'garith. 'However, even an emperor may make one such mistake in his life, and you have my assurance, Amnek, that I have learned by it.'

'Sire, forgive me,' the scientist said feelingly. 'Knowing you as I do, I am convinced that this touch of fallibility will only add to your future strength. I have always had the utmost faith in you and I will continue to do so.' Amnek was no flatterer, and rarely made such speeches.

Xaedrek was gratified, and the more so when Shavarish added, 'I too, Sire. Understandably, you feared that this incident would shake our belief in you. Rest assured that it has not; particularly as you have confided fully in us at the first opportunity. I would like to reaffirm my support for you.' She moved behind her husband's chair, and he clasped her hand in a gesture of concurrence.

'Thank you. I hope I shall prove worthy of it,' Xaedrek replied quietly. He moved to the window and turned to face them. In fact, he had confided anything but fully in them. He certainly did not wish it known that Ashurek's daughter, the true heir to the throne, was at large. It would only confuse matters. Nor did he mention his proposal of marriage. He had hinted that she was the result of a liaison between a Gorethrian soldier and a Tearnian woman, and that she had come from Tearn to investigate and sabotage Xaedrek's work, using her unique sorcerous powers. It was a mixture of truth and dissembling designed to answer any awkward questions. Now the delicate business of admitting his mistake was over, he could return – with relief – to practical problems.

'Now, it is a matter of urgency that we find Melkavesh at once. She is a powerful Sorceress and I do not wish to make light of the dangers of letting her escape. Baramek, please go at once and ask one of my captains to organise an immediate, full search of the city and surrounding area.'

'It will be my pleasure, Sire. I'll supervise it personally,' Baramek replied. He tucked his helm under one arm, saluted and swept out, his cloak swirling.

'Amnek, I want you to summon the other Inner Councillors and inform them of this unfortunate affair. Tell them I will meet them this evening to answer their questions. I'm sure you will handle it with the utmost discretion and ensure that it goes no further.' Lord Amnek nodded gravely. 'And as for the Senate, and court, I wish them to know as little as possible. Lady Melkavesh is being sought for some minor misdemeanour, that's all.' He moved over to them and put a hand on each of their shoulders. 'Amnek, Shavarish, I cannot tell you how deeply I value your loyalty. When you have been betrayed as I have, you fully appreciate the worth of true friends.'

Shavarish's blue eyes were full of warmth for the Emperor, and even Amnek verged on a smile.

'You may go,' Xaedrek said, 'Shavarish, return to the mansion. Our work must continue, whatever happens. It's more important than ever now.'

'Yes, Sire,' she said, and the two bowed and left the room. Now Xaedrek was alone with Ah'garith.

'"Confided fully in us",' the woman-demon mimicked as the door shut. 'Sire, you may not give me much, but you do afford me great amusement at times.'

Xaedrek turned to her, his eyes blazing with scarlet fury.

'You let her go,' he said in a low, dangerous voice. 'I called on you to help me restrain her and you did nothing. You stood and watched her running away and you laughed. I want to know why.'

'Because, Sire,' the demon replied sibilantly, 'you deserved it.'

'Deserved – By the gods, Ah'garith, whose side are you on?'

'Mine.'

'Naturally.' Xaedrek paced round the room. He was shaking with rage, and no matter which way he turned, he could still see Ah'garith's bland grin out of the corner of his eye.

'What did you expect, Sire?' the Shanin went on bitterly. 'You planned to get rid of me, to replace me with her. I suppose you thought I didn't know, but I am not that stupid. It is you who've behaved like an imbecile on this occasion.'

'I have great patience, demon, but it has a limit,' Xaedrek said warningly.

'Don't think to threaten me, Sire, when you've never had greater need of me. If only you had trusted me! As soon as I set eyes on her, I knew exactly who she was. You think I could ever forget Ashurek and Silvren, not recognise the taint of their blood when I see it? I could have told you this would happen. But, oh no, you could not trust me. You were too busy conspiring against me. Yes, yes, you deserved it!'

Xaedrek swung round and found the demon at his shoulder. Malice glinted like scalpels in the murky shallows of her eyes, and she smelled of clotted blood. She disgusted him to the core of his soul, and was beginning to make him deeply uneasy. In the garden, for the first time, she had disobeyed him.

'Ah'garith, calm down,' he said placatingly. 'You are right, of course. I made a mistake, I should have trusted you. I was wrong and I apologise.' It galled him to grovel to the Shanin, but, as an astute psychologist, he knew it was the only way to bring her to heel.

'You imagined you didn't need me,' she growled. He stepped back to avoid touching her.

'I was frustrated at our lack of progress. I thought Melkavesh could discover a way to far-see, that's all.'

Ah'garith laughed scornfully. 'Discover? Do you think she can't far-see already? Can a bird fly? Can a snake crawl?

211

What a fool she made of you. I will never forget how you've treated me, never forgive it. There's so much you did not tell the Inner Council, which I'm sure they'd love to know . . .'

With a great effort of self-control, Xaedrek continued in a soothing penitent tone, 'Ah'garith, please. I have wronged you, but I will make amends. Listen. If you obstruct me, you help her. And I'm sure you don't want that, because you obviously hate her.' This seemed to strike a chord, and the Shanin's ill-temper faded into a sulky silence. 'Assist me, please. I need you,' Xaedrek cajoled.

'As I am still yours to command, Sire, I have no choice but to help,' she grated sullenly. 'But be careful. It may not be so for ever.'

He remembered her disobedience, and knew he could no longer be complacent about his ability to control her. Suddenly he felt tired, oppressed. It was at such a time that he would once have sought solace in Kharan's arms . . . 'What do you want me to do?' he asked wearily.

'I demand simply that you treat me with respect and trust and never again try to dispose of me. Do you promise?'

'Yes, yes,' he said impatiently. 'I've said I'm sorry, Ah'garith. What more can I do?'

'Just keep the promise,' was the ominous reply.

He sighed and leaned on the desk. 'Now perhaps we can discuss –' he was going to say, 'something more important', but thought better of it, '– the finding of Lady Melkavesh. Could you locate her, by sensing her sorcery from a distance?'

'I might.'

'What does that mean?'

'If she was using her power nearby, I would know it.'

'How near? You can't sense her now, I take it?'

'No, Sire.'

'Well, this is hopeless. She may be miles away already.' Xaedrek walked slowly round the room, staring broodingly at the scenes painted on the walls.

'There may be a way . . .'

The Emperor looked up sharply. 'Don't prevaricate. What is it?'

'If you permitted me to take amulin, I am certain that my perception would be vastly increased. I can only draw the power, I cannot wield it, as you know. If only you'd allowed me amulin before, this need not have happened! So don't make things worse, Sire. Let me take it.' Xaedrek said nothing. He might have known this demand was coming, and he dreaded the consequences. But it seemed he had no choice. He turned away, feeling trapped and stifled by the room, by her. The delicate, silvery murals seemed suddenly garish, and he had the nightmare impression that the figures in them were moving, shouting and jostling. The demon murmured, 'Trust, Sire. You promised to trust me. And you wouldn't wish me to tell anyone she is Ashurek's heir . . .'

'Aye,' he said through clenched teeth. 'Very well. But the trust must be mutual, and you must not fail.' He went to a cupboard, took out a small phial, and added the contents to a goblet of water. Ah'garith curled a white hand round the vessel and drank greedily. He watched with distaste and a sense of resignation, cursing the circumstances that forced him to give way to her. But at the same time, the scientific half of his mind remained detached, watching her with great interest.

'Ahh,' the woman-demon gasped. 'The amulin is potent. I feel almost as I used to, before M'gulfn's death . . .' There was a sickly pale glow in her face, almost a ghost image just out of register with her body. And it was an image not of an old woman, but of a silvery-smooth, asexual being. It moved with her, leaving transient streaks of light in the air.

Xaedrek waited anxiously. Outwardly he appeared at ease, but his eyes were full of brooding fire. Not to be in control was an anathema to him, and he loathed being at Ah'garith's mercy in this way. He wondered if she would take advantage of the power to betray him at once. Perhaps try to kill him, or worse. Since he had planned to rid himself of her, he could hardly blame her. And how long would her newfound power last? A day, as with humans – or might the effects be permanent? Well, soon he would know.

'Yes, I have power now,' she said, her mouth stretched in

an ugly grin. 'Are you afraid, Sire? You should be.' She walked towards him, giggling, but Xaedrek stood his ground.

'The Lady Melkavesh,' he said softly. 'Do you not hate her more than you hate me? You must help me to find her.'

The woman-demon stopped and said in a wounded tone, 'I am about to, Sire. I was only . . . teasing you. How dare you still doubt me? I said you could trust me, and you can.'

'Of course,' Xaedrek said reassuringly. And he smiled to himself, because he had seen the truth behind the Shanin's petulant words: she could not destroy him, because she needed him too much. She was still at his command. Letting Melkavesh escape had not been disobedience so much as simple incompetence.

Ah'garith closed her eyes and stood motionless for two or three minutes, testing her ability to far-see. Then her lids flew open and she hissed, 'I sense a very strong power . . . It can only be her. In the mansion.'

'The mansion!' Xaedrek exclaimed. 'By the gods, what a fool I am! She has gone back there to destroy the machine!'

'Then, Sire, she must be prevented,' Ah'garith said, but the Emperor was already rushing from the room, shouting for guards. The woman-demon trailed on his heels, her hands clasped primly in front of her and her face set in a meek grimace. Although Xaedrek was running, she seemed to keep up easily at a kind of floating walk.

They arrived at the mansion too late.

The doors of the underground chamber burst open, and through them rushed Xaedrek, Ah'garith and six guards. The first thing they saw was the machine, half-wrecked, the metal tubes lying buckled and dented, the glass rods scattered broken across the floor. The marble tiles were covered with glass powder and splinters. Xaedrek's heavy workbench had been overturned as if by superhuman strength, and the debris glittered with spilt amulin.

And the culprit was still at work, tearing at the machine with bare hands and flinging the pieces across the room, apparently oblivious to Xaedrek's arrival.

It was not Melkavesh.

It was a tall, well-built man with strangely patterned skin, bronze hair and a long red beard; the Kristillian whom Xaedrek had brought to the room earlier. A greenish-copper glow surrounded him and Xaedrek realised at once that he had taken amulin. He strode over to him and commanded in a clear voice that cut through the sound of destruction, 'Stop.'

The man turned from the machine and launched himself at the Emperor. There was an explosion of power, black and green and copper, and Xaedrek found himself skidding across the debris-strewn floor until he collided hard with the wall. Four of the guards had been flung to the ground alongside him.

'Ah'garith, help me restrain him,' he cried hoarsely as he staggered to his feet. He could not believe how strong the Kristillian's power was, stronger than his own. Again he approached the man, unleashing a swathe of crackling energy at him. Normally it would have killed, but the man only staggered. Ah'garith converged from the other side, ribbons of sickly argent light rippling from her hands and curling round and round his body. He struggled, and bursts of dark fire emitted randomly from his hands and sweat-slicked chest. Obviously he had no skill in controlling the power, but it still took Xaedrek's and Ah'garith's combined strength to restrain him.

Finally the Kristillian stood rigid between them, his eyes wild and the cords in his neck and shoulders standing out, as if he were battling furiously against paralysis. But ropes of sorcerous electricity held him, and the guards surrounded him with swords poised.

Xaedrek faced the man and paused to get his breath back and pluck glass splinters from his bloodied hands. 'Well, Ah'garith, you've certainly made an excellent job of finding Melkavesh, haven't you?' he remarked caustically.

The demon seemed embarrassed. 'Sire – Sire – I sensed a great power – I assumed it was her. I never thought there could be another energy so great.' She looked sideways at the Emperor and rasped, 'Sire, let me punish him –'

215

'Curb your eagerness,' Xaedrek interrupted sharply. 'I need to question him first. He interests me.' Although he was inwardly furious, he could not let the Kristillian think he had achieved anything. He looked the man in the eye and asked in a matter-of-fact tone, 'What is your name?'

'Irem Ol Thangiol,' the man snarled. He tried to back away, but the demon's power held him.

'Well, Irem Ol Thangiol, I am pleased to tell you that your day's work has been in vain. It is an inconvenience, of course, but the machine is not, in fact, particularly difficult to rebuild. So tell me, how did you get the amulin?' A trace of fear entered the man's face, and his dark eyes kept swivelling to one side, as if he were trying to escape Xaedrek's unnerving gaze. 'Answer me. The truth, now.'

Irem Ol Thangiol clenched his teeth defiantly, but he could not resist Xaedrek's will. After a moment of struggle, he stammered out, 'A woman gave it to me. The one who was in here with you this morning. She healed me, then told me to try to escape.'

'But instead, you decided to come down here and sabotage the apparatus. Objectively, I have to admit that that was commendably heroic. I'm impressed, Ol Thangiol,' Xaedrek said, sounding thoughtful. 'Very impressed.' He turned away and walked slowly round the room, kicking at the debris of shattered glass and metal. 'The sooner this mess is cleared up the better.'

'I'll see to it at once, Your Majesty,' one of the guards replied; then, 'Your Majesty, what's wrong?'

Xaedrek had stopped in mid-stride by the overturned workbench, staring at something behind it. 'Shavarish,' he whispered hoarsely. 'Guard, come here, help me.'

The Lady Shavarish lay amid the wreckage behind the bench, her blue satin robe crumpled and her limbs at awkward angles. There were cuts on her face and arms from broken glass, but they no longer bled. Her head was tilted backwards and her sapphire eyes were wide and lightless. He bent to examine her, but to no avail.

'She is dead,' he said quietly. 'Take her to a room above.

And have Lord Amnek sent to me at once.' The guard bent down and lifted the body with exaggerated care. Her head rested in the crook of his shoulder, her hair clung to the dark curve of her neck, just as if she were a sleeping child. Xaedrek stared at her with numb disbelief; then the door opened, and the thin, dark figure of Lord Amnek stood there.

He saw his wife and went to take her from the guard before Xaedrek could stop him. For a moment he bent over her, assuming she was only unconscious; then the truth dawned, and he let out a single deep, hoarse cry of grief that was terrible to hear. Xaedrek went to him and placed a hand on his shoulder.

'Amnek, I have no words to express my sorrow at this dreadful event. I can only tell you what has occurred.' Briefly he explained about the Kristillian. 'Evidently Shavarish did her utmost to stop him, but he was crazed with amulin. He nearly killed all of us before we restrained him. She died a brave death . . .' but the words turned sour and empty in his mouth when he saw the terrible grief in Amnek's hawk-like face.

'There is only one person who is to blame for this,' Amnek said grimly. 'Melkavesh. And she is going to pay.' He turned and stalked out of the room, hugging Shavarish's limp frame to him.

'Well, Irem Ol Thangiol, this makes matters somewhat more serious,' Xaedrek said, pacing slowly towards the Kristillian. Now he knew why the man had kept glancing nervously to one side: he had been waiting for them to discover the body. 'Have you anything to say for yourself?'

'I did not mean to kill her, Emperor,' Ol Thangiol replied, trembling but defiant. His face was a mess; the burned layer was curling back from the healed flesh beneath, and sweat pooled and trickled between the flaps of skin. 'She got in my way. But one Gorethrian less can only be to Kristillia's benefit.'

Xaedrek restrained himself from hitting the man. He had always found physical violence unproductive and undignified. Nevertheless, it was only just that the man should suffer for

217

Shavarish's wanton murder. He said evenly, 'Ah'garith, can you restrain the man single-handed?'

'I can indeed, Sire, now that he's under control,' she replied.

'Good. Now listen to me, Ol Thangiol. I wish to interview you at length, but you are too dangerous in your present state. So I am going to leave you in Ah'garith's capable hands until the effect of the amulin wears off.'

Something in the woman-demon's eyes seemed to fill the Kristillian with terror; Xaedrek recalled the day she had first come to him, and he had found Varian sobbing with fear in her presence.

'Why do you not slay me?' he cried brokenly. His legs buckled and he fell to his knees. 'Don't leave me alone with that fiend . . .'

'You've committed a dual crime. For that, a double punishment. The effect of amulin upon you fascinates me, and I believe I can learn much from it. You don't deserve death, Ol Thangiol. Instead you are going to help me.' He bent over the man and put a hand on his head; and to Ol Thangiol, the hand felt like a black scorpion, and Xaedrek's eyes were poisonous red moons. 'You are going to help me find Melkavesh, and to conquer your beloved Kristillia.'

Xaedrek motioned the guards to position themselves at the door and added, 'Do what you will, Ah'garith, but don't damage him.'

'Oh, he will be safe with me, never fear,' she replied with leering delight. 'Thank you, Sire, thank you. I take back everything I said.'

It was the first time he had allowed her freedom with a prisoner, and he found her gratitude repulsive. 'Don't thank me, Ah'garith,' he snapped. 'I should be punishing your incompetence, not rewarding it.' He strode out of the room, but he could not avoid glimpsing the demon out of the corner of his eye, her soulless eyes and malevolent, sadistic glee . . .

He slammed the door behind him and leaned against it for a while, feeling exhausted, unclean, and sick to his stomach.

8

The Emethrian Mountains

MELKAVESH STEPPED quietly through Anixa's door and passed through the workroom, unnoticed by two courtiers who were browsing over bolts of cloth. Once safely upstairs, she dropped the guise of invisibility and let her power fade. She fell into one of the kitchen chairs, forcing herself to breathe deeply and relax while the pain – like metal rods stuck through her bones – gradually eased.

Kharan was preparing a meal, oblivious to her arrival. Her mind was elsewhere, and not on what she was doing. Over the past few days she had done her best to put Melkavesh and Xaedrek from her thoughts, and had largely succeeded. Things seemed less black, and she had begun to feel that she had a reason to live after all, someone to care for besides herself. In a strange way, she was almost content . . .

Then she turned, and saw Melkavesh, and froze with a ladle poised in her hand. 'Where did you appear from?' she gasped.

'Sorry if I startled you. I came in very quietly. Where's Anixa?'

'Downstairs . . . But your hair, Mel! What's happened?' A familiar feeling of dread crept over her, and her contentedness fled. 'Xaedrek has found out . . .'

'Xaedrek,' Melkavesh said offhandedly, 'has just asked me to marry him.'

The ladle clattered to the floor, and Kharan's expressive eyes widened with shock and betrayal.

'I don't know why you've come back here to tell me that,'

she said hoarsely. 'Unless you want to make him a wedding gift of my head. Of course, I should have foreseen this, except I was too busy trusting you. Well, I must say you are a perfect match. There's nothing to choose between you.'

'Kharan, wait,' Melkavesh exclaimed. She was taken aback by this outburst, but realised she had probably deserved it. 'Sit down and let me explain properly. I'll be brief, though, we haven't much time.'

As she related her confrontation with the Emperor, Anixa came into the kitchen, apparently not at all surprised to see her.

'And he asked you to marry him *after* he knew you'd deceived him?' Kharan asked incredulously.

'Well, it was quite logical. He wanted me on his side, knowing I'd be dangerous if I wasn't. I might have accepted his conditions, except that he would not agree to mine . . . To be frank, Kharan, I realise that I have been foolish. I thought I could persuade Xaedrek to see my point of view and become more humane. I was wrong. He is totally single-minded. It's not that he doesn't understand, he just won't compromise.'

'Good grief, Melkavesh, I could have told you that,' Kharan exclaimed with a bitter laugh. 'In fact I thought I had, several times.'

'You did, Kharan, but I'm afraid I never believe anything until I've seen it for myself. There's no question of compromise or marriage now – we've just made a fair attempt to kill each other. He'll be searching the city for me, and he won't rest until I'm captured. My only choice is to flee Shalekahh at once.'

Anixa came to her side and said, 'Don't worry, Lady Melkavesh. Everything can be prepared quickly. You'll need stout travelling clothes, and provisions. I anticipated this eventuality, and I have been storing food – cheese, dried fruit and suchlike – for you to take. I'll begin at once.'

'Anixa, you are wonderful!' Melkavesh exclaimed. 'Kharan, how quickly can you get ready? We should eat before we leave, it may be our last chance for some time. Have those courtiers gone?'

'Yes, my lady,' replied Anixa, as she busied herself with preparations. Kharan stood up and leaned on the table, staring at Melkavesh.

'What do you mean, *we*?' she demanded.

'You're coming with me, of course.'

Kharan seemed taken aback. After a moment she stammered, 'But I – I can't.'

'Don't be ridiculous, you must come! You were desperate to leave Shalekahh a few weeks ago!'

'That was before . . .'

'Before what? Surely you're not frightened?' Kharan turned away, shaking her head. Whatever her dilemma was, she refused to speak of it. 'Look, Kharan, you are coming with me if I have to tie you up and drag you. Xaedrek will search the city thoroughly. Every house. It would be disastrous for Anixa if you were found here – not to mention yourself.'

Kharan was silent for several seconds. Then, as if she had resigned herself to the situation, she lifted her head and said, 'It seems both options are as bad as each other. As you give me no choice, I'll come.'

'I only wish I had a choice, Kharan,' Melkavesh responded ungraciously. 'You are going to be a definite liability. You have put on weight, and look decidedly unfit.'

'Well, I don't know what you expect, when I've not set foot outside this house in a month, and had nothing to do but sew, sleep and eat,' Kharan retorted. 'And what about Anixa? Are you going to leave her here, in danger?'

Melkavesh pondered this. 'She may come with us if she wishes.'

'Thank you, my lady, but I see no point,' the dressmaker replied. 'Once you two are gone, I'll ensure there's no evidence that I have been harbouring anyone. I'll be in no danger. Besides,' she rested a hand lightly on Kharan's shoulder in passing, 'like you, Lady Kharan, I have served the Gorethrians for so long that I have lost all will and

221

incentive to defy them openly. All my rebellion is in thought, not deed, and will remain so.'

Like me? Kharan thought. Is that how she sees me? She felt at once infuriated by this judgement and guilt-stricken because she felt it to be true.

But Melkavesh said, 'You're a dark one, Anixa, and I don't altogether believe you. But you may have achieved more than you realise, just by helping me.'

'So I fear, my lady.'

'Fear?' Melkavesh exclaimed. 'Anixa, I am trying to help Kesfaline now, not Xaedrek.'

Kharan, who was hurriedly serving their meal, broke in anxiously, 'Mel, where are you planning to go?'

'Well, if we reach the mountains I'll think we've been lucky. After that, the logical place would be the only country which is free of Gorethria's rule and apparently still has some strength: Kristillia.'

'Do you know how far away Kristillia is?' Kharan gasped. 'It's at least four thousand miles! That's months of travelling –'

'So? We'll survive. I'm a Sorceress, remember?' Anixa brought them an armful of clothes and they began to change, in between seizing mouthfuls of bread and meat. 'Today's exchange brought it home to me that Xaedrek must be stopped, and he can only be stopped by force. I need allies.'

Kharan and Anixa looked at each other, and with a sudden chill, Kharan recalled the Kesfalian's words, *Perhaps it is Xaedrek who should stop her.* A vision of Melkavesh's vast ambitions took her breath away. She was powerful, and quite capable of starting yet another war, or worse. And Anixa expected Kharan to restrain her!

Then the Kesfalian woman stepped up to Melkavesh and laid a hand on her arm. 'Lady Melkavesh, listen to me. The sages of my country have long prophesied that one such as you would come. There could be danger in your going to Kristillia.'

'Anixa, I can look after myself –'

'Not danger to you, but to the rest of us! I'm sorry I can't

222

explain clearly enough to convince you. The reasons are known only to the sages of Kesfaline. Therefore, I implore you to go to them. No one should meddle in the powers of Earth without first seeking their guidance.'

'Really, Anixa, I have never heard of these sages and I can't see what they know of sorcery that I don't,' Melkavesh replied, bending to pull boots on.

'They hold the secrets of the Earth. The Kristillians do not. Please go to Kesfaline, my lady, and take their advice – to do otherwise could be disastrous,' Anixa persisted. The light shifted from blue to gold on her dappled skin, and her eyes shone like amber moons. Kharan found herself silently praying that Melkavesh would acquiesce to Anixa's plea; then, at least, she could feel less responsible for the fate that was shaping itself around them.

'All right!' Melkavesh said, realising that the simplest way to quiet Anixa was to give in. 'All right, we'll go to Kesfaline. If it means so much to you.'

'Not to me, to everyone, if only they knew it. Thank you, my lady,' Anixa said quietly, turning away to check the provisions. But as she did so, she caught Kharan's eye, and Kharan knew the look meant, *It is up to you to ensure that she goes to Kesfaline, and follow the sages' guidance.* Kharan stared back and gave a helpless shrug, *How can I?* But there was no sympathy in Anixa's face. Her gaze became hard and compelling, as if to say, *You must.*

Soon Kharan and Melkavesh were ready, dressed in riding gear of the dullest colours permitted by Gorethrian taste. Breeches of a hard-wearing double cloth, with a complex woven pattern of dark red and blood-red. Long, heavy boots of mulberry leather, with straps to support ankles and knees. Wide-sleeved violet shirts and tunics of a slightly darker shade, gleaming with purplish brocade, and over that, close-fitting, high-collared jackets of the same material as the breeches.

Anixa slung a pack of maroon leather onto each of their backs; each contained a supply of food, extra clothing, and a knife. 'My best cloth knives,' Anixa said. 'They are all I have to offer, I'm afraid.' Melkavesh also had a good map, purloined from the palace library, and some money, in case it was needed, but she left a generous pile of Gorethrian sovereigns – flakes of gold sandwiched between thin layers of pale blue crystal – for Anixa. The dressmaker accepted them with good grace.

Over the packs went voluminous black cloaks with sculpted shoulders and deep hoods, which were the best camouflage for Gorethria's dark mountains. Then they were ready, and there was nothing to do except say goodbye to Anixa.

'There are soldiers in the street,' Kharan said anxiously, looking out of the window.

'They won't see us. Don't worry.'

But then Kharan spotted an ominous flash of blue and white. 'Huntsmen,' she breathed. 'And six hounds! They'll scent you here –'

'Kharan, I can confound dogs as well as humans. Just stay very close to me. And have faith! Now, we must go.'

Anixa bade them farewell, and Kharan glanced round to see her watching them leave, a small, dark figure, her unsmiling face framed by raven-black hair. The longer Kharan had known her, the more the dressmaker had disturbed her; yet she would miss her, miss the security she had provided for the past few weeks.

Before they stepped out of the house, Melkavesh had cloaked them both with sorcery so that they could walk straight in front of the soldiers without being noticed. She could feel Kharan shaking, pressed very close to her as they left the garden and moved into the bustle of the street. Gorethrian citizens were watching the guards striding from house to house, but no one turned their head to look at Melkavesh and Kharan. Melkavesh ignored the soldiers, and made her way towards the pack of russet-and-white hounds, which were sniffing their way along the street. They could not see her, but as she approached they scented her, and began to give voice.

Melkavesh moved among them, and touched each of their heads in turn, numbing their keen sense of smell and replacing it with confusion. Their baying deteriorated into short, high-pitched yelps. Presently they were running in circles, following any scent they could find, unable to tell one from another. Then she seized Kharan's arm and hurried her away, with the infuriated exclamations of the huntsmen receding behind them.

A few minutes more, and the hounds would have traced her to Anixa's house. But now the dressmaker was safe.

Now no human or animal would hinder their escape; the danger was that her sorcery might leave a blazing trail for Ah'garith to follow. Still, the risk had to be taken. She was already tired from her expenditure of power against Xaedrek, and to conceal Kharan as well as herself was a great drain on her strength. She hoped she could maintain it long enough for them to flee beyond Shalekahh's outskirts. She knew ways of travelling very swiftly by sorcerous means, but she had nowhere near the strength needed to practise them. For the time being, their feet must serve.

Soon they left the white streets of Shalekahh behind, and there was crisp grass under their feet, plum-red trees around them. They were heading east, straight towards the river Kahh, beyond which were red forests, then the mountains. Kharan, already desperately out of breath, demanded a rest. As they paused, several Gorethrian officers rode past towards one of the nearby encampments, totally oblivious to them.

'They really can't see us. It's unbelievable!' Kharan whispered. 'I've underestimated you.'

'Don't say that too soon. We have to get across the bridge yet.' They walked on at a swift and steady pace, parallel to a wide paved road that led to the river. A continual stream of soldiers, slaves, carts and chariots moved along this road, for it led to the main bridge over the Kahh. Melkavesh held desperately onto the shield of sorcery, cursing whatever it was that so weakened her power, praying that it would last until they were safely in the forests beyond the river.

The weather had been hot and bright when they set out, but now clouds were flowing overhead, compressing the atmosphere. Lightning flickered in the periphery of their vision, and it began to rain. Unseen, they fell into the line of folk tramping across the bridge.

It was a glorious edifice, a testimony to the skill of Gorethrian craftsmen in centuries past; it had stood for eight hundred years or more, arching from bank to bank in a crystal-white curve, its high sides intricately fretted and inlaid with pale enamels. It was wide enough to take eight horses abreast. The river itself was a hundred yards wide, and its steep banks were lined with trees, which leaned out and trailed their fire-red leaves in the water. Great drops of rain began to churn the flat, silvery surface.

Melkavesh felt her enchantment sliding away, turning from gold to lead. She gritted her teeth and made Kharan walk faster. All around them there was more military activity than was normal, and the white and gold of palace guards was much in evidence. People were being stopped and questioned. The gentle green hill beyond the bridge looked like a mountain; the edge of the forest seemed ten miles distant, not one.

The sky cracked deafeningly, and a spear of scarlet lightning destroyed a tree on the far bank. Horses shied, and for a few moments there was chaos. Melkavesh began to run, hanging onto Kharan's arm, dodging between soldiers and horses. Her power was fragmenting now, and some of them must have seen a flash of black from the corner of their eye. To her dismay, she saw four red-cloaked guards patrolling the hillside. Xaedrek's own men. If her strength failed now, they would become visible in full sight of them; there was nowhere to hide.

They reached the end of the bridge and sprinted up the long green slope. Kharan was sobbing for breath, but somehow she kept going, alarmed by Melkavesh's urgency.

The riders were trotting northwards, so Melkavesh crossed behind them. Pain was singing in her bones, and the storm seemed to reiterate her discomfort, as if every lightning whip, every crack of thunder, was inside her. Soon they would be visible, soon the guards would turn and see them – and she had no strength to resist arrest.

Then her power died, carried away on a hot, stormy wind. The residue stayed with her for a few minutes, which meant that their forms would appear translucent and fragmented for a time – but clearly visible to onlookers.

The guard turned their horses, and Kharan realised what had happened. Panic flashed through her, and her whole body seemed weighted by iron chains. Warm, torrential rain began to pour down, while beryl-green forks of lightning played over the river.

And the storm saved them.

Just for the few minutes it took them breathlessly to gain the edge of the trees, sweeping sheets of rain veiled them – the same translucent grey as their forms – and they blended into the torrent. The guards saw nothing. When lightning flashed, the two fugitives were simply not there at all. Even the unnatural stirring of bushes as the two stumbled into the forest went unnoticed, shrouded by rain.

Melkavesh and Kharan lay on the forest floor, struggling to regain their breath, sobbing with exertion and laughing with relief at the same time. Water was running from their cloaks in rivulets; Melkavesh sat up and pulled up her hood, shuddering as a cold trickle of rain found its way down her back.

'We must go on, Kharan,' she said, standing up and pulling the An'raagan to her feet. 'They may be searching in the forest as well.'

'Are you all right? You look terrible, almost grey,' Kharan asked concernedly, brushing wet leaves from her cloak.

'I'll be fine. Using my sorcery tires me out. I'll soon recover, but I won't be able to summon the power again for an hour or two.' They struck upwards through the trees in the gloomy storm-light. Around them, the leaves and undergrowth glistened with rain. Kharan already felt raw, hot and exhausted, and the journey had barely begun.

Trying to lighten the mood, she said, jokingly, 'Well, which way is Kesfaline?'

Melkavesh replied, 'We are not going to Kesfaline.'

Kharan stared at her in dismay. 'But you said –'

227

'I know what I said. I had to humour Anixa, there wasn't time to argue.'

'But you promised her!' Kharan was deeply distressed. She had come to feel it was essential that they followed Anixa's advice, but she had a cold, helpless intuition that nothing she said would convince Melkavesh of it.

'I promised nothing. There's no point in going there; in fact, it would be suicidal, seeing as the place is overrun by Gorethrians. Anixa's superstitious, that's all. It's just as far as Kristillia, so I don't see why you're worried about it.'

Kharan argued with her, but Melkavesh remained unmoved, and eventually she realised she might as well give up and save her breath for the climb. Melkavesh took her no more seriously than she would a child.

'You've made up your mind then,' she concluded bitterly.

'Yes. Kristillia, Kharan.' Melkavesh gripped the An'raagan's shoulder. 'We are going to Kristillia.'

Falmeryn drifted in and out of unconsciousness for a very long time, days it seemed. There were stretches of oblivion, but he was aware only of the nightmarish, interminable intervals when he was half-dreaming, half-hallucinating. Time and again he was in the forest, running, his heart bursting – then falling with steel traps crushing his limbs and ribs, surrounded by creatures which resembled hounds, but were something worse. And there was always Kharan – but whenever he ran to embrace her, she would turn away, saying softly, *You let me die* – and then she would be at Xaedrek's side, leaning against him, her eyes the same ruby-red as his. And he would turn and run from them, only to find he had to battle across an entire continent before he could escape.

Sometimes he dreamed he was in Forluin, desperate to return to Gorethria because he had left Kharan behind . . . and all through this the pain of his physical wounds was a permanent background, each tear in his flesh metamorphosing into a mountain range that he must cross before he found rest.

There came a gentler vision: his mother, Arlena, was before him, her hand stretched out to take his, her pale, beautiful face framed by a mass of silver-blonde hair. 'There's nothing to fear,' she was saying. 'The Serpent tried to slay me. For weeks I lay as if dead – I was dead. Life returned to me, but I tell you in that time of death, I found nothing to fear. Give me your hand and let go. It is a falling into sleep.'

He reached out to her, gasping, *Mother . . . Mother . . .* but he could not touch her. Yet she remained with him, watching over him; and sometimes there seemed to be another with them, a girl of about five or six with long, red hair of indescribable richness. In the dream Falmeryn seemed to know who she was. Once Arlena looked at her and smiled and said, 'Always under my feet . . .'

Presently it seemed to Falmeryn that he was not dreaming, but awake. Arlena was still sitting beside him, but her form seemed distant, ill defined as fog . . . with a sensation like the sliding of ice down his spine, he realised it was not her. The figure seated by his bed was all grey, its head and whole body shrouded in layers of gauze; he got the unpleasant impression that it was made wholly of gauze, without any human flesh beneath the covering. Involuntarily, he emitted a hoarse cry and sat up.

There was nothing, no one there.

Trembling, Falmeryn leaned back onto one elbow. He felt frighteningly disoriented and for a time had no idea where or even who he was. Blankly, he studied his surroundings. He was lying on a low, wood-framed bed, covered with a warm blanket of some unidentifiable brown material. The room itself – no, it was not a room, but a small cave, roughly egg-shaped. The walls were a pale, mottled limestone, with patches of russet and green lichen blending softly into the rock. On the uneven floor, clumps of moss and ferns grew, and somewhere he could hear the musical trickling of a spring. A bland light filtered in through the open end of the cave, but he could discern nothing beyond it except white sky.

The air was cool, fresh and odourless, very different from Shalekahh's heat-heavy atmosphere. The feel of the place was unfamiliar, not like Gorethria or anywhere else he knew. Fragments of memory drifted back: Forluin, the dreams . . . and then, with a sickening jolt, he remembered what had gone before.

The hunt. Tearing jaws, curved ivory teeth slicked with blood – he closed his eyes convulsively at the memory. He should have been dead. Pushing back the cover, he swung his legs over the edge of the bed to sit up. Something so horrendous could have been no mere nightmare, yet he seemed to be uninjured. But when he inspected his body more closely, he saw the silver tracery of scars all over his chest, abdomen and legs. It must have taken weeks for the bite wounds to heal so completely. How was it possible?

He stood up unsteadily, his bewilderment growing worse as his mind cleared. He felt weak, but free of pain and fever. Picking his way over the uneven, rocky floor towards the back of the cave, he traced the sound of running water to a tiny spring cascading vertically from the roof to a clear, rocky pool below. The cave was deceptive, bigger than it looked. Falmeryn knelt to drink, discovering that he was desperately thirsty and that the water was as sweet as crystal and as strengthening as food. He put his head under the cascade, then finally slipped into the pool and let the water pour over him, icy and invigorating. Then he sat at the edge of the pool, trailing his legs in the water, and tried to think.

Someone or something had saved him. He was not given to pessimism; for some reason he had been given a second chance of life, and it was precious and not to be wasted.

But Kharan? he thought, and a wave of bitter memory and grief overwhelmed him. He saw images of her in the iron grip of Xaedrek's guards, being marched pitilessly towards a place of execution, the windowless fort that had haunted his nightmares – no, for Kharan there could have been no escape. A weight settled in his chest, a crushing sense of outrage and immedicable sorrow. His head dropped forward and a deep sob escaped him; then he jumped to his feet, scattering water, and half-ran to the cave entrance.

For a moment he stood poised in horror; then he drew back from the entrance and pressed himself against a wall, breathing shallowly. He had expected to find a hillside of some sort outside; instead, there was nothing. The cavern seemed to be set in a sheer wall of rock, and outside, in every direction, a pale fog swirled. The diffuse light that shone through it was of even brilliance and never changed.

Now Falmeryn felt inclined to panic, but he controlled himself. To do so would achieve nothing. He walked back to the centre of the cave, trembling, half-way between grief and fear. Feeling suddenly cold, he pulled the brown cover from the bed and wrapped it round himself. As he did so, he became aware of something moving near the back of the cave, and he heard a voice say, 'It pleases me that you have recovered.'

Falmeryn started violently, and stared into the recesses behind the rock pool. From them emerged a creature which, he realised with a shiver, must have been there all the time, watching him. It was human in shape, but it stood at least seven feet tall, and had four arms, one pair below the other. Its skin was as black as polished coal on which transient sheens of purple and bronze shifted. Its face was long, sombre and handsome, refined beyond being male or female, as some statues are. The eyes were like jet, whiteless. It wore a short tunic of a stuff so dark that no light seemed to return from it at all. It was wholly alien, yet somehow familiar; Falmeryn had never seen its like before, but he clearly remembered Kharan describing such a being, the one she had released from Xaedrek's custody.

The creature said, 'My appearance seems to alarm you. Be assured, I offer no harm.' Its voice was beautiful, at once rich and light. Falmeryn found his tongue and stepped cautiously towards it.

'You are a – a being from one of the Planes, aren't you?'

'Yes. The Black Plane Hrunnesh. My name is Raphon.'

Then Falmeryn remembered: during the Quest of the Serpent, Estarinel had gone to the Black Plane and encountered the Hrunneshians. They were a peaceful race, devoting themselves entirely to philosophy. And they were nemen, a third, asexual gender which also occurred in humans in some parts of the Earth.

'Raphon, I am Falmeryn of Forluin. Can you explain to me how I came to be here? The last thing I remember, I was being savaged by a pack of hounds. Now I find myself here, and it makes no sense . . .' Falmeryn was instinctively well mannered even in the worst of situations, a fact which had afforded his captors in An'raaga much amusement. But Raphon's tone was gentle, not mocking.

'Yes, I understand that you find it strange and disquieting. I will explain. The hunters left you for dead – indeed, you would have died, had you not been rescued at once. But I found you, and brought you here.'

Falmeryn dragged a hand through his wet hair and tried to take this in. 'But why? I mean – how did you find me?'

'To answer that, I must first explain my presence on Earth. A human called Xaedrek came to Hrunnesh and induced me to go back to Earth with him. It was a fascinating experience, despite being uncomfortable. He was what might be called a philosopher of the physical, eager to investigate the functioning of my body rather than my thoughts. At first I did not object to participating, but I began to die, and discovered that I wished to live. I was fortunate. A human freed me from my bonds.'

'A woman called Kharan,' Falmeryn put in. 'I know, she told me. And she helped you find a small black stone . . .'

'That is so. A lodestone, with which I hoped to find my way back to Hrunnesh. I owe my life to her. But as I pursued the Entrance Point along its axis, I discovered your injured body and transported you to this place.'

'And where are we? This is not the Black Plane.'

The neman retreated to the back of the cavern, waded through the water, and seated itself in a shadowy recess. Falmeryn followed and stood on the edge of the pool. 'Forgive me, but I have need of darkness and moisture, conditions which are closest to those of my own Plane,' Raphon explained. 'No, this place is not Hrunnesh, nor is it the Earth. It is another domain, a place of healing.'

The knowledge that he was not on Earth gave Falmeryn a weird sensation of vertigo, as if he suddenly found he was not on solid ground, but flying. 'How long have I been here?' he called over the splashing of the spring.

'Some forty days, by Earth reckoning,' the neman replied. 'Your injuries were terrible, and no human physician could have healed you. Here there is a higher power. All the same, this is not H'tebhmella, where healing is all but instant. You have endured many days of pain.'

'And you nursed me, Raphon?'

'As best I could. I would also have died if I had not come here.'

'Of course, Kharan told me Xaedrek had inflicted dreadful injuries on you. Have you recovered from them?' Falmeryn asked concernedly.

'Yes, I am quite whole.' The term sounded strange, but the Hrunneshians were not human, and the idea of 'health' was abstract to them.

Falmeryn hugged the cover round himself and was silent for a while, watching the water splashing fragments of shattered light on the neman's sable skin. Then he said, 'Raphon, I must thank you. It was very kind of you to give me such care.'

'Kindness is a human concept which I have no means of judging or measuring,' Raphon said thoughtfully. 'Yet it is also an idea, and there is nothing more powerful than a pure idea . . .' The Hrunneshian's whiteless eyes were no longer focused on Falmeryn, and he sensed that it had drifted onto a train of philosophical thought from which it would not be distracted. Despite its friendly manner, its alien aura was overwhelming, and he felt suddenly, horribly alone.

'Raphon, there's more I must know,' he said urgently.

'Go and rest, my friend,' was the benign reply. 'You must recover your strength in sleep, as I must regain mine by solitary thought. Then we will talk again.'

233

'Raphon. Raphon!' he called, but the creature did not reply. Falmeryn wandered restlessly round the cavern for several minutes, like a prisoner pacing a cell. But there was nowhere to go, nothing he could do. At last he threw himself onto the bed and, despite his agitation, fell into a deep, refreshing sleep.

When he woke, the neman was sitting by his bed with its chin on its dark fist, its other three hands resting with limp grace on its knees. Falmeryn sat up, startled. Raphon bent to pick up a wooden dish from the floor, and handed it to him, saying, 'The water has sustained you for a long time, but now you must eat.'

He stared at the dark bread, cheese and honey in the bowl and exclaimed, 'Where did this come from?'

'It was here all the time. You did not look,' Raphon replied. Falmeryn was sure he had studied every inch of the cave, and could hardly believe it, but he was too hungry to dwell on the mystery. He offered the dish to the neman, but it declined, saying, 'My thanks, but I do not require food. Water and moist air are all I need to sustain me.'

When he had finished eating, he looked at the Hrunneshian and said, 'Well, Raphon, what happens now?'

'We return to Earth,' the neman replied simply. 'However, I have something to ask you first. I have an errand to undertake, and I would be grateful if you could assist me in it.'

'What sort of errand?'

'I am not yet clear of its nature. But that is a shortcoming in myself, the gulf between Hrunneshian thought and human experience. While I waited for your wounds to heal, it came to me that I must journey to a country called Kesfaline, and there discover a secret locked within the Earth.'

'What sort of secret? Something physical?'

'Or metaphysical? Both, I think. When we arrive, the answer will await us,' Raphon replied. Falmeryn, totally at a loss to understand this strange being, did not know what to say. He felt there was some purpose to his having been rescued, but the neman's words had not enlightened him.

Far from it; he no longer even knew what questions to ask. There were no simple answers; all seemed complex, muddy and obscure, and he felt that the more he struggled to understand, the deeper he would be drawn under the surface.

'I don't know, Raphon,' he sighed.

'If you do not wish to come, I cannot and would not compel you. I shall return you to Forluin, and go to Kesfaline alone.'

Forluin! That would be a miracle unlooked for. Falmeryn stood up and went to look at the nothingness beyond the cave, needing the unnerving touch of fear to sharpen his thoughts. One thing he knew: by saving the neman, Kharan had indirectly saved him. And what had he done to help her? Nothing. He rested his head against the limestone wall. Now she was gone, he needed a purpose to fill the void; and he could never return to a peaceful life in Forluin while knowing that Xaedrek's atrocities continued unchecked.

Besides, he owed his life to Raphon. As alien as the Hrunneshian seemed, Falmeryn knew instinctively that it was a good and gentle creature which had put caring for an injured human before its own concerns. To help it in return was the least he could do. Perhaps he had been given a second chance of life for a reason.

'All right, Raphon, I'll come with you. I'd be glad to help,' he said, walking to the neman's side and placing his hand on its shoulder. Already he felt a strange kind of sympathy and concern for the being. 'I don't even know where Kesfaline is. When do you want to go?'

'As soon as you feel strong enough,' Raphon answered.

'Then I am ready to leave now, if you wish.'

The neman's expression did not change, nor did its posture, but Falmeryn somehow sensed that it was profoundly relieved. 'I am grateful, Falmeryn of Forluin. You cannot know how much I will appreciate your company.'

Falmeryn went to bathe in the spring. When he returned, to his amazement, there were clothes lying on the end of the bed. 'The garments have also been here all the time,' Raphon said dismissively. Falmeryn felt puzzled and disturbed, but he sensed he would gain nothing by pursuing the matter.

With a resigned sigh, he began to dress. There was a fawn shirt, trousers, boots and tunic of creamy-brown leather, and a wide belt with a bronze buckle. Over that went a long white cloak with a deep hood, soft as the finest wool and gossamer light. Raphon put on an identical one, its whiteness a vivid contrast to the gleaming black skin beneath. Falmeryn also found a leather flask, which he filled from the spring and attached to his belt.

'If you are ready, we shall depart,' Raphon said.

Falmeryn followed the neman to the cave entrance and they stood together on the brink. The pale mist of nothingness confronted them like a wall, and a sick sense of dread rose unbidden in his chest. Did Raphon really expect him to step into that? The neman outstretched its four hands in an eerie, sinuous gesture, and he saw five pointed grey stones floating above the palms, swivelling like compass needles as if to point out unseen pathways. Lodestones. Falmeryn stared at them as if hypnotised, and as he did so, he became aware that the cave no longer seemed as motionless and solid as Earth. It was falling. Overwhelmed by a sinking sense of dizziness, he reached out for the cave wall – and his hand passed through it.

'I know little of Earth's geography, but the lodestones will return us as close as possible to Kesfaline. They will aid me to sense our location,' Raphon said in a matter-of-fact tone, as if nothing was happening. Falmeryn grabbed the neman's arm, and at last found solid flesh beneath his hand. But the horrific falling sensation worsened. They were weightless, spiralling through a white void. He felt Raphon step forward, and he had to follow or lose his hold – but he was not aware of leaving the cave entrance. The nothingness had already swallowed him.

And suddenly, it was gone. There was firm ground beneath his feet. The Hrunneshian was beside him and he was still clutching its arm. For several seconds his head continued to spin, and he could see and hear nothing; the first thing he became aware of was a warm, dry wind blowing into his face, catching at the cloak. Then vision returned, like a white

236

membrane splitting and peeling away to reveal the scene beyond. They were on a wide, smooth plain which undulated gently in every direction. A rich, indigo dome arched overhead, shading to violet near the skyline. The horizon in front of them was rimmed by apricot light which blended with the violet, heralding a rising sun.

They stood alone in a desert, and the only sound was the faint rising and falling sigh of the wind.

'Raphon, do you know where we are?' Falmeryn whispered. The sand slid and crunched beneath his boots as he turned to look around.

'On Hrunnesh the concept of geography is an abstract one. How interesting it is to experience the reality.' As the neman spoke, a brilliant spike of light appeared on the horizon. Falmeryn pulled the edge of his hood down to shield his eyes, but the neman turned away with a cry, as if the sun caused it physical pain. 'Alas . . .' it groaned. Its head dropped forwards and its lofty shoulders sagged.

'Raphon! what's wrong?' Falmeryn exclaimed in alarm. The neman leaned on him, and its other three hands emerged to pull the edges of the cloak together and draw the hood over its head.

'Alas, my friend, we have been led amiss. We are not close enough to Kesfaline.' The Hrunneshian stretched out a hand and the five lodestones began to spin above the palm. Evidently Raphon had the ability to sense their whereabouts because its perceptions were on a different and more acute level. Falmeryn held its arm to support it, made anxious by its distress.

'Then where are we?' he asked.

'We are in a country which lies some four hundred miles south-west of Kesfaline. I believe it is called Ungrem.' Falmeryn had heard of it: Ungrem of the Swallowing Sands, it was called. When the wind blew, its great desert flowed like liquid, drowning all who walked unwarily on the treacherous surface. Raphon went on, 'I am sorry, Falmeryn of Forluin. I had not foreseen this. We Hrunneshians are ill suited to survive on Earth in the best of conditions. A place that is hot and without water is fatal to us. Already the light weakens me. Within a few hours, I will die.'

'No!' Falmeryn cried. 'I won't let you die . . .'

The neman sighed. Its sombre face was like that of a statue carved in an expression of mournful sadness. 'The extinguishing of thought and awareness is not a prospect I welcome. Now I understand that all human experience is coloured by the knowledge of inevitable death. I am only saddened that I will not have time to devote sufficient thought to this revelation, nor relay my conclusions to my fellow Hrunneshians.'

'Raphon . . .' Falmeryn said helplessly. But he saw that the neman was in earnest, and it seemed there was nothing he could do to preserve its life. The sun was rising swiftly, there was no protection from it. The desert was unexpectedly beautiful in its slanting rays; long shadows slid over the dunes, and here and there a haze of sand rippled, lifted by the wind. *We have been led amiss,* Raphon had said . . . but by whom?

'Raphon, lean on me, we must at least try. There may be shelter and water over the horizon,' Falmeryn urged, but the neman's reply was calm and unyielding as obsidian.

'No. I would slow you down. Only let me tell you what you must seek in Kesfaline, then you must go on alone. Perhaps you will have a chance of reaching the edge of the desert before the wind blows in earnest, and the sand swallows us both.'

The forest was dark. Somewhere below, horses were crashing through the trees, and the occasional blaze of a torch could be seen, leaving streaks of flame hanging in the air. Half-way up a steep hill, Melkavesh and Kharan crouched in a clump of undergrowth, praying that the search party would pass by. Once the horses halted and milled around in the trees, and it seemed they would turn uphill, but after a minute there was a command from the officer-in-charge, and they took a downward path.

Melkavesh's eyes were closed, for she was using her higher, sorcerous senses to watch the patrol. Yes, the men were retreating, but there were others searching . . . Hounds! How had they picked up the scent? She could sense them and see them in her mind, russet and curd-white beasts with malevolent eyes, trotting softly through the undergrowth. There were four, but she sensed no humans with them. Obviously they had been trained to hunt independently.

'Is it safe yet?' Kharan mouthed in her ear. Her shoulder was pressed to Melkavesh's, and she was trembling.

'Hush. Wait,' Melkavesh silenced her. Praying that she had recouped enough strength, she waited for the hounds to draw closer. Leaves stirred around them, disturbed by a breeze – or by the approach of the four massive canines. The scent of hot, meaty breath and of damp fur infiltrated the air. Kharan drew in a sharp breath of fear, but Melkavesh hissed, 'Keep quiet,' and stood up boldly.

The first hound saw her and sprang, but a spear of energy felled it in mid-leap. The others did not even have time to give voice; a surge of amber electricity crackled from her hands, lighting the forest for yards around. When it faded, the hounds were nowhere to be seen. All was dark again, but she knew their bodies lay somewhere in the undergrowth, limbs awry, coats matted with leaves, wet tongues lolling onto the earth.

'Now we must run,' Melkavesh said. 'When they find those hounds, they'll know which way we came. And I have no more strength for sorcery tonight.'

Kharan felt she would die if she did not rest soon, but Melkavesh forced her on at a punishing pace. All afternoon they had fled upwards through the forest, and the way was growing steeper and steeper as they approached the Emethrian mountains. Melkavesh insisted that they continue all night, and only rest at dawn. 'We can't risk moving in daylight this close to Shalekahh,' she said. 'We'll find a hiding place for the day, and go on tomorrow night.'

'Mel, if you don't stop soon I'll be in no state to go anywhere tomorrow night,' Kharan gasped.

But somehow, by taking brief rests along the way, she managed to keep going. An hour before sunrise they found a cleft in the hillside, overhung by vegetation. Here they ate and rested, although Kharan was at once so exhausted and so nervous that she found it almost impossible to sleep. The day seemed a grey blur of insomnia and discomfort as she tried to find rest on the hard earth floor, her pack like a boulder under her head. When Melkavesh asked her to take a turn at keeping watch, Kharan found it more restful to sit at the edge of the cleft, peering out into the trees.

The forest was beautiful, but also deadly. Light filtered through layers of red foliage, forming pools of ruby light between the trunks. Jewel-like colours gleamed amid giant ferns and other, stranger plants. Kharan saw vibrant-hued birds swoop down on animals twice their size and kill them with a beak through the eye; she saw giant, venomous lizards basking in a shaft of sunlight a few yards from their hideout; she watched at least a dozen huge insects, whose bites she knew to be fatal, marching along twigs inches from her face.

'If we even survive this forest, it'll be a miracle,' she thought gloomily.

Evening came too soon for Kharan's aching limbs. She had stiffened up during the uncomfortable day's rest, and every step brought throbs of pain to her legs, shoulders and blistered feet. But Melkavesh was merciless, and forged on swiftly through the treacherous vegetation. After her own encounter with a spider when she had first come to Earth, she was only too aware of the dangers of Gorethria's wildlife. As they went, she cast around with a net of sorcery which kept away the nocturnal biting insects and also gave a faint light by which they could see their way. Great ferns stroked them as they passed, moisture fell on them from the trees, and fungi burst under their feet, scattering spores.

Kharan was almost asleep on her feet, trudging onwards like an automaton, when a flapping thing came screeching at them out of the night. Melkavesh saw it off with a well-aimed fireball of sorcery, but from that moment on Kharan's tiredness fled, and she jumped at every cracking twig, saw monstrous shapes lurking in every shadow.

'Calm down, it was only a bird,' Melkavesh said with a touch of irritation.

'A dear little bird,' Kharan responded acidly. 'I've been watching such birds putting the eyes out of foxes and deer all day.'

'Don't exaggerate,' Melkavesh snapped. 'And come on, you must be able to walk faster than this . . .'

But Kharan could not. The going was uphill, and the ground was criss-crossed with deep furrows which were covered by undergrowth. Despite her sorcery, even Melkavesh stumbled at times. When they rested at the top of a particularly steep incline, Kharan was gratified to observe that the Sorceress was out of breath.

'I don't like this,' Melkavesh muttered. 'Whenever I use my power it makes us vulnerable to being located by Ah'garith. Still, at present we have to take the risk.' Kharan shivered. The alternative to the ghost-light that protected them and made sinister shadows leap out of every tree, was total darkness in which huge, poisonous insects lurked. She gritted her teeth and swallowed her panic, as she had done many times that night.

The darkness terrified her and she longed for the dawn; but when it came, things seemed no better. Her imagination transformed the sway of branches and rustle of leaves into Gorethrian soldiers with giant hounds. She almost wept with relief when Melkavesh found a dry hollow concealed by bushes, and pronounced it suitable for them to hide for the day. This time she slept as if dead, and only woke with extreme difficulty when Melkavesh roused her to keep watch.

When the third night came, and most of it was still ahead of them, Kharan was actively wishing she was dead. She felt totally unsuited for such travelling; there was no part of her body that did not ache and tremble with exhaustion. Her eyes hurt, her throat was raw and she had a perpetual stitch. Fear itself was as tiring as physical effort, yet it was fear that made her struggle on when her body cried out to give up, to collapse against a tree and escape into sleep or death. Thus she forced herself on through the blackness of that night; and just when it seemed it would go on for ever, a rosy twilight shimmered through the crimson leaves, and they saw the edge of the forest ahead.

'Wait,' Melkavesh said, and she closed her eyes and cast about with her far-seeing ability to check if there were any Gorethrian patrols nearby. Presently she said, 'It is safe. Come on.'

'But it's nearly light. Hadn't we better stay in the forest until evening?'

'Oh, we can soon find somewhere to sleep. I want to look at the mountains first.'

Kharan was not sorry to leave the blood-red forest behind, but she would have slept better that day if she had not first been induced to gaze on the dreadful terrain which lay ahead of them. They emerged from the trees onto a sweep of rough grass, carpeted with spear-shaped purple flowers. It stretched towards the skyline, narrowing in the distance to a track leading between two great soot-black knolls of rock.

The sight of them filled Kharan with dismay. 'Well, you've seen them. Can we rest now?' The wind found its way to her sweat-damp neck, and she shivered.

'Not yet. I want to climb higher. I can't see anything from here,' Melkavesh replied. She had a faraway look in her eyes, and Kharan knew it would be a waste of breath to try to dissuade her. The Sorceress strode briskly up the sweep of grass, and presently struck up the side of the nearest knoll until she had gained the peak. Kharan toiled after her, cursing.

And from the knoll, it seemed they could see the world. The forest lay below them like a blanket of crimson velvet, softened by a dawn mist. To their left and right, it lay in tongues between the folds of the mountains; to the West, from whence they had come, it stretched almost as far as they could see. In their headlong flight, they had not realised how far they had come from Shalekahh and they were both amazed to see the city shining on the far horizon, a pearl set

242

in an oyster-shell haze. They had put fifty miles between themselves and Xaedrek.

Then they turned to look eastwards at what lay ahead, and Kharan's heart sank. The mountain range rose like a wall in front of them, thousands of feet of sheer coal-black rock towering grimly against the violet sky. The Emethrian mountains, which must be negotiated before they would be free of Gorethria.

And do I want to be free? Melkavesh thought. Bitter-sweet emotions turned in her chest; she loved Gorethria, loved Shalekahh and the way of life, the history and the colours and the mood, everything that made Gorethria what it was. But because of Xaedrek, she must turn her back on her country and even – her heart lurched – betray it. Yet something else was calling her. Involuntarily she raised her hand to touch the double-orb talisman which Irem Ol Thangiol had given her, and she remembered the sweet Kristillian hills reflected in his eyes. And behind everything, her own sorcerous destiny loomed like a vast backdrop against which the Earth itself was dwarfed. There was darkness, but it was not frightening or suffocating; rather, it was as clear and boundless as space, a glassy midnight sky in which moons sailed joyfully. Whatever lay ahead was both inescapable and desirable, and its exhilarating essence seemed to be captured within the mountains. As soon as she laid eyes on those peaks, she loved them, and she could not wait to set foot on their slopes and feel the frosty wind on her face.

Kharan, by contrast, instantly loathed them. With the sun behind them, they seemed to consist not of rock, but of black nothingness. Gloom and reasonless fear filled her, and she pulled her cloak round herself and clasped her arms over her stomach. The mountains seemed to swallow all light, and she had a petrifying intuition that they would also swallow the only thing that had made her life seem worth clinging to.

Melkavesh made an eerie figure, as dark as the rock on which she stood, except for the golden hair framing her face. She turned to smile at Kharan, and her green-gold eyes shone with excitement. 'Aren't the mountains beautiful? Xaedrek and all his legions cannot stop me now!' she exclaimed, and laughed.

I know. That's what I'm afraid of, Kharan thought, but dread clogged her throat and she could not speak.

Irem Ol Thangiol lay on a couch, restrained by thick leather straps. His face was set in a grimace of pain, and his head was thrust back as his muscles convulsed involuntarily against his bonds. Amulin raged in his veins like molten glass; the euphoria of power had long turned to agony.

Xaedrek sat by the couch, watching him impassively. The lighting in the room was dim and brassy, and it came from a source which Ol Thangiol could not see. It backlit the Emperor's hair with a coppery halo and gave a sheen to his dark skin. His face had a strange carved beauty, and he looked . . . serene. Yes, Ol Thangiol thought bitterly, he observes my suffering and he is serene.

Vapours floated in the air and all seemed the colour of old bronze and tarnished gold, blurred and claustrophobic and thick with tainted sorcery. Amnek was somewhere in the chamber, but the Kristillian was beyond registering his presence. He could only see Xaedrek.

'Now, shall we try again?' the Emperor asked in a pleasant tone. Ol Thangiol felt the knife slicing into his arm, and he felt his blood draining from the wound. His arm seemed to be on fire, and the room turned grey. When he came round, Xaedrek was stemming the flow with a tourniquet, and he could see the ornate bronze bowl standing on a table nearby. It brimmed with ichor, and the red surface swirled with streaks of gold.

'The amulin changes your blood, Ol Thangiol,' said Xaedrek. 'I have never encountered this effect in anyone else. You are also unique in that the more amulin you are given, the more powerful you become. I'm afraid I have given you far too much, and it is causing you pain – if so, I apologise. This is our last experiment for today. Afterwards, you may rest.'

But these solicitous words sounded like ghoulish mockery to the Kristillian. For days Xaedrek had forced him to take huge doses of the powder, and the result had been terrible agony, like lava boiling within him. As for the power it brought, they had made sure he was unable to use it. Ah'garith had induced such terror in him that it had removed his will to resist. Since then, Xaedrek had kept him under control by the use of various drugs which dulled his wits. Kristillia, Melkavesh, everything he believed in, were still within him somewhere, but blurred and buried deep. On the surface all was confusion and agony, and he could barely gather his thoughts to understand what was happening, let alone fight it.

He felt he had lain on the couch for eternity with Xaedrek bending over him, conducting an endless chain of painful, meaningless experiments. Yet he sensed the Emperor's mood changing, becoming quieter and more intent. A discovery was imminent. Through his swollen, tear-misted lids, Irem Ol Thangiol saw Xaedrek stand up and cradle the bowl of blood carefully in both hands. It looked like red wine.

'Well, if this works, I will have Melkavesh to thank for the gift of far-sight,' he said thoughtfully.

Irem Ol Thangiol found the anger to rasp, 'I pray that you fail.'

'Don't pray for that, Kristillian,' Xaedrek replied indifferently. 'For if I fail, my experiments upon you will continue until I succeed.'

9

A Sorceress Born

ALL NIGHT Kharan and Melkavesh scrambled around the base of the forbidding mountain wall. Out of the forest, the starlight was clear enough for them to see their way, so Melkavesh did not need to use her power. The mountainside gleamed like obsidian in the faint radiance, and it was rough and cold under their hands. Millions of years had weathered scars and faults deep into the rock, so that the surface was scored by ink-black shadows. Kharan followed Melkavesh with her heart in her mouth, convinced that they were certain to plunge into a chasm at any second.

But Melkavesh seemed confident and climbed on without hesitation. Presently she turned to the left and began to forge steeply upwards, and Kharan was forced to follow, fighting her reluctant, trembling limbs at every step. Finally, to her relief, the ground levelled out; Melkavesh had found a pass into the range. It was a relief to be able to walk upright, although the path was treacherous with loose stones.

Just before dawn they came out into a valley. The Emethrians soared all round them, hostile and barren, but on the valley floor there was grass, and Melkavesh pointed out a sparkling cascade of water at the far end.

'We can follow that stream into the heart of the range. That will solve several problems for us.' Kharan was too tired to do more than nod in acquiescence; she yearned for the moment when they found a suitable hiding place, and she could slough off her pack, curl up in her cloak, and sleep.

Gorethria had very little farmland; most of their food came

from the fertile bowl of Patavria, which had been under Gorethria's domination long before the rest of the Empire was taken. However, herds of goats were kept by certain wealthy families who lived on the fringes of the Emethrians, and wild antelopes roamed the mountain valleys. Although the heart of the mountains would be deserted, as yet they were only just within the edge of the range, and Melkavesh knew there would be numerous Vardravian goatherds and Gorethrian hunters about. They must be cautious. The stream would be essential to their survival, but it was also a magnet to anyone else wandering the mountains.

At twilight the next evening they emerged from their rock cleft and struck upwards alongside the noisy torrent of water. Hardy trees leaned at grotesque angles from the bank, heavy with heart-shaped amber nuts. On either side of the stream were sloping fissured walls of jet-black rock. It was an unfriendly environment which Kharan could not stand, but Melkavesh strode briskly through it like a queen surveying her realm.

'Mel, you seemed to know this stream was here, but I've never seen you look at the map,' Kharan said. 'Is that part of your power?'

'I studied an art known as the Way between Worlds. It's related to sorcery, certainly, though not quite the same. But it enables me to sense the geography of an area from a distance, without prior knowledge. So don't fear, Kharan, we can't get lost.'

'Well, it's comforting to know that one of us knows where we're going, at least,' Kharan grimaced. As she spoke, Melkavesh's face changed and she seized her arm.

'Someone's coming. Quickly.' Swiftly the Sorceress cloaked them both against being seen, and half-pushed, half-dragged Kharan up an outcrop of rock to the side of the stream. There, sweating and breathless, they heard the clatter of hooves on rock, and they saw six riders pass below them.

It was an Imperial patrol. The horses glowed fiery-gold and the guards' cloaks gleamed palely in the half-light. Kharan

247

thought she would faint with terror as her heart struggled feebly to pump the blood round her body. She hung onto Melkavesh's arm, but when the patrol had cantered out of sight, she forced herself to control her fear and remark calmly, 'Mel, we should have stolen a couple of horses. We could have travelled so much more swiftly.'

'Yes, but think: on foot we can go where horses can't follow. Besides, they need a lot of looking after, and would only make us more visible.'

Kharan parted her lips to reply, but at that moment the retreating hoofbeats became louder again. The patrol was returning. Evidently the path had become too steep for the horses. As the six riders clattered below them and disappeared into the gloom, Melkavesh grinned at Kharan and winked. 'You see? They've had to turn back. The deeper we go into the range, the harder it will be for a mounted party to follow us.'

'They can always get off and walk,' said Kharan gloomily.

'It doesn't matter. Don't you see? If Xaedrek is still sending soldiers after me, it means that he and the demon have failed to locate me by extramundane means! Come on. It's safe to go now.'

They scrambled down from their refuge and trudged on. Towards the end of the night the way widened, but still those sable peaks loomed above them, and Kharan shuddered at the sight. Tiredness oppressed her spirit, and she felt as though the mountains went on for ever, and she would never escape them. She ached to the very core of her bones, her feet burned and she was wretched with fatigue, but Melkavesh seemed to be suffering no discomfort at all, as if her mind was on higher things and she could walk for ever without food or rest. At times, Kharan could not help wondering if she was truly human. Undoubtedly Melkavesh's feelings for Xaedrek were stronger than she would admit; how then could she appear to be so unaffected by what had happened between them? But Kharan quickly came to realise that Melkavesh had an ability to sever herself from her emotions, and channel them into positive action. Just as

Xaedrek could. Perhaps those suppressed feelings would one day recoil upon her; or perhaps at the core of her being she was truly heartless. Whichever was the case, it made her a dangerous woman.

Kristillia lay in central Vardrav, east and somewhat north of Gorethria. There was one easy way to it; a route known as the Vardrav Way, which led north from Shalekahh, past the black city of Zhelkahh, and thence through the soft green country of Omnuandria. It was a broad, easy route which avoided the forests and cut between two mountain ranges. But it swarmed continually with Gorethria's legions, merchants, and other travellers, so Melkavesh had chosen to take the difficult path, turning east through the depths of the Emethrians and thence through Mangorad. A path suicidal to an ordinary traveller, but she was not an enchantress for nothing.

'When you originally came to Shalekahh, was it through Omnuandria?' Melkavesh asked as they resumed their journey the next night.

'No, I came across the South of the continent, from Bagreeah,' Kharan answered. 'I thought that journey was bad enough. But at least we travelled at a reasonable speed in daylight, and were able to make a proper camp every night. This is going to kill me, Mel.'

'Nonsense. You're unfit, that's all, you'll soon get used to it,' Melkavesh replied unsympathetically. 'Listen, this is the easy part of the journey. Further on the mountains may be totally hostile – no food, no water, icy weather. If it comes to it, I know ways of travelling swiftly by sorcery, but I don't have the strength for that at present. So unless we become desperate, we have to rely on our feet, and you'll just have to put up with it. We'll survive.' Kharan felt disgruntled at her lack of concern, but then she recalled the pain that Melkavesh suffered, uncomplaining, every time she used her sorcery. She felt slightly ashamed. Her self-respect stirred, and she became determined that, however wretched she felt, she would prove that she was not such a 'liability' after all.

Thus their journey began. As the days went by, their

path diverged from that of the stream, but the mountains abounded with springs and they rarely found themselves far from water. They harvested nuts from the hardy waterside trees as they went, and so were able to conserve their provisions. Nevertheless, they both felt perpetually hungry and even the rough, slightly bitter flavour of the nuts seemed increasingly palatable. Sometimes they caught fish from the stream, and Melkavesh would light a small fire – using a spark of sorcery – on which to cook it.

Soon they were beyond even the most isolated human habitation, and Melkavesh deemed it safe to travel by day. As soon as it got light, they would set out and march steadily for four or five hours, then rest for an hour or so while they ate. After another five hours' walking – with brief rests along the way – they would find a suitable place to make camp for the night. It was not hard to find niches in the mountainside in which to sleep, usually not far from water, but there was never any relief from the discomfort of resting on hard rock. They took it in turns to keep watch in four-hour stretches, but Melkavesh always let Kharan sleep first, and often did not wake her at all. Alone, she could have travelled much faster, so keeping to Kharan's pace she did not become so tired.

Sometimes she felt impatient with Kharan's slowness; the mountains exhilarated her, and she felt she wanted to run, ascend the highest peak she could see, and shout for joy. The physical discomfort of the journey meant nothing to her, which was due partly to a naturally tough constitution, and partly to her sorcerous training. She tried not to take her impatience out on Kharan; but she would often leave her side to run or climb ahead, as much out of excitement as to see what lay in front of them.

Kharan, by contrast, was suffering. She could not understand Melkavesh's high spirits, and resented her apparently boundless energy. To her the journey was something to be endured, not relished. After the initial agony of fleeing Shalekahh, she had become fitter; her raw feet had toughened, and her legs no longer ached and trembled with

250

weariness at the end of a few hours' walking. She had even become used to sleeping on a hard surface with only her cloak to cushion her. Her terror of being pursued had subsided in the daily, rhythmic monotony of walking, but it was replaced by a feeling of permanent fatigue and hunger. She was surviving, but only just, and she knew in her heart that she would never fully adapt to the rigours of the mountains. In spite of Melkavesh's sorcery – without which the journey would have been impossible – she felt that if they did not reach civilisation soon, she was certain to fall ill, even die.

But worst of all were the mountains themselves. Every morning when she woke, the grim peaks confronted her; all day they surrounded her, while she tramped wearily over their cold, rough slopes; at night they rose like slabs of ebony shadow against the sky, a midnight abyss that flowed all around her to the edge of the world. They seemed at once impassive and voracious, oblivious to her, yet intent on swallowing even the smallest spark of life that dared to stray among them. They even haunted her dreams, and their weight seemed to be pressing down on her head, and she would wake weeping.

But she did her best to bear up and tell herself that things could have been harder. Melkavesh's wayfinding ability was invaluable in guiding them through the range. Sometimes she would consult the map to ensure that her skill was not misleading her, but mostly she went by instinct. She tried to minimise the amount of climbing they had to do by keeping to valleys and passes between peaks. Often it was impossible to avoid ascending a steep slope, but she always found a way that Kharan could manage, and they never had to retrace their steps.

So far the weather had been kind to them. Gorethria's climate was hot, if highly unpredictable, for most of the year. Here in the mountains it was much cooler, which made it comfortable for travelling, but not enough to chill them at night. There had been no more storms since the day they had fled. Melkavesh loved to watch the changing skies as she walked and breathe in the different atmospheres. To her the

251

mountains were always beautiful, whether gleaming like roughly faceted jet under a china-blue sky, or looming massive and purplish through layers of billowing mist, or dusted by starlight. The map told her the name of every peak, and she recognised each one as it came into view in the distance, to draw nearer day by day until at last they were scrambling over the rocks beneath its lofty summit. The Hunter, the Eagle, Ordek's Peak, Mount Eskesh . . . she knew them all by heart, like old friends.

Since they had hidden from the mounted patrol on their second day in the mountains, they had seen no signs of pursuit. Melkavesh cast about with her far-seeing skill at regular intervals, but there was no one within a hundred miles of them in any direction. Kharan did not exactly feel relieved by this piece of good news; to know that they were so isolated from other humans only served to make her feel eerily alone. Although grass still grew sparsely in the more sheltered valleys, here there were no domesticated animals, only herds of small black antelopes. Sometimes birds of prey hovered overhead, watching the herds but never attacking them. It seemed no human hunters pursued the antelopes this far into the mountains; the creatures only had feline predators to fear. Melkavesh and Kharan often saw mountain lions on the prowl, beautiful animals whose black coats were striped with golden yellow and a rich, smoky blue.

Once they frightened one off its prey, and it fled with a snarl of rage, flicking its tail. The rest of the herd were still bounding away in the distance, clinging surefootedly to the sides of a steep gully. They were well camouflaged against the dark rock. Melkavesh knelt down by the fallen antelope, ran her hands over its smooth, black coat, and said, 'Those mountain cats are skilful killers. It's dead.'

'Well, help me carry it over to those bushes, and I'll make a fire,' Kharan suggested, but Melkavesh shook her head. 'What's the matter? I for one am sick of nuts, and we can't waste this chance of a good meal.'

'The simple fact is, Kharan, I don't know what to do with it – how to skin it, or whatever. So we'd better leave it.'

'Just because *you* don't know –' Kharan gasped, half-amused and half-annoyed. 'Listen, I am not as useless as you seem to think. I was not always a "lady of leisure", and I haven't forgotten the few skills I acquired as a slave. Now, are you going to help me carry it or not?'

While Melkavesh built a fire from the sparse supply of wood and lit it by sorcery, Kharan took Anixa's knife and expertly prepared the antelope for roasting. They ate well that night, and there would be enough meat to sustain them for the next two or three days.

Melkavesh looked at Kharan, no longer rosy-faced but drawn and pale in the fire-glow, and decided she had underestimated her. Melkavesh was not totally insensitive; she knew the An'raagan was having a hard time, but felt that showing sympathy would not help. Kharan often protested at the speed at which they had to travel, or expressed a desire for several days' sleep in a soft bed, but there was always a touch of self-deprecating humour in her complaints – and sometimes anger. While she could laugh or get angry, Melkavesh knew that her spirit was intact, and that she would survive. But at other times Kharan seemed deeply depressed, and Melkavesh suspected it was more than exhaustion that put her in a black mood. She had tried asking her what was wrong, but Kharan would only turn away, murmuring, 'Nothing. I'm just tired.' So now Melkavesh no longer asked, telling herself that it was undoubtedly continuing grief over Falmeryn. She worried about Kharan more than the An'raagan could have guessed. Still, the important thing was that Kharan – despite pessimism about her stamina – had kept going with a stubborn determination that Melkavesh admired.

'I think I've misjudged you, Kharan,' she remarked with a grin. 'You're tougher than you give yourself credit for.'

'Let's hope so,' Kharan replied, licking meat juices from her fingers. 'Listen, this is the first time I've felt replete since we started this wretched journey. Why can't we hunt instead of scratching about for nuts?'

'Do you happen to have a bow and arrow about your person?' Melkavesh said, raising her eyebrows.

'But we don't need one. You're a Sorceress.'

'My Oath forbids me to use sorcery to slay animals,' she answered sharply. 'I may hunt for food by normal means, but not using my power.'

'You killed those hounds,' Kharan pointed out.

'That was self-defence, which is permitted.'

'This is another kind of self-preservation.'

'Perhaps.' Melkavesh's tone was low and troubled, full of conflict. 'But I have broken my Oath so many times since coming to Earth. I have taken memory, which is forbidden. I have stolen and practised deception. I have aided evil, and I've attempted to kill. The School would strip my white mantle from me and disown me.'

'With such incredible standards of perfection, I don't see how they can expect people to accomplish anything at all,' Kharan said. Melkavesh did not seem to appreciate this remark, and glared angrily at her.

'You don't understand. The Oath is everything. The Oath makes me a Sorceress. If I have not the strength to keep it, then I do not deserve to be called by that exalted title.'

'But you only did what you had to, and if you've made a few mistakes –'

'Mistakes!' Melkavesh cried. 'I've had ten years to make my mistakes. The Oath should only be taken by those who have achieved perfection. On Ikonus I would be called a renegade now. I did not come here to become a renegade. I will not break my Oath again.' She was still staring straight at Kharan, but her green-gold eyes had become glassy. Kharan knew that she was lost within her own thoughts, and was not even seeing her.

'You're right, I don't understand,' she muttered. And suddenly she sensed acutely the gulf that lay between them. How distant Melkavesh seemed, how far removed from human concerns; she lived in another world, a world of cold, high places, of incomprehensible Oaths and esoteric principles. It was as if Melkavesh stood on a mountain top

254

with nothing between herself and the stars, and she could stretch out her arms and embrace their incredible power, comprehending that which ordinary mortals could not even see. Like a god, she understood all and was afraid of nothing, not even the fierce winds of space. And Kharan meanwhile crawled about the base of that mountain like a mouse, for ever unable to touch that glory or even understand it.

She bowed her head, clasped her arms across her stomach. A mist began to fall like fine rain, and on it she could taste the bitterness of granite and imminent bereavement. The fire went out. Night towered around her. *I should have told her*, she thought. *I might have told her, except* . . . Except that now Kharan knew there could never be any real communication between them. Melkavesh lived on a higher plane, divorced from mundane problems, and there was nothing to be said.

Then Kharan understood something (or thought she did, for fear and fatigue had drained her of rationality): Melkavesh belonged to the mountains, heart and soul, but she, Kharan, was an intruder who was bound to be punished for trespassing among them. Punishment, that's what it was. And Kharan hugged her stomach and thought, *Oh my love, forgive me. Forgive.*

They had now been in the mountains for about fourteen days. As Melkavesh had predicted, the going was becoming much harder. The valleys were as bare as the slopes above them; the nut-bearing trees grew more and more stunted until they ceased altogether; there were no antelopes on the rocks, nor fish in the streams. It grew colder and colder, and the air seemed thin. Melkavesh still strode on as if nothing could daunt her, her hair flowing like a golden flag over her black cloak. But when they had tackled a particularly steep rock-face, she was unusually breathless and even admitted to feeling dizzy. Her fitness might have been insufferable, but Kharan found any signs of vulnerability in her alarming.

The weather changed. Banks of sullen cloud would frequently roll over the harsh peaks, while a bitter, dank wind blew rain into their faces. If they were unlucky, a thunderstorm would break, forcing them to take shelter under an overhang or in a cleft. There they would remain for hours, watching lightning flickering from the dense purple clouds to cast an eerie, multi-coloured glow onto the mountainside before them.

'Xaedrek used to say this weather was due to the Earth changing, some sort of manifestation of power,' Kharan remarked, huddled miserably with her hood drawn up against the rain dripping into their shelter. 'Well, you know about such things, is it true?'

'I don't know enough,' Melkavesh sighed. 'But the weather, sorcery, sunlight, everything – they're all part of the same power. So Xaedrek is right. But on this Earth, there is some secret to the power which I've yet to unlock.' Again she became lost in thought, and Kharan regretted mentioning it.

That night – their sixteenth in the mountains – Melkavesh had a strange dream. She could see nothing, but felt she was lying on a wooden raft on an ocean, drifting with the gentle swell. Presently she became aware of stars, one or two bright points at first, then scores, then thousands, as though her eyes were slowly adjusting to the night. But something was wrong. In two great, round areas of blackness, no stars were visible. It was as if something had swallowed them.

Then she realised that she was not seeing circular voids, but two spheres obscuring the starlight. These two great globes of rock seemed at once very close to her and very far away, and at the sight of them a mixture of fear and excitement caught in her throat. The spheres were jet-black, but now she could perceive starlight glimmering round their edges, and could sense the mass of them; millions of tons of rock poised to crush her.

She tried to cry out, but could not. The weight was on her chest, and slow, heavy waves of luminosity were pounding through her, emanating from the spheres. The raft beneath her capsized, and she felt the cold waves swallowing her. The heavy beats of energy were forcing her deep into the black water and she began to drown. In panic, she flailed and struggled; and suddenly, although the sensation of pressure and drowning persisted, she could see clearly.

Rippling as through sunlit water, there was a female child with red hair, and perched on her hand was a bird the colour of dark red amber, and Melkavesh heard the words, *I am very close to you now* – and just as she understood the significance of the dream, she woke up violently, and the meaning was lost.

She sat up, trembling. So real and terrible was the dream that she could not dismiss it as mere fancy. She remembered how she had dreamed of Xaedrek – and he of her – long before she knew he existed. But however hard she tried, she could not regain that last, poignant moment of understanding. Cursing, she climbed to her feet, stepped over the sleeping Kharan, and scrambled over the boulders which lay in the entrance to their cleft.

Dawn was just coming to the mountains, giving the faintest rosy sheen to the higher peaks, while the valleys remained in inky shadow. She climbed a few yards up the mountainside and stood with her hands on her hips, a chilly breeze blowing at her cloak and hair. They were in the heart of the Emethrians now, a hostile, black stonescape where no one wandered without dire need. There was frost in the air, and the mountains were harsh as a starless winter night, with no snow to relieve their starkness. They formed an effective barrier that protected Gorethria's long border. Surely no one could survive what lay ahead? Melkavesh reached out with her senses, and saw a network of chasms, and sheer, unscalable walls. Every path they might have taken petered out on the brink of an abyss or under a vertical rock-face. There were no springs nor sources of food, nothing but ancient rock. Freezing cold gales hurtled across the peaks and the clouds were swollen with hail. If they were to traverse this cruel land and survive, everything depended on her power – the capricious power on which she could no longer rely. Yet the mountains did not frighten her, or if it was fear, she relished the cold, sharp taste of it. This was still Gorethria, and she loved its savage wildness as much as she loved the civilised beauty of Shalekahh. Her heart had never been in the gentle valleys of Ikonus. It was here.

The two moons were visible as lacy crescents blending into a violet sky. Melkavesh gazed at them, drawing her cloak round her against the wind. There was a single bird up there, drifting in silhouette on the high air currents. An eagle, by the look of it. She watched it for a while, then turned and went back to the shelter.

She woke Kharan, then foraged in their packs for something to eat. Kharan surfaced reluctantly from sleep, not wanting to face another day's walking through the heartless mountains. Her neck was stiff, her back and stomach ached, and she was cold. She dragged herself into a sitting position, while Melkavesh created a sorcerous fire from a single twig. It was more a glow than a flame, but it was enough to warm them, and to heat water with herbs to make a sustaining hot drink.

'You look pale,' said Melkavesh. 'Are you feeling unwell?'

'It's just so cold,' Kharan sighed, hunching up in her cloak. 'I'll be all right when I've eaten something. Gods, how I hate these mountains. I'd do anything to be whisked back to Shalekahh. I'd happily be Xaedrek's kitchen maid for ever!' She grinned, doing her best to make light of her discomfort. They divided a ration of nuts, dried fruit and cheese between them, but Melkavesh noticed that Kharan was eating slowly, without appetite.

'Are you sure you're all right?' she asked. The last thing she needed was for her companion to become ill.

'Yes!' Kharan snapped. 'I've got a chill on my stomach, that's all. I'll be perfectly fine.'

'I hope so,' said Melkavesh, giving her a curious glance, 'because we are going to need all our strength for the next part of the journey. From here on there is no vegetation, and no water – except what falls out of the sky as ice. And the mountains are becoming all but impassable.'

'Oh, good,' Kharan said drily. 'It wouldn't do for things to get too easy for us, would it?'

Melkavesh smiled. 'Before you start cursing me, I've some better news. I told you I know ways of travelling swiftly. I've been saving my strength for this part of the journey. We'll be on the other side of the mountains in days, not weeks.'

Kharan's large eyes met hers, shining in the firelight. 'How?'

'The simplest method is one I found easy on Ikonus. It may be more difficult here, it depends on how much it drains my strength. When we're ready to leave, I'll show you. It's easier than explaining.'

Soon they had shouldered their packs and were standing on a bleak stretch of rock. The sun took a long time to rise above the mountains, and although it suffered the eastern sky with a lemon glow, the travellers were still engulfed by shadow. Kharan looked up, and felt mist sifting onto her face, and saw a black eagle circling high above them. She felt numb. She desperately needed to believe that they would escape the mountains after all, but hardly dared hope for anything.

Meanwhile, Melkavesh was lashing together some slender branches, which she had been carrying, without explanation, for two days. At each end of a central branch, about four feet long, she attached two similar lengths. Then at one end she tied a third, slightly curved limb, at an angle to the others. Severing the twine with her knife, she carefully arranged the wooden frame on the ground. 'This nut-wood is not ideal, it was hard to find pieces long enough. But it doesn't matter, all that's needed is a light, basic skeleton to channel the energy.'

When she said 'skeleton', Kharan realised that the branches resembled, very crudely, the structure of a horse – neck, back, four legs . . . She watched in amazement as the Gorethrian woman grasped the 'spine' and began to summon her power. A familiar aureate glow surrounded her dark hands, spreading slowly along the branches. Presently she straightened up and lifted the skeleton so that it stood squarely on its four stick-legs. The whole thing was now glowing with a misty, golden radiance that gave off a slight warmth. Melkavesh's hands rested on the spine, and her eyes were closed, yet Kharan got the unsettling impression that her irises were shining through the lids.

Soon she let go of the branch-skeleton, and stepped to Kharan's side. The structure stood without support, and the radiance continued to swell and become – not brighter, but richer and more intense. And when Kharan blinked, she was certain that she could see the transient image of a true horse's skeleton within the glow. Not sticks, but bones; the great vertebrae of the spine and arched neck, the sloping scapulae and the big joints in the hips and legs. Light filtered through the ghostly silhouette of a rib cage, shone from the eyeless sockets of a huge, dark skull.

Kharan stared at it, her mouth dry.

Somehow she expected it to transform into solid flesh, but it did not. The radiance took on the shape of muscles, then the contours of skin, even a plume of light where the tail should have been, but it remained transparent. It stood before them, motionless. Then she heard Melkavesh whisper in a strange language, but somehow she knew that the words meant, 'Now I command you to live.'

And the sorcerous steed bent its neck and lifted its feet and turned towards them, prancing a little. Saffron light streamed like pollen from its mane, pale fire splashed the rocks under its hooves.

Melkavesh grinned broadly at Kharan's expression of astonishment. 'Now, are you ready?' she asked. Her eyes were brilliant in the golden glow. 'I'll mount first, and you can sit behind.'

'But – I – you mean it can bear our weight?' Kharan gasped, shaking her head. The horse turned side-on to them, and stood patiently while Melkavesh vaulted onto its back, just as if it were a flesh-and-blood steed. With her hair flowing palely against her black cloak, the sorcerous charger beneath her, she made a weird and other-worldly sight. Kharan could hardly find breath to speak. 'But how are you doing that?' she demanded.

'Extramundane energy gives the horse its shape and mass.

260

My thoughts control its movements. So come and jump on behind me, it won't throw you.' Melkavesh smiled and winked. 'Unless, of course, I want it to.'

'This is the most incredible thing I've ever seen. Xaedrek never did anything like this.' Kharan approached the horse's flank nervously, took Melkavesh's hand, and vaulted on. Beneath her, it did not feel exactly like a real horse – there was no texture of hair, no real solidity. It was real, yet insubstantial, like air contained within a bubble. She held firmly onto Melkavesh's waist, feeling decidedly precarious.

At the Sorceress's command, the spectral steed began to canter forwards. Its hooves made no more than a faint scraping sound on the stone. As it gathered speed, Kharan squeezed her eyes shut, trying to forget that nothing more than a bubble of sorcery kept her from being flung onto the rocks. When she dared to open them again, her stomach sank. The ground appeared to be some eight or ten feet below them. The horse was skimming the air at twice the pace of an earthly steed, and over Melkavesh's shoulder Kharan saw a vast black abyss ahead of them.

She gave a strangled exclamation, bit her lip, held her breath. The chasm swooped beneath them, its sheer sides plunging into a bottomless well of shadow. Vertigo seized her and she clung convulsively to Melkavesh's cloak. But the Sorceress said calmly, 'It's all right, Kharan. You won't fall.'

Suddenly they were on the other side, effortlessly ascending a rugged slope of rock which would have taken them hours of toil on foot. 'To avoid that chasm, we would have had to have made a detour of some fifty miles,' Melkavesh informed her. 'And there are more ahead.'

'Oh. I see,' Kharan whispered with what little breath she had left. The words ended in a strangled gasp of horror as a sheer black cliff hurtled towards them. She pressed her face into Melkavesh's cloak and braced herself for the impact, only for her stomach to lurch as they swerved wildly, upwards. After a moment she raised the courage to look, and found they were ascending an all but vertical rock-face.

Her fingers locked rigid on the Sorceress's waist, and she wondered if she would ever breathe again.

'Don't look down,' Melkavesh suggested, although what use she thought this inane piece of advice was, Kharan did not know.

'I'm trying not to look at all,' she replied through clenched teeth. And just as the rock levelled out, and she began to sag with relief, another abyss sliced through the mountain, and her heart turned over again.

Thus their strange flight continued. It took Kharan perhaps an hour to believe that they really were not in imminent danger of falling, and another to become used to the horse's strange galloping motion. When she did, she began to find the movement lulling and dreamlike. Presently her fear faded altogether and she kept falling asleep, her cheek resting against Melkavesh's back. As she dozed she remained vaguely aware of the black mountains rolling thunderously beneath them, the sullen clouds resting on their peaks, and an ice-filled wind stinging one side of her face. But it all seemed distant, a dream landscape which could not harm her. For a few hours she basked in a warm sense of security . . .

'Kharan, wake up.' Melkavesh's voice roused her. She looked around groggily and found they were at a standstill on a night-black mountainside, with the horse glowing like a dying fire under them.

'What's wrong?'

'Nothing. We've been travelling all day and it's time to rest, that's all. Jump down so I can let the horse go.' Kharan slid to the ground, and even as Melkavesh dismounted, the pale outline of the creature flickered and faded and was gone. A loose skeleton of branches lashed together with twine clattered onto the rock. The Sorceress picked it up, and Kharan shook her head in awe, unable fully to grasp the miracle she had experienced. She was about to ask why they could not have travelled like that from the beginning, then she saw the greyness of Melkavesh's face, and the painful slowness of her movements, and she knew the reason.

'Mel, how are you feeling?' she asked anxiously. 'Very tired?'

Melkavesh nodded. Her bones felt like granite and there seemed to be steel spikes impaling her forehead. She moved like a dotard, gnarled and crippled. Such was the penalty for extended use of her sorcery. But she gritted her teeth and said, 'All I need is food and a good night's sleep. We've travelled a very long way – two more such days should see us beyond the mountains. I'm optimistic. I could never have done so much with my power when I first came to this Earth.'

It was not that the pain had grown less, just that she could wield her theurgy for longer before it forced her to desist. Desperate to find rest, she began to limp slowly up the mountainside, where she had sensed the presence of a suitable cave. It was almost dark, but there was still a stormy light in the clouds, enough to show the sharp, black silhouette of an eagle circling overhead.

For no particular reason, Melkavesh suddenly felt suspicious and stopped to look at it; then realisation hit her, a great, cold wave of dismay. 'Gods!' she breathed. 'By the Sphere!'

'What is it?' Kharan cried, alarmed.

'Kharan, quickly, run for that cave,' Melkavesh rasped urgently. 'No, not that way, damn it, can't you see it?' Seizing her arm roughly, Melkavesh hurried her towards an inky slit in an outcrop, hardly visible to Kharan's eyes. It was further than it looked, and the way was steep. Slithering on loose stones, bruising their limbs and grazing their hands, they scrabbled breathlessly into the entrance.

It was only a narrow corridor running back into the mountain, but it provided a feeling of security, solid rock walls to shield them. Melkavesh collapsed onto the stone floor, so drained by this last effort that for several minutes she could do nothing but lie on her back, sucking in ragged breaths, her eyes squeezed shut against the knives throbbing in her head. Kharan watched her anxiously in the gloom, feeling an icy sense of panic. Presently the Sorceress managed to sit up, and open her eyes. Her chest rose and fell convulsively. Kharan held a flask of water to her lips and she swallowed several mouthfuls before gasping, 'That eagle.'

'Yes, I saw it. What about it?'

Melkavesh coughed and drew in a deep, uneven breath, fighting her debility. 'Why didn't I realise earlier? It's been following us. All day.'

'Surely not – what makes you think it's the same one?'

'By sorcerous instinct, far-seeing, of course!' she snapped. She was furious with herself. 'I should've known the moment I saw it. But I didn't, I was too busy thinking about the horse. Now, because of that so-clever horse, I've cut a blazing trail for anyone with far-sight to follow. And so they have.' She gripped Kharan's arm painfully hard, and said grimly, 'Xaedrek's found a way to watch us.'

'How?' Kharan exclaimed. It was all but dark in their refuge, and shivers ran along her limbs as if dark wings were rustling around her, fanning her with icy air.

'I don't know yet.' Melkavesh's voice was rough with suppressed anger. 'And I won't know until I've recovered my strength. I need to far-see properly, to find out what Xaedrek is doing, and how. But that takes energy, and at present I have none. Damn him. Damn my stupidity!'

'Will the eagle attack us? Or is it just spying?'

'For heaven's sake, Kharan, *I don't know*!'

'There's no need to bite my head off,' Kharan said indignantly. Despite her fear, she had a strong need to prove that she could cope. She took her cloak off, removed her pack, and produced a packet of flat, close-textured cakes made mainly of flour, oil and dried fruit. 'Obviously there's nothing we can do at present. Have something to eat, and get some rest. I'll keep a look-out.' She gave a cake to Melkavesh, took one herself, and went to crouch just inside the entrance, staring up at the darkening sky.

Clasped in one hand she had a knife, and the cake from which she took intermittent mouthfuls. In the other she held her cloak. For a time, all was quiet; she could see nothing, and hear only the desolate moaning of the wind and the

264

rattle of hail on the rocks. Behind her, Melkavesh had fallen into a deep, much-needed sleep.

When the attack came, she found there was no time to think about being frightened. First she felt the air current on her face; then came the sound of slow, ominous wing-beats, descending towards the refuge. She strained to see into the darkness, but could perceive nothing. She stood up, gripping the knife and cloak, her whole body poised to defend herself, adrenaline pounding through her to transform her terror into anger and determination to fight.

The flapping was close now; she made a wild guess, swung the cloak in a desperate arc, and bruised her hand against the rock wall. She cursed, but hardly registered the pain. The eagle was just above her, she realised, and it was huge. She swung the cloak again, and this time she felt it catch in the bird's claws. For a moment they engaged in a frantic tug-of-war, and she found out with a shock just how strong the bird was; it felt like two men pulling against her. She braced her legs and leaned back, but she was being dragged into the open — then the cloak suddenly came free, and she staggered backwards into the cave. She heard the heavy whirr of wings as the eagle sought to recover its balance and circle round for a second attack. Its wing span seemed vast. Undoubtedly it was too big to fly into the narrow cave. If it landed and tried to walk in, she could only do her utmost to try to drive it out.

The eagle made no sound as it swooped again; it would have seemed less sinister if it had squawked its aggression. Kharan felt the cold air fanning onto her face, sensed the huge black shape descending towards her, the outstretched talons. Despite the chill in the air, her skin prickled with sweat. She could hear her own pulse thudding in her ears, and her breathing seemed unnaturally harsh and loud. She gripped the cloak, trying to judge the eagle's position. But judgement was impossible. It was almost on her, and she felt paralysed, off-balance, as if she were caught in a strong underwater current. Feathers rustled round her head, claws caught in her hair. Desperately she flung out the cloak and lost hold of it. There was a faint sound of flapping, something turning over and over in the air. Then silence.

Kharan crouched down in the entrance, listening. All she could hear was a variety of rushing noises on different levels; the wind, hail, her own heart pounding. Her cloak lay somewhere on the rocks, but she dared not creep out to find it. And somewhere above, Xaedrek's eagle glided in circles, biding its time.

All night she stayed awake, huddled anxiously in the mouth of the shelter, alert and poised against another attack. All night her senses played tricks on her, telling her that a dark shape was flapping down to attack her, or that something was scraping and clattering towards her over the rocks. Each time her heart would leap, her muscles clench in readiness; and each time nothing happened. Her imagination magnified the weather sounds, and her skin was over-sensitised to every stirring of the icy air. And although she knew this, she dared not risk relaxing her vigilance; and so she remained at her post, shaking with cold, tension and fatigue, throughout that interminable night. And Melkavesh, meanwhile, did not once stir from sleep.

Sorcery, Melkavesh dreamed, was like the sea. The tide came in and went out. And she needed this long, deep sleep of utter exhaustion while the tide of power flowed slowly back into her. Ah, but what controls the ebb and flow of the sea? The moons, her dream-thoughts reminded her, the two sweet ivory moons whose names were just on the edge of her memory . . .

The dreams that plagued her – while Kharan fought a different battle in the conscious world – were not nightmares, but they were frightening. Over and over again, she dreamed of the ocean and two great and terrible globes of rock. And she dreamed of Xaedrek. *The Empress Melkavesh's secret was simply that she would do anything, anything at all for Gorethria*, he was saying. He was pointing, not to a portrait, but to a woman, and that woman was herself, dark-skinned, golden-haired, dressed in Imperial robes. *I will do anything for what I believe in*, she said; and Xaedrek replied, *Then remember that Gorethria tolerates no half-measures*.

Ashurek and Silvren were in the dream, confronting her, and with them was a silver figure which she knew to be Ah'garith. *This is an abomination*, Ashurek said, glowering at the demon. And Silvren added with despair in her voice, *You should have destroyed the demon. You must destroy it. It cannot be suffered to live* . . . the dream went on and on, a long, repetitious and painful journey, and waiting at the end, as Melkavesh had known she would be, was the red-haired child. But this time she was not distant and serene; she was close and real, and she turned to Melkavesh with fear in her eyes and cried out, *Help me*.

Melkavesh woke up violently and found Kharan bending over her. 'Mel, what's wrong? You called out.'

'Did I?' She sat up stiffly and rubbed her eyes. 'I was only dreaming. Oh, it's dawn. I can't remember the last time I slept so deeply. Did you sleep well?'

'Oh, wonderfully,' was the sarcastic reply. 'I've spent all night frozen stiff in the entrance, watching out for our aquiline friend. He made two or three attempts to visit us, and I don't think it was to discuss the weather.'

'Why on earth didn't you wake me up?' Melkavesh exclaimed.

'Because you needed to sleep.'

'You should have woken me up!' she blazed, jumping to her feet. 'To face it alone, all night, was sheer, reckless stupidity.'

'Oh, was it?' Kharan retorted. She stretched her stiff limbs and ran her fingers through her hair, which was becoming long and shaggy. 'Has it struck you that if you hadn't had enough rest last night, you wouldn't have had the strength to travel today? That would've been even more stupid. Just because you're annoyed with yourself for not being perfect, there's no need to take it out on me.' She turned away and went to look out of the entrance, her arms folded.

It seemed she had hit a sore point with Melkavesh, for the

Gorethrian fell broodingly quiet. After a few seconds she went to Kharan's side and said in a quiet, cold tone, 'Well, where is it now?'

'The eagle? I don't know. It only got light a few minutes ago, and I haven't been stupid enough to go outside yet.'

Melkavesh glowered at her, and shook the creases out of her cloak. 'Well then, we'd better go and look for it,' she said brusquely.

There was no sign of the bird in the sky, so they began to venture cautiously down the mountainside. Presently Kharan spotted her cloak, lying in a crumpled mound and crusted solid with hail. It could have been taken for a rock in the half-light. 'How did I manage to fling it so far?' she muttered. She strode over to retrieve it; but at the last moment she jumped back with a strangled cry. The cloak was moving.

Melkavesh caught her up and saw the reason at once. The eagle was underneath, tangled up in it. Only one wing was visible, outstretched and trailing on the ground, the primary feathers broken. But it knew they were there; the cloak lurched violently, and the fierce head with its iron-harsh beak was thrust out at them. Kharan retreated rapidly. There was something pitiful about the bird, despite its great size. She realised that the last time she had flung her cloak at it, it had been knocked out of the air and entangled in the garment, and had been struggling all night to free itself.

'Didn't you know you'd grounded it?' said Melkavesh in surprise. 'Well, come on, let's catch it.'

'Is that wise? It still looks dangerous to me . . .'

'I need to investigate the creature more closely. I must find out how Xaedrek came by this power, and how much he knows. Get round the other side of it. When I give the signal, we'll pounce.' Kharan edged reluctantly closer to the eagle. Its huge beak stabbed at their legs and its eyes blazed with black fire, but the cloak hampered it and it could not touch them. Together they seized the bird, and Melkavesh succeeded in folding its injured wing into place and bundling it up in the garment. With its eyes covered, it stopped struggling, but it still took both of them to lift the creature and manhandle it back to their shelter. They put it down carefully in the centre of the cave, and Melkavesh told Kharan to hold firmly onto it while she freed its head from the cloak.

The eagle stared angrily at them, opened its beak and uttered a sound somewhere between a hiss and a squawk. It was a magnificent creature, ebony-dark with beautiful grey markings on its neck and feathered legs. But Kharan could not pause to admire it. Even injured, it was tremendously strong, and she could only just hold it still by wrapping her arms round it and half-lying on it. She could feel its talons digging into her arm, even through the thick material of the cloak and her jacket.

'If it can see us, Xaedrek will know I'm alive, won't he?' Kharan gasped as she struggled with the eagle.

'Not necessarily. It may only be able to "see" my powers. Therefore if I don't use them, I become "invisible",' Melkavesh said. 'Of course, I have to use some sorcery to see into its mind – that can't be avoided. Don't worry if I appear to go into a sort of trance, but don't speak to me, and at all costs don't let our friend go!'

Kharan watched anxiously as the tall Gorethrian settled herself in a cross-legged position. The bird was half on her lap and she was cradling its head in her hands. Her liquid-gold hair hung over her face as she bent dangerously low over the aggressive, open beak. She looked considerably better than she had the night before, although she was obviously still deeply tired, but Kharan found it hard to feel any real sympathy for her. When Melkavesh uttered words of concern, Kharan sensed there was no real feeling behind them; and the Sorceress wanted no sympathy for herself. True friendship, even a degree of affection between them, seemed impossible. Melkavesh was too distant, too wrapped up in higher concerns. She only spoke to Kharan to give orders, and Kharan only replied to argue with her. What had made her think that a Gorethrian, even a half-Gorethrian, could ever be a true friend? she thought bitterly. Not that she really

269

cared; it was just one more thing to make the journey colder and lonelier.

Melkavesh looked into the bird's round black eyes, slowly losing herself in their depths. Then she let go of the physical world and loosed herself on a shaft of sorcery into the creature's mind.

The creature was in pain and afraid, but it was a simple matter to release healing energies which soothed it. As the bird became quiescent, she sensed the emotionless, fierce hunting instinct that lay beneath the surface. Now its mind lay open to her, and she knew that she had not been wrong. This was no ordinary wild creature, but one whose hunting instinct was triggered by sorcery, and whose only prey was her . . . She drifted deeper through the layers of its mind, becoming lost in the labyrinth. The eagle had no conscious memory as such, but there were sense memories, the feeling of wind under outstretched wings, and beyond that, a feeling of imprisonment in an alien place, human hands and faces around her. She was now seeing the past through the eagle's eyes, using the creature as a vessel to filter out the precise information she wanted.

The scene slowly became clearer, but it had a curious quality of distortion. She saw figures in a dim room – which she realised was one of the subterranean chambers within the mansion – but it all seemed two-dimensional, elongated and flattened. The air had a rippling, underwater quality and the illumination was the colour of brass. Vapours writhed sluggishly about the ceiling as a tall, thin figure slanted across her vision. It was Amnek. She wondered briefly why Shavarish was not there. Then she saw Xaedrek sitting by a low black couch, intently watching the prisoner who was strapped to it . . .

With a shock she recognised the Kristillian, Irem Ol Thangiol. Why had he not escaped? She had healed him, yet now he lay prostrate with sweat pouring from him and his muscles stretched taut as wire. He was clearly in terrible pain. Xaedrek was bending over him, apparently draining a large volume of blood from a knife wound in his arm. Far-seeing was an objective process in which it was all but impossible to feel emotion; reaction would come later, but for now she could only observe. And she saw Xaedrek cradle the bowl of blood in his fine, dark hands, and she heard him say, 'If this works, I will have Melkavesh to thank for the gift of far-sight.'

'I pray that you fail,' Irem Ol Thangiol gasped, and Xaedrek replied, 'Don't pray for that, Kristillian. For if I fail, my experiments upon you will continue until I succeed.' He was drifting towards her now, saying, 'Amnek, assist me with the eagle, will you?'

With a great effort, Melkavesh practised a technique known as 'mirroring', which meant that although she was still within the eagle's mind, she could see the scene from outside, as if looking in a mirror. And she saw the proud, beautiful eagle chained to a perch in the corner of the room. Amnek was holding its head and prising the beak open with a gloved hand, while Xaedrek balanced the bowl on one hand and carefully filled a glass dropper with the red liquid.

'This magnificent creature was netted on the edge of the Emethrians two days ago, on my command,' Xaedrek said. He gently slid the dropper into the beak and let the blood trickle down its throat. 'I gave him a mild drug to quieten him, but that will wear off soon. I think he is hungry . . .' The Emperor continued to feed it with droppers of blood until the bowl was almost empty. The eagle showed no ill-effects; if anything, it seemed to relish this liquid meal. Xaedrek put the bowl down and absently stroked the feathered head with one finger. 'Now, we will see.'

A door opened and Ah'garith drifted like a fish into Melkavesh's field of vision. 'The rebuilding of the machine is progressing well, Sire,' she said. 'It will be ready for use tomorrow.' Even through the dense, brassy atmosphere, Melkavesh saw at once that there was something different about her, a glow of amulin power.

'Good. Well, Ah'garith, you are just in time to witness something interesting.'

'What are you doing, Sire?' the demon hissed.

'The principle is simple. Explain to Ah'garith, would you, Lord Amnek?' Xaedrek said, moving towards the couch and looking down at Irem Ol Thangiol.

'Of course.' The distortion of the scene made Amnek's unnaturally tall, lean frame seem even more sinister, like the elongated shadow of a gargoyle. With him, too, something had changed; there was emotion in those usually cold, scientific eyes, a haunted look of bereavement. 'As you know, amulin lends curious qualities to the Kristillian's blood. Our experiments have led us to believe that if the blood is given to another creature, there is a linking of minds. Whatever the eagle sees, Irem Ol Thangiol can also see.'

'Ingenious,' Ah'garith muttered, standing in front of the eagle. 'If it works.'

Xaedrek bent over the Kristillian, whose eyes were squeezed shut. 'Tell me, Ol Thangiol, what can you see?'

His jaw rigid, the prisoner choked out, 'I see the demon.'

Amnek raised his eyebrows. Ushering Ah'garith out of the way, he stood before the bird himself and said, 'Ask him what he can see now.'

'Nothing,' was the reply. 'But the demon is still there . . . silver. A silver lamp.'

'I was right,' said Xaedrek thoughtfully. 'He sees Ah'garith's power, not Ah'garith herself. But it's enough. Now, Ol Thangiol, I want you to tell me if you can see the Lady Melkavesh.'

The Kristillian groaned and twisted in his bonds. 'Distant. A golden glow, no more than a star. She's gone, you won't find her.'

'Ah, but I will. Listen to me, Irem Ol Thangiol.' He held the Kristillian's sweat-drenched face between his hands. The man's heavy lids half-opened, revealing yellowish, bloodshot crescents. 'We are going to release the eagle now, and you are going to pursue that golden star in your mind. And when the eagle catches up with her, you are going to tell me exactly where she is.'

'No,' he gasped. 'I will never tell you that.'

'Ah'garith.' Xaedrek beckoned with a light, graceful gesture. The Shanin floated through the honey-thick air and put her face near to Ol Thangiol's, smiling benignly. She did not touch him, but Melkavesh sensed terror oozing from him like sweat. To him the demon's human form was a flimsy illusion behind which there was a creature of nightmares, a grinning thing without a ghost of conscience or reason. Even in the emotionless vacuum of far-seeing, Melkavesh shared a moment of his dread, the excruciating point at which control is lost and only unconsciousness or insanity can follow. She shuddered with sickness.

'So you see, Ol Thangiol, either you tell me or I leave you with Ah'garith again,' said Xaedrek flatly. 'Until I find a better method, you will be my eye upon the world. Once we have located Melkavesh, you will cause the eagle to kill her.'

Amnek shook his head. 'She deserves worse, for Shavarish's death . . .'

'She deserves worse for existing!' the demon added.

Xaedrek turned slowly, and even through the dim, rippling atmosphere, Melkavesh saw those familiar features clearly. How calm, gentle and magnanimous his face seemed; yet what power radiated from those beautiful jewel-like eyes. 'I will have no talk of revenge. A swift, clean end is all that is required,' he said quietly. On the couch, the Kristillian's large frame began to shake convulsively. With his brow knotted and his lips drawn back from his teeth in a terrible grimace, he was weeping like a child.

There was more Melkavesh needed to know. She sifted through scenes past and present, gathering the scraps of information to complete the picture. And when she knew enough, she allowed herself to drift back into the eagle's mind and sail with it on the wind currents as it winged its way across the Emethrians. Clouds rolled around it, rain lashed its feathers, but neither the weather nor the hostile

273

landscape below could daunt it. The mountains were its kingdom. And its flight was guided by a golden beacon which drew it, burning now bright, now dim, sometimes lost altogether, then flickering to life again. The beacon was her sorcery. And suddenly the light became dazzling; that was the moment at which the eagle had sighted them, and Irem Ol Thangiol had been able to tell Xaedrek exactly where she was.

Could he see her now? she wondered, allowing herself to slide into the present. For an eerie moment, she saw herself through the bird's eyes, her dark face intent, her green-gold eyes brilliant but unfocused. Then she travelled back along that blazing beam of sorcery, and found herself in Irem Ol Thangiol's confused and tormented mind, felt his lips part and heard his voice shaping the words as if she had spoken them herself: 'She has captured the eagle. She knows . . .' Then she saw Xaedrek's face, just as if he was really there and very close to her. And in an intense, un-nerving moment of mutual recognition, she knew that he had seen her. The Earth paused in its orbit and ceased to exist; they were two souls flying through space, all conflict annihilated.

Melkavesh fell backwards with a cry, bruised her head on the rock, and came back to herself. Squirming away from the eagle, she pressed her hands over her face and shuddered with dry sobs for several minutes, unable to stop. Kharan, still holding onto the bird, stared at her in alarm.

Finally Melkavesh regained her self-control. Panting hoarsely, she pushed her dishevelled hair back from her face. Her eyes were so wild that Kharan recoiled, almost releasing the eagle; and in the same instant, Melkavesh plunged forward without warning, seized the eagle, and, with one deft movement, wrung its neck.

There was a silence. Kharan swallowed. The bird was dead, but she was still hanging on to it as if by reflex, not registering that it was safe to let it go. Presently she croaked in a small voice, 'Why did you do that?'

Melkavesh took several deep breaths before she was able

274

to reply, 'I had to. Xaedrek could see me. If we'd let it go, it would have continued to follow us. In fact, we're lucky it didn't kill us.'

'By the gods, Mel, you look absolutely petrified,' Kharan exclaimed. 'What on earth did you see?'

Still visibly trembling, Melkavesh stood up and tried to shake some life into her numb legs. 'Let's throw the bird outside. Then I'll tell you. Poor thing, it was the most innocent party in this, but it's the one to pay.'

'That's typical enough,' Kharan said bitterly. The eagle's body tumbled limply onto the cold mountainside; a wind stirred its feathers, and in death it looked smaller, rather pitiful. Hail began to crust its glossy black wings. Kharan shook out her cloak, but could not bring herself to put it back on for the time being. They returned to the shelter, and Kharan asked, 'Well, what happened?'

'By the Sphere,' Melkavesh said, rubbing her forehead as if to erase the lines of distress. 'I don't know where to begin. The Kristillian I told you about, Irem Ol Thangiol, he took the amulin I gave him, but instead of escaping, he went down and wrecked Xaedrek's machine.'

'Good for him!' Kharan exclaimed.

'No, it wasn't. In the process, he killed Lady Shavarish.' Kharan was about to acclaim this news as well, but Melkavesh's expression made her think better of it. The Sorceress went on hoarsely, 'I liked Shavarish. I never planned for anything like this to happen. I can't believe she's gone. Her husband, Lord Amnek, is absolutely distraught. I thought he had no feelings, but I was wrong. He blames me for her death, and he is right, I suppose. Irem Ol Thangiol is another innocent who is suffering for what the rest of us have done. I gave him the amulin to help him, but obviously that accursed stuff can help no one. Xaedrek captured him and discovered that it gave him a special power which could be used to far-see. Now he is Xaedrek's prisoner.' She knotted her hands together and stared down at them. 'Gods, Kharan, if you had seen him! He was in agony. Agony,' she ended in a whisper.

'I'm sorry,' Kharan said faintly. 'But at least he destroyed the machine . . .'

Melkavesh shook her head. 'They've rebuilt it since. The amulin process goes on. And Xaedrek is more deeply entrenched with the Shanin than ever – he's started to let her take amulin. No good can come of it. But the Kristillian . . .' It was the nearest Kharan had ever seen Melkavesh to tears, and her eyes were shadowed by exhaustion and distress. 'Xaedrek will gain further powers from him, I know. Next time there will be five eagles, or ten, or something worse. And when Ol Thangiol is dead, there'll be other Kristillians . . . Come on.' She suddenly jumped to her feet, her manner switching in a flash to one of businesslike urgency. 'The sooner we go, the sooner we'll be in Kristillia.'

As Kharan stood up and put on her travel-worn cloak, Melkavesh was already outside, conjuring the supernatural horse. Only in the clear morning light did Kharan notice that the mountainside on which they stood angled into a chasm below them and a vertical wall above; without sorcery, they could not have escaped it. Hail clattered against the sable rocks, and the wind stung her eyes. The weather was turning noticeably colder. She hugged herself against the persistent ache in her stomach and thought with longing of fire, hot food and a warm bed.

Yesterday's journey, once she had got used to the mode of travel, had seemed almost pleasant; today's was hellish. Melkavesh was tired from far-seeing, and the horse was very insubstantial. She seemed to have less control over it, and instead of skimming smoothly over the edges of chasms, it would drop sickeningly before she could straighten it out. Kharan hung on until her arms went numb, praying for it to be over. She felt ill, and pain clawed at her abdomen; several times she had to fight not to pass out. Melkavesh seemed to be pushing herself beyond her strength, and Kharan knew that if her power failed for an instant, they would both be killed. But – as always – she was wholly at the Sorceress's mercy. And Melkavesh was in such a black mood that Kharan did not even dare to suggest that they stopped for a rest.

276

The black mountains veered dizzily beneath them. Gusts of ice-cold wind buffeted them. Then they galloped into a storm, and everything was obscured by billowing iron-grey clouds. Dazzling spears of white and blood-red lightning rent the atmosphere with ear-splitting cracks. Wild air currents flung them from side to side, sucked them up through the clouds, then dropped them again. Kharan's terror began to approach hysteria, and only the fact that she was paralysed with fear and cold prevented her from screaming and flinging herself off the steed.

Then it began to hail. This was no light covering, but a punishing deluge; the air was suddenly thick with stones of ice, pelting down on their cloaks and stinging their faces. Soon the hailstones became pebbles, then great chunks, and Kharan cried out with pain as they battered down on her cloaked head.

'Mel,' she whispered desperately. Her throat was sore, her voice almost lost. 'Mel, you must stop!'

She thought the Sorceress had not heard, or was deliberately ignoring her. She felt the horse lurch, but between the solid wall of hail and the blinding flashes of electricity, she could see nothing. They were travelling upwards again – and suddenly, there was blackness and comparative silence. The horse vanished, and Kharan crashed to the ground with a gasp of shock and pain.

The next thing she knew, Melkavesh was bending down and pulling her to her feet. A burst of lightning flickered on damp rough rock and Kharan hazily registered their surroundings; they were in a cleft, sheltered from the storm. Outside, the hail roared onto a grim mountainside.

'For once I agree with you,' Melkavesh said breathlessly. 'I couldn't sustain my power through that. I sensed a cave nearby, so here we are.'

'And where are we?' Kharan asked, pulling back her hood and rubbing at her bruised head with cramped fingers. 'Not that knowing will make any difference. My sense of direction deserted me days ago.'

'A peak called Mount Karvish. It's the greatest mountain

in the Emethrians.' From nowhere a faint, bluish sphere of sorcery appeared, its light revealing that the cleft led back into a cave. 'I thought so,' Melkavesh said. 'Come on, at least we'll have room to rest comfortably tonight.'

She led the way into the cave, moving as stiffly as an old woman. After only a few minutes the glowing sphere faded; she did not even have the strength to sustain it. They sat on the rock floor in darkness, with only the flicker of lightning on the rough, coal-black walls to give them light. Melkavesh stretched out on her back, utterly spent.

'You'd have tried to go on through that storm if I hadn't said stop, wouldn't you?' Kharan said. 'Melkavesh, you're pushing yourself too hard.'

'I'll be the judge of that,' she replied abruptly. She was inwardly frustrated at her lack of stamina, furious with the power itself for causing her such pain. 'Damn it, I need my power. I can't afford this weakness. What the hell is causing it?'

'I don't know. But getting angry and fighting isn't going to help. More likely, it will kill you.'

'Kharan, I really would be grateful if you'd keep your thoughts to yourself,' Melkavesh snapped. 'You don't know anything about it. Go to sleep.'

'All right, I will,' she retorted coldly, turning away. She heard Melkavesh taking a ration of cake and cheese from her pack, but Kharan's stomach turned at the thought of food. Having eaten, Melkavesh lay down and fell asleep almost at once, but Kharan could not sleep. She hunched up miserably in her cloak, but the cold seemed to have penetrated to her bones. Whether she lay down, sat up or even walked round the cave, she could find no comfort. Every part of her was bruised and aching, and she could not stop shivering. Worst of all was the persistent, sickening cramp in her back and abdomen.

In her wretchedness, she began to suffer the distorted perceptions of a fever; it seemed she could feel the massive weight of the whole mountain above her, and that weight was slowly crushing her stomach. From the first moment she saw the mountains, she had known that they would drag her into their starless maw and obliterate her. Now it was happening. Mount Karvish was extracting its terrible, impersonal revenge and she was as helpless to prevent it as an insect ground beneath a boot. Yet it was not herself she feared and wept for, but another. One who was more innocent than the eagle.

Melkavesh woke up suddenly from a deep sleep with the distinct impression that someone had cried out. She sat up anxiously but could see nothing amiss. It was dawn, and a misty light was filtering along the narrow cleft into their cave. Outside, the storm persisted; she could hear the wind moaning and hail lashing against the frozen rock. Kharan was sitting huddled up on a rock, her arms clasped across her stomach.

'Did you call out?' Melkavesh asked. Kharan shook her head. 'But I heard – oh well, I must have been dreaming.' She stood up and stretched; then noticed with a shock that Kharan was deadly white and her eyes sunken with pain. 'Whatever is the matter?' she exclaimed. 'You look absolutely dreadful.'

'I feel it,' the An'raagan replied through chattering teeth.

Melkavesh went up to her and looked closely at her. 'You really are in pain, aren't you?' she said quietly. 'I think it is something worse than a chill.'

'I know it is,' Kharan said. She lowered her head stiffly and squeezed her eyes shut. 'I have had these pains for days, and I hoped it would pass off. But it's been getting worse all night.'

'Well then, what's causing it?' Melkavesh demanded impatiently.

'You're not going to be pleased.'

'For heaven's sake, Kharan, if you know what it is you must tell me!'

'All right.' She seemed to be struggling to find the right words. Finally she said, 'I was going to have a child. No more, it seems.' Tears oozed between her long lashes and ran down her face.

279

'What?' Melkavesh cried. 'Why on Earth didn't you tell me before?'

Kharan's eyes met hers, burning with defiance. 'Because it was nothing to do with you. Nothing to do with anyone.'

'Don't be so ridiculous. You knew this journey would be arduous. To embark on it, knowing you were pregnant, was stupid beyond belief –'

'Don't call me stupid!' Kharan flared. 'I couldn't stay in Shalekahh, I couldn't leave – but I had to choose one or the other, and it was you who insisted I come with you, if you remember. I wouldn't mind being insulted, if you were doing it out of concern for my welfare. But I know for a fact you're only angry because this threatens to interrupt your precious journey.'

Melkavesh's anger subsided abruptly at this. She asked in a low voice, 'How long have you carried the child?'

'Nearly four months,' Kharan replied through clenched teeth.

'And is Xaedrek the father?'

'No, he is not!' she answered with icy rage. 'The child is Falmeryn's.'

'I can't imagine what possessed you to be so careless,' Melkavesh commented. 'If I'm to help you, you must come and lie down.'

Kharan did not move. 'I'll tell you something, Melkavesh. It was not carelessness. I think I always knew I was going to lose Falmeryn. I wanted something by which I could remember him, hold on to him. For a time after you rescued me, I no longer cared about the child, but when you'd gone to Xaedrek and I thought you weren't coming back, it started to matter again. All that kept me going was thinking, "At least now our child will live." But now even that is being taken from me. I know I should have told you, but I couldn't. My life has always been commanded by others – the Gorethrians, Xaedrek, you. Falmeryn and his child were all I had that were truly mine. My secret. Now I pay.'

Melkavesh put an arm round her shoulders and said gently, 'Kharan, I'm sorry. I'm more concerned about you than you realise. Perhaps it's my fault for not showing it. Gods, if only you'd told me before!'

'I don't see what you can do about it. It's inevitable. I knew it would happen from the moment I set eyes on these accursed mountains,' she muttered.

'Have you forgotten than I am a healer?' Melkavesh cried, exasperated. 'Now do as I say. You'll have to undress, and we'll wrap you in both cloaks. Lean on me.'

Kharan let herself be helped to a low shelf of rock which jutted out from the back of the cave. With one of the packs under her head as a pillow, she lay on her side, doubled up and shaking. Melkavesh examined her and said in a gentle and grave tone, 'There is blood. The child will leave your body very soon now. I want you to understand that I can do nothing to save it, it is too late. All I can do is ease your pain and heal you. You'll fall asleep, and when you wake you'll feel much better.'

I don't want to wake up, Kharan thought. Never had she felt more wretched than at this moment; even the time when she knew Falmeryn was dead, and had thought her own life about to end, had seemed less black than this. Her mouth was full of the bitter taste of the storm, and the walls of a lightless abyss reared around her. *I should have told her. Too late, too late . . .*

Thoughts echoed round her tormented mind as she felt the spark of life leaving her. The last thing that linked Falmeryn to the world and to her was dying, slaughtered by the lofty, pitiless mountains, or by Xaedrek, or by herself . . . Whose fault it was no longer seemed to matter. All bereavements are hard, but this was unbearable, because she had not understood just how much she needed the child until it was too late. *I'm sorry, so sorry*, she said to the unborn baby, over and over again; and at last, *if you die, my love, I will die also*. And so she gave herself up to the abyss.

Melkavesh knelt over her, saddened. If Kharan had a fault, it was that she lacked self-esteem. She believed herself to be weak, so in compensation she had become too stoical. And I have not helped, Melkavesh thought. I have not been a friend to her. I've treated her hardly better than a Gorethrian his slave. No wonder she could not confide in me.

With this thought, she bent to the task of healing Kharan. Tragic as the loss of the baby would be, she told herself, perhaps it was for the best. An infant would only have complicated Melkavesh's plans. A silver-blue radiance emanated from deep within her and glowed softly around her hands, gradually spreading to envelop Kharan's whole body. Melkavesh closed her eyes and left the physical world behind, letting her senses drift out on a beam of theurgy to discover how ill Kharan was and how best to heal her. The storm raged on outside their refuge, but she was oblivious to it. She was floating in a warm darkness like the pulsing of blood across her own eyelids, seeing nothing, aware only of a rhythmic, searing ache which was mindless yet utterly set on its one goal of extinguishing life.

Ah, there was the child. To Melkavesh it appeared as a mere light-mote in a swelling ocean of crimson, a tiny, fluctuating spark. Soon it would wink out altogether. It was too far gone to be saved, and the Sorceress knew she could do nothing to restrain the savage red waves which were thrusting it prematurely into the world. It was almost over. She could only assist the process, making it gentler and less agonising; and this she was doing, when a dazzling arc of light streaked across the darkness and plunged into her mind.

It was the greatest shock she had ever had, either mental or physical. Astonishment made her helpless; she knew what she had seen, but she could not believe it. Fragments of a dream flickered round her, a voice whispering, *I am very close to you now*, imploring, *Help me . . .* But the voice came from inside herself, not from the child. Such a tiny speck could not even know that it needed help, let alone call out for it. And yet it could contain that brilliant, unmistakable light which was the last thing Melkavesh had dreamed of witnessing.

Within the embryonic child was the latent gift of sorcery.

Incredulity and excitement danced through her. It would

be the first natural Sorcerer on this Earth since Silvren, the *first*. Melkavesh had come to Earth to assist the birth of sorcery, though she had never expected it to be so literal an event. This was it, the beginning – and at once, her joy was flooded away by panic. The baby, from being merely inconvenient, had become unique and precious beyond description – and it was about to miscarry and die. There was nothing she could do. Even as the revelation came, there was a surge of blood and the helpless scrap of life was expelled.

No. I will not let you die, she shouted inwardly. At once she withdrew her attention from Kharan and focused it all on the foetus. Hardly visible, hardly human; yet the faint pink glow of life had not quite left it. She seized on that atom of vitality, fed it with her own power, like a breath of oxygen reviving a dying fire. But what use was it? No baby so premature could survive. There was only one way to save it, which was to instil the child with all the energy and nurture it should have received during its natural term within its mother.

Impossible. Even on Ikonus, she had never heard such a feat mentioned, let alone attempted. Yet it was her one, fragile filament of hope, and in her desperation she would have tried anything. This was more than a mere child. It was the very essence of the Earth's future.

She cradled the bloody scrap of flesh in her palms. Power flowed from her in streams of gold, silver and blue fire, power crashed and curled about the cave, power eclipsed even the lightning. The storm fed the current of magical electricity until her whole form glowed like a white sun. Never before had she dared to summon such theurgy. Power rained on the foetus in dazzling crystal arrows; power transported them both beyond the tangible world to a dimension of pure light.

For hours Melkavesh poured her strength into the child. She sweated and bled sorcery, far beyond caring about the physical pain or even noticing it. Even when she had wrung herself dry, from somewhere she found a hidden reserve, and she drew herself up, breathed in lightning and began

283

again. And in her hands, the foetus began to grow. The minuscule body blossomed like a red flower, putting out tiny limbs, becoming more recognisably human. It began to move. Hope and excitement filled her, and she poured out a torrent of amber and azure light as if she meant to shred and sacrifice her very soul to create the miracle.

It was not enough. Even as hope grew, it faded. The foetus had increased in size, but still it was barely longer than her hand, too tiny and frail to survive. She needed three, four times the amount of power to bring it to term, and she was all but spent. The light of sorcery faded. A gloomy twilight settled in the cave. Melkavesh returned to reality and saw nothing but greyness and blackness, and Kharan's body bent in the angles of troubled sleep. She became aware of the excruciating hardness of rock digging into her bruised knees, the leaden weight in her spine and the knives stabbing into her head. She could hardly feel her arms and legs, they were numb. But none of it mattered, because she could not save Kharan's child.

She looked down at her hands, and for the first time saw the body with real rather than sorcerous vision. It was perfectly formed and struggling feebly. Melkavesh's tears fell onto the child, and she whispered, 'Oh, you have the gift of sorcery too. Give me an idea, an inspiration. I would do anything to save you, anything.'

Kharan had hoped not to wake up, but she was disappointed. When she opened her eyes, she could not tell whether days or minutes had passed, but it did not matter. Nothing mattered. The weight of the cloaks warmed her, and she was no longer cold or uncomfortable; but she felt sore, exhausted and too weak to move. Now she knew what it meant to lose the will to live . . . She closed her eyes again, trying to recapture oblivion.

'Kharan, don't go back to sleep,' a voice said. She looked up reluctantly and found Melkavesh sitting cross-legged next to the low shelf of rock. 'It's evening. The storm has ceased and the sun's out.' A golden square of sunlight had found its way to the back of the cave, making everything look different; a small miracle in itself. 'How do you feel?'

This question did not even deserve an answer. When she said nothing, Melkavesh half-smiled and reached out to brush strands of dark brown hair from her forehead. 'You will feel better, after a couple of days' rest. And so will I.'

'Mel, I don't want you to think me ungrateful,' Kharan murmured through dry lips, 'but I've decided it would be best if you went on alone. You don't need me, and I would quite like to die.'

'Don't say any more.' Melkavesh put a finger on her lips. 'I've got something to tell you. You'll find it hard to believe, but it's true. Your child is not dead.'

'Gods,' Kharan gasped, as if this was one more thing to torment her. Then a glint of life returned to her eyes, and she raised her head stiffly and exclaimed, 'What do you mean?'

'It's all right. Listen to me. The child miscarried, but I saved its life by sorcery.'

With a superhuman effort, Kharan sat up. 'It's alive? I don't believe you. How can you say such a thing? You've gone mad.' But Melkavesh's eyes were serious, intent, gathering the evening sunlight and reflecting it back like two glittering seas of hope. After a moment Kharan breathed, 'You mean it. I don't – I don't understand. Show me.'

'I will. Be warned, the baby looks strange, but don't let it alarm you.' Melkavesh raised her other hand, which had been out of sight in her lap. And in it lay what looked like a gleaming, pale red cocoon, no more than ten inches long. Very slowly, Kharan lowered herself on one elbow, as if afraid to look closely at it. Then a shuddering breath escaped her. A tiny, perfect infant lay wrapped in layers of a glistening, red membrane. Its eyes were shut but its arms and legs were moving under the transparent covering. It was like a chrysalis.

'By sorcery, I tried to make the babe grow large enough to survive. I tried too hard, and failed,' Melkavesh explained.

'I was on the point of despair, then the idea came to me: all I had to do was find a means of keeping it alive until I had rested and regained my power. So with the little strength I had left I created the membrane, a sort of caul of sorcery to preserve the child's life.'

Kharan reached out tentatively and touched a fingertip to the hairless, shining head. Her eyes were enormous, her whole expression one of awe and rapt disbelief. In a small voice, she asked, 'Can it live?'

'Just listen, I haven't finished,' the Sorceress said, breaking into a smile. 'You see, I never stopped to think that in the ordinary way, we had no means of feeding an infant. But then it struck me that it doesn't matter. Kharan, this is the best thing of all: the baby can stay within the membrane indefinitely, nurtured by sorcery, until the journey's over. Do you see what this means? The child is going to live!'

'He or she?' Kharan exclaimed. 'Don't keep saying "it".'

'She. And there's more. She is a latent Sorceress.' But Kharan hardly registered the last statement. Her arms were round Melkavesh's neck and she was weeping and laughing at the same time, tears of incredulous joy rolling down her face. If she had any clear thoughts at all in that breath-stopping tumult of emotions, it was that Melkavesh was not heartless after all. She could so easily have let the inconvenient speck die; instead, she had almost given her life to save it. Kharan had never known that such happiness could rise like the sun out of such black despair; nor that she could be proved so wrong about someone. For a long time she and Melkavesh hugged each other, all differences forgotten, with the chrysalis-child cradled between them.

Eventually Kharan drew away and took the infant in her own hands. The membrane felt strange; rubbery and slightly moist. But within it the baby felt surprisingly heavy, soft and alive. It filled her with awe to realise that this was no anonymous atom of life, but Falmeryn's daughter. Theirs. Remembering all that had happened, she wept afresh, but every sob seemed to renew her spirit, not drain it. She embraced Melkavesh again and whispered, 'I don't know

286

how to say thank you, Mel. There are no words to match this. No words at all.'

'I know,' Melkavesh said softly. Moving to sit beside Kharan, she rearranged the cloaks so that the An'raagan was better wrapped against the chill air. 'Look, if anything I owe you an apology. I am not the easiest of people to get on with, I know, and I've been very hard on you. That night you defended us against the eagle, I had no right to say you'd been foolish. The truth is, I couldn't believe how courageous you'd been. You must never, ever call yourself a coward again. To face it all night, alone, was incredibly brave.'

'Brave?' Kharan laughed. 'I've never been so frightened in my life. With one or two exceptions.'

'That's true courage.' She put an arm round Kharan's shoulder and kissed her cheek. 'And now, we must eat. I'm sure we haven't come through all this only to expire from hunger.'

Both grimy, sore and exhausted, they huddled together for warmth and shared their provisions. There was only enough food for a few more days, but they ate a substantial meal of cheese and Anixa's nourishing cake. The glow of unlooked-for joy made tiredness and discomfort recede, and it seemed impossible that they would not survive the rest of the journey through the mountains. They both desperately needed time to rest and recover, but the thought of facing the mountains again no longer filled Kharan with foreboding. Despite all their efforts, the dark peaks had lost the battle. They had failed to steal her daughter.

No barriers could survive the bond that had been forged between Melkavesh and Kharan, and for the first time there was warmth between them, and real friendship. In a way Melkavesh felt humbled, because she knew – as did Kharan – that whatever befell them in the future, however many grand designs she achieved, nothing would ever compare with the simple, miraculous joy of one tiny Sorceress's birth.

'You'll have to give her a name,' Melkavesh said.

'Yes.' Kharan hesitated, then said, 'I had already decided what to call her actually. Falmeryn told me of a ship called

The Star of Filmoriel, and I thought it was the prettiest name I'd ever heard.' It was appropriate, too. This was a miracle, there was no other word to describe it; a miracle like the first lambent dawn after the Serpent M'gulfn's death, as sweet and unlooked-for as the appearance of Miril to someone in the depths of a personal hell. Kharan looked at the infant and smiled. 'Her name is Filmoriel.'

10

Mangorad

MOUNT KARVISH was shaped like a tooth, and it soared for thousands of feet in an improbable spike whose tip was wreathed in mist. Looking up at it made Kharan feel dizzy, but it was hard to tear her eyes away. Now that she no longer feared the mountains, she began to taste some of Melkavesh's fascination with them. They were like monoliths of frozen midnight, ancient, eternal and oblivious to the upheavals of the world.

The day was overcast but calm as she and Melkavesh emerged onto the mountainside. A cold wind gusted spasmodically around them, catching at their travel-soiled cloaks. It was the third morning since the birth of Filmoriel, and although they were both far from fit, they were in danger of starving unless they moved on. 'I can do many things,' Melkavesh sighed, 'but the conjuring of food from thin air is beyond even the High Master, unfortunately.'

By partially dismantling her pack, and using the needle and thread that the ever-practical Anixa had provided, Kharan had fashioned a kind of sling which held the child securely against her stomach, leaving her hands free for climbing. She needed that freedom; confronting them was a barrier of tumbled rocks which they had to negotiate before they could find a clear path down the mountain.

Once on top of the barrier, they paused to stare in wonder at the view. Mount Karvish seemed to extend as far beneath them as above, its skirts sweeping down to intersect with other mountains in a confluence of knife-sharp valleys.

Clouds drifted below them as well as overhead. The Emethrians marched endlessly north, west and south, as otherworldly and intriguing as another plane.

To the East, however, they seemed less severe. On the horizon, in a gap between two peaks, Kharan was certain she could discern a line of purplish vegetation. She clutched Melkavesh's arm and exclaimed, 'Mel, I can see the end of the mountains! Oh, tell me I'm not seeing things!'

Melkavesh smiled. 'No, you're not. I told you we would cover a great distance by swift travelling. In a day's time we'll be beyond the Emethrians, in Mangorad.'

Mangorad, Kharan recalled, was a country of jungle. Reaching the far side of the mountains had seemed so impossible that she had given no thought to what they would have to face beyond. Suddenly the prospect daunted her, and her optimism faded; the jungle could be just as hostile as the mountains, and in more insidious and unpleasant ways. Putting a protective hand round Filmoriel, she asked, 'Do you know what to expect in Mangorad?'

'I gather it's rather thinly populated. There is only one city, Gholeth, which is under Xaedrek's rule. But we shan't be going anywhere near it. The jungle won't be so bad, Kharan, there's nothing to fear,' Melkavesh replied cheerfully, and Kharan tried to respond with a confident smile. 'We've survived the mountains, haven't we?'

'Yes, you said we would, and we have,' Kharan affirmed. The glow of good spirits which had followed Filmoriel's birth was still with them and it would take more than the thought of Mangorad to diminish it.

Before beginning the descent, Melkavesh cast around with her inner senses to ensure that there was nothing following them, no eagle hovering above. But for the first time, she could not be sure. Her usually clear sight kept shifting and blurring, and her head ached. The birth of Filmoriel had drained her so profoundly that even after three days, her power had not returned. At present she could barely near-see, let alone conjure the spectral horse; what little sorcery she could muster was needed to sustain the child. She felt handicapped and horribly vulnerable. The pain of using sorcery she could bear, but to have hardly any power at all was an anathema to her. Not knowing when, if ever, it would return, was intolerable. However, defeatism was not part of her nature, and setbacks only served to make her more determined. Today her power would return, she was certain of it.

'I won't conjure the horse as yet,' she said lightly. 'I want to conserve my strength.'

'There isn't another eagle, is there?' Kharan asked suspiciously.

'No. There's no danger,' Melkavesh replied, managing to sound convinced. She took a deep breath, trying to draw strength from the mountain's wildness and forget her anxiety. Then she began to pick a way down between the boulders.

As she did so, she felt a distinct, icy shift of the atmosphere that was not so much physical as in her mind. She paused and looked around, but could detect nothing amiss. Surely, she thought, even without her witch-sight, she would still sense danger? Reassured by this thought, she went on more confidently. But the way was steep and as slippy as obsidian, and it was not long before Kharan had to stop and rest.

'I'm sorry, Mel, I feel worse than I thought I would,' she said apologetically. 'I keep going dizzy. If I fall –'

'You won't. Lean on me, and we'll go down as slowly as you like.' Thus they negotiated the next half-mile of huge, jutting rocks and precarious ridges, both privately longing for the spectral horse. At length they reached a spring – no more than a glassy trickle bubbling from the rock – and flopped down beside it to rest.

As they sipped the ice-cold, slightly effervescent water, Melkavesh noticed with concern just how ill Kharan looked. They had only been travelling for about an hour, but already her face was ashen and her eyes bruised with tiredness. The truth was, Melkavesh had been so concerned with Filmoriel that she had failed to heal Kharan fully. She was certainly in no fit state to go on much further, and again Melkavesh cursed her lack of sorcerous power. It was appalling to think they could be stranded, so close to Mangorad.

Melkavesh reached out and touched the minute baby on her soft, hairless head, sustaining her with faint flames of sorcery. Then she put her hand on Kharan's forehead likewise, but her power faded almost at once. Kharan met her eyes with grim understanding, and said, 'I will be all right. The water has refreshed me. Save the power for Filmoriel.'

Presently they refilled their flasks, and resumed their slow march towards the valley. Kharan leaned on Melkavesh's shoulder with her right hand as they went, supporting Filmoriel against her chest with the left. Within the life-preserving membrane the child neither cried nor opened her eyes, and seemed to require nothing other than Melkavesh's sorcerous touch every few hours. Perhaps because this strange state of affairs made Kharan feel oddly superfluous in caring for her, she could not bear to let the precious infant out of her sight for a second.

Kharan's eyes were fixed on the path as she struggled to keep her feet, fighting bouts of faintness. She paid no attention at all to the weather until she suddenly felt the air turn thick and wet. Then she looked up, and found grey thunderous cloud swirling all around them.

'It's a storm,' Melkavesh announced gravely. 'It would be best to go back up and get above it, but as things are, we'll just have to carry on.' Even as she spoke, a whip of lightning cracked deafeningly across the cloud in front of them, and Kharan felt her hair stand on end. Then the rain began to slant across them in cold sheets, turning to ice as it hit the rock. With their hoods pulled up, they slithered onwards down the glassy path, hanging onto each other for support.

The sudden, violent assault of their senses by thunder, lightning and ice was too much even for Melkavesh, and it was purely instinctive to try to summon a protective aura against it. But no golden sorcery flooded her. Instead, all she felt was a juddering, jarring pain like a saw being drawn across her bones. She cried out and staggered, almost sobbing with rage, and what followed was a nightmare.

She saw shadowy figures drifting around them, then dissolving into the cloud – only to reform further ahead. But Melkavesh's senses were confounded, and she could not understand what this meant, let alone protect herself. There was no time for thought. A sudden gust of turbulence snatched them, the path was no longer there, and she and Kharan were falling.

They did not fall far. Almost at once they tumbled onto the rock, and slid out of control down the mountainside for a few yards; then the slope mercifully flattened out, and they came to rest at the foot of a great boulder. Filmoriel was uninjured, having been cushioned in Kharan's arms; and Kharan was only stunned and winded. But Melkavesh's body was a mass of pain, and she was so disorientated that she could not even speak, let alone move. And it was not the fall that had disabled her, but her last, excruciating attempt to use sorcery.

For a time they could do nothing except lie helpless against the rock, lashed by sleet and deafened by thunder and wind. The storm began to slacken off and recede towards the West, with lightning forks flickering along its edge. Mount Karvish reappeared from the storm-haze, towering over them in its awesome beauty; then it was lost again as a dense mist flowed around them.

And in the mist were those same, shadowy figures, dissolving and reforming, moving a little closer each time until they were all but surrounded. Illusion, Melkavesh thought struggling to sit up; then she experienced for the second time a weird shift of the atmosphere, and she realised the danger was not illusory but real. Her witch-sight had failed her, and now it was too late. She was as helpless to protect her companions as Kharan's baby . . .

'Kharan, I'm sorry,' she whispered. 'I've led you amiss and I've failed you . . .'

The sun appeared and turned the fog to a silver-white haze, and this time the figures did not vanish; they became clearer, like silhouettes painted on gauze. Melkavesh heard Kharan's terrified gasp, and suddenly there were faces looming all around them, glinting eyes and unsmiling mouths and the gleam of blue gems. Hands reached out to seize them and drag them upright. Melkavesh lost her footing on the icy rock, but the grip on her arm remained firm, and her shoulder was wrenched painfully as she was jerked back to her feet. She was spun round roughly, and then she saw Kharan standing rigidly in the grasp of two tall warriors, white and expressionless with shock.

In a moment of utter stillness, a gust of wind swept the mist away and revealed the valley in an ice-clear light, giving Melkavesh a vivid view of their captors. There were twelve – seven men and five women – and they were tall and muscular with slate-blue skin and fierce, strong features. Their eyes were indigo or black under slanting brows, and they had high cheekbones, large noses and pointed chins. Without exception, they were hairless, yet there was something oddly beautiful about their long, tapering skulls and shining scalps. Both sexes alike were clad only in pectorals and loin-coverings of intricately carved blue stones, held together by bronze links. The triangle and the serpent were recurring motifs, and some had bejewelled snakes twisted round their wrists and ankles. All were armed with javelins.

By now Melkavesh had recovered her wits, if not her strength. 'Can't you see we're too weak to fight you? Let us go!' she demanded, but none of the tribe replied or moved, except for one man who was approaching Kharan, staring ominously at the makeshift sling which contained Filmoriel. Kharan watched in blank horror, realising what he was going to do but unable to prevent it. Without a word, he thrust his hands into the sling, seized the cocooned infant, and wrenched it away from her.

At that, Kharan burst into life and gave a hoarse scream, She struggled, she kicked at the warriors' legs, she cried out desperately. Once she almost broke free, but they held her. The man was walking away with her child, and there was nothing she could do. For a few seconds she continued to thrash wildly against her captors, and Melkavesh also began to struggle, shouting furiously, 'What the hell is this?'

Still no one replied. Kharan suddenly went limp and slumped forward. Melkavesh thought she had fainted – until she felt a smarting pain in her own wrist, and looked down to see that one of the women was holding what looked like a plant stem. It had been sliced through at a knife-sharp angle, and a white sap oozed from the cut end. White sap and her own blood. Even as Melkavesh stared horrified at it, she felt paralysis creeping through her.

She did not lose consciousness, only the power to move and speak. Her cloak and pack were pulled off and flung away. Then, utterly helpless, she was lifted up and thrown over the shoulder of one of the men. Having manhandled Kharan in the same way, the warriors fell into line and began to walk through the silver mist, their bare feet making an eerie slapping noise on the rock.

They descended deep into the valley and moved along the base of Mount Karvish, heading eastwards towards Mangorad. Melkavesh, paralysed and hanging upside down with the beads of her captor's garment pressing painfully into her face, could see almost nothing. She lost her sense of direction, then her sense of time. Only when it grew dark did she realise that the tribe had walked all day without rest.

Nightfall left her suspended in limbo, with only the vaguest impressions by which to judge their progress. They must be walking through the foothills of the Emethrians, and the motion of the warrior striding along beneath her told her they were moving steeply downwards again. Lulled by the steady, hypnotic rhythm and unable to help herself, she fell asleep.

At some stage the tribe must have stopped to rest, but when she returned to consciousness it was daylight, and they were on the move again. For a time her head cleared, and she became aware that their path was angling down into deeply carved valleys thick with trees. But her captors must have realised she was reviving, because she felt the sting of another stem in her arm, and the unpleasant numbness of paralysis worsened. Twilight . . . the second night passed in confusion, with fragmentary impressions of a river bank, starlight gleaming on a blue-black surface, the soft, clear lapping of water as the tribe waded to the other side. Beyond, the blackness of a jungle swallowed them. They were in Mangorad.

Melkavesh only knew she had been asleep for several hours when she became aware of dim light filtering through the leaves. It was morning, and she knew that the tribe had walked all night and that the Emethrian mountains had long been left behind. The atmosphere was different, softer and warmer. Somewhere within her, a touch of resentment stirred that she had been deprived of a last look at those mountains, the chance of a dignified farewell. The image of Kharan and Filmoriel lanced into her mind, compelling her to action; but the paralysing sap was still in her veins, and she could not move.

Everything looked blue. Not the sweet, clear sapphire of H'tebhmella, but a muddy, underwater blue, the colour of a dense jungle seen through steam. The air was thick and humid, and they were surrounded by rubbery vegetation. Huge leaves stroked her as she was carried along, moisture dripped from beards of hanging moss, and somewhere a bird was repeating the same haunting, discordant notes over and over again. There were hisses, rustles, creaks.

Then the undergrowth spun round wildly, and she was lying on her back on a carpet of succulent plants with tiny round leaves. Her head fell to one side, so that her vision was obscured by the blue-green blur of vegetation. All she could see was what looked like the base of a pyramid the same deep, rippling blue as the jungle. Something was marching across her field of vision, just far enough away to be seen in alarming detail: a huge, thick-legged lizard, armoured with pewter-grey scales. She could pick out every one of those scales, and even see the green iridescence on their edges. There was a jewelled collar round its neck and a leash that disappeared beyond her sight. It walked past as if in slow motion, to be replaced by a pair of bare, human feet . . .

And then she felt hands seize her armpits, and she was dragged to her feet and held upright like a rag doll. Kharan was beside her, hanging limply in the grasp of two women, but she could not see the man who had taken Filmoriel. A hand seized Melkavesh's hair, her head was pulled back roughly, and at last she had a clear view of their surroundings.

They were in a jungle clearing. Steam hung in the air, and all around them rose great plants as tall as trees, with rubbery stems and fleshy leaves. Moss and bromeliads hung profusely from them. The vegetation was all of the same muted, jade-blue, gleaming dully with moisture. Within the clearing itself were several stepped pyramids of various sizes, built from blocks of a grey-blue stone.

More of the blue-skinned people were emerging from the pyramids and coming forward to stare curiously at the two captives. Soon a crowd surrounded them, all with the same slaty skins, harsh features and bald, tapering heads. There appeared to be a hierarchy among them: they were all dressed similarly, but some costumes were far more elaborate than others. At close quarters, she could see that most of their garments were made of interlinked tablets of bone, stained and polished to resemble semi-precious stones, but some – elders and priests – were adorned with actual gems. Those who were obviously most senior in rank led great lizards on leashes. These creatures stood about three feet high at the shoulder, and their scales gleamed steel-grey or bronze with blue and green lights reflecting on them. At once ugly and beautiful, they gazed around with unblinking golden eyes as they stalked ponderously alongside their handlers, testing the air with ever-flickering tongues.

These strange people were now walking round and round the captives, staring at them; their low voices mingled into an incomprehensible murmur. They seemed to be waiting for something. Then the conversation died down, the crowd fell back and parted, and between their ranks marched three magnificent elders. The most imposing of them was leading a lizard of remarkable size and beauty whose scales shone metallic blue. The man himself was not tall but he was massive, almost corpulent in appearance, although the weight was obviously muscle. A pectoral of jade, turquoise and bronze glinted on his chest, and over that he wore a lizard skin of the same brilliant blue as his pet, still with claws and head attached. Jewelled serpents were twined round his arms.

With his two companions – a woman and a younger thin-faced man – he approached Melkavesh and gave her an appraising stare. His slate-blue face was fleshy, but strong-featured; his brows were deeply indented with a permanent frown above a great beak of a nose, and the wide cheeks were graven with lines. His mouth was thin-lipped and sullen, his chin square, and his eyes almost lost in folds of flesh. Nevertheless, they were keen, and Melkavesh read every negative emotion in their wet, black depths. Scorn, ignorance, cruelty, self-righteousness . . . Then he barked out a question in a harsh language which she had never heard before.

Instinctively, she tried to reply. For a moment she gagged against paralysis; then her jaw moved stiffly, and the words emerged in an indistinct mumble, 'I don't understand. Does no one here speak Gorethrian?'

The elder – or King, as he appeared to be – frowned more deeply and turned to the woman at his side. She stepped forward and said in heavily accented Gorethrian, 'I am U'garet. I am the only one who speaks your language. Therefore I will translate.' She was obviously of high rank, from her bearing and the elaborateness of the pectoral that covered her breasts and shoulders. The design was of several stylised serpents, intricately worked in ivory and gems; a bronze lizard skin was thrown over one shoulder, and she wore a long skirt of interlinked flakes of bone that clicked softly as she moved. Her face was smooth, harsh and proud, and there were five triangular turquoises adorning her forehead.

'What do you want with us?' Melkavesh asked as clearly as she could. The King looked sneeringly at her, then made a pronouncement in a gruff strident voice.

'N'gudam informs you that the blood of nullifidians is less

worthy than that of believers, but still acceptable,' the woman translated.

'Please inform King N'gudam that I don't know what he's talking about,' Melkavesh said through a clenched jaw. As the translator relayed this to the King, the scorn in his narrowed eyes grew more intense.

'N'gudam asks if you are a fool,' said U'garet.

'I don't know about that,' she grated. 'Ask him why he captured us, and what he's done with the baby they took from us.'

'The infant is unnatural, but its blood is also acceptable,' was the answer. 'N'gudam wishes to know if you are from the city of Gholeth.'

'No, we are not.' Life was returning slowly to Melkavesh's paralysed limbs; she still could not move, but her whole body itched and tingled, and her captor's grip on her hair was becoming nauseatingly painful. Doing her utmost to order her thoughts she held N'gudam's gaze and said, 'Let me explain. I know I must appear to be a Gorethrian agent, but I am not. I am Emperor Xaedrek's enemy. We came across the mountains to flee Shalekahh, and we mean you no harm at all. All we wish is the safe return of the child, and to be allowed to go on our way.'

The translator looked astonished at this, and spoke rapidly to N'gudam and the thin-faced man. They murmured together for a few seconds; then N'gudam shook his head, and barked another statement at her.

'Your face is Gorethrian,' said U'garet.

'But my hair is not!' Melkavesh exclaimed. The King looked confused, and he was the sort of man who reacted to confusion with anger. When the other two began to express their bemusement, he raised an irritable hand to quiet them, and roared at Melkavesh.

In an incongruously calm tone, U'garet translated, 'Gorethrian or not, all are nullifidians who do not share our beliefs. Therefore you will all be forfeit.'

'You mean you're going to kill us?' Melkavesh croaked. 'Oh, you are making a great mistake. I could help you against

Xaedrek —' This seemed to infuriate N'gudam, and he lunged forward and gave her a vicious slap across the mouth. Blood ran from her lips.

'The prattling of nullifidians in the attempt to save their lives tires N'gudam. Mangorians shed their souls in brave silence. You should learn from this,' said the translator icily.

Melkavesh struggled furiously for breath and forced the words past her stinging lip. 'Why does he keep calling us "nullifidians"?'

U'garet stared at her as if she could not quite believe the question. Through the rippling jungle light Melkavesh could see the rest of the tribe grouped round the clearing, as motionless as statues carved from living rock. And a cold, viscid sense of shock flowed through her as the translator replied, 'All are nullifidians who do not worship the Serpent M'gulfn.'

Kharan hardly took in any of this conversation, nor of what followed. The drug in the plant sap seemed to have paralysed her mind as well as her body, splitting her perceptions in two as if with a sheet of white glass. The scene passed before her as if it were happening to someone else; it seemed no more real than a play she could not understand, or a distant scene in a mirror. Her true self was far away, weeping and raging for the loss of a tiny child who should not even be born, yet had already been snatched from her. But she was adrift in a vacuum, and there was no one to hear her.

N'gudam's anger meant nothing to her. Nor did she care when he turned and strode away, and their captors dragged them to the smallest of the stone pyramids. They were pulled through a narrow opening and dumped unceremoniously on a bare earth floor. As a stone door slid into place, sealing them in darkness, it seemed to her that she had been sealed within her own head.

For a long time she lay helpless on her back. Some time later she found herself curled up on her side, and shortly after that, the effects of the sap wore off and her perceptions returned abruptly to normal. She sat up, shivering and drenched with sweat.

'Melkavesh?' she cried out anxiously.

The Sorceress had already recovered and was on her feet, feeling her way cautiously around the inside of the pyramid. But on hearing Kharan's voice, she quickly knelt down at her side and said, 'Kharan, thank goodness you're recovering. By the Sphere, you're shaking like a leaf. I think you've got a fever.' She clasped the An'raagan's damp hands and tried to soothe her.

Kharan drew in several convulsive breaths. 'So this is Mangorad,' she said bitterly.

'Yes,' Melkavesh sighed. 'It's my fault this has happened. I was over-confident, careless.'

'They took Filmoriel.'

'Yes, I know.'

'How long –' Kharan's voice almost broke, but she mastered herself. 'How long can she live without your sorcery? That is, if they haven't already –'

'She's still alive, I'm sure of it,' Melkavesh said firmly, putting an arm round her shoulders. 'It would be several days before she weakened. And we'll have her back long before then, Kharan. Believe me.'

'They must give her back,' the An'raagan said faintly. 'Mel, what's been happening? All I remember is falling on the mountain, and those blue-skinned people seizing Filmoriel. The rest was just a nightmare. What did they say to you out there?'

Melkavesh hesitated, and took a slow breath. 'I can't see any use in trying to protect you, Kharan, but I warn you, none of it was pleasant.'

'I can take it,' Kharan replied. 'It's Filmoriel I'm worried about, not myself.'

'Well, these people worship a god, namely the Serpent.'

'Worship it? That's obscene. Besides, don't they know it's dead?'

'Obviously not. It seems to be a religion they've had for centuries. They believe they must appease M'gulfn by sacrificing people to it. The priests select the weakest members of the tribe, two or three each month as they deem fit. They regard everyone else – Gorethrian or otherwise – as unbelievers, "nullifidians". We do not make such worthy sacrifices as the Mangorians themselves, but we're better than nothing. Acceptable enough to spare two of their lives.'

Kharan swallowed, and said in a dry, husky voice, 'How is it done?'

Melkavesh had resolved to be frank, feeling that if she hedged around it, Kharan might grow even more alarmed. 'They shut the victims in a temple much like this one, and release their pet lizards in with them. The lizards are starved for three days beforehand. If any of them gorges itself and dies, it is regarded as a good omen.'

'Gods,' Kharan whispered. 'To think I was worried about being beheaded. And that's what they mean to do with us?'

'Not if I can help it. But it is their intention, yes. In three days' time.'

'Filmoriel, too?' Kharan's voice rose with terror, and she did not wait for an answer. She scrambled to her feet and began to beat at the blind rock of their prison, yelling, 'Let us out, you monsters! Where's my child?' Melkavesh leapt up to restrain her, and she turned, shuddering, to bow her head against the Gorethrian's shoulder. Presently she said in a quiet, flat voice, 'To find her, then lose her like this is unbearable. I can't and won't bear it. I must get her back, if it's the last thing I do.'

'Listen to me,' Melkavesh said, giving her a gentle shake. 'Come and sit down again. They've left us a couple of bowls of food and water. We must try to regain our strength.' Kharan sat down wearily on the earth floor, while Melkavesh groped in the darkness until she found the stone dishes, saying as she did so, 'No one is going to kill us, Kharan. You must believe that. If Xaedrek couldn't manage it, this wretched tribe certainly can't.'

'I'm sorry, Mel,' Kharan said, wiping her damp forehead and pushing back her hair with a grimy hand. 'It's just –'

'I know. Try to eat.' The water tasted musty, and the meat

in the other dish was tough and slimy. Melkavesh could guess which animal it came from, and suspected that it was raw. But they forced it down, knowing it was all they would get.

'Apparently these people are refugees who fled from the city of Gholeth when Xaedrek's troops invaded it a few years ago,' Melkavesh went on. 'Their deepest objection to the Gorethrians is that they suppress the Mangorians' religion.'

'In what way?'

'Destroying their temples, breaking up their gatherings, preventing sacrifices.'

'Well, that's ironic,' Kharan said with bitter humour. 'The so-civilised Gorethrians doing their utmost to stop these barbarians killing people.'

'I don't suppose there's anything moral in it. Mangorad's religion is the pivot of their unity and power, so naturally Gorethria wants to destroy it,' Melkavesh sighed. 'Barbarians they may be, but some kind of negotiation with them would seem to be our only chance. If only we had something to negotiate with.'

They were silent for a time. The rough smell of stone, damp earth and decaying vegetation was as overwhelming as misery, and words of mutual encouragement seemed to stick in their throats. Melkavesh would rather die than admit failure, but she could see no way out; they were nothing to King N'gudam, nothing except flesh to slaughter.

Then Kharan said, 'Why don't you tell them that the Serpent is dead?'

'What good would that do?' Melkavesh asked in surprise. 'They'd probably regard it as blasphemy.'

'But if you could make them believe you – oh, I don't know. I suppose it is a ridiculous idea.'

Hours passed and Kharan fell asleep, but Melkavesh lay awake, thinking. Her over-confidence had betrayed her, though this seemed a hard way to learn the lesson. She seemed to see Xaedrek's face in the darkness, heard his voice saying, 'Without your power, you are nothing.' The idea was intolerable – but what if it was true? The moment her sorcery

303

had failed, she had been captured like a wounded bird. The strength was not within her, but borrowed from the Earth . . . A wave of angry denial went through her, and she involuntarily gripped the talisman Irem Ol Thangiol had given her, feeling the little orbs cold and hard between her fingertips. There were other powers: physical strength, which had a limit even in the strongest, and power of personality . . .

At some stage she must have dozed off, because she awoke to the sound of a stone door scraping open, and a shaft of light falling across her face. There was a female warrior in the entrance, placing more bowls of food on the floor. Melkavesh jumped up and said urgently, 'I must see the translator, U'garet, immediately.' The woman brandished her javelin and affected not to understand. Melkavesh could see two further guards at the entrance, and thought better of trying to overpower her. Putting on her most commanding tone, she repeated, 'U'garet. U'garet,' and gesticulated to show what she meant.

She was still not sure the Mangorian had understood; but several minutes later the stone slid back again, and U'garet stood silhouetted against the steamy blue light. Melkavesh could only just perceive the shape of her smooth head, the faint sheen of gems on her shoulders.

'U'garet, I must see N'gudam again.'

'You have had one audience. He will not permit a second.' A grey lizard wound past her legs and quested into the darkness. Kharan, who had woken and was standing behind Melkavesh, recoiled from it. That it was restrained by a leash gave her no confidence at all.

'I think he will. I have something very important to tell him. It concerns the Serpent M'gulfn.'

U'garet paused, caught between duty and curiosity. 'You can tell me. I am a priestess.'

'Believe me, it is of such importance that I must tell N'gudam directly.' Her tone became confidential, flattering. 'You will still be the first to hear it, because you will translate. I tried to tell him before, but he wouldn't listen. You can persuade him to hear me out, can't you? You must surely have great influence with him . . .'

'I am a priestess,' the translator replied with an inclination of her head. She hesitated. 'Very well, I will inform him of your request. Wait, I will return.'

'What are you going to tell him?' Kharan asked as soon as U'garet had left.

Melkavesh shrugged and answered matter-of-factly, 'The truth.'

Several minutes later, U'garet returned with two male warriors. Gripping Melkavesh roughly by the arms, they dragged her outside, but when Kharan made to follow, she was shoved back inside the pyramid. Her desperate entreaties to know where Filmoriel was were cut short by the stone door being pushed back into place, yet they continued to haunt Melkavesh as she crossed the clearing, like echoes of guilt. In response, her mood became grimmer and more determined.

It was morning again, to her surprise, which meant they had been imprisoned for a whole day and night. Glancing around, she noticed a group of men and women seated on a large, rough-woven mat in the centre of the clearing. They were occupied in skinning the corpses of lizards. Children sat around the edge of the mat, threading pieces of bone together to make garments. On one side of the clearing, some youths were engaged in a violent, strangely spiritless mock spear battle. Many of them turned to watch Melkavesh as she was led towards the largest pyramid, and she thought what a joyless people the Mangorians seemed to be. But between the Gorethrians, the jungle and the Serpent, perhaps it was not surprising.

As they reached the pyramid a section of stone slid out on wooden rollers, and Melkavesh was ushered through the entrance into a huge chamber quite unlike the bare temple prison. It was some sixty feet square, with walls built of great blocks of stone sloping upwards and inwards to an apex high above their heads. Each block was carved with images of lizards and coiled snakes. The floor was of the same slate-grey stone. The dim blue light of the jungle filtered through window slits, supplemented by torches at intervals along the walls. The ribbons of smoke drifting from them made the atmosphere thick and hazy and lent a certain eeriness to the pyramid's grandeur.

There were already several people in the pyramid, grouped around a low dais in the centre of the chamber. Some were warriors; others Melkavesh recognised from the richness of their garb as being of the priestly caste. The huge King N'gudam sat on a long stone seat on the dais, magnificently costumed in lizard skin and semi-precious jewels, with the thin-faced man who had accompanied him the previous day seated at his side. It was warm in the pyramid, and perspiration gave a soft sheen to their bare heads and limbs. Their skin was the same deep grey-blue as the rock itself.

As U'garet led Melkavesh forward, the others surrounding the King looked round at her and fell silent. She detected a mixture of curiosity and irritation in the King's tar-black eyes as he signalled them to stand aside so that she could be brought to the dais. U'garet bowed and spoke a few words, while the two warriors maintained a painful grip on Melkavesh's arms. The priestess's tame lizard was tugging at its leash; looking around, Melkavesh noticed at least ten more of the reptiles wandering loose in the chamber.

Finally N'gudam deigned to utter a few gruff words, and U'garet translated, 'N'gudam wishes to know why the nullifidian has requested this audience.'

Only one chance. That is all I have, Melkavesh thought. She drew herself up, willing herself to forget her captors, and recall instead how adeptly she had deceived Xaedrek, who was infinitely more intelligent than this tribal King. And this time, no deceit was needed; the truth itself was powerful enough for her purpose.

'You know that I am no ordinary unbeliever, King N'gudam,' she said in a calm, clear tone. 'You know it, or you would not have agreed to listen to me. I have a task, which is to spread knowledge across Vardrav, and your people are privileged to be the first to hear it.' As the priestess translated, Melkavesh stared straight into his eyes, but N'gudam would not hold her gaze and she saw that she was making him uncomfortable.

She went on, 'I am not a "nullifidian". I know, as you do, that the Serpent existed. But a creature which lives may also die, and I have come to tell you that M'gulfn is dead.'

U'garet stared at her. Her voice was tight, almost faltering, as she relayed this statement to the King. No one spoke, but Melkavesh sensed a thickening of the atmosphere, and felt the glare of the many eyes upon her becoming keen and dangerous. The lizards seemed to sense it too, and the patter of their feet on the flags became frantic.

'Some might not call it a death, but a change,' she went on, improvising wildly but with total conviction. 'And this change has brought a new power to Earth, a power which will help to free you from Gorethria's tyranny.'

N'gudam leaned forward, resting his great hands on his knees. His eyes swivelled from side to side and she sensed that he was longing to hit her again, anything to silence her. But something stopped him. Like Xaedrek, Melkavesh had a very compelling presence, and when she spoke, people could not help but listen. Perhaps the King did not want to let her go on, but he was perceptive enough to realise that his priests and warriors might rebel if he did not.

He barked a question, and U'garet translated, 'By what authority do you bring this news?'

'It was my own father who slew the Serpent. But I am answerable to no one, and to nothing – except to the power itself. I am an enchantress, a wielder of the power, which some might call magic.' Such was her air of conviction that some of the warriors actually began to edge away, looking at her with wide, suspicious eyes. N'gudam saw this and yelled at them, clearly telling them not to be such cowardly, gullible fools. U'garet flinched, and lizards scattered to all corners of the pyramid.

'If you think to mock me with this rash boast of being a –' U'garet re-translated 'enchantress' as 'demon' – 'then you will pay,' he shouted.

'How can you accuse me of mocking you when I have offered to help you?' Melkavesh blazed. Now she was in her stride, it was obvious to U'garet and the others that she was not in the slightest degree intimidated by him, and they seemed astonished. 'We have received the wretchedest of treatment from you. Do you think you can afford to make an enemy of me?'

N'gudam licked his lips and swallowed, but his eyes still glinted wetly with rage. 'If you have such power, why have you not used it to escape? Demonstrate this magic. If you do not, we will know you are lying.'

'If I used my power now, it would kill you all and raze this chamber to the ground,' she replied sternly. A huge azure lizard brushed against her legs and she resisted the urge to push it away with her boot. 'I have shown forbearance as a sign of my faith that you will eventually believe me and become my allies. But you have already seen my sorcery. How else do you think the child you took from us is kept alive?'

At this, N'gudam leaned forward and muttered to a female warrior. She strode to a far corner of the chamber, lifted something from a stone table, and brought it to the King. Melkavesh's heart jumped as she saw the red cocoon, saw that the child was still moving and breathing within it.

N'gudam bent over the baby and poked at the membrane. Melkavesh instinctively lurched forward to stop him, but her captors held her back. 'Is this unnatural child not from the Serpent? Are you not from the Serpent, sent to punish us?' he said in a low, troubled tone.

'The Serpent is no more,' Melkavesh replied. Perhaps that was why they had not harmed or killed Filmoriel: they feared her. 'The power is in the child as well as in myself. I know this is hard for you to believe in such a short time; I ask only your patience. Let us live, for in time your wisdom will conquer your fear, and you will see that I speak the truth.' As U'garet translated, her eyes were fixed on Melkavesh as if she half-believed her already. The King muttered angrily to himself, clenching and unclenching his fists, while his subjects waited anxiously for his judgement.

Suddenly he stood up and began to roar such a stream of abuse at Melkavesh that she could barely hear U'garet's translation. But the sense was plain enough. 'The nullifidian speaks heresy. The Serpent cannot die. She is telling these vile lies to save her wretched life – you can all see she has no power. Take her away!' As the dark hands tightened round her arms, he added in a low, venomous tone, 'You will be put to sacrifice immediately – the serpents are hungry enough. If you are a demon as you claim, you will be able to save yourself. Then and only then will we believe you. I am a fair man.' He sat down and nodded emphatically as if pleased with this pronouncement.

Around her the blue-skinned people shifted uneasily and looked from her to the King, their eyes unreadable in their harsh blue-grey faces. Her two captors bowed smartly to N'gudam and made to pull her backwards from the dais, but at that moment the thin-faced man at the King's side, who so far had not spoken a word, made a statement that plainly meant, 'I believe her.'

N'gudam turned to glare at him, shaking his head in furious disbelief. Then he bellowed an angry string of words, which U'garet faithfully translated as, 'Anyone else who believes the nullifidian can show their faith by putting themselves to sacrifice alongside her!'

No one moved. The King roared U'garet into silence. Melkavesh found herself being pulled backwards across the chamber, her shouts of protest ignored. She watched the massive frame of N'gudam receding from her, with the woman holding Filmoriel and his priests and soldiers grouped around him like a tableau. Then the huge stone door creaked into place, and she was outside, the audience over. And she had achieved nothing except the loss of three days' grace in which her power might have returned.

While Melkavesh was away, Kharan's anxiety began to verge on panic. The blackness of the prison was pressing on her eyes, and whether she opened or closed them she could not escape the dreary colours bursting across her vision. The sound of insects scratching about on the floor made her shudder. Her bones still ached from the fall on Mount Karvish, but she was unable to find rest and wandered restlessly round the pyramid. The atmosphere was chilly and damp and claustrophic; the mountains, however alien they had seemed at the time, now took on an aura of sweetness and freedom in her memory. But the real cause of her wretchedness, which exacerbated every discomfort to a torment, was Filmoriel. Until she could believe that the child was safe, and see her again, she existed in a nightmare.

It seemed unbelievable that she could have awakened from one bad dream, only to be plunged into another. And again she was powerless, and again only Melkavesh could save them. The knowledge left her poised half-way between fury and blind terror. And if she verged on madness, it was only the thought of Filmoriel that drew her back from the brink. For her sake, she must survive.

Presently the stone door scraped open, and a sliver of bluish light dazzled her. A spear tip prodded Melkavesh through the crack. Kharan flew to her and implored in a voice raw with desperation, 'Did you see her?'

'Yes,' Melkavesh said in a strange, tight voice. 'She is alive.'

'Thank goodness!' Kharan cried. 'Oh, Melkavesh, won't they let me see her? What do they want with her? I'm doing my best to stay calm, but I think it's only fair to tell you that if they don't let us out of here soon, I am going to go mad.'

But Melkavesh did not reply at once, and Kharan's panic rose anew. 'Mel, what's happening?'

With obvious difficulty, Melkavesh said, 'Kharan, they're going to sacrifice me now. Not you or Filmoriel,' she added hurriedly. 'Just me. My power hasn't returned, so I can do nothing. It's up to you to save Filmoriel.'

'No – Mel, they can't –' but even as she spoke, there were shadows in the entrance, shadows moving forward to seize Kharan and drag her out of the temple. Melkavesh tried to

310

follow, but U'garet blocked her path and said in an impersonal, ominous tone, 'I almost believed you. Be calm, for if you survive, all will believe you, but if you perish, nothing is lost. Now the ritual will begin.'

Then the tribespeople began to file in, and there were torches crackling in the darkness, filling the air with magnesium fire and heady smoke. As soon as the pungent vapour touched her nostrils, Melkavesh began to feel dizzy, and the scene became dreamlike, distorted and senseless. She stood under the apex of the pyramid as if drugged, while figures moved round her in a slow, swaying dance. Torchlight cast alarming shadows on the dark, angled walls; it flickered on domed heads, shimmered on lizard scales, flashed on metal and jewels. The blue-skinned people were moving in threes, leading one lizard between them and dancing in the same graceful, slow-motion rhythm as the reptiles themselves. Their voices moaned a low-pitched chant, the polished bones of their garments clicked softly, the lizards' claws scraped on the bare earth floor. Everything became the colour of light shining through blue smoke, bleached and ill-defined.

The hypnotic ritual went on for so long that somewhere in her smoke-fogged awareness, Melkavesh came to understand it. It was a rite of transformation. The people danced with the lizards in slow, complex patterns, they sang ancient words whose meanings were lost, and in the nightmare ecstasy of the ritual they believed that each of the reptiles changed and became the Serpent itself. Like the Serpent, they would consume human flesh and be appeased. A superstition, perhaps, but one deeply drawn from reality and, at this moment, as fierce and terrifying as an Arctic wind. These people were more than mere primitives. Somewhere in their past they had touched the dread reality of M'gulfn, and it had shadowed their lives down through the centuries ever since.

Dark faces were weaving closely around her, and the stench of smoke and sweat and musty soil overwhelmed her. When the dark hands reached out for her, she fell into them as if fainting, and did not resist as they stretched her out on the floor and bound her hands and ankles with creeper. She recognised only U'garet, and the pinched face of N'gudam's companion. A long, green-blue plant stem was held in sharp focus before her eyes, dripping white sap. Someone lowered it towards her arm, but she did not feel it enter the flesh; nor was she aware of the paralysis creeping through her muscles, for she was already beyond movement. The priests stared down at her, their eyes like black glass. The voices of the worshippers rose and fell like the sea, speaking the name over and over again, *M'gulfn. M'gulfn. M'gulfn.*

For a few minutes, her trance became a vision: snow was whirling around her, and she was transported back to the extreme youth of the world. There was a perfectly flat plain of snow, and over it arched a dome of black crystal in which two perfect white moons shone. But somewhere on the ice lay the Serpent, brooding torpidly on its domination of the world, and a grey figure rose out of the plain, and she heard a voice say, 'It waits for the Last Witness, and then it can sleep.'

A sense of the unutterably weird caught in her throat, and she felt the ice-cap fracturing, the ocean dragging her down and swallowing her, the moons falling. Everything turned grey, and now the only reality was a dull plain on which two figures stood, one light grey and one dark grey. Between them there was a woman robed in white with a blue light shining from her, and she was going from one figure to the other, imploring, 'Why? Why have you done this?' Every shade of loss and grief was in her voice, but neither figure would answer her; and when one did not reply she would return to the other and ask again; and so it became a ritual dance that would continue through eternity . . .

And Melkavesh opened her eyes, and found the worshippers gone and the temple once more in darkness. But the darkness was full of sound: the dry rustle of lizards stalking to and fro on the floor, circling round and round her. Once or twice she felt the flicker of a tongue on her face. The scented smoke of the torches had cleared, and as the drowsiness began to leave her, she drew a deep breath and went into a long spasm of coughing.

312

Her hands and feet were still tied, numb. And she vaguely remembered that they had injected her with the paralysing sap. It seemed an act of incredible sadism, to render the victim unable to move but fully conscious while the reptiles gnawed at the flesh, mouthful by tiny mouthful. They had left her fully clothed, no doubt to make the process as long as possible. Even as these gloomy thoughts were drifting through her mind, she felt the pain of jaws in her hand. She started, cried out – and involuntarily sat up.

Praise the Sphere, she was not paralysed after all. Yet she had seen the poisonous plant-stem being lowered towards her arm . . . Puzzled, some instinct made her reach behind her with numb hands and feel about on the earth until she found it; a long, pliable stem with one end cut to a sharp point. Someone had dropped it by accident – or left it there deliberately?

From that moment on, Melkavesh did not feel a trace of fear, only total, single-minded determination. Given the tiniest chance of survival, it was her nature to use it to the utmost limit. Now the lizards were chewing her boots, sniffing her hair, snapping at her hands. It was hard to estimate how many there were, and with her ankles bound and her hands tied behind her back the slightest manoeuvre was a painful effort. The initial effort of turning the stem until she was holding it in the right position made her fingers stiffen and cramp. All the time the lizards were butting at her shoulders and hands, tearing at her sleeves with sharp teeth. There seemed to be about six, but that was enough; they were as large and strong as dogs. She could kneel, but not stand up, so she was barely able to evade them or push them away, and with every move she made to shake them off, she risked spiking herself with the stem, or breaking the essential sharp end.

But at last she felt one move behind her, and as it lunged at her wrists, she jerked her hands backwards and drove the stem into its neck. After a moment she heard a slithering thud as it stumbled and fell onto its side. A gasp of relief escaped her; the sap's effectiveness was not restricted to humans. Whether there would be enough to disable all the reptiles, she could not guess, but there was no time to worry about it. She concentrated on manoeuvring until she could reach the next one and pierce its delicate skin.

Her breath hissed in and out between her clenched teeth; her mouth was dry and her throat sore. Hair stuck to the sweat coursing down her face, and she could do nothing to brush it away. Her whole body became gnarled with tension and exertion, but her ability to transcend discomfort did not fail her, it seemed the creatures could not match her iron determination to win.

When she had dispatched five, there was silence. Only five? For a long time she remained poised on her knees, straining for the faintest sound of claws in the darkness. The stem was blunted and split, and the sap had run onto her fingers and numbed them. She could hear nothing. At last she was convinced that all the creatures had fallen, and only then did she drop the stem and collapse onto her side, exhausted. After a few minutes she stirred and made a final, agonising effort to scratch a hollow in the floor in which to bury the stem. She hoped that if she concealed the evidence, N'gudam would not guess how she had survived.

Hours went by, and she began to wonder how long it would be before they opened the temple to see if she was dead. It was possible that if they waited much longer, the lizards would revive, no doubt feeling very much hungrier. Desperate for water, and far beyond clear thought, she drifted into an unpleasant state of half-consciousness. Eventually, a noise intruded on her distorted dreams; the stone door sliding back on its rollers. All at once there were lights and faces round her, awe-filled whispers echoing in her ears.

She revived, tried to sit up, and failed, but it was enough to show that she was alive. U'garet and N'gudam loomed above her, surrounded by at least twenty priests and warriors. All were staring at her with a kind of dark awe that gave her the sensation of insects running over her skin. No one approached her. Then N'gudam let out a guttural cry, swung round and marched out of the pyramid.

A moment later, her hands and feet were free, and she was being helped to sit up, and there was a bowl of lukewarm water at her lips. She drank deeply, compulsively; the musty taste seemed as sweet as an Emethrian spring in her clogged mouth. It was N'gudam's narrow-faced companion who was helping her; the others were moving about the chamber, collecting up the paralysed lizards.

'I said I believed you. Now I am proved right,' he said.

She stretched her tormented limbs and found her voice. 'You do speak Gorethrian,' she whispered.

'Yes, but my father would not permit it if he knew,' he replied.

'Your father?'

'I am N'gudam's son,' he replied with a touch of surprise. 'My name is N'golem.'

'I am Melkavesh.' She spoke softly so that only he could hear. 'And it was you, wasn't it? The stem.' He nodded. 'Why?'

'I will tell you later. But you are unwell. First you must rest and eat.'

'Where are Kharan and Filmoriel – my companion and the child?'

'They have not been harmed.' N'golem helped her to her feet and led her to the temple entrance. He was the same height as Melkavesh, and despite the gauntness of his hollow-cheeked, pinched face, he had the muscular build typical of his people. Polished blue stones gleamed against his slaty skin, and he wore a shining green lizard hide over one shoulder.

Outside, it seemed the whole tribe was waiting. Word had spread that this yellow-haired Gorethrian claimed to be a demon who had slain the Serpent, and N'gudam himself had pronounced that if she survived, they must accept her claim as true. First they had seen N'gudam marching dumbstruck from the temple; then they witnessed a procession of priests, each carrying an apparently lifeless reptile; and now they saw Melkavesh herself emerging, blinking dazedly at the light and weak with exhaustion – but alive! A ripple went through them of such amazement that it took her aback. But she knew she had a role to fulfil. Shaking off her tiredness she walked between them with her head held high and as much majesty as she could summon. And as she passed, many of them fell to their knees and laid down their javelins before her.

N'golem and U'garet accompanied her to another small pyramid, but at the entrance the priestess paused and said, 'How you lived is beyond my understanding. I was wrong to doubt you. But be warned, N'gudam is angry.' With that, she turned and walked away, while N'golem took Melkavesh into the pyramid.

A dim light filtered into the chamber through a number of embrasures, and there were rows of mats lined up on the stone floor. Obviously this was a sleeping place for the tribe, though at present it was deserted – except for one small figure, curled up on her side in the far corner.

'Kharan!' cried Melkavesh. The An'raagan woke, dazed for a moment; then she leapt up and flew into Melkavesh's arms, crying out with relief.

'Where's Filmoriel?' Melkavesh asked.

'They've still got her. They wouldn't let me see her,' Kharan replied in a tight voice. 'But your power's come back, hasn't it?'

'Not yet, but don't worry. It won't be long. N'golem, are we still under guard?'

'No. You are no longer prisoners. N'gudam would not dare harm you now.'

'That's a relief. I must sit down before I fall down,' Melkavesh sighed, subsiding into a cross-legged position on one of the mats. Kharan sat beside her, N'golem facing them. A young tribesman entered bringing them some slabs of solid black bread and a bowl of sour plant-milk. It was not the most pleasant meal they had ever eaten, but it was, nevertheless, far more palatable than the previous one had been.

When she and Kharan had finished eating, Melkavesh

316

said, 'N'golem, I want you to know that I did not lie about my power. There were reasons – which I won't go into – why I couldn't use it. But you didn't know that, so why did you save me?'

'Because I knew that you spoke the truth. I left the drug sap for you, but only someone of great wisdom and strength could have used it. I knew you would pass the test, because the moment you came to us I saw that you are . . . I do not know the word. A prophet.'

Kharan raised her eyebrows at this, but Melkavesh only smiled.

'I gather the King sees me as a threat to his authority,' she said.

'The King?' N'golem's narrow forehead contracted in a frown.

'N'gudam.'

'We have no King. N'gudam is our high priest. All are subordinate to him. Perhaps this seems strange to nullifidian Gorethria. The high priest commands the people, orders our lives and deaths. As his son I have certain duties but no true authority.'

Melkavesh heard the resentment in his voice and sensed the undercurrents of a power struggle between N'gudam and N'golem. He went on, 'My father knows well enough that you are a true prophet, therefore he fears you. For if the Serpent is dead, there will be no need for priests, and the loss of faith may destroy my people. N'gudam grows old and set in his ways, and will try to deny the future, but I have waited long for this change, and now that it has come, it is my duty to safeguard my people from his ignorance.'

'Even if that means seizing power from him?'

'I will do so if necessary,' he said softly. 'I have waited long . . .'

'But if you've worshipped the Serpent for centuries,' Kharan broke in, 'how can you be so quick to believe it's dead?'

N'golem gave her the briefest glance, as if he had only just realised she was there, and returned his attention to

317

Melkavesh. 'I think there is much you do not understand about our beliefs. The Serpent is a tormented god which punishes the world for the pain it suffers. Our purpose in worship is to appease it and soothe it into a slumber from which it will never awake. In our rites, we believe that each of our lizards becomes the Serpent. When they eat human flesh, they become slumberous, and if any gorge themselves to death, it is a good omen that M'gulfn itself is nearer to eternal sleep.

'Some years ago, there was a terrible time of storm and pestilence in which it seemed we had failed and made M'gulfn angry. We prayed and sacrificed night and day, and at last the time of storms ended. Then the priests said that our efforts had calmed it, but that our worship must continue or it might wake again.'

'You must believe me,' Melkavesh exclaimed. 'It is not merely asleep, but dead.' She told him, as briefly and simply as possible, how Ashurek, Medrian and Estarinel had slain M'gulfn, and of the extramundane power that had been released as a result. N'golem listened in silence, his head bowed gravely.

When she had finished, he looked up from beneath his slanting brows and said, 'It is as though I have known this in my mind ever since the time of storms. I was only a child then, so I dared not speak my doubts. But now I know I was right.'

'And you wish to free yourselves from Gorethria, don't you?'

'Our greatest wish is to recapture our city, Gholeth, and drive them from our borders once and for all.'

'I want to help you,' Melkavesh said in a quiet, intense voice.

'I believe you. But if the others do not, I cannot make them. That is up to you. I am going to speak to N'gudam now, make him understand that you have come not as an enemy, but to lead us to freedom. He must allow you to speak to all our people together.'

'Thank you, N'golem. If only I can speak to them, I know I can make them understand,' she said, and Kharan shifted uneasily as a crusading gleam appeared in her bright eyes.

'There is only one thing: do not mention the three who slew the Serpent, but make it seem that their own efforts and sacrifices are what sent M'gulfn into eternal slumber.'

Melkavesh considered this, and exclaimed, 'That's brilliant. People are always more inclined to believe what they most want to hear. You're a much cleverer man than your father, N'golem, and I'm glad to have you on my side.'

He stood up and bowed to her. 'I will return when you have rested for a few hours, and I will have more food sent to you.' But as he turned to leave, Kharan jumped up and seized his arm.

'Wait – you still have my child. I must see her. Please –'

He regarded her coldly. 'You will see the infant later. Not now.'

'But you said we're no longer prisoners,' she said angrily. 'Which means that we could leave now, doesn't it?'

'Yes, but I think you will not wish to leave without the infant.' He strode out of the temple, leaving Kharan aghast.

'The bastard,' she breathed. 'Did you hear that? How can you trust him now?'

'Be patient,' Melkavesh said soothingly. 'I told you, Filmoriel is all right. They daren't harm her. Everything will work out for the best – in fact, it will be even better than I'd imagined.'

'Oh, will it?' Kharan spat, pacing across the chamber. 'The only thing he's interested in is deposing his father.'

'What if he is? If they're too involved with their own tiny power struggles to see the larger issues, it only makes my task easier.'

'But what about Filmoriel?' she cried. 'They're using her to manipulate us. A tiny child, barely five days old. They're using her!'

They slept for several hours, woke and ate again. Melkavesh asked for bowls of water to be brought so they could wash.

Their Gorethrian travelling-gear was worn and grimy, its rich hues reduced to a dull grey-brown. Naturally fastidious, Kharan was slowly giving up hope of ever being really clean again, but at least a perfunctory wash was better than nothing. The pure relief of being released from the temple was enough to revive their strength and spirit, and Melkavesh – despite her ordeal, and Filmoriel's predicament – seemed positively buoyant.

Then N'golem came, and led them out into the clearing. Kharan was surprised and vaguely alarmed to find a great throng of the blue-skinned people waiting outside. There were perhaps a thousand in all, far more than could live just within this one village. There must be Mangorians scattered throughout the jungle. The mingled sound of their voices, murmuring in their own harsh tongue, hardly sounded human; she was unpleasantly put in mind of snakes hissing. But Melkavesh was undaunted, and strode among them with an unselfconscious air of authority.

N'golem led them to the largest pyramid, and they ascended the side like a giant staircase, block by block. N'gudam and U'garet were waiting, flanked by two lesser priests and two warriors, on a ridge some ten feet above the crowd's heads. N'golem ushered them along the next step down to stand below and in front of the high priest. With a shock, Kharan saw that N'gudam was holding Filmoriel in his huge, fleshy hands, but N'golem prodded her out of his range and told her brusquely to keep quiet. She looked pleadingly at Melkavesh, but realised that for the time being, there was nothing she could do.

'As you have passed the test of your power, N'gudam permits you to speak to his people,' U'garet said, adding ominously, 'They will judge you.' Kharan noticed that N'gudam was not looking at Melkavesh, but glaring at his son, N'golem. For all his huge bulk and intimidating presence, he looked oddly helpless, and the ghost of a smile flickered on N'golem's narrow face.

Melkavesh looked out over the crowd, her hands on her hips. She was a travel-dusty figure, and even her hair was by no means impressive, being lank with dirt and humidity. But her eyes were as brilliant and compelling as ever Xaedrek's had been, and the power of her personality shone like an aura. A thousand pairs of eyes were fixed on her, wide with expectation. Even before she began to speak, they were hers.

It did not matter that they did not understand her words, nor that U'garet's translation was delivered in a flat, dry tone; the mere sound of her voice, the passion and utter conviction of her delivery, were enough to convince them. She spoke of the Serpent and its death, which the tireless work of the Mangorians had helped to bring about; she spoke of the glorious, mysterious power of sorcery; she spoke of the evil of Gorethria's oppressive rule, the need to rise up and unite against Xaedrek. The Mangorians hung on her every word, as if N'golem's description of her as a prophet had been no exaggeration.

And Kharan, watching her, was astounded. Melkavesh had always been strong-willed and vivacious, but now she saw her in a new light. The spark of leadership had been dormant within her, and Kharan had barely noticed it. Now it burned like a fire, transforming her into a preternatural figure whose will could not be resisted. Kharan was more than impressed; she was awestruck, her cynicism washed away by a wave of excitement. For a few wild minutes, she understood and shared the crowd's exhilaration.

Melkavesh knew the effect she was having, and she revelled in it as if she had been waiting all her life for this moment. And as she spoke, there was another revelation: at last, at last, she felt the sweet golden tide of sorcery flowing gently and surely back into her. It returned almost jauntily, as if it had never been lost, driving out her weariness and filling her veins with a fierce and joyful fire. But she restrained herself from letting the Mangorians see any outward sign of it. It meant a lot to her to know that she had swayed them by charisma alone.

As her speech ended, Kharan expected tumultuous cheers. Instead, there was an eerie silence in which the only sounds were the creaks of jungle vegetation, the chirping of insects and fluty bird-calls. And one by one, the tribespeople were falling to their knees and stretching out their hands. Kharan caught her breath. It seemed an act of devotion more profound than any vocal expression, and it made her stomach churn with a mixture of emotions.

Melkavesh, though she did not show it, was even more deeply affected. It took her a moment to realise that N'gudam was speaking to her, and U'garet translating, 'N'gudam requests you to inform his people that we begin preparations tomorrow to march upon Gholeth and seize it from the Gorethrians.'

Melkavesh turned to look at N'gudam, who was standing behind her on a higher block. 'No, N'gudam, that would be senseless. We are no match for the Gorethrian army, and I know Xaedrek. Even if we did repossess the city, he would simply send more and more troops until he defeated us.' She made to explain further, but N'gudam's face darkened and he shouted her down.

'You promised us your help. Do you now go back on your word?' He actually brandished Filmoriel's tiny form in the air. Kharan lunged towards him, furious, but N'golem caught her and held her back. Melkavesh could not make herself heard, so she concentrated patiently on U'garet's translation. 'You have made it clear that this unnatural child is of great value to you. You will use your power to help us retake Gholeth, or the child will be slain.'

'You damnable fiend!' Kharan cried. She struck out at N'golem, but he twisted her arm and thrust her down, so that she almost tumbled off the side of the pyramid. She saved herself and scrambled away from him, shaking with anger and shock. She made to climb up towards N'gudam, only to see that Melkavesh was confronting him, her whole form suffused by a cloak of lemon-gold light.

Looking steadily at N'gudam, the Sorceress stretched out her hands and said, 'Give the child to me.' At the unexpected, visible evidence of her power, his face distorted into a grimace of incredulity. Until now he had suspected she was a clever liar, and that his son had saved her by underhanded

322

trickery. He had been waiting for a chance to denounce her – but the sight of that crackling veil of stars changed everything. Melkavesh did not even need to wield the power against him. His anger fled, superstitious fear paralysed him, and he relinquished the infant without another word.

Still radiant with power, Melkavesh put out a hand to help Kharan to her feet, and placed Filmoriel in her hands. Now even U'garet and N'golem were on their knees, while the tribe bowed their heads and offered up their spears. Melkavesh suddenly felt strangely embarrassed, overcome by this unforeseen adulation and dizzy with the responsibility, the vastness of what she was taking on. Raising an army to lead against Gorethria – her throat was tight and dry. What would Xaedrek say if he could see her now? More than that, what would Ashurek have thought?

Recovering herself, she went on in a calm, clear voice, 'I appreciate your eagerness to return to Gholeth. But you must understand that Mangorad alone cannot rout the Gorethrians. Xaedrek can only be defeated if every race under his domination rises up against him as one. To this end we must leave Mangorad and seek the most powerful allies we can find. Beginning in Kristillia. It may be a long time before you return to victory to Gholeth, but be assured that your time will come. Will you follow me?'

This time it was N'golem who translated to the crowd, thus showing them – and his father – his support for Melkavesh. His voice seemed to break their trance of silence, and at last they began to voice their passionate concurrence. Only they did not so much cheer as sing, each on one long, deep note, on and on until the pyramids reverberated deafeningly with the sound. Melkavesh and Kharan unconsciously moved closer to each other as if pinned together and paralysed by the exaltation that shook the very air around them. From here, destiny would begin to shape itself around Melkavesh like a whirlwind, and no one – least of all Kharan – had the power to prevent it.

11

The Swallowing Sands

'IN KESFALINE you must seek a place called Imhaya. The Circle of Spears,' Raphon gasped. The neman's tall form was prostrate on the sand, and it was all Falmeryn could do to support its heavy shoulders and head.

'I will not let you die,' he repeated. The neman's hood fell back, but he drew it up again to protect its head from the swiftly ascending sun.

'My skill in argument has deserted me. I do not know what to say to make you leave me. I can only implore you, Falmeryn of Forluin, to go to Imhaya.' The Hrunneshian's tone was deep and calm, as if it were relinquishing life without a struggle, but suddenly it reached up and gripped Falmeryn's arm, gasping, 'Ah – it is no good. Imhaya is a secret place. Only I can guide you there. You will never find it alone –'

'Raphon, save your breath.' The wind flung sand in his face, but he scrubbed it away and fumbled for the water flask at his belt. Uncorking it, he poured a few drops into his hand and began to bathe the neman's face and neck.

Almost at once, Raphon revived visibly, only to begin protesting at the waste of water. Falmeryn ignored its objections, and continued to moisten its coal-black skin. But Raphon was right, this was futile. As long as he kept the neman's head and torso wet, it would live, but as soon as the water was gone, they were both bound to die. The situation was hopeless, yet while there was the slightest chance of keeping his companion alive, Falmeryn could not give up.

But the wind was rising, moaning louder and louder as it

hurtled towards them across the desert. The soft haze of sand sliding over the dunes began to stream outwards in great plumes. The air became dark and harsh with stinging particles that obscured the sun. Falmeryn turned his back to the sandstorm, pulled his cloak tightly around him, and cradled Raphon's head in his lap. All around them, the dunes were moving – not just shifting forwards under the force of the wind, but undulating like a honey-gold sea.

One moment the ground under him was firm. The next, the surface opened into a funnel, and he and Raphon were sliding down a slope with tons of sand curling above them like a wave. It happened so quickly that Falmeryn did not even have time to feel afraid. He was sinking in a thick, dry ocean, hanging wildly, uselessly, onto Raphon's shoulders. Sand accumulated round his face, covered his mouth. He seized a last breath, and just before his nose and eyes were submerged he saw every grain of sand in detail, each one like a tiny glass pearl, filled with rainbow colours. Then the whole surface of the desert seemed to heave and turn over, and the swallowing sands of Ungrem claimed them.

Falmeryn did not lose consciousness at once. This was worse than drowning; it was slow and choking, and even struggling was impossible. He was being crushed by a huge weight of sand, and it was dark and cold and his lungs were bursting. Any moment now, he thought quite calmly, I will be dead; and he felt nothing but longing for that moment, relief from the terrible weight on his body, the pressure in his head and lungs.

The moment did not come. His agony went on. He felt the sand churning all around him, as if huge creatures were moving through it. Then it seemed that he was no longer sinking deeper through the sand, but resting on a firm, warm surface. Undoubtedly his imagination was playing tricks. Now he felt that he was rising, while the weight slowly decreased. A hissing noise filled his ears, drowning the sound of his own labouring heart; it was sand, sifting away as he was borne upwards. Suddenly a dazzling, red-gold light burst

325

across his eyelids, and he felt warm air on his face. He sucked in a huge breath – only to be half-choked by sand.

A violent fit of coughing shook him, and it was several minutes before he recovered enough to take in what had happened. When he did, he found that he was not merely on the surface of the desert – but several feet above it.

The air was still full of flying sand but he seemed to be above the worst of it. Where was Raphon? Pulling his hood up and holding it over his nose and mouth, he sat up and looked around. His eyes were full of grit, streaming and smarting, and it was all he could do to see anything, but after much painful blinking his vision cleared slightly, and he began to make out where he was.

He was on the broad, flat back of an enormous animal. The only detail he could make out clearly was its skin, which lay wrinkled in thick folds and covered with short soft fur like velvet. Turning, he found Raphon lying a couple of feet behind him, about to slide off over the creature's tail. Falmeryn leaned forward, seized the neman, and dragged its heavy frame into a more secure position. The Hrunneshian was very weak, almost insensible, but mercifully, still alive.

All around them the desert of Ungrem was rising and falling like a sea, and swimming through that sea was a herd of strange animals. Falmeryn blotted the water from his stinging eyes and gazed at them in wonder. There were about twenty in all. They stood ten feet high at the shoulder and walked not on the sand but through it, on eight thick legs. Their table-flat backs tapered along a horizontal neck to a small, sheep-like head, and in colour they were a milky-beige that blended with the landscape. They were moving eastwards with their eyes closed against the wind.

'Raphon. Raphon, you must hang on now.' Falmeryn shook the neman's arm. To his relief, the flask was still attached to his belt and corked, so they had not lost the precious water. He poured a little onto Raphon's lips and forehead, then took a mouthful himself. 'We've been given a chance. Someone must be protecting us – perhaps the Lady

326

of H'tebhmella herself.' It was said lightly, but Raphon stirred and gave him a strange, sombre look.

'No, not the Lady of H'tebhmella. However, I share your hope. Ah, how intriguing to philosophise upon the nature of hope, having experienced its reality for the first time . . .'

But they were still under the sun's burning rays, hundreds of miles from Kesfaline. Raphon would still die soon if they could not find water and shelter. Falmeryn leaned over the Hrunneshian to shield it from the worst of the heat, and endeavoured to keep its face and chest moist. As he was brooding upon their dilemma, he received yet another shock. From nowhere, a man was climbing towards them up the creature's side.

He was shrouded from head to foot in creamy-fawn robes, with only his forehead and dark brown eyes visible. His skin was dark copper with a bluish sheen, graven with deep lines from years of squinting against sun and wind.

Falmeryn's first response to a stranger was to show he meant no harm; not out of cowardice, but a simple instinct to seek friendship and – in this case – help.

'I am Falmeryn of Forluin,' he began, using the language common to Forluin and Tearn without thinking. 'We are stranded, and my companion desperately needs water.' The man, who was clinging to the skin folds on the animal's side, stared at him with no sign of understanding. Falmeryn repeated himself in Gorethrian, but there was still no response. He noticed that another of the huge beasts was converging from the right, and as it drew close, a woman and a boy of about eleven – also wrapped in creamy robes – jumped from its back and landed alongside him. Then he saw that about half of the creatures now had people sitting or standing on their backs, one or two on each.

The man and woman spoke to each other in their own language, while the boy stared at Raphon. Finally the man said in excellent Gorethrian, 'The desert swallows outsiders. But fate has spared you, so we are bound to help you.'

'He has a kind face,' said the woman, sitting cross-legged next to Falmeryn. The wind was dying, so she pulled the headdress away from her face. Her features were broad, weather-beaten but gentle. 'But the other one, is he Gorethrian?'

Raphon, still lying flat out, turned feebly to look at her. The cloak fell open, revealing coal-black skin, four sinuous arms and whiteless eyes. The man and woman recoiled, but, to Falmeryn's surprise, Raphon began to speak quietly to them in their own language. After a few moments they relaxed and came closer, their fear gone.

'My companion is from the Black Plane,' Falmeryn said. 'We're trying to reach Kesfaline, but Raphon will die without water and shelter. Please, can you help us?'

'Yes, we will,' the man replied, nodding calmly. 'Your friend has told me that you offer my family no harm, and we see that he is ill. The desert is cruel to those without a janizon.'

'A janizon?'

The man patted the animal's velvety, wrinkled back. There was tenderness and pride in his voice as he said, 'This beast we call a janizon, and she is my family's life, food and shelter. We rejoice in her. There is no sweeter, nobler animal in all the Earth. This our doe is named Cuhla.'

Falmeryn could not help smiling. 'And your name?'

'I am Ahn Hrav, my wife is Dhrua, and this is our son, Ahn Bhen. Now, Raphon must climb down with me and I will take him to safety.' The Hrunneshian was very weak, but was able to cling to the beast's side and follow Ahn Hrav as he climbed agilely round the huge, rippling shoulders. Falmeryn followed, holding onto the velvety folds of flesh with one hand and supporting Raphon with the other. Cuhla, meanwhile, plodded on undisturbed.

When he reached the chest, Ahn Hrav swung between the moving front legs – and vanished. But a moment later, his head and arms reappeared, and he reached out to help Raphon climb beneath the doe's belly. Dhrua and the boy climbed round from the other side to lend a hand, while Falmeryn, hanging precariously onto the wide chest, saw that Raphon was clambering between folds of skin into a pouch beneath the stomach. Ahn Hrav was already lying half in it, helping the neman inside.

The woman laughed at his expression and said, 'You have never seen such a creature as this before, have you? Your friend will be safe in Cuhla's pouch. It is dark and although there is no water, there is milk, which is better.'

Falmeryn soon came to understand the mystery of the herd's eruption from the desert and the sudden appearance of Ahn Hrav and the others. The people lay inside the pouches – which trapped enough air for them to breathe for several hours – while the janizons dug themselves into the sand, thus avoiding the intense heat of the sun and the cold at night. They surfaced only in the morning and evening, so it appeared to be pure chance that Cuhla had caught Falmeryn and Raphon on her back and borne them to safety.

When Ahn Hrav emerged again, he was holding an armful of robes and a soft leather flask full of milk, which he gave to Falmeryn. It was strong-flavoured, creamy and delicious, quite unlike anything he had ever tasted before. As they returned to the janizon's back, Dhrua explained, 'Our does bear their young only once every four years. In between, their pouches and their milk sustain us.'

'When the sun becomes too hot, we will go under the sands again,' said Ahn Hrav. 'Before then, you must change into these robes. You will be more comfortable so.'

'Thank you. I can't tell you how grateful I am for your kindness.'

'Cuhla saved you, not we, and who are we to go against her judgement?'

For a time, Falmeryn sat on the doe's flat back with Ahn Hrav and his wife and son, lulled by the gentle swaying motion into a sense of complete peace. Perhaps it was the narrowness by which he had escaped death that drove out all thoughts of the past and worries about the future; but for a time he thought of nothing except the janizons. Individually, they were ungainly beasts, yet the sight of them moving soundlessly through the desert as a herd was one of sheer beauty, silvery giants in a beige mist. It made no difference to them whether the sands flowed or remained still; they were as much at home in the desert as whales in the sea.

All too soon the heat of the sun became unbearable, and Ahn Hrav told Falmeryn to join Raphon in the pouch. 'More than two is uncomfortable, so I will go with Dhrua and Ahn Bhen to another janizon,' he added. Dhrua clapped and called, and another doe marching alongside Cuhla came close enough for the three of them to jump onto her back. Meanwhile Falmeryn, now dressed in the cream-coloured robes Ahn Hrav had given him, climbed down Cuhla's chest and eased himself through the lip of the pouch with apprehension. As he had suspected, there was only room inside to lie down – or half-sit up at best – and the thought of being trapped in the dark pocket many feet under the sand was an unpleasant one. Within, it was warm, leathery, moist and filled with a pungent, animal aroma, mixed with the stench of stale milk. A dome-shaped concavity below the rib cage held some air, and also bore the teats from which Ahn Hrav's family obtained their milk.

'Raphon?' Falmeryn whispered, trying to make himself comfortable.

'I am alive, my friend, and will remain so if we can travel in this manner to Kesfaline,' said the Hrunneshian.

'I think they'll do anything they can for us . . . Perhaps too much,' Falmeryn murmured, half to himself. 'Raphon, how on Earth did you know their language?'

'No sound for the communication of thought is foreign to me,' Raphon replied, as if surprised at the question.

Falmeryn could feel the janizon shifting and swaying as she burrowed down into the sand, and he closed his eyes and tried not to think of it as burial. Surely if ever one of these creatures died below ground, the people within would be trapped . . . Then he became aware of a strange sound above him, and almost laughed. A continual gurgling and grumbling noise emitted from the doe's stomach, and far from being disturbing, there was something decidedly soothing in this cacophony. Presently his fear left him, and he fell asleep. As

330

Dhrua was to tell him later, the Ungremish themselves found the noise as sweet as a lullaby, for it was a sure sign that their janizon was in the best of health.

When evening came, Falmeryn was woken by the sudden movement of the doe ploughing her way up to the surface. As soon as he felt fresh air entering the pouch, he climbed out and scrambled up her side onto her back. The sun was low, the desert all violet and silver and the air completely still. Cuhla was one of the first up and it was a remarkable sight to see the ground undulating and erupting, the huge beasts rising out of it with sand streaming from their wrinkled coats.

Dhrua and Ahn Hrav waved from the other doe's back, and presently jumped across to join Falmeryn. As the sun set, even Raphon emerged for a short time, seeming much strengthened. Word of the two strangers had spread, and the copper-skinned folk were all eager to see them. Guiding the janizons close together, young and old alike leapt from back to back until they were grouped around Cuhla, although Ahn Hrav would allow no more than two at a time onto her back. Raphon spoke softly to them in their own language, which seemed to delight and fascinate them.

They shared a supper of milk – which was their only food – and then Ahn Hrav said, 'You told me that you wish to go to Kesfaline?'

'Yes. To the hills in the North,' Raphon replied.

'We can take you only to the edge of the desert. The janizons are travelling south-eastwards, but we can ask them to turn more to the North, so that we may take you as close to Kesfaline as we can.'

'Are you sure?' Falmeryn said uneasily. 'That you've saved our lives is enough – I wouldn't want to put you to such trouble.'

Ahn Hrav replied simply, 'The janizons will decide. You must trust their judgement, as we do.'

Then Ahn Hrav climbed along Cuhla's neck and turned her head to the North-East, thus telling her that he wished to change direction. The whole herd obeyed quiescently. It was not until two days later that Ahn Hrav expressed surprise

331

that they were keeping to the new course and had not drifted back to the original one. But Falmeryn felt a touch of unease which he could not explain. Changing the migratory route of the janizons seemed as unnatural as diverting a river for convenience' sake, and their placid acceptance of it struck him as wrong in some way. But events were beyond his control, and he did not feel able to voice his doubts to Raphon. The neman rarely emerged from the pouch and seemed to spend most of its time in philosophical thought.

In the following eight days, Falmeryn learned much about the Ungremish. They were a generous and open-hearted people, wholly devoted to their janizons. But he soon realised that the herd did not belong to them; *they* belonged to the herd. The janizons were nomadic, and wherever they went, the Ungremish went with them. At certain seasons they travelled to the edge of the desert, grazed until they had stored sufficient water and fat to survive for several months, then returned to the Swallowing Sands. They were intelligent, placid beasts who seemed to regard their human companions with affection. Falmeryn sensed an almost telepathic communication between them.

When Ahn Hrav spoke of his family, he did not just mean his wife and child; he meant everyone. There were thirty-seven altogether, all blood relatives, a true family tribe of the desert, one of many such tribes in Ungrem. Their lives were so ordered by the herd that they needed no human leader, although there were respected elders such as Ahn Hrav and Dhrua. There were only four children, and no adult much over fifty, for they endured a punishing existence which only the toughest survived. For many hours of each day and night they were entombed beneath the sand, and their limited time above ground was spent in burning heat, wind and sandstorms. They never left the janizons, any more than a sailor would leap from his ship; the risk of being swallowed was too great. They would often ride precariously on the neck or leg, or clamber nonchalantly all over the animal, but they never set foot on the sand.

All the animals in the herd were does. The male janizons

ran wild in groups and were another source of danger, particularly in the breeding season which occurred every four years. Then while the does carried their young, the tribe could come close to starvation from the shortage of milk. Throughout their months in the desert, they were wholly reliant on the janizons for their survival. Yet despite the severity of their life – or in compensation for it – they were a vivacious people who found great joy in life. While above ground there was continual coming and going, people leaping from one doe to the next to talk, sing and tell stories.

Not all of Ungrem was desert, so Falmeryn could not help wondering why they chose to live like this when they might have had an easier life elsewhere. The answer, he soon discovered, was straightforward and grim. All the habitable parts of Ungrem were under Gorethria's rule. The desert was the only place where the Ungremish could be free of them.

'And here we are truly free,' Ahn Hrav told him. 'Even the Gorethrians cannot follow us here. Why should we wish for a life that is "less hard", when we have exactly the life we desire? We have our freedom, we have the desert, and most of all we are blessed with the janizons. I think we are more fortunate than any Gorethrian in his marble palace.'

Children and adults alike shared a childlike fascination with the outside world, and asked Falmeryn questions hour after hour. Some had never been out of the desert, and were intrigued by his descriptions of lands that were permanently green, of mountains and snow and oceans.

'One day I want to go out of the Sands, and see the places you describe,' said Ahn Bhen, an intelligent and thoughtful boy. 'Mother and father have been beyond the desert edge, but I haven't. Are the green lands and the seas really there?' Falmeryn assured him that they were, but the boy frowned and became quiet. Later, when he and the Forluinishman were alone on Cuhla's back, he confided, 'There are many who live beyond the desert and fight the Gorethrians. I want to join them. But father says we must stay in the sands to stay free.'

'He's right, in a way. The Gorethrians would destroy you.'

'Why are they so strong? All of Ungrem should be ours, not just the Sands. They have no right to be here. Someone should show them,' Ahn Bhen said belligerently.

'It's not that simple,' Falmeryn replied, resting a sympathetic hand on the boy's shoulder. 'But I understand.' Ahn Bhen nodded, and did not speak of Gorethria again.

Falmeryn no longer found the long hours spent below sand frightening, but they were oppressive, and he longed to reach what the Ungremish called 'land' – just as if the desert really were an ocean. Yet while he was above ground, soothed by the dip and sway of Cuhla's back as she waded onwards, he knew there was much he would miss. The dunes stretching to the horizon, utterly still in the twilight, or rippling like amber waves in a brilliant, windy dawn. The sight of the janizons looming massively through the sand-haze as they plodded on their silent, mystical migration. Even the now-familiar, cheesy scent of their milk, which pervaded everything. But most of all he would miss Ahn Hrav, Dhrua and Cuhla, and he could not in honesty say he would miss the humans more than the animals, because tribe and herd were inseparable.

So it was with mixed feelings that he saw the greenish rim of 'land' appear on the horizon. In eight days they had covered roughly three hundred miles, but Raphon said that once in Kesfaline, it was still several hundred miles to their destination.

'This is a part of the desert edge that we rarely go to,' Ahn Hrav said. 'It is too close to Kesfaline.'

Falmeryn was thinking of Gorethrians, and said quietly, 'I don't want to put you in any danger.'

Ahn Hrav's dark, weather-beaten face crinkled in a half-smile. 'We live our lives in danger. If the janizons go willingly, there is no risk.'

'Besides, this part of the land is richer than our usual grazing place,' Dhrua added. 'We will all be glad of that.'

It rained in the night, and when they surfaced the next morning, it was as if the edge of the land had flowed out to

334

meet them in a green tide. Overnight, the sand became carpeted in tiny, fresh green shoots, some flowering and seeding in the space of hours. The janizons began to graze as they went along, rejoicing in this sudden feast.

By evening the sand began to give way to dry earth, and there were rocks and bushes strewing the landscape, which sloped gently towards distant hills. The janizons moved awkwardly on land, and Falmeryn noticed for the first time that they had large, spade-shaped feet, designed for ploughing through sand – not walking on earth. For several hours they grazed on the bushes and young shoots, while Ahn Bhen and the other children jumped to the ground and ran about barefoot, laughing at the novelty of it. But as the sun sank, the herd came to a halt and Ahn Hrav said, 'We will go no further inland. We must return to the sand so the janizons can submerge during the night. They will not sleep on land, and nor will we. It is not safe. Will you leave us now, or in the morning?'

'Now would be better for Raphon, I think,' Falmeryn replied.

'You are right,' said the Hrunneshian, as it climbed from Cuhla's pouch. 'I can travel while it is dark and cold, but not in the heat of the day.'

'Very well. We will give you flasks of milk to sustain you on your way.' Falmeryn changed from the loose robes back into his leather tunic and breeches, sorry that the time of parting had come so quickly. He felt he had been in the desert for ever, and it was unpleasant to be severed from the security and rhythm of tribal life. The rich smell of milk had permeated his and Raphon's cloaks, and would be a constant reminder of that strange, other-worldly time.

The whole family gathered to watch them depart, their creamy robes fluttering in a light wind. They were unusually subdued, and the sadness in their eyes showed that they did not really want Falmeryn and Raphon to leave.

Even the janizons seemed aware of what was happening. Cuhla nuzzled at Falmeryn's shoulder, and he reached up to stroke her head, with its large, round eye and velvet-soft skin.

'You have been welcome visitors in my family,' Ahn Hrav said. 'I hope you will find whatever it is you seek in Kesfaline.'

'I don't know what it is myself, yet,' Falmeryn replied, smiling, but Raphon said nothing.

'We will never forget you,' Dhrua added.

'Nor I you. I'll miss you all.'

'You are going to fight the Gorethrians, aren't you?' Ahn Bhen asked suddenly, with an almost painful note of envy in his voice. Falmeryn shook his head sadly.

'Perhaps. I don't know.' Their farewells over, he embraced Ahn Hrav, Dhrua and Ahn Bhen, then he and the neman turned away and began to walk up the dry slope towards the hills.

The sun was still above the horizon, casting long thin shadows from the tiniest rock and grass blade. The air was blurred and golden, as if full of sand or mist, a strange light in which it was impossible to see clearly. When Falmeryn turned to look back at the tribe the janizons were no more than vague shapes sketched on the haze, and he could not make out the people at all. A cloud of dust appeared to be rolling towards the tribe from the North, churned up by an errant gust of wind. Falmeryn shielded his eyes and squinted against the dazzling sunset to see it more clearly.

No, the cloud was too purposeful to be caused by the wind. And now he could hear the faint thunder of hooves on rock, and perceived the shapes of horses, flying cloaks and helmeted heads through the dust. The outlines were horrifyingly familiar and quite unmistakable. A division of Gorethrians was bearing down swiftly on Ahn Hrav and his people.

For a moment Falmeryn stood rooted to the spot by disbelief. 'Raphon,' he said hoarsely, gripping the Hrunneshian's arm. The tribe were unarmed, and despite their size, the janizons were too slow to outpace the horses. There was not even time for the tribe to climb onto the does' backs before the Gorethrians were upon them. Dust plumed up into a huge cloud which obscured everything, and the air was pierced by shouts and screams and sounds of violence. In horror, Falmeryn bent and seized a rock, and then he was running, running wildly down the slope towards them.

Within a few easy strides, Raphon caught up with him, stretched out all four arms and virtually lifted him off the ground. Falmeryn struggled violently, but the neman was inhumanly strong and hung onto him with determination. 'For the Lady's sake, Raphon, let me go!' he cried furiously. 'We have to help them, you can't –'

'There's nothing you can do,' the neman replied in a calm and logical tone. 'If you go among them, you will be killed. Whom will that help?'

Suddenly the light changed, and the scene became horrifyingly clear. The attack had taken the tribe completely by surprise; fire-gold horses were milling around them, and all was confusion. The soldiers' winged helms were sharply silhouetted against the sky, and their swords shone with the heavy brilliance of amulin power. Some of the Ungremish tried to flee, only to find their way blocked by plunging horses. Others launched themselves at the Gorethrians with bare hands, and were cut down.

The janizons had no aggressive instinct, and could only sway from side to side in their distress, or turn in ponderous circles. But Falmeryn clearly saw Cuhla swing her head at one Gorethrian, unhorsing him, and he saw another turn and bring his blade down vengefully on her neck. She stumbled and fell heavily onto her side. With a scream that was terrible to hear, Ahn Hrav flew at the Gorethrian and was felled instantly. Dhrua and Ahn Bhen rushed towards him, but were seized by another soldier and thrust away.

After that, a strange kind of peace fell. The surviving Ungremish – perhaps twenty-five or so – had been captured, and stood in shocked silence within a circle of Gorethrian horses. Two of the does lay on their sides, dead; the rest had broken away and were charging headlong back to the desert. The Gorethrians were nonchalantly sheathing their swords and calming their highly strung steeds.

Then Falmeryn stopped struggling against Raphon. The rock fell from his hand, and he wept.

'Come,' said the neman, pulling him along by the arm. 'We must escape before they see us. We must go to the Circle of Spears.'

Falmeryn knew Raphon was right, that there was nothing they could have done and that they must flee or be killed, and the knowledge only made his grief worse. He had no choice but to follow Raphon towards the hills, but he ran mechanically, half-blinded by tears. Behind them, the Gorethrian horsemen were intent on herding their prisoners northwards, and did not spot two figures escaping into the eastern hills.

Falmeryn only glanced back once, and that was not to look at the Gorethrians but at the janizons. They were in the distance now, wading through the sand as swiftly as their thick legs could bear them, necks outstretched and ears flattened. And as they ran, they began to give voice to a forlorn, hoarse bugling noise which stabbed his heart with renewed misery.

It was the first time he had ever heard them make any sound at all. He had never been sure quite how intelligent they were, but now he knew. The janizons were not merely frightened. They were bereaved. Long after he was out of earshot, those despairing cries still followed him, and he knew they would continue to follow him for the rest of his life.

It was not rare for Anixa to be summoned to court, but she had never before had to attend on the Emperor himself. A robe was needed for a ceremony, and his own dressmaker was ill; thus she found herself in a chamber within the palace, in Xaedrek's presence for the first time. He stood obligingly still while she draped the rich green and gold brocade around him and secured it with pins, but otherwise he seemed quite oblivious to her.

The High Councillor Lord Amnek was also in the room,

338

seated at a small desk in the corner and applying his seal to various documents. Anixa was uncomfortably aware that the two were not speaking to each other because she was in the room. She held a position of trust, but it was not done for the Emperor to discuss anything in front of an outsider, Gorethrian or otherwise.

A thought passed through Anixa's mind: a single poisoned pin, and she could have slain Xaedrek then and there. But it was only a thought, she would not have done it. Perhaps, in that, the Gorethrians who trusted her knew her better than she knew herself. Dismissing the fancy, she went on with her work.

Xaedrek, meanwhile, was thinking of Melkavesh. He was not thinking of her with hatred or even anger, but with the same kind of brooding obsession that had driven him to restore the Empire. Amnek hated her, because he blamed her for Shavarish's death, but Xaedrek could not find it in himself to hate her. She was a fascinating duality. In one aspect, she was Ashurek's daughter, a pursuer of wild, mis-guided ideals that could only bring ruin. Yet in another she was as much a child of Gorethria as himself, descended from the Empress Melkavesh and with the potential to be as great.

A second eagle sent after her had lost her, as if her power had suddenly winked out and died. He had not dispatched a third. He was beginning to accept that he could not defeat her simply by killing her. She was too complex, and the implications of her presence on Earth were of something greater than herself, which could not easily be swept aside. Although he had resigned himself to letting her live for the time being, he was in no doubt that she must eventually be destroyed, or the outcome would be disastrous. But just as he had summoned Ah'garith in full awareness of the risks, the same objective curiosity now compelled him to wait and see what she was going to do, however much danger there might be.

Besides, Irem Ol Thangiol had become too ill to make any more progress with the experiments. Until more Kristillians were captured and brought back to Shalekahh, he was indispensable, so Xaedrek had been forced to allow him a few days' rest. In the meantime, his mind had been working along different lines which he had not even revealed to Amnek, let alone Ah'garith.

Contrary to his fears, the woman-demon had been absurdly obedient of late, despite taking further doses of amulin. But there was something repulsively sinister in her subservience, and he never let himself become complacent about her intentions. In some intangible way it seemed she was slipping away from him, and he loathed nothing more than that feeling of being not quite in control.

As he was thinking of Ah'garith, the ornately panelled door swung open, and she entered. It was not his imagination; she seemed physically changed in some way, and the change was becoming more marked each day. Her body seemed less solid, and there was a horrible luminescence about her, like a sickly white fish from the depths of the ocean. No one else seemed to have noticed.

'What is it?' he demanded.

She ignored his abruptness, seeming unusually elated. 'Sire, if you can spare me a few minutes of your precious time, there is something I wish to show you. Something I have been working on —'

'Ah'garith, we are not alone,' Xaedrek said sharply. She fell silent and turned to glare at Anixa who had paused in her work, transfixed by the sight of the white-haired old woman. Melkavesh had sometimes spoken of Xaedrek's demonic companion. She was nothing to look at, but her eyes — her eyes were like lenses onto a world where nothing existed except malice made physical, a sickly grey ocean where the human soul could drown for ever without dying . . .

Anixa fainted.

'Well, that's dealt with her,' said Ah'garith nastily.

'That was quite unnecessary.' Xaedrek felt wearied by the demon's gratuitous spite, but refused to let her think she had succeeded in annoying him. Calling a guard, he said calmly, 'The dressmaker is unwell. Please take her to the adjoining

340

chamber and let her rest until she has recovered. Irem Ol Thangiol is there, but he is in a coma. She will not disturb him. And go and bring her some refreshment.'

Ah'garith watched the guard carrying Anixa's slight frame out of the room, and said, 'Now will you come with me, Sire?'

'Can't it wait? Or can you not tell me what it is?'

'No, Sire, I would much prefer to show you. It is not a trivial matter, I assure you, but something of great –'

He cut her short with a wave of his hand. 'Very well. Go on to the mansion, Ah'garith, and we'll join you in a few minutes.'

'Ah – not the mansion, Sire. The dungeons beneath the Fortress of Execution.'

'The dungeons?' exclaimed Xaedrek, looking up in surprise. 'Who gave you permission to work there?' But Ah'garith was already slipping out of the room, pulling the door closed behind her. Xaedrek sighed and went to sit in a chair facing Amnek. 'Do you still think I'm right to work with the Shanin?' he asked.

Amnek put aside his seals and papers, and folded his bony hands. 'I believe I share your feelings, Sire. I dislike the creature, but she has proved useful. You have her under control.'

'Even though she has been taking amulin?'

'She has not disobeyed you.'

Xaedrek raised his eyebrows. 'But she is trying to.'

'Perhaps you are too strict with her. Perhaps she speaks the truth when she says that she must take amulin in order for us to make scientific progress.'

'Well, I hope so, my friend. I hope so.' Xaedrek began to disentangle himself from the half-finished robe, cursing as the pins scratched him. In its place he put on a garment of quilted purple satin, with a design of hawks worked in black and gold beads. 'By the way, Amnek . . . Baramek and I have decided to delay the invasion of Kristillia.'

As he had anticipated, Amnek reacted with shock. He

341

stood up, stooping to glare into Xaedrek's impassive eyes. 'Why, Your Majesty?'

'Because, as we have said many times, Kristillia has some hidden source of strength, and until we have a new and effective weapon to use against them, all attempts to invade are simply a waste of troops. Baramek agrees. All our strength must be put into developing hyperphysics.'

'But we have been saying that for months – years – and there has been no progress,' the Councillor said shortly.

'There will be progress soon.' Xaedrek paused, fastening a golden belt. 'I have an idea, Amnek. I think we've been too embroiled with the unreliable human element. My thoughts are taking another direction. However, there's no point in us discussing it until the theory can be proven.'

Amnek smoothed the folds of his grey robe, and unnecessarily busied himself in tidying the desk. Since the death of Shavarish, a certain coldness had developed between him and Xaedrek which both of them regretted but could do nothing to avoid. Presently he asked tightly, 'And what of the Lady Melkavesh? Surely it is essential that you send another eagle after her?'

'There is no need. I know where she's gone. She was in the centre of the Emethrians – heaven knows how she survived there, but it doesn't surprise me – so where would she be going, except Kristillia?' Xaedrek fell silent, wondering – as he had done many times – if she really was capable of betraying her Gorethrian blood and siding with his enemies.

'And you are just letting her go? But it is imperative that we know exactly where she is and what she is doing.' Xaedrek did not reply, and suppressed anger began to enter Amnek's voice as he went on, 'Sire, I am dismayed that you have so far failed to find and destroy her. It would take much to shake my faith in you, but –' Xaedrek glanced sharply at him. At that, the Councillor seemed to lose control, and all but shouted, 'Must I do it myself?'

Xaedrek's tone was placatory but his eyes were ice cold as he replied, 'Amnek, you give the impression that you are seeking personal revenge against her. I hope I am mistaken,

342

because I hardly need to point out how unworthy of you such a motive would be.'

Shaking with rage, Amnek brought his fists down on the desk, scattering papers everywhere. 'Shavarish was my wife, damn you!'

There was a silence. Xaedrek said quietly, 'I know. And my friend.' His sympathy might be genuine, but to the Councillor it seemed hollow. Amnek had not realised how much he had loved and relied on his wife until she was gone. He had thought science the motivating force of his life; now he realised, too late, that he was wrong. It was Shavarish who had sustained him with her fierce love of life and her joy in Gorethria's strength. It was she who had helped Xaedrek to reshape the Empire. Without her, nothing seemed real to Amnek, and nothing seemed to matter – except destroying Melkavesh. Xaedrek had disposed of the Lady Kharan without a second thought, and was apparently able to put Shavarish from his mind with equal coldness. Yet he had a strange reluctance to kill Melkavesh and forget her, and Amnek was growing increasingly bitter and suspicious of his attitude.

Xaedrek, however, saw it differently. The loss of Shavarish was cause for great sorrow, but sorrow must never be allowed to come between him and his duty. So he was disappointed in Amnek, who was becoming obsessed by grief to the exclusion of Gorethria's welfare. He despised the desire for vengeance in anyone; in Amnek, that most single-minded of scientists and his closest colleague, it was intolerable. Thus their relationship had turned sour, and was unlikely to improve.

Finally Xaedrek broke the strained silence. 'I agree with you, Amnek. We must find a way to watch Melkavesh, but it must be something more precise than an eagle, which can only see a golden blur. We need to use a human. If only there was someone she knows and trusts, whom we could send to spy on her without arousing her suspicions. Unfortunately, Irem Ol Thangiol certainly will not suffice, and I know of no one else . . .' He sighed, and turned to the door.

343

'Well, Amnek, we may as well go and see whatever it is that Ah'garith wishes to show us.'

'Yes, Sire,' Amnek replied, his hawkish eyes boring into Xaedrek's satin-clad back as he followed him out of the room. 'Let us hope it is something worthwhile this time.'

When Anixa came round, she found herself in a large room, lying on a couch which was fashioned in the shape of a leopard. Everything was in shades of gold: heavy curtains, delicate furniture, the bejewelled cover of a large bed on the far side of the chamber, even the air itself seemed golden. But it was a faded, ochreous hue, as if the room had not been used for many years. The strange insight she possessed told her that this had once been the bedchamber of the insane Emperor Meshurek.

She sat up, trembling, feeling strands of icy sweat branching down her back. She rubbed convulsively at her throat, but that only worsened the pressure that threatened to choke her. Meshurek's aura was still in this room, and the hideous memory of Ah'garith's eyes was so vivid that she felt the demon might slip through a crack in the atmosphere at any second. The air seemed brittle with blood and pain, taut with the unheard cries of all those who had suffered at the hands of Xaedrek and his ancestors.

And there was something moving on the bed.

She clutched the carved leopard's head with a damp hand, willing herself to regain control. She thought of Kesfaline, trying to lose herself in the gentle philosophy of her land and fill her thoughts only with images of the two dove-white moons that governed their lives . . . But the moons kept transforming into the demon's malignant eyes, and black panic swept through her like nausea. She lurched off the couch and staggered to the bed, under a fearful compulsion to find out what lay there, however terrible it was.

It was a man, only a man. She held onto the jewel-studded canopy in relief, fighting off another wave of faintness. Her breathing slowed and the imminent hysteria subsided, but the evil atmosphere continued to press down on her. The man was a Kristillian. His red-bronze hair was damp with sweat, his marbled, brown-gold skin disfigured by scar tissue. His eyes were closed and he moaned and writhed in a coma, locked within his own hellish phantasms. A coppery-black, unnatural power flowed from him in waves, and his torment seemed palpable.

Anixa's eyes burned with pity. She was far beyond understanding or even trying to, and everything she did was by instinct. She reached out and pressed her trembling fingers to his forehead, and his writhing ceased at once. He awoke, parted his swollen lids and looked at her.

'Xaedrek has done this to you,' she whispered.

Irem Ol Thangiol swallowed, and stared at her. He thought he was hallucinating. For weeks he had existed in a haze of amulin intoxication. The only faces he had seen were Gorethrian ones, looming over him with the sinister indifference of torturers' masks. Or worse, he had woken from many a nightmare to find the demon leering at him, revelling in his pain. A kindly face, words of comfort – such things were lost to him, so deeply buried under the weight of horror that they might as well never have existed. So when he found the small, dark Kesfalian woman looking down at him, he could not believe she was real. A dream? A new kind of torment? Her expression was at once solemn and fearful, but there was tenderness in the pale amber eyes, and her presence was like a calm, sweet breath of sanity. He felt like a child whose mother had suddenly appeared to tell him that everything was all right, it was over and she had come to take him home . . . He tried to reach out to her, and she seized his nerveless hand and held onto it, tight. *She was real.*

Then they both discovered that the ancient, mystical attachment between Kesfaline and Kristillia was no myth. They had never met before, they knew nothing of each other, yet understanding flowed between their eyes like a diamond-clear stream. The empathy they shared was deep and instant, and needed no words to strengthen it. But it was only a tenuous thread in a chasm: far from being comforted, each

345

of them saw the cause of their terror accentuated in the other's eyes, and Anixa knew that if she did not speak, they would be overcome by mutual despair.

'I didn't know,' she said in a dry, choked voice. 'I mean, I knew Xaedrek was evil, but it has never touched me before – not like this.'

'Who are you?' he gasped. He was aware that they were the first coherent words he had spoken in days.

'My name is Anixa. I am a court dressmaker, but . . .'

'I am Irem Ol Thangiol of Kristillia,' he said, startled to find that he still retained some sense of identity.

Anixa recognised the name. Melkavesh had spoken of him just before she left; she had given him amulin in the hope that it would give him the strength to escape, but evidently she had failed. This was the result; he had become a wretched victim of Xaedrek's vile experiments.

'You know Melkavesh,' she whispered.

'Yes!' he exclaimed, raising his head from the pillow as if the name itself had given him strength. 'How do you know of her?'

'The sages of Kesfaline have predicted her coming. She is the Sorceress who will help us, then destroy us.'

'No. She will save us.' He hung onto her hand and hauled himself into a half-sitting position, his voice fervent. 'Our priests have also spoken of her, the enchantress who is a child of the moons, whose power will prevail even against Gorethria.'

'Oh, I hope you are right,' Anixa said softly. 'I trusted her and helped her. I don't want to believe I was wrong to do so. Irem Ol Thangiol, have you the strength to walk?'

'I – I don't know. I doubt it. Why?'

'Because we are going to escape. I cannot work for Xaedrek any longer, I cannot bear to think that because I have been untrue to myself for so many years, it is too late to make amends. I cannot leave you here in this pain. Come with me, and I will hide you.'

'But . . .'

She found a robe lying on a chair, and gave it to him. 'Put

346

this on, and get up. You can lean on me. There were very few guards in the corridors when I came, and if we meet anyone, I can say that you were helping me carry some cloth. They know me, I come and go from the palace without being challenged.'

Irem Ol Thangiol was weak, but the few days' grace Xaedrek had given him had restored him more than he realised. He pushed back the bedcover and swung his legs over the edge to sit up. His limbs ached and trembled and he felt light-headed, but he found the strength to wrap the green satin robe around his large frame. Then he stood up unsteadily, leaning on the wall. Anixa was peeping through the door into an anteroom, whispering, 'I can see no one. Come with me.'

The truth was, Anixa was deluding herself. If she had stopped to think, she would have realised at once that they could not possibly get more than a few yards without being stopped. It was a long way to the outside of the palace, absolutely impossible to traverse without encountering any number of guards and courtiers on the way. Even if Irem Ol Thangiol was not recognised as a known prisoner – which he certainly would be – he still looked too obviously ill, fevered and unsteady to pass unnoticed. But Anixa was not in a rational state of mind. Her encounter with the demon and her subsequent terror had unhinged her, and she was acting upon the kind of logic that held sway in dreams. All she knew was that she must rescue Irem Ol Thangiol, thus fulfilling the age-old vow of fellowship between their two countries.

The Kristillian, likewise, was in no condition to make sensible judgements. He could not resist the promise of freedom. Anixa was a breath of life in his hellish world, and he would have followed her anywhere, done whatever she asked, anything not to lose her. He leaned on her shoulder, noticing that her bones felt as delicate as a bird's through the plain black material of her dress. She raised a hand to support his arm, and they began to make their slow way across the anteroom.

There was another panelled door in front of them, beyond which lay an archway, then a marble corridor. Anixa made Ol Thangiol wait while she looked out, but the guard who had taken her to the chamber had been dispatched to bring her a drink, and had not yet returned. All was quiet. She took Ol Thangiol's arm, swung the door open, and led him out into the corridor – precisely in the same moment that Xaedrek and Amnek chose to emerge from the adjoining room.

Both parties stopped and stared at each other. There was a long, frozen moment, in which Xaedrek gazed at the small dressmaker and the tall, ravaged form of Irem Ol Thangiol with astonishment, and they returned the look with dread and utter, heart-stopping dismay. Then the Emperor came forward slowly, his arms folded and his eyes glowing crimson under half-closed lids.

'Lord Amnek, please would you summon the guards?' he said in a calm, almost casual voice which made Anixa feel that a block of ice had formed in her stomach. What a fool I am, she thought, closing her eyes. At once, rationality returned to her and she saw her half-formed plan in all its rashness and futility, but too late. Fear gripped her like a collar of black iron – then it was gone as suddenly, leaving her calm and empty.

'Madam Anixa, I'm sure there is an explanation for this, and I would be very interested to hear it,' Xaedrek said. He was not surprised when she did not reply. 'You know, it is very strange. This man has been in a deep coma for three days, despite the physician's efforts. Now, suddenly, he feels well enough to accompany you in a stroll. You obviously have a healing touch.'

Four guards came pounding down the corridor and halted smartly by Xaedrek, saluting. He raised a hand, telling them to wait, and took a step closer to Anixa. Sharply, he demanded, 'Do you know this man?'

'No, Your Majesty.'

'Good. I like a clear answer. He is a very particular guest of mine, you understand, and I do not care for him to be

348

removed from his room without my authority – especially as he has been so unwell.' His voice was light and pleasant, yet she found it as menacing as an instrument of torture half-hidden in shadows. 'If you do not know him, what are you doing with him?'

Anixa did not answer. She could not.

Xaedrek persisted, 'Where were you going?' The Kesfalian remained obdurately silent, expressionless, her pale apricot eyes fixed sullenly on his. With anyone else he would have grown impatient and given her over to the guards by now, but there was something about her that intrigued him. 'Well, madam, your silence is leading me to think there is an element of Kesfalian and Kristillian subterfuge against Gorethria in this. Perhaps I should remind you that there are extremely unpleasant penalties for such activities. So some kind of explanation – which will no doubt convince me of your innocence – can only be to your benefit. I ask again, why were you removing this man?'

But as far as Anixa was concerned, there was nothing to say. She could not throw herself on his mercy, pleading terror of the demon, the aura of Meshurek's room and the obscene amulin power. Nor could she bring herself to mouth lies which he would see through at once. In fact, she felt that he already saw through her; that he understood her fear, her deep-rooted hatred of him, all the impulses that had driven her to attempt the rescue of Ol Thangiol – and in understanding her, he despised her. What they said of him was true: he had the percipience to see into his enemies' minds, to dissect and paralyse their spirits without resort to physical torture. He was impossible to defy.

Anixa knew she could not win, but neither would she admit defeat. Her only defence was to withdraw into herself, curling protectively around her soul so that whatever happened to her, no one – not even Xaedrek himself – could violate her essential spirit.

'For an extremely capable and intelligent woman, you are acting very foolishly. You have served the court well for years, so I can't imagine what has possessed you to throw away such a privileged position . . . Well, perhaps I can, but I will not put words in your mouth.' The Emperor half-smiled chillingly. Then he asked suddenly, 'Does the name Melkavesh mean anything to you? Never mind.' He signalled to the guards. 'Place Madam Anixa and Ol Thangiol in the chamber under guard. Have a physician attend both of them, and see that they receive rest and a good meal. I will return and talk to them later.'

When the guards had led Anixa and the Kristillian back into Meshurek's chamber, Xaedrek and Amnek continued on their way to meet Ah'garith in the dungeons.

'You are too lenient with them, Sire,' Amnek said sharply. 'The woman made a blatant attempt to free your most valuable prisoner. Perhaps it was pre-meditated.'

'Nonsense. Nothing so clumsy could have been planned in advance,' Xaedrek said benignly.

'All the same, it was treasonable. She should be imprisoned, induced to talk, and appropriately punished. Instead, you give her – both of them – all the comforts accorded to visiting nobles!'

'Not quite. By the Serpent, Amnek, can't you see it? It is simple psychology. Two souls, both alone and under great stress and fear. When Anixa was taken to the room, they had never met before. By the time they emerged, they were half-way to being in love. Was it not obvious to you?'

'No, Sire. Not really,' Amnek said acidly.

'Then take my word for it. If we separate and punish them now, that is exactly what they expect, and we'll gain nothing by it. But if they are left together indefinitely, in a reasonable degree of comfort, but in continued anticipation of a horrible punishment . . . do you see?' Xaedrek grinned, feeling more cheerful than he had done since Melkavesh's departure. 'In no time at all they will be desperately in love, wholly dependent upon each other, inseparable. That is the lever by which we manipulate them to do whatever we wish.'

'You have lost none of your brilliance,' said Amnek grudgingly. 'But how do you hope to use them? The woman's only a dressmaker.'

350

'No one is "only" what they do. Where would we be without our craftsmen?' Xaedrek mused. 'No, Amnek, she intrigues me. There's something within her. Did you not see how she reacted when I mentioned Melkavesh?'

'I saw no reaction at all.'

'Ah well, it's only an intuition. Maybe it will come to nothing. It's of no consequence. Besides, I can't have her put to death – she hasn't finished that wretched robe yet.'

They went to the lowest level of the palace and made their way through a series of locked and heavily guarded doors where even Xaedrek himself must give a password. This was an entrance to the network of dungeons that stretched underground from the palace to the Fortress of Execution. Few knew of it and only certain members of the palace staff were allowed to use it; all others who had business in the dungeons must enter through the Fortress.

After descending a long, narrow flight of steps, two guards opened a final door and stood rigidly to attention as Amnek and Xaedrek passed through into the dungeons. As with the whole of Shalekahh, the cells were kept fanatically clean – mainly by the prisoners themselves, under duress – but that did nothing to make them less sinister. Torchlight flickered on pale grey walls which were built of stone but had a peculiar sheen that made them look like metal. A corridor lined with black doors stretched as far as the eye could see, like the infinite reflection of one mirror in another. Here, the monarchs, war leaders and governments of conquered countries were imprisoned alongside errant slaves, Gorethrian wrongdoers, and whose guilty (or suspected) of conspiring against Gorethria. Few who were held here were ever released, and most were eventually executed in the grey Fortress that Kharan had so narrowly avoided.

Xaedrek and Amnek strode swiftly along the corridor until it intersected with an identical one, and there they saw Ah'garith waiting by a cell door a few yards away on the left. She was chafing her palms together with obvious impatience. 'At last,' she exclaimed, her voice echoing unpleasantly in

351

the confined space. 'I thought you were not coming, Sire, Lord Amnek.'

'I don't recall giving you permission to work in here,' said Xaedrek brusquely. He found the mingled stench of dampness, scrubbed stone and human exudations unpleasant.

'Sire, when you agreed to let me experiment alone, you placed no restriction on where I might work, nor on what I might do,' the Shanin pointed out.

'Well, that's true,' Xaedrek acknowledged reluctantly. 'So, what have you done?'

With what seemed to be a parody of a nervous, obsequious confession, Ah'garith muttered, 'I found three Kristillians down here, Sire. Before you curse me for not handing them over to you, let me explain that they are not prisoners of the recent war, but ones who had been here since Meshurek's time. They were old and weak, so I took the liberty of using them for my own experiments.'

'That was a liberty indeed.' Xaedrek's lightness of heart vanished and his mood turned dark, oppressed by the dungeons and by Ah'garith. He glanced at Amnek, but the Councillor's fierce eyes were avidly intent upon the demon.

'Wait until you have seen what I have achieved. Sire, you will see that I have not betrayed you. You will not be sorry that you trusted me enough to let me take amulin. Far from it, you will rejoice.'

'Enough of these flowery promises,' the Emperor sighed. 'Just show us what you are talking about, and let us judge for ourselves.' Ah'garith nodded, and moved eagerly to the unlocked cell door. As she pushed it open, a throbbing, pinkish-white glare burst across their eyes, painful in its intensity. Other colours flickered within it, the mauves and greenish-yellows of a fading bruise. The brassy amulin stench was so overwhelming that even Xaedrek, who was used to it, could not help gagging.

They stepped into the cell and saw that almost the whole floor, except for a rim of stone round the edge, had been cut away and replaced by a large circular lens. Like the smaller

352

one that he and Ah'garith had made in the mansion, it was striated with iridescent blues and greens and had the texture of living muscle. From the centre, concentric rings of light pulsed slowly outwards, radiating a vile, blood-tinged glare.

And on it lay not the three Kristillians, but three monstrous creatures joined together – or one creature divided into three lobes, it was hard to tell which. Each was bloated, shapeless and corpse-pale, sweating a sickly light as its sides rose and fell with its laboured breathing. Yet they emanated power – such power that Xaedrek staggered under the force of it. Yes, Ah'garith had not been boasting: she really had used the amulin to unlock the flood of necromantic energy that they had been seeking. For the first time Xaedrek tasted all the power he could have desired, and more.

And he felt nothing but disgust.

The sight of the creatures repulsed him, as if everything he loathed about Ah'garith was distilled in them. He had seen and caused much pain in his time, and been coldly unmoved by it – but this was different. It was un-Gorethrian, unclean. He remembered the sickness he had felt when he had first allowed Ah'garith to torment Irem Ol Thangiol, and now that feeling threatened to overwhelm him again. He fought to control his nausea, to prevent himself from rushing from the cell in horror.

Whatever those creatures were now, they had once been men. Each still retained a rudimentary face, tilted upwards, flattened and half-hidden between the swollen shoulders, but still recognisably human. They *were* the three Kristillians. However great the power that Ah'garith had created, the obscenity of her method was more than even Xaedrek could stomach.

12

Ferdanice of Kesfaline

WHEN FALMERYN and Raphon left Ungrem behind they kept up a swift pace for most of the night. There was no clearly defined border between Ungrem and Kesfaline. The desert blended into bare, bony hills, then a plateau of sparse grassland. Beyond was a chain of greater hills, their stark outlines blurred like sheeted ghosts in the starlight. All night Falmeryn and Raphon toiled through them, increasing the distance between them and the Gorethrian raiders mile by mile.

Had his companion been human, Falmeryn would have tried to be stoical and hide his distress at the attack on the Ungremish. But Raphon was not human, and had no particular expectations of him, and somehow this made it easier for him to express his misery and rage.

'I knew it was wrong for Ahn Hrav to bring us so close to Kesfaline,' he cried. 'I knew it! So why did he agree so easily? If he was so certain the janizons would sense danger, why didn't they? I should have insisted they kept on their original course.'

'My friend, I know not why humans feel the need to blame themselves for the destructive acts of others. It cannot change what has happened.'

'I'm not blaming myself, Raphon,' he said angrily. 'For that, I would have to feel that I was in control of things, and I don't. I feel that something is controlling me. Something with no regard for the consequences of anything it does.'

He looked accusingly at the Hrunneshian, hoping it would say something to throw light on events, but it only replied,

'This is also a common feeling, one responsible for the invention of gods.'

'I don't think we need to invent them, Raphon.' Falmeryn fell silent, until a long time later he murmured, 'Why – by the Lady, why?' and began to weep convulsively without tears. But the dry sobs were the shock waves of grief being hammered deep into his soul, and rather than alleviating his pain, they only chafed it raw.

The Hrunneshian showed no reaction at all to his grief; no sympathy, no embarrassment, no disdain. Its neutrality was the only thing that made the situation bearable. But later, it began to talk softly of philosophical matters, setting one argument against another, carefully considering all possible motives for and reactions to the attack, both Gorethrian and Ungremish. Then Falmeryn knew that, despite its emotionless exterior, it had been deeply affected after all. While he found no comfort in its words – there was no comfort for the raw brutality of what had happened – there was something in them that wrung his grief dry, so that he faced the dawn better able to go on.

After two days in the hills, the landscape changed dramatically. They were on a high point, below which Kesfaline lay spread out like a mosaic of bronze, green and amber. Dark green forests flowed around rich farmlands, threatening to reclaim them. Acres and acres of fruit-rich orchards shimmered with ever-changing tints of green, gold and red. The landscape was dotted with villages of rust-brown stone, and in the distance the hills blended to deep blue, with terraced fields marked out as if by white pen-lines. Some of the hillsides nearer to them bore the black scars of open-cast mines, for Kesfaline was a mineral-rich country that Gorethria had plundered for centuries.

And it was a land with a powerful aura, which affected Falmeryn strongly. Closing his eyes, the peaceful landscape before him was replaced by an image of violence. There were fields afire, and through the haze of smoke and charred straw a legion of Gorethrians was charging down to engage the Kesfalian army. They were a small, dark people, clad in uniforms of dark green and violet leather. Some were mounted on ponies, most were on foot. They seemed no match for the tall Gorethrians in their black armour and bright swirling cloaks, with their broadswords, crossbows and dauntless war-horses; yet they fought bravely, with the ferocious skill of desperation.

Falmeryn did not know whether he was seeing the first invasion of Kesfaline, centuries ago, or the more recent one by Xaedrek; it did not matter. The spirit was the same – the fierce pride of both sides, the exhilaration of the first engagement followed by the mess, confusion and agony of battle. Inevitably, the Kesfalians were driven back. Few Gorethrians fell, but many a green and violet tunic was blackened with blood, and the groans of the wounded were ignored as the battle became a massacre . . .

Falmeryn's vision changed, and he saw cottages spewing smoke and flame, families fleeing in terror, some cut down as they fled and others seized and herded into abject groups of prisoners. And now he saw a paved road with lines of gibbets stretching to the horizon. On them hung the broken bodies of those who had tried to regroup the Kesfalian army after the invasion, labelled rebels and traitors to Gorethria – a dire warning to others who considered defying their conquerors. Past the gibbets trundled great pony-drawn carts, laden with fruit and grain and precious minerals, bound for Shalekahh. Tiny figures in silhouette were chained behind the carts, some walking with proud defiance, some shuffling with bowed heads, some stumbling and crying. They were men, women and children who were being taken to serve Gorethria as slaves.

Falmeryn opened his eyes, and the vision ended. He pressed a hand to his forehead, swaying slightly. Ghostly and unreal as the visions had been, he knew they were a true picture of what had happened in Kesfaline, and the reality of the attack on Ahn Hrav's people was still with him, keen as a sword-cut.

'I wish I knew what to do,' he said faintly. 'Estarinel said it was a shock to him when he realised that not just Forluin was suffering under the Serpent, but the whole world. Now I feel the same. Forluin is safe, but Ungrem and Kesfaline aren't. How can we enjoy our good fortune in Forluin, when this is happening in Vardrav? At least Estarinel knew what he had to do – destroy the Serpent. If only things seemed as clear and straightforward now. What should I do, Raphon?'

'There are endless possibilities in answering that question. It would delight me to debate them with you, but the sun is rising . . .'

'It's just as well. I'm in no state to debate anything,' he replied with a grimace. 'Let's find shelter.' They descended the hill and entered the dense cover of a forest. Dawn drew rich, earthy tints from its depths, and delineated the dark green roof of leaves with emerald light. Birds chorused loudly in the branches, occasionally flitting out of the shadows in a flurry of black and honey plumage. There was a fresh scent in the air that reminded Falmeryn poignantly of Forluinish woods after rain.

Presently they found a stream flowing between deep, undercut banks, and decided to rest there until the evening. Raphon did not need sleep as such, but craved refuge from the daylight and time for solitary thought, so while the neman settled itself in a deep hollow under the bank, with its feet in the stream, Falmeryn found a drier place between the roots of a huge tree, concealed by bushes. He had hardly eaten for three days, but could not bring himself to drink the milk Ahn Hrav had given him. Instead, he poured it away into the stream, watching the bluish-white cloud swirling and dispersing until the current had obliterated it completely. Then he pulled his cloak round him and fell into a tormented sleep, in which the ground seemed to rock under him like a janizon. Over and over again he saw a robed figure felled by a Gorethrian sword, and each time he would rush over and pull the headdress from the corpse's face – only to find it was not Ahn Hrav, but Kharan.

He woke in the late afternoon, unrefreshed and in low spirits. While he washed in the stream and filled his flask, Raphon sat cross-legged on the bank studying the five pointed lodestones floating above its outstretched palms. Falmeryn had forgotten about the lodestones, and was suddenly struck by the eerie shifting quality they had, as if they were of another Plane. Presently the neman announced that it had decided on their direction and slipped the lodestones into a pocket in its tunic. Before they went on their way, Falmeryn suggested that they discard the white cloaks, which had been useful in Ungrem but would offer no camouflage in Kesfaline. The dull brown of his clothing and the black of Raphon's tunic were better protection against being seen. Then they set off north-eastwards through the forest, heading for the secret place Raphon called Imhaya, the Circle of Spears.

It was still some five hundred miles to their destination in the North of Kesfaline, but the going was relatively easy, and covering at least thirty miles a day, they would be there in sixteen days or so. For once, food was not a problem. The trees soon gave way to farmland, terraced hills rich with grain and vegetables, and miles of fruit-heavy orchards.

But Kesfaline held other hazards. Being a rich country, it was heavily populated, and the Gorethrian army was much in evidence. Falmeryn soon realised that although Raphon might have an almost psychic knowledge of where they were meant to be going, it had little appreciation of practical dangers. Falmeryn had to keep a continual look-out, and guide them safely round farm dwellings and villages without being seen. The Kesfalians they saw were mostly farmers at work in the fields and orchards, but wherever there were Kesfalians, there were also Gorethrian overseers. Falmeryn often had to drag Raphon out of sight while a group of peasants or an Imperial patrol passed by. If anyone did see them, it was too much to hope that they would just be ignored.

Moving in secret, however, was not Falmeryn's only concern. They travelled in the dark as much as possible, avoiding the sun, and trying to stay near water. But despite these efforts, Raphon was growing weaker every day. Its skin was taking on the translucent quality of black glass, and the colours that glided over the surface, like the rainbow sheen of oil, had an unhealthy look. It often seemed tired, its eyes unfocused and its movements uncoordinated. When Falmeryn expressed his worry, it replied, 'As I have told you, all the beings of the Planes are ill-suited to survive on Earth. On our own plane we are immortal – whatever that means, for it can never be proved – yet we are physically vulnerable, as if . . .' The neman paused in thought. 'As if we were human beings replicated in crystal. Like crystal we may endure for ever, or we may be shattered or dissolved.'

'But isn't there anything I can do to help you?'

'You are doing all you can. It is a matter of time. I can only hope to complete my task before it is too late.'

'Is what you're looking for in Kesfaline so important that it's worth risking your life? Can't you return to the Black Plane?' Raphon said nothing, but fixed him with a peculiar, rather sad look. 'Forgive me, Raphon, but you've told me almost nothing. All I know is that you appear to be suffering needlessly.'

'I must complete the journey. That is why I need you, Falmeryn. But do not fear for me, I have survived ten days, and seven more will bring us to the Circle of Spears.'

But seven days seemed for ever with the neman fading before his eyes. For two more days they made good progress through orchards, seeing few Kesfalians and no Gorethrians at all. Falmeryn sustained himself on fruit, and they managed to find adequate hiding places in which to rest. But then they came to the first of a network of roads heavily used by Imperial troops and traders. Walking under a canopy of olive-green leaves and plump, russet fruits, they heard the rattle of carts some time before they reached the road. Raphon made to walk straight out of the fringe of trees, but Falmeryn anticipated this and was ready to seize its arm and guide it to a clump of tall grass from which they could watch the road in safety.

The sun was low in the sky, a huge, deep orange globe which gave a jewel-like scarlet tip to every leaf and grass blade, and lent a rosy cast to the wide, paved track. The road was quiet apart from a group of Kesfalian peasants. But as they waited, there was a clatter of hooves in the distance, and presently a full division of Imperial cavalry came into view.

The Kesfalians fell aside as the conquerors rode past, all strength and careless arrogance, their copper-gold horses striking showers of sparks from the track. Again Falmeryn felt emotion pricking his throat. They were like demons of fire and black metal, unassailable and supremely confident of their right to subjugate others. Although it was an anathema to him to hate anything, he was being slowly forced into it against his will. But hatred alone was not enough. He could not forget the helplessness he had felt when confronting Xaedrek, the absolute impossibility of defying him no matter how fiercely he had wanted to. If Gorethria's power had survived the Serpent itself, surely no force in the world could dislodge them.

When the Gorethrians had gone, the Kesfalians moved back onto the road and went on their way, shaking their heads and murmuring bitterly to each other. Falmeryn did not need to understand their language to guess what they were saying. Sighing grimly, he looked into the trees on the other side of the road – and caught his breath. Standing amid the slender, dark trunks was a figure from his dreams, a young girl with long, plum-red hair.

Afterwards, he could never recall exactly what she had looked like. Her form was glassy and translucent, yet she had a vital quality, as if she was very much alive but on another Plane. One hand hung white and slender at her side, the other was raised to her shoulder where a bird nestled almost invisibly in her hair, its feathers the same deep red. Could she see him? Of course not: she did not exist. Yet every line of her form seemed to be imploring him not to go any closer to the Circle of Spears. Forgetting everything else – including the need for caution – he rushed wildly across the road towards her.

He was fortunate. The group of peasants had passed by and did not notice him or Raphon, who had leapt up to pursue him. His only thought was to speak to the girl, but

360

when he reached the place where he had seen her, she was gone. He looked round wildly, saw her walking away through the deep shadows of the grove, and hurried in pursuit.

Just as a dreamer may realise he is dreaming, he knew she did not exist, but that did not make her seem any less real. He was compelled to follow her. She was always just ahead of him, vanishing, reappearing, drawing him on like a lodestone but impossible to catch up, however fast he ran. While he pursued her he felt quite calm, but as soon as Raphon strode after him and grasped his arm, a terrible feeling of anxiety came over him. He tried to pull away but it was too late, the girl had gone.

'My friend, what is wrong?' the neman said. 'Where are you going?'

'Let me go,' he said savagely. 'Didn't you see her – a child with red hair? I must find her.'

'I saw no one. But evidently she was real to you –'

'Don't get philosophical with me. We must follow her. I don't know what this means, but she's leading us somewhere.'

'But you were going in the wrong direction – away from Imhaya . . .'

'Then she must be telling us not to go there!'

'I don't understand you. I must take you to the Circle of Spears,' said the neman in a flat, almost sinister voice. It closed two hands firmly on Falmeryn's arm so that he was forced to walk alongside. He protested and struggled for a minute or two; then all at once it was as if he woke from a trance, and felt that he was behaving ridiculously.

'I'm sorry, Raphon. I don't know what came over me. You can let me go now, I won't run off.' The neman released his arm, saying nothing. He did not see the girl or the bird again, but his sense of unease and wrongness worsened until the whole grove seemed to be spinning darkly around him.

It was fear he felt, yet he could neither identify the cause nor shake himself out of it. He was locked into the strange rhythm of destiny, with images of Xaedrek, Kharan and Ahn Hrav looming in his memory, dark trees all around him,

Raphon stalking like a gaunt, black ghost at his side. Forluin seemed so far away that he could barely remember it.

In the next four days there were more roads to cross, Gorethrians everywhere. They came to the end of the orchards and began to ascend a series of terraced hills, where it was so hard to find hiding places in which to rest that Falmeryn had hardly any sleep at all in that time. And Raphon grew weaker every day. Its body did not waste like a human's; rather, it seemed to become transparent, and its eyes, once as vivid as black opal, took on a matt, greyish cast. Falmeryn did everything he could to help the Hrunneshian, but secretly he was beginning to despair of its life.

Now the carts trundling along the roads bore cargoes of newly mined minerals, and were heavily guarded. A track winding round the flank of a hill divided the farmland below from a mine-scarred slope above, while in the distance the rich Kesfalian landscape lay like an undulating quilt of blue, gold and green. They crossed the track to the left of the mine, where there was some tree cover, and climbed upwards as swiftly as Raphon could manage. Once or twice, where the trees thinned out, Falmeryn could see that scores of Kesfalians were toiling in the great gorges of black earth, overseen by a large number of Gorethrian soldiers. The Kesfalians were a spirited and rebellious race, despite centuries of subjugation. On the crest of the hill, a Gorethrian supervisor appeared to be showing a party of visiting nobles around. They were clad in robes more suitable to the graceful halls of Shalekahh than a muddy hillside, and Falmeryn would have laughed at them picking their way fastidiously over the grounds – if he had not been so incensed at their arrogance.

Soon they were beyond the mine, walking north-eastwards through folded, tree-covered hills. Raphon studied the lodestones frequently, ensuring that they were on the right course. From a knoll they saw that more hills rose ahead of them, shimmering from black to green under an ocean of dark trees. Raphon pointed to them and said, 'Imhaya lies within those hills.'

'We could be there by tonight, if you can keep going all day,' Falmeryn said hopefully. 'It's cloudy, and it's cool and dark in the trees . . .'

'I will try,' the neman said, its voice as faint and dry as a leaf. Its weakness was progressive, and not much relieved by resting. As they walked onwards, it began to stumble, until Falmeryn had to take its arm and guide it step by step. They went on slowly for two or three hours, but he began to lose hope of reaching their destination by evening.

Meanwhile the forest grew thicker and darker around them, and the atmosphere became close and stifling with the stench of decay and animal droppings. There was no sound except the piping of a solitary bird. Falmeryn became disorientated, and the forest seemed like a maze of shadows in which they were walking in circles.

He grew angry at the irrational fear that nagged at him, but could do nothing to suppress it. His throat felt dry and thick, and every movement of the foliage made him think of Gorethrian hounds. Then Raphon fell to its knees and said quite calmly, 'If we can find some water, I may live a few hours longer. But without moisture –'

'It's all right. I think there was a stream to our right a few minutes ago. We'll have to retrace our steps.' He hauled Raphon to its feet and began to trudge over the soft forest floor, with the neman leaning across his shoulders like a dead weight.

The stream was hardly more than a strand of water in a red clay ditch, but Raphon fell headlong into it in relief. Falmeryn jumped down the bank and knelt on the mud beside the neman, swishing water over its body until it began to revive slightly. He got the horrible impression that beneath the skin its substance had crystallised into a mesh of glassy strands, and if it dehydrated any more, a breath of wind would be enough to tear it apart like a mass of cobwebs. Once its body was saturated it sat up, but a tremor shook its limbs and it was in obvious distress. It took out the lodestones determinedly, but its hands were too feeble to control them, and they fell through its fingers into the stream. Then it uttered a sigh of deep exhaustion and its head lolled forwards as if it had even lost the strength in its neck. Falmeryn's eyes stung with pity.

'My friend, I have failed. I am lost, I cannot read the lodestones,' Raphon whispered.

'Then we'll have to find the place without them,' Falmeryn said, scooping up handfuls of water and tipping them over its head and neck. 'Raphon, you can't give up when we're almost there!'

'Ah, but the measurement of distance is more subjective than physical. A bare few miles, yet it might as well be half-way across the Earth, for all I am able to traverse it.'

Falmeryn carefully plucked the lodestones out of the water and pressed them into the neman's hand. 'Try again,' he said firmly. 'All you have to do is tell me which way to go. I'm going to carry you.'

From somewhere above, a strange voice remarked, 'That will be an interesting spectacle.'

Falmeryn looked up sharply and saw a Gorethrian officer standing on the bank.

The face beneath the hawk-shaped helm was sharply chiselled and handsome. He had one foot resting on a rock and was leaning casually on the raised knee, revealing a vivid kingfisher-blue lining to his black cloak. His dark war-gear was faded and battered from much travelling and fighting, and with him were six equally seasoned men. With a sinking heart, Falmeryn stood up very slowly, his arms outstretched to show that he was unarmed. The officer put his hand to his sword hilt briefly, then let it fall, grinning. 'Well, you are no Kesfalian, my fair-skinned friend. Do you speak Gorethrian?'

'Yes.' One of the other soldiers jumped down into the stream and looked curiously at the neman, still half-lying in the water.

'What the devil is this, Captain Oromek?' he exclaimed.

'There you have me, Malmek. I've seen many strange things, but that is the strangest,' said the officer, shaking his head. 'Still, we will soon find out.' Looking at Falmeryn, he asked, 'Where are you from?'

'Forluin.'

This brought a ripple of surprise. 'Well, and what brings you to the middle of the Empire?' Falmeryn swallowed a rising wave of dread and did not reply. What could he say? But his silence antagonised Captain Oromek. 'Come now, have you some reason to fear answering a few simple questions? Just tell me straightforwardly who you are, where you are going, and why, and it will save us all a lot of grief.'

'I don't think I can. It's a long story, and even if I tried, you would never believe me,' Falmeryn said, looking straight at the Gorethrian with his clear, grey-violet eyes. He did not mean to sound insolent, but an undercurrent of defiance came through in his voice, and the officer's smile vanished. The Forluinish were characteristically a friendly, gentle race, and Falmeryn was no exception, but where Gorethrians were concerned, his gentleness had been replaced by a single-minded, hard intolerance. Oromek sensed it in his upright figure and clear-featured face, a powerful aura, not of hatred, but of something far more unnerving. He began to feel personally offended by the Forluinishman.

'That was a singularly foolish thing to say,' he remarked in a dangerous tone.

'Sir, shall I bind him – and the creature?' asked one of the soldiers.

'Not yet. I've a mind to have some sport with him,' said Oromek, his dark green eyes narrowing. 'I heard the Forluinish were a sweet-natured race. What happened to you? Surely you were not born hating the Gorethrians, like a common Vardravian?'

'No. I learned it,' Falmeryn replied quietly, folding his arms. 'It was not very hard to learn.'

At that, Captain Oromek suddenly wrenched his sword from its sheath. Falmeryn caught his breath but the officer paused, testing the point against the tip of his thumb. 'Can you fight with the sword, Forluinishman?'

'In Forluin, we learn to fence as a sport.'

Oromek grinned. 'Not quite the same thing. Still, I've no wish to have an unfair advantage over you. Climb out of that ditch.' Falmeryn was reluctant to leave Raphon, but as there were soldiers all round him, he had no choice. As he hauled himself onto the bank, two Gorethrians moved alongside him and gripped his elbows. Oromek, meanwhile, drew a glass phial from his belt and held it up to the light. A pale gold powder glistened within it.

'Do you know what this is?'

Falmeryn had an idea, but he said, 'No.'

'It is amulin. It is not a drug, but it gives supernatural strength. As I have already taken some, it is only fair that you take some also. Then we will be evenly matched.' Falmeryn knew the amulin was a product of Xaedrek's evil sorcery, and the last thing he wanted was to take it. But the soldiers manhandled him, forcing the dry powder into his mouth, then holding a flask of water to his lips until he was forced to swallow it or choke. Captain Oromek added, 'Now you will have the pleasure of venting your anger against me, and I will have the pleasure of killing you.'

'Before I've answered your questions?'

'I suspect your friend can tell me more than you can,' Oromek replied, indicating Raphon with a callous gesture that chilled Falmeryn. 'But it depends on how you fight. Do well and you'll receive a swift, noble death. Do badly and I'll have you bound and tortured for as long as it pleases me. Malmek, give him your sword.'

Falmeryn felt the padded hilt of a broadsword in his hand, much heavier than he had anticipated. It was an effort to hold it upright. The six soldiers stood aside and watched, laughing. Around them the atmosphere seemed to grow tighter and thicker, filled with the rustle of dark trees, the soft crunch of boots on the leaf-mould, the faint splashing of water as Raphon struggled feebly in the stream to keep itself alive. Falmeryn's senses seemed to become painfully vivid, and distant birdsong pierced his ears like the ringing of a crystal glass.

Oromek flung off his cloak and began to circle, making a

few taunting strokes in the air. Falmeryn had no wish to fight, for it was against his nature; apart from that, he had not even fenced for some years and stood no chance against the skilled Gorethrian. But as he faced Oromek, the memory of Ahn Hrav burst into his mind with the violence of lightning, radiating through his body until his arteries seemed to pulse with sun-bright power. The amulin was taking effect. Suddenly the heavy blade became as light as a fencing foil in his hands, as keen and precise. The feeling of strength was unexpected, devastating; he felt no exhilaration, nor did his grim mood change, but it was as though he were suddenly divorced from conscience and inhibition. He swung the sword in an arc above his head, shouting.

As he did so, Oromek lunged at his unprotected stomach. But the amulin compensated for his lack of experience. His reactions suddenly as fast as light, he sidestepped easily and struck out at the officer's shoulder. His blade met leather and glanced off, and there was a cry of surprise and pain. Oromek's handsome face set in an expression of determination, and he began to fight in earnest. His sword swept down but Falmeryn brought his blade up to meet the blow, and there was a loud clang of steel. Oromek struck again and again, but the Forluinishman blocked every stroke, and the rhythmic clash of metal drowned all other sound. Falmeryn was aware that his heart was pounding, sweat springing from his forehead, yet he felt no discomfort at all. It was a dance, moving with delicate grace towards a sinister conclusion.

Their weapons seemed to move of their own volition, filled with the hyperphysical fire of their wielders, shedding fragments of green and copper light on the forest floor. For a while they seemed evenly matched because it was some time since Oromek had taken amulin and its effect had begun to fade slightly. The Forluinishman was light on his feet, but Oromek possessed greater skill. They clashed again, and suddenly they were wrestling hand-to-hand, each trying to force the other to drop his sword. They broke apart, and Falmeryn found the officer's blade swooping towards his head. He ducked, leapt out of the way and rolled back to his feet, breathing hard.

'You fight well, Forluinishman,' said the Gorethrian, grinning. 'You surprise me.' But Falmeryn was not to be distracted by conversation. Quickly wiping his forehead, he stepped forward and lunged straight at Oromek's heart. The officer twisted out of the way and slashed Falmeryn's left arm. The shock of being hit sobered him and he staggered backwards, feeling sick as his shirt-sleeve became wet and sticky. Ducking Oromek's sword a second time, he regained his balance and began to parry him stroke for stroke.

But the Gorethrian's greater skill was beginning to tell. Now he had got his opponent's measure, he could begin to employ tricks, make misleading strokes, or simply wear him down with unrelenting blows. Smiling to himself at the cheers of his men, he began to drive Falmeryn further and further back through the trees. Despite the amulin power, Falmeryn knew he was losing, and desperation began to sap his strength. He was wholly on the defensive. The fire in his veins seemed to become slow and viscid, faced with the greater power of his opponent. The ground was treacherous, and it seemed at any second he would stumble on a tree root and be slammed to the ground with Oromek's sword at his throat. Manically, automatically, he struck out to block every blow, while the ringing of steel became a torment to his accentuated hearing.

Then, incredibly, Oromek made a mistake. Falmeryn was caught off-balance, unable to swing his sword back into position. Oromek took the chance and lifted his blade in a high curve, ready to bring it down on Falmeryn's head; but he had not allowed for the low branches of a tree just behind him. The sword caught in them, showering leaves and twigs – and Falmeryn seized the opportunity. He thrust forward wildly, and the amulin-enhanced blade cut clean through the leather plates of Captain Oromek's uniform and sliced deep into his abdomen.

Oromek fell heavily, releasing a sanguine flood onto the forest floor. His eyes were wide open with astonishment and disbelief, and he struggled desperately to keep hold of his sword and get up. He could not accept that it was over. His limbs twitched and his mouth worked as he made a last effort to speak – but to no avail. He could not move. Falmeryn watched, paralysed, as his dying agony dragged on for several terrible, endless seconds. Then blood ran from his lips, and he died.

And there were six grimly enraged Gorethrians bearing down on the Forluinishman, swords drawn. The power blazed in him anew, and he turned to face them with his own blade poised, knowing he was about to die but determined not to give in without a struggle. The first flash of steel descended, his sword swung up to meet it, and sliced through – nothing.

The Gorethrians and the forest were gone.

He stood alone on a flat, grey plain with a jet-black sky overhead, and an amber radiance pulsating around the horizon. He was still gripping the sword, but before he had time even to move, the scene changed again.

Now he was in total darkness, but the air echoed with the slow, persistent drip of water in a cave. He straightened up cautiously, blinking against the darkness. The sword glowed with a faint, rusty light which was too dim to illuminate the surroundings. Lowering the point to the ground, a slight reflection revealed that he was standing on dark rock. The air was icy cold, and the wound in his arm was throbbing painfully, exacerbated by the amulin-fire in his veins. Everything had happened so fast that he had not had time to think; now, in the darkness, the shock began to recoil slowly on him.

'Falmeryn?'

The voice made him start so violently that he thought his heart would fail. Yet it was a familiar, welcome sound.

'Raphon?' he exclaimed. 'Raphon, is it you?'

'Yes, I am here.'

Falmeryn turned round in the darkness, and took a few cautious steps towards the sound of the voice. 'But where are we?'

'We are in Imhaya, not far from the Circle of Spears.'

'We're – but how in the Lady's name did we get here?'

'I – I cannot say,' Raphon answered quietly, making it seem that it probably knew, but was not going to tell him. As it spoke there was a hissing noise, and a spurt of yellow flame appeared in the blackness as if suddenly lit by an invisible hand. By its light, Falmeryn saw the neman lying in the centre of the small cave, like a strange statue that had sprouted from the rock itself.

He quickly went to kneel by its side. 'Raphon, how are you?' he asked anxiously. 'Do you feel any stronger?'

'A little. Now that I am protected from the sun's rays, I will survive a while longer.'

'Well, it's certainly as dark and wet in here as you could wish.' He put the sword down and gingerly probed the blood-soaked slit in his jacket to discover how bad the cut was. At once he wished he had not; it was like touching a wound in his mind. 'Gods,' he muttered.

'My friend, are you hurt? I think you have taken a blow.'

'It's not that. Raphon, I killed him. I've never killed anyone,' he exclaimed. 'The worst thing is that I wanted to. I was thinking of Ahn Hrav. Ahn Hrav, and . . . Kharan.'

'But he would have killed you.'

'I know, but all I was thinking of was revenge. It wasn't me wielding that sword, it was a stranger. Someone sick.'

'I think I understand your pain. There is no logic in slaying one man to make amends for the actions of others. No logic at all,' Raphon said with its usual lack of emotion. 'But the substance they made you take may have affected your reasoning.'

'I hope so,' he murmured. 'By the Lady, I hope that's what it was.' He sank down onto the floor next to Raphon, and they rested for a time in silence. It was oddly peaceful in the cave, and Falmeryn felt so numb that he did not even care that they might be trapped. His physical situation meant nothing to him.

But after a time Raphon said, 'I have recovered enough to go on. We must find the Circle of Spears before I grow

370

weak again. And you must have your arm attended to.'
Falmeryn climbed to his feet, dizzy and cold from loss of
blood. He could still feel the amulin-fire burning in him, and
the sensation sickened him like a touch of pure evil.

Walking over to the yellow flame, he found it to be a torch
resting in a bracket on the cave wall. He lifted it up, returned
to Raphon's side and helped the neman to its feet. Shadows
grew and shrank like living things with every slight movement
of the torch, and he could see no way out. Raphon, however,
now seemed sure of where they were and guided him to a
sliver of shadow which turned out to be a narrow tunnel.

'Had we not been brought here by higher means, we would
have had to find the hidden entrance from the outside,' said
Raphon. 'Only a very few know of the Circle and the secret
way to it. Thus the sages of Kesfaline preserve their wisdom.'

'You speak as if you've been here before,' Falmeryn
remarked, but the Hrunneshian did not reply. As they made
their way along the narrow tunnel, he was uncomfortably
conscious of the hard walls pressing on them, the great weight
of rock overhead. In the glow of the torch flame, he saw that
the rock was not black, but a soft brown with other hues
shimmering on the surface – soft reds, silvery greens, muted
pinks and blues.

Suddenly the tunnel divided, presenting them with a choice
of two ways. 'Now where do we go?' he exclaimed.

'We are in a maze, designed to confound unwanted in-
truders,' was Raphon's discouraging explanation. 'But do
not fear, I know the way.'

'You have been here before,' Falmeryn muttered accusingly. Raphon made for the left-hand opening, but before
they reached it, Falmeryn stopped in astonishment. Standing
in the entrance to the other tunnel was the red-haired child.
The torchlight did not touch her, for she was illuminated by
the soft light of another time and place. Her presence was
calm and silent, yet inexpressibly disturbing. As he stared at
her it seemed to him that she was no longer a child, but a
woman; unknown yet familiar, connected to him in some
sweet, intimate way he did not understand. And her eyes

were imploring him not to go a step nearer to the Circle, but to turn back – to avert fate. *Her fate.*

Falmeryn gripped Raphon's arm and said hoarsely, 'Can't you see her? You must be able to.'

'I can see nothing, my friend.'

'Something's wrong, I know it. She's warning us not to go to Imhaya. We must turn back.'

Raphon turned slowly and fixed him with impassive eyes. 'We are already in Imhaya. We cannot turn back.' Falmeryn stared helplessly as the girl's form became transparent, like a faint reflection in glass, then vanished altogether. But he still hesitated, while a terrible feeling of disquiet and wrongness swirled within him. The neman added, 'We must go on, or I will perish.' It tugged gently at his arm.

Raphon was right, of course; the girl was illusory, but the neman was real and in danger of dying. Falmeryn had no choice but to turn away, dismiss her from his mind, and take the left-hand tunnel. But as he did so he felt as if he had committed an act of betrayal without knowing it.

As if in confirmation, there was a movement like a rush of wings behind him, and he felt the torch knocked from his hand. It spluttered on the rock floor and died, leaving them once again in blackness.

'Raphon –' Falmeryn cried, overwhelmed by a wave of terror.

'There's nothing to fear. I can still see,' the Hrunneshian said calmly. Its grip on Falmeryn's arm was feeble but compelling. Breathing deeply and trying to slow his pounding heart, he took charge of his emotions and let himself be guided along the tunnel.

At intervals Falmeryn would feel the movement of dank, cold air on his face, and would know they had reached another junction of passages. After a time he began to notice a metallic thrumming in the air, as if someone was beating a distant gong – or the rock itself was vibrating. The effect was unpleasantly dizzying. It was a complex labyrinth, and he could not guess whether it was the work of men or nature; both seemed impossible. Anyone who did not know it would have wandered there for ever. But Raphon unhesitatingly chose the correct opening each time, leading him slowly and inevitably towards the Circle of Spears. He did not see the girl again, but the sense of unease continued to plague him. *She has warned me twice*, he thought suddenly. *If I did not take heed, what more can she do?*

'We are almost there,' Raphon announced. As the neman spoke, a vivid yellow flame ignited in the darkness some yards ahead and began to sway slowly towards them, trailing ribbons of smoke. Falmeryn cursed himself for having left the sword behind in the cave. As his eyes grew accustomed to the brightness, he saw again the soft colours glowing in the rock walls, and perceived that the torch was being carried by a gaunt, middle-aged man.

'Welcome to Imhaya,' he said in a deep, clear voice. To Falmeryn's surprise he spoke not Gorethrian, but the Common Language. 'I am Ferdanice.'

He was about the same height as Falmeryn – tall for a Kesfalian – and he was clad in a calf-length robe of brown linen, tied in by a belt. His colouring was typically Kesfalian: black-bronze skin dappled with lighter patches which reflected a faint blue-gold sheen, changing with the light. His black hair hung to his shoulders in braids, and his eyes were as pale as lemon in a heavy-boned, hollow-cheeked face. Two ivory orbs, the size of plums, hung round his neck on a strip of silk.

He came up to them, and said jovially, 'Well, Raphon, and how have you been for the past – what is it? Three thousand years?'

'Time has little meaning upon Hrunnesh. However, it is evidently of great importance upon Earth. I have cause to feel that my days are numbered here, and Falmeryn has a wound which must be healed.'

'Ah yes – Falmeryn,' said Ferdanice, looking thoughtfully at the Forluinishman. 'I am so glad you could come with Raphon. You have undoubtedly been invaluable to each other.'

Falmeryn had now begun to feel that he must get a grasp

of the situation or go mad. His instinct to be friendly to strangers had deserted him. He asked sharply, 'Ferdanice, do you and Raphon know each other?'

The Kesfalian sage hesitated. 'Yes – indeed, you could say we are very old friends,' he smiled.

'And you were expecting us to arrive?'

'Yes.'

'Raphon, why didn't you tell me?' Falmeryn exclaimed angrily. 'All along I've had this vague feeling that you were hiding something, but I gave you the benefit of the doubt and said nothing. I've travelled with you in good faith – now I think I deserve some sort of explanation.'

'Don't blame Raphon,' said Ferdanice. 'I asked him to bring you here, and I also gave him instructions not to tell you anything. He was only doing as I asked. It's not his fault.'

The thrumming in the air grew more insistent, and Falmeryn felt as though the ground were tilting from side to side. Spikes of pain radiated from his wound, and he had to fight not to pass out. 'You asked – I don't understand any of this. Who are you? I thought Raphon was coming here for his own reasons. I wish you'd explain what's going on.'

Ferdanice put out a hand to steady him. 'I apologise, Falmeryn. I will explain, of course – if you'll just bear with me. The reason I came down to meet you is that I want to show you both something which will go some way to explaining why you are here. It won't take long, then I'll take you up to the Circle of Spears where you'll receive rest and refreshment.'

He turned and led them along the tunnel, which, after a few twists and turns, opened out into a vast cavern. They had come to the end of the maze, and were now on a ledge half-way between the roof and floor, which were lost in echoing shadows. As if Ferdanice had given a silent command, torches flared suddenly around the walls, drawing rich, deep hues from the russet stone. Even in his present state of mind, Falmeryn could not help but marvel at the beauty of the cave. Stalactites caught flashes of flame on

374

their wet surfaces. Parts of the cave angled away into intricate honeycombs of caverns which seemed to hold the promise of unearthly secrets. Water dripped constantly into unseen pools far below; water gave everything the sheen of glass with colours locked deep inside it.

'I hope you can manage some steps,' said Ferdanice. Not waiting for an answer, he began to descend a roughly hewn, dangerous staircase which led from the ledge to the floor of the cave. The neman went next, then Falmeryn, both of them clinging to the wet rock-face on their right as they edged down cautiously.

'Ferdanice, I have come here as you asked, but the journey has already been too long,' said Raphon.

'Yes – I am sorry about that,' the sage answered vaguely. 'Miscalculation.'

'If I remain on Earth for much longer, I will perish. I wish to finish the task quickly.'

'That's impossible,' Ferdanice said flatly. The callous note in his voice astonished Falmeryn. 'It can't be done quickly, and I'm about to show you why. However . . . you will survive a while longer if you stay down in the caves, won't you?'

'Yes. Here in the darkness, I may live for several weeks . . .' and there was such a peculiar quality of self-abnegation and acceptance of pain in the neman's voice that Falmeryn almost cried out in protest. But the cause of his anger was so nebulous that he could only swallow it, and say nothing.

When they reached the cave floor, the light of Ferdanice's torch revealed that it angled downwards, undercutting the ledge and leading into a further, deeper cavern. They squeezed between huge stalagmites and scrambled over steep masses of rock until Falmeryn was quite lost, and knew he would never find his way back to the great cave alone. Finally the Kesfalian led them down a glassy, steeply angled stretch of stone to the brink of a chasm. 'Careful you don't fall,' he said. 'Now look.'

Falmeryn knelt down on the edge but could see nothing

in the darkness. Only the hollow echo of water told him that the bottom was at least a hundred feet below. Ferdanice knelt down beside him and held the torch out over the brink. Falmeryn discerned a few faint glimmers of light reflecting from what looked like a great pane of glass far beneath them. It could have been ice or clear rock crystal.

'Can you see it, Raphon?' asked Ferdanice.

'Yes. It is still there.' The neman sounded as exhausted as when it had collapsed in the forest. 'This is the secret for which we have travelled to Kesfaline, Falmeryn.'

He was about to ask what they were supposed to be looking for, when he perceived something glowing under the crystal pane. It was just a fuzzy disc of light, silvery-grey in colour, but it could not be mistaken for a reflection of the torch. It emitted a radiance of its own, and gave the disconcerting impression that it was pulling him towards itself. He hurriedly moved back from the edge, but felt induced to lean forward and look at it again.

'You see how far away it is,' said Ferdanice. 'We have to wait for the pull of the moons to draw it to the surface before we can recover it. That may take many days. So you see, Raphon, the task cannot be rushed.'

'What is it?' asked Falmeryn.

Ferdanice pursed his lips with a touch of irritation before replying. 'If I tell you, you must swear to speak of it to no one.'

'Very well, I swear.'

'It is stone from the Moon, Fliya. Some three thousand years ago, a particular conjunction of the Planes allowed someone to pass through Hrunnesh to Fliya and bring the moonstone back to Earth. Raphon helped to conceal the stone deep within the Earth, but the time is now coming when it must be . . . moved. So I asked Raphon to come and assist with it again. I also need your help. I hope that you will stay with us until the stone rises within reach, and can be recovered.'

'Do I have a choice?'

'Of course.' Ferdanice sounded surprised. 'Why, have you

some reason for not wanting to help us? There's nothing dangerous in it, I assure you.'

'I wasn't thinking of danger. But all of this feels wrong to me. Completely wrong.'

'Oh, Falmeryn,' sighed the sage, putting a fatherly hand on his shoulder. 'What assurance can I give you that far from being harmful, what we are doing is essential for the Earth's benefit?'

Falmeryn shook his head, feeling that the amulin had indeed affected his mind, making him unnaturally hostile and suspicious. Ferdanice seemed friendly and genuine enough; yet there was his lack of concern for Raphon, and a hint of irritation every time he was asked a question. Falmeryn got the impression that the sage would be much happier if he would only keep quiet and do as he was told – but he would not. 'You must explain the significance of the moonstone, why you want it moved, and where –'

'Yes, yes, Falmeryn, and so I will. But it is a long story, and your immediate need is for rest and healing.' The Kesfalian's tone was soothing. 'Suffice it to say that there is a power in the stone that . . . well, that the Earth needs.'

'But what about Raphon? You must realise that he'll die if he doesn't go back to the Black Plane.'

'Don't be concerned. Ferdanice is right,' said the neman. 'I will survive as long as I remain in the caves. I will stay here, and restore my strength by reflecting on our journey. My friend, I apologise that I could tell you nothing of the nature of the task, but that is for Ferdanice to explain. I must complete it, and I still need your help.'

'And I still want to help you,' Falmeryn answered softly. The neman seemed to trust Ferdanice, and Falmeryn's instinct was still to trust Raphon. Perhaps he was being ridiculously suspicious after all. He was exhausted, not rational. 'I'm sorry, Ferdanice. I'm not myself. I just need time to rest – and to ask some more questions.'

'Of course, of course. We'll talk again. Come now, let us leave these dark caves.' He took Falmeryn's arm, helped him to his feet, and began to lead him away from the chasm.

Falmeryn looked back anxiously at Raphon, but the neman's form was already invisible in the darkness.

As they made their way through the complexities of the cave, Falmeryn brooded on the strange events of the journey. He had been rescued from the hunt by some supernatural agency, healed of fatal wounds in a domain that was not of Earth. Then they had landed in the desert, and Raphon had said, *We have been led amiss*. Yet the janizons had saved them, and then walked into danger as if some higher power had directed them to take the travellers to Kesfaline, regardless of the perils. And just as Falmeryn and Raphon had faced death again, they had been snatched from danger and spirited into the caves of Imhaya. In spite of that, nothing had been made easy for them. It was as if something had wanted them both here, and did not care how it was achieved, or what anyone suffered in the process.

Falmeryn now knew enough of the Hrunneshians to realise that they were a passive race who lived to observe and reflect – not to initiate action. None of what happened had been Raphon's doing. On the contrary, the 'power' – whatever it was – appeared to be manipulating them both. It was something without conscience or any grasp of human feelings . . .

When they reached the large cave, the welcome sight of the torches flickering on the walls greeted them. But he noticed at once another source of light there, an unexpected radiance that emanated from a cloud of sparkling blue light drifting across the floor of the cavern. It was strange and beautiful, but to Falmeryn's surprise, the sight of it caused the sage to utter a curse.

'What is it?' Falmeryn asked. Ferdanice ignored him and strode purposefully towards it. As he did so, the whole cave suddenly lit up with a brilliant sapphire light, and a tall figure appeared before them.

An image of the ruby-haired girl went through Falmeryn's mind, but this time it was not her. This was no dream figure but a stately, ethereal, and very real being, robed in white with a long blue cloak. Beams of azure light flowed from her, curving and dancing into every corner of the cave. Her hair was brown, her eyes the colour of dew, and her face the most exquisite he had ever seen. And although Falmeryn had never set eyes on her before, he knew precisely who she was at once.

She was the Lady of H'tebhmella.

There was nowhere sweeter than the Blue Plane H'tebhmella, no one more revered by the Forluinish than the Lady herself. Awe and an incredible sense of joy filled him – but Ferdanice seemed anything but pleased at her appearance. Seizing Falmeryn by the arm, he thrust him hurriedly towards the base of the steps, muttering angrily to himself.

'Stop,' said the Lady. Her gaze was stern, her voice clear and compelling. But to Falmeryn's utter disbelief, the sage ignored her.

'Go up to the ledge. I will deal with her,' he said grimly.

'What are you saying? She's the Lady of H'tebhmella!'

'I know who she is. She cannot be allowed to interfere!'

Incredulous, Falmeryn tried to break away from him and go to her, but suddenly there were other Kesfalians on the steps, and Ferdanice was pushing him into their hands and ordering them to take him above ground. For a second, the amulin blazed in him, and he tensed himself to throw them off. But as their hands closed on his arms, an excruciating pain stabbed through the sword wound, and he half-fainted, losing his strength. He was hardly aware of being dragged up the steps, but he clearly heard the Lady's voice as it rang out.

'Why must you persist in evading me, Ferdanice? It is imperative that you listen to me.'

'And let H'tebhmella wreck the natural evolution of sorcery? I know what you have to say, but nothing is going to stop us, not even you. You are above yourself in this, my Lady. Now I command you to depart.'

Now Falmeryn knew for certain that his first instinct about Ferdanice had been right. The red-haired child had tried to warn him. If the sage was opposed to the Lady of H'tebhmella, what he was doing could only be wrong. But there was nothing he could do, his brain was clouded by pain and he could barely hang onto consciousness. Somewhere below him there was an unearthly cry, and the azure light fluctuated and vanished.

13

To the Crystal City

KHARAN COULD not decide what she hated most about the jungle: the insects, which were even larger and more aggressive than those of Gorethria; the tiny snakes that slithered around them while they tried to sleep; the rank, soupy rivers where slug-like creatures lurked under the surface; or the unrelenting humidity. It was all equally loathsome, and the end of it was so far away that she could not even visualise escaping. Melkavesh estimated it would be another thirty days before they reached friendlier country.

They had left N'gudam's village several days ago, Melkavesh leading a small 'army' of Mangorians. When she had begun to make plans for the journey, she had discovered that in addition to their pets, the tribe kept lizards, known as U'adruils, which were large enough to ride. There were only twenty, but it meant Melkavesh, Kharan and the more senior members of the tribe could travel in reasonable comfort. The whole tribe had been almost too eager to uproot themselves and follow her, and it had taken some persistence to convince them that a relatively small party of the fittest would be better. A vast entourage trailing into Kristillia would have been vulnerable to the Gorethrians, whereas a group of only a hundred or so could be disciplined to travel swiftly and in secret, when necessary. Once Melkavesh was established in Kristillia – she hoped – the rest of Mangorad could be mobilised.

Her embryonic army was more symbolic than functional – but it was an impressive symbol. The tribe continued to find her as inspirational as when she had first spoken to them, seizing their imaginations and hopes. Her hair, even when lank with humidity, drew them on like a golden banner at the head of the column, and she was perpetually full of energy and laughter. Even the dour Mangorians began to smile more often under her influence.

Her effect on the tribe, however, had placed the high priest, N'gudam, in an awkward position. He and his son N'golem could not both go to Kristillia with Melkavesh. If N'gudam went with her, he was certain that N'golem would usurp his authority in his absence. But if he stayed, and his son went instead – he felt that N'golem and Melkavesh were sure to conspire against him as they travelled. With these thoughts in mind, he had fallen into a black mood punctuated by explosions of temper, which would normally have filled the tribe with terror.

But for the first time, they had seemed unmoved by his outbursts; their thoughts, hearts and hopes were all focused on Melkavesh, and even N'gudam himself had become secondary. Once he had been high priest of a great city, Gholeth; now, since Melkavesh's appearance, he could not even control the miserable remnants of his people. He had not the intelligence to be analytical about this, or to discern the larger issues; but he had sense enough to perceive that as long as he remained with her, he would always be in her shadow, his own power reduced to nothing. So he had decided to stay in the village and try to recapture his authority. At least, if N'golem went with the Sorceress, the immediate threat would be removed. But he knew in his heart that the spirit of his people was with Melkavesh's army; and if they believed their god M'gulfn really was dead, its high priest could retain little credibility.

Melkavesh was aware of his predicament and understood his bitter feelings, but she could find no sympathy for him. He was the worst kind of leader, a conceited and ignorant bully. She was only glad that she would not have to endure his glowering presence on the journey.

The jungle area that formed Mangorad stretched for some

eight hundred miles, and at best, they covered only twenty or so miles a day. The vegetation was thick and the lizards slow-moving. Like their smaller cousins, they were mostly iron-grey or bronze, with a few blues and greens. They were each about the size of a fourteen-hand pony, but far less intelligent and much harder to control. Melkavesh soon learned the knack from the Mangorians, and Kharan was given a bronze creature that placidly followed Melkavesh's blue one wherever it went. The saddles were made of reptilian leather with a high pommel and deep seat, which made them comfortable and secure. The bitless bridle and reins were decorated with pieces of polished bone, and panniers hung from the saddle for the carrying of provisions and weapons. Fully equipped, the lizards were an awesome sight.

At the head of the column rode Melkavesh and N'golem, followed by Kharan and the priestess, U'garet. When necessary they were preceded by warriors hacking a path through the foliage. Then came a hundred young, strong men and women on foot, with the rest of the mounted reptiles placed at intervals in the column so that their riders could keep discipline. As the days passed, they encountered more Mangorians scattered through the jungle in small tribes, and soon their number had swelled to nearly two hundred. They formed a great, slow-moving snake winding through the dense vegetation towards Kristillia; a land that lay besieged without any idea of the strange source of aid that was on its way.

The jungle was never still, never silent. It creaked and hissed and rustled; it dripped endlessly with rain and sticky exudations; it flashed with brilliant-coloured birds and bizarre, short-lived flowers. There was a continual chorus of insects, overlaid by weird, haunting birdsong and the cries of unseen animals. At intervals, their route coincided with the course of a winding river which gave off a stinking miasma of decay, and the air was filled with plopping sounds as amorphous creatures poked their heads through the turgid surface, gulped oxygen and submerged again. The river was fringed by trees of vast size which had straight, blue-green trunks and aerial roots that curved down from the bole many feet above their heads to stand in the earth like pillars. The travellers moved between them as if through a lofty, columned hall, while the lizards' feet squelched in black mud, leaving water-logged footprints in which pale invertebrates could be seen writhing. Kharan had never been more grateful for not having to walk.

As she had envisaged, Mangorad's jungle would swiftly have proved fatal to an unprotected traveller; if insects or snakes did not kill them, parasites or disease-infested water certainly would. But now Melkavesh's sorcery had returned, it was easy for her to produce an aura that kept insects and other predators away from herself, Kharan and Filmoriel. It did not distance them from the general miseries of the journey; the creatures still came unpleasantly close and the humidity was unbearable, but at least it preserved their health.

The Mangorians, of course, were seasoned jungle dwellers and largely impervious to most of its afflictions. They had their own remedies for illness, insect-stings and snake-bites – most of which were evil-smelling or painful, if not both. Kharan could only be glad that she was under Melkavesh's protection. The blue-skinned tribe were able to garner food from the most unpromising sources; they knew which plants yielded milk, where to find edible roots or stems, which fruits were poisonous and which were safe. They also hunted all manner of animals and birds, although cooking was unknown to them. However famished Kharan was, she found eating this fare a major effort.

Nevertheless, she forced herself. Having survived this far, there was something dogged in her soul that would not allow her to give up. In spite of Xaedrek, the mountains, and Mangorad, she was still alive – and more importantly, so was Filmoriel. Every day she grew tougher in body and stronger in mind, and the gradual strengthening was wholly for her daughter's sake. Now Filmoriel was safe, she was determined that no one would ever threaten, harm or use her again.

384

Kharan still felt the occasional touch of resentment that they were so dependent on Melkavesh for their survival, even a pang of envy at the enchantress's own power and freedom – but she did not dwell on such thoughts. She still found frequent cause to argue with Melkavesh, but at heart she loved and trusted her. Her own lack of independence meant nothing, as long as Filmoriel survived. There was much she could have brooded on, but instead she devoted all her energy to protecting her daughter.

The infant was still in her protective cocoon, but growing daily. Melkavesh nurtured her with extramundane energy every day, and she was already almost the size of a new-born baby. She kicked energetically within the membrane, and her eyes sometimes fluttered open briefly – long enough for Kharan to see that they were the same colour as Falmeryn's – but it would be a long time before she could emerge and live as a normal child. Meanwhile she travelled in the sling on Kharan's chest, mercifully oblivious to the unpleasantness of the surroundings.

The Mangorians seemed to need little rest and sometimes, if they could not find a dry place in which to sleep, they would walk all night, while Kharan dozed in the saddle. They still seemed so alien to her that she felt she would never grow used to them. She particularly disliked N'golem, and was unable to forgive him for trying to use Filmoriel. Melkavesh, on the other hand, appeared quite at ease with the Mangorians while remaining in full command, and Kharan could not help admiring her for it. She was an inspirational leader, and however physically uncomfortable the journey was, a mood of optimism and excitement prevailed.

There was only one good thing about the jungle. It did not go on for ever. When they had endured thirty days of the steamy heat and dripping vegetation, their surroundings began to change slowly. There was no immediate relief, and nothing to raise Kharan's spirits; if anything, the journey became more unpleasant. The river became wider and shallower, fanning out into a network of waterways between vegetation-choked islands. Eventually they were forced to

385

wade, but those on foot were instantly attacked by leeches and other creatures in the water. After that, Melkavesh insisted that everyone be carried across by lizard, however long it took.

There seemed to be an endless series of waterways to cross as they moved from grove to grove, while the vegetation became stunted, the islands flatter, and the water shallower. A day later the transformation of the landscape was complete. They were no longer in the jungle, but crossing a vast, flat swamp.

'This is horrible,' Kharan said vehemently, staring around her. 'I was so keen to escape Mangorad, I never thought there might be something worse beyond. At least we had cover in the jungle. Here, we seem so exposed.'

Fingers and walkways of boggy land rose barely a few inches above an expanse of still, shining black water. The only vegetation was grass, reeds, and a few skeletal trees sticking grotesquely out of the ground. A perpetual bluish mist swirled everywhere, giving the effect of permanent twilight. It was a wild, bleak and eerie landscape, and even Melkavesh shivered at the sight of it. But she was adept at hiding her own doubts.

'There's nothing to worry about. No eagles, no one within miles,' she said reassuringly. 'We'll soon be across it, and that much nearer to Kristillia.' She tapped her lizard with a short stick, and it lumbered into a slow trot ahead of the others.

'Well, at least it doesn't smell any worse than the jungle,' Kharan said, wrinkling her nose.

Melkavesh drove the lizard onwards, feeling the need to be away from the others and on her own for a time. Its feet squelched in the waterlogged grass, and spray flew up, soaking her legs. It would be dark soon, and if they could not find a dryish place in which to spend the night, they would face another night's walking. At least the swamp could be crossed on foot . . . As these thoughts passed through her mind, something caught her eye; something pale, gleaming just under the surface of the water a few yards away. She pulled at the lizard's rein and cajoled it to the right so she could take a closer look.

The pool was black and glassy as obsidian, casting a reflection of the spiky tree that leaned over it. The thing in the water was half-obscured by reflections and mist, and she could just make out a large rounded object, so white that it seemed luminous against the dull tints of the swamp. She climbed from the lizard's back, crouched down and craned her neck over the pool. It was bobbing as lifelessly as a corpse, but it was too big to be human. It was more like some strange water-dwelling creature she had never seen before, repulsive in its alienness. It was a bloated, fleshy, three-lobed beast, but each lobe had four rudimentary limbs and – and a flattened, distorted, but recognisably human face.

Melkavesh recoiled, letting out a single cry of horror.

'Melkavesh? Is something wrong?' Kharan was approaching on the bronze lizard, but the Sorceress hardly noticed. She was lost in shock and disgust, shaking violently as she began to understand.

As real as the monstrosity in the water seemed, she knew it was only an illusion; an involuntary far-seeing vision which any Sorcerer might experience when there was dire need. She knelt down on the soaking ground, sobbing with revulsion as she forced herself to look at it.

It was something to do with Xaedrek, of course. Three humans, vilely warped into a different form, perhaps still conscious, but gravid with unfurled, evil power. Never had anything struck such blackness into her soul as the aura of misery and despair that radiated from those wretched souls. It was like a lingering brushstroke of acid painted on her heart, and she felt sick, violated – and helpless. The three faces were turned to her in supplication, as piteous as animals about to be slaughtered; and as she watched, the bloated form spun round slowly and began to sink into the dark water.

Gods, she thought. *What has Xaedrek done?*

She felt a hand on her shoulder, looked up, found Kharan

standing by her. But even faced with her friend, she could not control her trembling limbs or convulsive breathing.

'Mel, what on earth's wrong?' Kharan cried concernedly. Receiving no reply, she crouched down and put her arms round Melkavesh, holding her as she shook and sobbed. The lizards obscured them from the sight of N'golem and the others. 'What is it? Hush – it's all right. Calm down. That's it . . .' Gradually Melkavesh took charge of herself, but she could feel her own eyes wide open and stinging with fear, and she felt paralysed. For the first time she was desperately grateful for Kharan's presence, her comforting arms and voice.

'Evil. Evil,' she whispered. 'It's just a word, "evil", and it is used so often that it becomes meaningless . . . but what other word is there? There's nothing, nothing else that explains how I feel. It's vile. I can't express it. But it's there.' She struck her heart.

'Mel, you're frightening me,' Kharan said. 'What are you talking about?'

'Can't you see it?'

'See what?'

Melkavesh looked into the water again, but the swollen white apparition had vanished. Kharan had seen nothing. 'It – it was just –' she sighed and shook her head. 'Oh, I might as well tell you. I had some sort of vision. Present or future, I don't know, but it meant that Xaedrek has finally made a new breakthrough to power. It's something so vile and degrading that it can only be the demon's doing.'

Kharan had never seen Melkavesh so blatantly upset and frightened before, and her distress was infectious. She felt fear catch in her own throat, and almost panicked at the thought of being trapped on the swamp. Swallowing, she said, 'Come on, Mel, he was bound to discover something awful. You must have anticipated it.'

'I don't know – I thought of it, but this artificial creation of sorcery is so unnatural to me I can hardly grasp it. It's impossible, but it's happening. You're right, though. As long as he went on working with Ah'garith, this was bound to

388

happen.' Another shudder went through her, and she hung her head. 'The Lady help Kristillia. I don't know whether I can fight it.' She looked up, reached out to the infant, and added, 'Poor Filmoriel.'

A defensive light came into Kharan's eyes. 'What do you mean, "poor Filmoriel"?'

'She is a Sorceress. It will be her battle as well as mine.'

'What are you talking about?' Kharan demanded. Melkavesh stood up shakily, stretching her stiff limbs. The setting sun appeared through a thin patch of mist and the swamp took on a brief, eerie beauty. The blue mist was flooded by a rose-gold haze, silhouetting the trees and turning the pools to golden glass.

'I should not have said anything.' Melkavesh sounded tired and abstracted. 'I don't want you to worry needlessly. It won't be until she is a grown woman. Perhaps never. Oh, take no notice, Kharan, I'm just –'

Kharan took her arm, her eyes softening with concern. 'Just what?'

'Scared,' Melkavesh admitted.

'I didn't think you were frightened of anything.'

'There's always a first time.' At last, something like calmness and clear thought were starting to return to her and she put an arm round Kharan's shoulder and said, 'Come on, let's go back to the others. I trust they saw none of that, or they'll think I'm losing my mind. I'm afraid we'll have to travel all night again; I want to put this swamp behind us as quickly as possible.'

Kristillia was bordered by mountains in the North and East, by the river Omnuandrix in the West, and by hills in the South. It was along the southern border that she was most vulnerable, and there the Gorethrian troops were massed, biding their time until Xaedrek ordered them to strike.

Somehow, Melkavesh must lead her army through the Gorethrian lines unseen. It was a daunting prospect and it would stretch her far-seeing skills to the limit, but it was not impossible. No army, however mighty, could form an unbroken chain across two thousand miles of wilderness.

Even the stoical Mangorians were made uneasy by the swamp, and they were relieved to leave it behind a day later, and enter a marshy forest. Here they rested – some on the damp ground, some wedged in the branches of trees – while the great lizards moved slowly to and fro on their tethers, grazing on insects and amphibians. In the morning, a herd of ferocious black pigs came crashing through the trees, killing a man before they were driven off by spears and sorcery. The tribe gathered up the pig carcasses and proposed to feast on the meat, but Kharan drew the line at eating it raw. She insisted on the building of a fire, and showed them how to roast it.

As they were taken further away from their native jungle, the Mangorians seemed to lose confidence and become even more reliant on Melkavesh's leadership. Even N'golem and U'garet, so proud and self-assured on their own ground, became strangely quiescent and rarely argued with Melkavesh's decisions. Kharan could appreciate the weight of responsibility the enchantress had taken on; the welfare of two hundred people was in her hands, they relied wholly on her for guidance, protection and inspiration. Every choice she made had to be the right one, and she could never show weakness, indecision or flagging spirit.

To Kharan's growing admiration, Melkavesh proved more than equal to the responsibility. She treated it not as a burden but as a challenge, to be met head on with vigour and exuberance. She swiftly recovered from the disturbing event in the swamp, and even the perceptive N'golem seemed to have no inkling of it – on the contrary, she seemed more energetic and inspirational than ever, fully confident that everything would go to plan. She already had a good command of the Mangorian language – acquired sorcerously, Kharan suspected – and was teaching some of them to speak Gorethrian, so they would be understood in Kristillia. She seemed indomitable.

Kharan, however, knew only too well that she was human. She saw the signs of tiredness which the others did not notice and knew when she was suffering the pain of using sorcery. It was only natural that she should do all she could to help her.

Once beyond Mangorad, Kharan's health began to improve, and she gradually found herself taking a more active part in leading the tribe. Suddenly she was no longer a passenger on the lizard; control of it came automatically as she rode up and down the column, relaying Melkavesh's instructions to them and urging them on. No one was more astonished than herself to find that they responded to her and respected her. Perhaps, she thought self-mockingly, they were endeared by her broken Mangorian.

They were several days in the forest, where it rained non-stop. The light was a drenched, glittering green under a canopy of emerald foliage, but there was nothing attractive in the liquid mud through which they had to splash their way. Still, the rain washed off the worst of it, and Kharan was now so used to being perpetually hot and soaked to the skin that it hardly bothered her. The forest was full of tiny lakes where large, brown animals wallowed in the water, occasionally raising their heads on extraordinarily long necks to peer through the curtain of rain at the travellers. They appeared too placid or lazy to attack. The only danger was from marauding pigs, but the tribe were not taken by surprise again. They ate well, cooking the flesh on sorcerous fires that burned even in the rain.

After about ten days, the forest became drier and sparser, until at last it gave way to a great stretch of grassland, the Plain of Rubnali. The skies cleared, the air was fresh and light after weeks of humidity, and Kharan felt a distinct lifting of her spirits. This was another world, a lifetime away from Shalekahh and the nightmare of the Emethrians and Mangorad. The grass was long and golden, rippling in a warm wind, and the landscape was dotted with pale green trees. In the distance a herd of wild oxen, creamy-white with long, gilded horns, were grazing their way slowly across the plain. A flock of white birds moved with them, circling overhead or perching on their backs.

Melkavesh made the tribe wait in the last of the tree cover, and let herself drift deep into witch-sight, carefully perceiving what lay ahead. They were still some seven hundred miles south of Kristillia's border, and she could discern no immediate Gorethrian activity. Vardravian hunters had once lived on this plain, but they had been dispersed and taken into slavery in centuries past. Now it was uninhabited, under no one's domination – except that of the Gorethrians, who might cross it as they pleased without being harassed by rebels. While Kristillia remained unconquered, it served as the main route into Kesfaline.

Further to the north-east, lying directly across Melkavesh's path, was the Plateau of Parua. The Gorethrians came and went below its edge, so once they had reached it, they would be relatively safe until they reached the hazardous Kristillian border.

Casting her senses further afield, Melkavesh could sense the dark mass of forces in Kesfaline, the legions ranged like storm-clouds on the far side of the Plateau, others discernible as a blur at the far western range of her vision – returning home to Shalekahh from a tour of duty, no doubt. But for the moment, the grassland was deserted and therefore safe.

So they began the journey over the undulating, golden plain, a procession of dark warriors and huge lizards, led by a Gorethrian woman whose bedraggled state in no way dimmed the light of purpose and determination that shone from her. They marched swiftly now, unhampered by vegetation or treacherous ground, in a state of exuberance. Even Kharan felt energetic and cheerful at times. She was even ceasing to be intimidated by the Mangorians; they were only human beings, after all.

'I really am quite proud of you,' Melkavesh said one day. 'I thought I would have to do everything myself, but you're proving indispensable.'

'Hm, no one's never called me that before,' Kharan smiled. '"Indispensable". Such praise could go to my head.'

'Well, I've always known I was going to need a right-hand woman. I didn't realise I'd already found her.' Kharan grimaced at this; there was a certain black humour in the idea of her being to Melkavesh what Amnek was to Xaedrek, and she did not know whether to be amused or horrified.

Herds of wild animals roamed across their path as they travelled, a continual source of pleasure to Kharan and Melkavesh. Besides the oxen, there were tall, slender creatures with impossibly long legs and necks and tiny, delicate heads. In colour they were a dappled russet, and they moved as if in slow motion, all stately elegance and grace. When they had gone, a livelier group came into view; wild horses, some relation to Gorethrian war-horses but smaller and paler. They were as golden as the grass, with pearl-white manes and tails. Melkavesh laughed with delight as they galloped in circles, twisting and leaping with sheer joy in life.

The herds were pursued by predators, of course. Several times they saw slender, creamy-golden leopards on the prowl, inducing panic until they had made a kill. But the Mangorians themselves, as they trekked across the plain, were responsible for slaying more wild oxen than any leopard. The army had to eat.

On their ninth day on the Plain of Rubnali, they glimpsed the edge of the Plateau, a green escarpment stretching from north-west to south-east, edged with glittering white limestone. By evening they had made camp at its base, and the next morning they began the slow ascent of the slope. It was steep, but fortunately the U'adruils were good climbers, and the long-limbed Mangorian men and women had no difficulty in gaining the top.

The Plateau was perfectly flat, spreading out in a golden-green mantle under a breathtakingly vast sky. Herds of oxen, horses and other creatures grazed slowly across the land, while fluffy pyramids of cloud reflected their lazy progress on a greater scale across the heavens. Birds wheeled in the clear, warm air. It was a vista so exquisite that Kharan felt tears pricking her eyes; tears, because Filmoriel was too young to share it with her, and Falmeryn was not there and never would be.

There was nothing in the world that mattered more than the world itself, and it broke her heart that such as Xaedrek and Melkavesh could not see it.

The crossing of the Plateau seemed slow and dreamlike, and Kharan almost wished it would last for ever, so that she would not have to face what lay beyond. Seven days passed like no time at all as they walked through the warm, blue days and slept comfortably on soft grass at night. Then, all too soon, they found themselves on the northern edge, looking towards the pale green hills of Kristillia.

Gorethrian encampments could be seen quite clearly, black as flies dotted here and there on the distant slopes. There were watchtowers at intervals along the horizon, almost certainly in Gorethrian hands and well equipped with signalling devices.

The senior members of the tribe lined up their lizards alongside Melkavesh's to take in the view. Presently N'golem spoke. 'There are very many of them. You did not lead me to believe there would be so many. A few folk on foot could slip through, perhaps. It is impossible that all my tribe can pass unseen.' He sounded sour, disillusioned.

'They will see us from the towers,' U'garet added.

'You must trust me,' Melkavesh said firmly. 'This is the hardest thing we have yet faced, I admit, but I never pretended this journey would be easy. I promise you we will get through.'

The warriors nodded and fell silent, accepting this reassurance. But as they dismounted from the U'adruils and made to rest and eat, Kharan joined Melkavesh and said quietly, 'You sound very confident. Are you?'

'For their sake, I have to be. But . . .' she sighed. 'Well, I've never done anything on quite this scale before. Of course, I can't be sure I'll succeed. But two hundred people depend on me for their lives . . .' She turned away, her eyes introspective with anxiety and determination. Kharan shivered, doing her best to suppress a pang of dread which was not unlike the anticipation of being executed. She knew very little about Kristillia, and could not visualise ever getting beyond the hills to find out what was there.

They waited until dusk, so no Gorethrian would glimpse a dark snake winding its way down the distant escarpment. Then they began a slow march across the valley, wading a shallow river and keeping to what tree cover they could find. Melkavesh led them with her eyes closed, using her far-seeing skills to sense the exact location of the Imperial troops. There were two encampments nearby. It was too dangerous to pass between them, but all she had to do was lead the Mangorians more to the East, thus giving both camps such a wide berth that even in broad daylight they would not have been seen.

The night was so still that every sound seemed magnified; the cavernous breathing of the U'adruils, the soft rustle of many feet on grass, the occasional whispered exchange. Melkavesh's senses were attuned to the slightest noise and movement, sifting the innocent ones from those that might be significant. There was some faint starlight, but she could not risk lighting their way by sorcery. They faced hours of creeping along through darkness.

Melkavesh had discovered by far-seeing that although the Gorethrians patrolled Kristillia's borders continually, there was no fighting. Two attempts at invasion had already been repelled, and although the Kristillians were not strong enough to drive them away completely, every engagement had ended in stalemate. So for the time being there was an uneasy truce. Every Imperial division that moved was shadowed by a Kristillian one just inside the border, but the Kristillians never attacked unless the Gorethrians intruded onto their territory. Baramek's instructions were simply to protect Xaedrek's existing conquests until means could be found to defeat Kristillia once and for all.

They were level with the camps when Melkavesh perceived movement ahead of them. A night patrol. Dismayed, she halted the column and ordered them to wait in silence while the group of ten Gorethrians passed by. They were about a quarter of a mile away, but to Melkavesh they seemed distressingly close. When they had ridden a couple of miles to the East, she deemed it safe to move – but just as she was about to give the order, she saw them in her mind's eye turning and coming back. Cursing inwardly, she resigned herself to waiting a while longer. They passed closer to the column this time, but instead of going straight by, they halted for no apparent reason. She held her breath, inwardly willing them to move on; instead, they dismounted to talk and take some refreshment.

Melkavesh felt like screaming. There was nothing she could do except grit her teeth and ensure the Mangorians remained quiet and still. The U'adruils shifted and sighed from time to time, but it was unlikely that the patrol could hear them. At long last the patrol remounted and went on their way towards the nearest encampment – but by then Melkavesh had lost an hour, and it was unlikely that they would be in Kristillia before dawn.

'Time to move off. We must make haste,' she whispered grimly. Kharan and U'garet trotted back along the column to relay the message and urge the warriors to hurry.

They almost succeeded. They were well past the encampments, and there were no other Gorethrian legions for several miles. There was only a single watchtower to pass, and in the dark, partially concealed by trees, they would not have been seen. They had raced against the sunrise all night, but time remained doggedly against them. Just as the last of the column trailed past the tower, the sun appeared like a brilliant topaz and glinted on lizard scales and slate-blue skin, flashed on polished beads.

Melkavesh's consciousness was focused wholly on the white stone tower. The top was encircled by a low wall, with a wooden roof on struts to shelter it and a large signalling mirror and beacon in the centre. The four Gorethrians manning it were sitting languidly on the wall, bored, tired and not expecting to see anything. Then one of them – a woman – leapt up and leaned over the side, exclaiming, 'By the

Serpent, what's that? Some sort of army? I've never seen anything like it!'

The words cut into Melkavesh's stomach like an icy knife.

She came back to herself, opened her eyes wide, and whispered to Kharan, 'They've seen us.'

Above, she could sense the grinding of cogs as the large mirror was turned into position. They were going to send a message to the encampments.

'Keep going!' Melkavesh shouted. Then to Kharan and N'golem, 'Make them keep going, fast, as fast as you can!' She pulled her lizard round and urged it back along the column at the fastest trot it could manage, all the while yelling at the Mangorians to run, *run*!

Even as she reached the base of the tower she was out of the saddle and standing upright on the U'adruil's back. She looked up at the astonished face of the woman officer staring down at her, and in a sorcerous vision overlaid on the first, she saw the others struggling with the signal. And in the same instant she flung up her hands and released four tiny golden comets of power.

Each met its mark, a Gorethrian skull. Four bodies fell insensible to the floor; no signal was sent, and when they regained consciousness they would have no memory whatever of having seen a procession of blue-skinned warriors led by a Gorethrian Sorceress with golden hair.

'Where will you lead us now, Lady Melkavesh?' N'golem asked. They had rested for several hours in a tree-filled cleft, but the mood of triumphant exhilaration was still with them. Melkavesh's dispatch of the watchtower guards had made her seem even more awesome in the Mangorians' sight.

'We are going on to the capital city, Charhn.'

'How much further is it?' Kharan asked casually. She had had some vague notion that the moment they stepped into Kristillia, they would be back in civilisation. Just reaching it had seemed so impossible that she had never pressed

397

Melkavesh to explain exactly what she intended to do when she got there. Now she laughed at her own foolishness; Kristillia was a large country and nothing, of course, could possibly be that simple.

'We should reach it in no more than seventeen days.'

Kharan groaned inwardly. 'Thank heavens we aren't heading for Alta-Nangra. Mel, we've dodged the Gorethrians, but what about the Kristillians themselves? They won't know we're friendly. We certainly don't look it.'

Melkavesh glanced around at the harsh-faced, sinister-looking Mangorians and had to agree. 'Do you think I haven't thought of that?' she said with a grin. 'I had already checked there were no Kristillians within five miles of us. There are some on the border and some about forty miles to the North; we're still safe. No one is going to impede my progress until I arrive in Charhn and present myself to the sovereign in person.' Kharan said nothing, only lifted a sceptical eyebrow, which had the effect of deflating Melkavesh instantly. She gave a self-deprecating grin and added, 'Don't worry, Kharan, you'll love Kristillia. I've seen enough of it by far-seeing to know it's a beautiful country.'

That much was true. They were now moving through wide, winding valleys in a chain of hills whose misty green slopes swept up to summits of pale quartz. The gleaming tors gave a hint of Kristillia's great mineral wealth. Copses spilled down their flanks, the foliage a mingling of green and warm russet. Kristillia was as lovely as Gorethria, but in a fresher, less exotic way. Kharan had never seen such a vast sky; a fragile blue, streaked with cirrus, it seemed endless. Though it was hot, the air was fresh and light, and so far there was no hint of the eccentric weather that Shalekahh suffered.

Peach-coloured finches chirruped overhead, and a herd of white cattle stood swishing their tails on a distant riverbank. Melkavesh sensed the presence of isolated dwellings here and there, but she was not unduly worried about the possibility of being seen by farmers. Sometimes she wished she had the power to cloak the whole column against being seen, or to conjure a spectral steed for each of them, but her power had limits, and she had to accept it and curb her impatience. As they went on, she still perceived no danger of being challenged, and perhaps grew over-confident. Plenty of animals, a few farmers; nothing to fear. After two days the valleys grew narrower, and they found themselves walking through winding green chasms, thick with vegetation. It was a peculiarly rich, secretive environment, offering lush cover to the travellers.

Sitting at ease in the saddle, one hand supporting Filmoriel and the other resting on her lizard's scaly neck, Kharan never tired of looking around at the rich tints of green in the grass and bushes, the light shining through endless layers of leaves, the trees bending protectively over them against a broad ribbon of sky. Wet foliage brushed against them as they passed, and there was always the soothing sound of leaves rustling and streams bubbling over crystal beds.

A dreamlike mood settled over the tribe. Even Melkavesh was relaxed and not anticipating anything when they rounded a bend in the chasm and were confronted by an astonishing sight. The leaders stopped short in wonder, causing the column to bunch up behind them.

A huge pillar rose from the centre of the chasm, unquestionably the work of man though of incredible proportions. The stone of which it was made was like nothing Melkavesh had seen before; it was smooth and shiny, with rich blues, greens and reds blending together in a marbled pattern. The base of it fused with a plinth which had been partially reclaimed by soil and trees. Melkavesh stared at it for several seconds before she realised she was looking at the ankle of a giant statue.

Following the huge, sculpted limb upwards with her eyes, she saw that it rose vertiginously for some three hundred feet – then ended, abruptly, at the thigh. There was no second leg, no giant trunk and massive head to complete the marvellous figure, but there undoubtedly had been in ages past. A colossus had once stood across the ravine, like an awesome gateway to the heart of Kristillia. The air seemed to quiver

399

with loss, as if a vacuum existed where the statue by rights should stand.

Her U'adruil shifted impatiently beneath her, and she calmed it with a hand on its metallic-blue scales. After a long time she said softly, 'I wonder what happened to it?'

'Perhaps the Gorethrians destroyed it,' Kharan murmured beside her.

'Possibly. Unless it was the effect of time and nature. Let's go closer.'

The soil that had shored up against the plinth formed a gentle hill, and it was easy enough for the Mangorians to climb the slope and work their way past the colossal leg on either side. While they marched by, Melkavesh, Kharan and N'golem rode up to the very base of the statue and looked up in amazement at the huge, perfectly sculpted toes, the veins in the feet as thick as tree trunks.

'I thought my people skilled with stone,' said N'golem. 'But this surpasses even the greatest of Gholeth's temples.'

'I don't think even Gorethria itself has anything like this,' Melkavesh said quietly. A strange sense of time and destiny subdued her and her mind slid gently towards witch-sight as she caught oblique glimpses of other dimensions, lost stories and meanings. But she could discover nothing about the colossus itself. Or perhaps she was not really trying, because the very mystery of it was such an acute, haunting pleasure.

It also disturbed her. There must be a reason why she had not sensed it in advance – even relaxed, she should have known they were approaching it. It was many minutes before she could tear her eyes away, and when she did, it seemed the surroundings had changed in some indefinable way. The greens of the undergrowth seemed dimmer, the air smoky. At once she extended her sorcerous vision outwards in every direction, but she could sense nothing threatening. On the contrary, everything seemed too quiet.

'Be on your guard,' she said to the others, urging her lizard into a trot away from the statue and back to her place at the front of the column without further explanation. But as she rode on, the feeling of unease continued to nag at her.

Shadows danced across her mind until her head ached. She had been sure they were heading north, yet the points of the compass now ceased to make sense to her and she began to experience the uncomfortable sensation that the world had closed into a circle. Beyond the ravine, there was nothing but grey fog.

Two hours went by. Then they rounded a bend, and found the foot of the colossus ahead of them a second time.

They stopped in disbelief, and Melkavesh said, 'We can't have come in a circle. It's impossible.'

'What does this mean?' N'golem asked.

'I don't know.' Experimentally, she raised a glow of sorcery along her limbs. She had not lost her power, yet something was clouding her far-sight, and she could see no way out of the ravine. 'We will have to try a different way, going back, or climbing up the sides.'

As she spoke, she felt Kharan's grip on her arm. 'Melkavesh, look,' said the An'raagan in a strangled voice.

The creatures were invisible to her witch-sight, and therefore should not have existed, but physically they were undeniably real. All along the edges of the ravine, clinging to its steep sides, and scattered throughout the trees, were scores of cat-like animals the size of lions. In colour they ranged from silver-fawn to a deep, coppery red, with a dappled appearance as their coats caught the light at different angles. They had delicate, pointed faces and huge golden eyes, and the males had long manes. They were crouched as if to spring, their elongated pupils fixed on the tribe, quite motionless except for the slow flicking of their long, sinuous tails. Into the silence, one of the lizards let out a hissing squawk of fear.

No one, not even Melkavesh, had been aware of their noiseless approach, and now the tribe were surrounded.

'Lady Melkavesh, use your power to destroy them!' N'golem cried.

'No, don't! Don't hurt them,' Kharan responded by reflex. Her grip tightened on Melkavesh's elbow, until the Sorceress jerked herself free, irritated.

'Be quiet, both of you. I could kill or frighten them, but I won't,' she replied. 'Look at their eyes. They are intelligent, and we are on their territory. We've come to Kristillia in friendship – we can't attack the first creatures we see. So keep your people in check, N'golem, and don't let them harm the cats.'

Several minutes passed by, but the animals made no move to attack them. The U'adruils, however, grew more and more restless, so in the end Melkavesh cautiously signalled the column to move. As she had anticipated, the cats began to shadow them, padding softly all around them. They made no attempt to hinder the Mangorians, but were impossible to shake off. And still the geography of the area made no sense to Melkavesh, and she dreaded passing the colossus a third time.

Now she found she could just perceive the leopard creatures as faint shadows in her mind, and she had the impression that several had detached themselves from the pack and were moving swiftly towards the nearest division of the Kristillian army, the one she had been so careful to avoid. Straining to far-see, she found the mind-numbing fog beginning to clear, but too late; the army were moving, and a large number of horsemen had detached themselves from it and were riding towards them at speed.

In as calm a tone as she could muster, she said to N'golem and U'garet, 'I am afraid we will have more company soon. The Kristillian army are riding to meet us.'

'Can we not avoid them?' said N'golem angrily. 'You said –'

'I know what I said. Listen. The Kristillians have some power I know nothing about. I can't even feel it, but it's there. Somehow it has constrained us within this ravine, while the leopards – or whatever they are – have called the army upon us. It's too late to evade them, the best thing is to go and meet them in peace.'

'We have time to prepare an ambush,' U'garet muttered.

'In peace, I said!' Melkavesh replied sternly.

Barely an hour passed before a band of about a hundred

Kristillians came cantering towards them, mounted on stocky brown horses that had thick, arched necks and feathered heels. The men were dressed in tattered gear of leather and bronze, and they had tangled beards and long, reddish hair. As they approached, Melkavesh commanded her army to halt, and she noticed the cats falling back slightly and crouching down as if in anticipation. The men were bearing down swiftly with swords drawn, so it was with great apprehension that she urged her lizard forward to stand and face them alone.

Her courage paid off. Their Commander saw that she was unarmed, and he ordered his men to halt while he came forward to meet her, sheathing his sword. He was aged about fifty, handsome but for an overlarge nose with wide nostrils. His horse pranced under him but he re-strained it with one hand as he looked Melkavesh up and down.

'We thought your Emperor had given up,' he said sourly. He spoke Gorethrian, which was widely used in the more civilised parts of Vardrav. 'What will he try next?'

'I know I appear to be Gorethrian from my face, but I am nothing to do with them. These people with me are from Mangorad. We have come to Kristillia in friendship, to offer you our help.'

The man looked sceptical, and shook his head. Rough and battle-hardened as he was, Melkavesh sensed that he was a straightforward, good-hearted man, so the look of suspicion and hatred in his eyes was far more unsettling than it would have been in a Gorethrian. At once she realised she had underestimated what a disadvantage her face would be – indeed, she had probably underestimated the Kristillians themselves.

'I don't like this,' he said. 'I must warn you, lady, that I have another four hundred armed men to hand. If you try to overcome us, the moon leopards will attack you and our army will be upon you in no time. Now, I am taking you all prisoner, and I advise you not to resist.'

'We will come with you willingly, and I hope you will take

that as proof that we come as friends,' Melkavesh answered calmly. 'We are heading for Charhn.'

'Indeed you are, for that's where we're taking you!' the Commander snorted. 'Who are you, and what do you want there?'

'I will only explain my purpose to the Sovereign himself.'

He gave her a scornful look, and replied, 'You have a high opinion of yourself, Gorethrian. You can stay silent for all I care, because there are those in Charhn who will make you talk; but I can assure you here and now, the last person you'll be allowed to see is the King. Now, order your people to surrender their arms.'

N'golem was riding up beside her, exclaiming fiercely, 'Show them your power!'

Melkavesh turned on him, furious. 'N'golem, please be quiet. The slightest sign of aggression could ruin everything. You've been too long in the jungle, and you don't know how to co-operate with other races – it's time you learned. Tell them to lay down their spears.'

The tribe did as Melkavesh said and accepted their situation stoically. But there was an undercurrent of apprehension and disappointment, and she could only pray that an opportunity to restore their faith in her would occur very soon. As they moved off, her sorcerous vision cleared, her sense of direction returned, and whatever power had kept drawing them to the statue released them. The moon leopards – as the Commander had called them – dissolved away into the undergrowth. But she felt hemmed in, oppressed by the Kristillian soldiers surrounding them. Holding her head high and refusing to be disheartened, she said, 'They're only being cautious, N'golem. You can't blame them.'

The Mangorian glowered at her, not quite meeting her eyes, and said, 'My people will never forget that they came to Charhn as prisoners.'

Their first sight of Charhn was of a profusion of exquisite towers and spires crowning a vast hill that could be seen from miles around. Unlike Shalekahh's towers they were smooth and simple, with no elaborate decoration, yet they were perhaps more beautiful for that. Each was a different pastel colour: there were pearly blues and peaches, almond greens and delicate tints of rose. Every hue of rock crystal that Kristillia could yield had been lovingly employed to create a marvel that was a testimony both to the country's beauty and to the skill of its inhabitants. As they drew nearer, the colours changed with the light, shining against the sky like a pale rainbow within a prism. It was easy to see how the Crystal City had come by its name.

The towers formed Charhn's Inner City. The Outer City, which spilled down the sides of the hill, was more prosaic, a jumble of plain, square buildings made from white and creamy-grey quartz. They were low-roofed, cleanly built but quite unimaginative. It was as if the technology that produced the Inner City had been lost and never recaptured, no doubt due to centuries of subjugation by Gorethria.

Surrounding the hill on which Charhn stood was a chain of vast fells, rolling eastwards in shades of misty green towards distant mountains. Mineral-rich outcrops jutted from them, echoing the hues of the Crystal City, and lush woodland flowed between their peaks. To the West lay a tapestry of farmland.

It had taken twenty days to travel from the border to Charhn, most of that time as prisoners of the Kristillian army. Physically, they had no cause for complaint; they had been humanely treated and well fed, but it irked Melkavesh deeply that the glory of arriving in the city independently had been taken from her. During the journey she had done her best to make friends with the Commander and establish herself as his equal, but he would have none of it, and she had had to admit failure.

As they approached the city, most of the Mangorians were led off separately to an enclosure surrounded by a high, white wall. The U'adruils were confiscated and taken to a stockade. This left Melkavesh, Kharan, N'golem and U'garet alone and on foot, being led towards the city by a guard of twenty Kristillians, including the Commander. It was only then that the gravity of the situation hit both Melkavesh and Kharan, and they exchanged grim, speaking looks. Melkavesh experienced a shiver of helplessness, knowing that if she could get no-one to listen to her, the Mangorians were doomed to remain 'prisoners of war' indefinitely.

Charhn was surrounded by a wall built of huge quartz blocks, entered through a well-guarded gateway that was rimmed by a design of moons carved in the stone. Beyond it, Melkavesh and her companions were taken along a pale street that wound upwards to a large, square barracks built of ivory-grey rock. As they walked, she observed that the city had a certain air of untidiness that she had not anticipated; grass grew through cracks in the paving, saplings had sprung up at random between houses, and greyish drifts of silt – washed down the hill when it rained – had been left to stain the ground. Nevertheless, it possessed a pleasant and welcoming aura. Mature trees shaded the buildings, rustling in a gentle breeze. It was a warm, blue day, fresh from the previous night's rain, quite out of keeping with the grimness of Melkavesh's mood.

At the barracks, Melkavesh was separated from the others and taken into a room on her own.

'You will remain here until someone comes to question you,' said the Commander.

'Won't you wait with me?' she asked, in a last attempt to win him over.

'And tell them what a model captive you have been?

That's for you to tell them, lady. Not that I'd deny it. Incidentally, it doesn't matter that you would tell me nothing, my duty was only to bring you here. But as for those who'll question you, it *is* their business and you can be sure they'll extract it from you.' With that, he strode out, slamming and locking a heavy door.

Melkavesh walked round the room, brooding. It was obviously a guard room, not a cell. It was plain, with greyish quartz walls and floor, one square window, a table and two benches of scarred wood. Several plates and tankards bearing the remains of a meal had been left there, and the sight turned her stomach. The corners of the chamber were stacked with military gear – saddles, cloaks, bucklers and the like – and the place smelled of ale and old leather.

She leaned against the barred window and looked out at the street. With a sinking heart, she had to admit to herself that she had never felt lower or less confident. She was in no physical danger, indeed, she was probably safer now than she had been since she first set foot on Earth, and she could have escaped by sorcerous means at any moment she chose. Perhaps that was the problem. Her whole stay on Earth had been full of challenge and danger, and she had visualised only glory of her arrival in Kristillia. Now, here she was, and it had been such an anticlimax that she could have wept. To be ushered in like a commonplace captive, refused an audience with the King – she felt humiliated in such an oblique, intimate way that she could not even define it.

The fact was, all the sorcerous power in the world would not avail her now. These people were not Mangorians, to be frightened and bullied into submission by a display of supernatural strength. She knew instinctively that even the slightest show of power, made to impress them or establish her authority, would only alienate them. And as for escaping and rescuing Kharan and the others – she might as well make an open declaration of war. She could only win the Kristillians over by talking – but again, charisma and oratory would not help her. Only honesty would win them over. And what if they did not want to listen?

It came to her then, like a leaden yoke being dropped on her shoulders, just how much she wanted and needed the Kristillians as allies. But what if they did not want her? They had their own strength. One Sorceress – a Gorethrian at that – might be the last thing they needed.

She had been so confident . . .

She pulled a bench out from the table and sat down on it, looking down at the faded material of her breeches. It was weeks since she had had more than a perfunctory wash, and she looked and felt filthy. If only she could have a bath, and know that at least she looked presentable, it might restore her spirit.

After about an hour the door opened and a man entered, flanked by two guards. He was not an officer, but had the look of a priest about him. He was tall and plump, clad in a dark orange vestment with an indigo chasuble over it. He was beardless, and his hair was hidden by a tall, dark blue headdress on which two tiny crescent moons were the only adornment. Like Irem Ol Thangiol, his skin had the marbled quality of brown, gold and ivory swirling together, so that he could be called neither dark-skinned nor fair.

She stood up, feeling an urge to kill him but forcing herself to be friendly and polite.

'Well, lady, I have heard much about you from Commander Istrel. My name is Irem Ol Melemen. He has informed me that your name is Melkavesh. A singularly unfortunate name for a Gorethrian trespassing within our borders.'

She closed her eyes briefly. Perhaps it was somewhat tactless to have taken the name of the very Empress who had first conquered Kristillia. 'If my name gives you offence, I apologise,' she said, masking her unease with calmness. 'I am only half-Gorethrian, and I have no connection with Emperor Xaedrek. I have come here in peace to help you against him. I would very much like to see your King, so that I can explain myself in full.'

The priest frowned, and she wondered what was going through his mind. Was she a spy? Was this some bizarre ploy of Xaedrek's to infiltrate Charhn? Did she want to assassinate the Sovereign?

'That is out of the question, of course. You can explain yourself to me,' he said in a kindly but reserved way that put her in mind of a physician.

'No, I cannot. It is so important that the King really ought to hear it himself.' Even as she said it, she knew she was wasting her time. She cursed herself. At present she felt she had as much charisma and persuasive power as a dead snake.

'You must know that the Mangorians are Xaedrek's enemies. They trust and follow me. We come to join Kristillia as allies against Gorethria.'

'There is little affinity between Mangorad and Kristillia. During the collapse of the Empire in Meshurek's time, they gave us barely any help at all in driving Gorethria out. However, this is confusing the issue. If you want to tell your story, lady, you had best tell it to me. You will have no other chance. We abhor the use of torture in Kristillia, but for intractable Gorethrian spies we have been known to make exceptions.'

The thought of torture did not worry Melkavesh. She could protect herself. It was purely the knowledge that Irem Ol Melemen was the only person she could talk to that changed her mind. With a sigh of resignation, she replied, 'Very well, I'll tell you everything. On one small condition.'

'What is that, lady?'

'Please let me have a bath and some clean clothes first.'

Ol Melemen looked surprised, but he agreed readily enough. So far she had seen no female soldiers, but two now appeared and took her to another room where they ordered a kitchen boy to fill a stone tub with hot water. Then they waited grudgingly while Melkavesh took as long as she possibly could to scrub herself down with fine, cleansing sand and swill the grime out of her hair.

The clothing they gave her was shabby by Gorethrian standards; a rough cotton robe, patchily dyed to a nondescript orange-brown. But it was clean and blissfully comfortable after the travel-worn riding gear, and as she ran her fingers through her hair to dry it, she began to feel human once again. The Kristillians were certainly not unkind to their prisoners; the two women brought her some bread, cheese and ale before they escorted her back to the guard room, and after that she felt far more able to put her case to Ol Melemen.

The table had been cleared, and he was sitting at it with his arms folded on the scarred top. He indicated for her to sit opposite, and said, 'I hope you are feeling better now, lady.' She noticed that even as he tried to concentrate his mind on questioning her, he could not take his eyes off her hair, which had billowed out in an extraordinary golden cloud.

'Much better, thank you,' she replied, absently raising her hand to toy with the chain round her neck.

'Then we shall start again. From the beginning. Who –' he suddenly stopped in mid-sentence, staring at the hand that was poised at her throat. Then, to her astonishment, he reached out and grabbed her wrist. The movement was so sudden that she could not even draw back, and had to restrain the instinctive flood of sorcery which rose to meet such an attack. Gripping her hand, he prised the talisman from her fingers so eagerly that she had to lean forward to prevent the chain from cutting into her neck. 'Where did you get this?' he cried.

It was the double moon talisman that Xaedrek's Kristillian prisoner had thrust on her when she had healed him. She had worn it ever since, finding that to touch it sometimes helped concentrate her thoughts. Apart from that, she had barely given it a moment's thought. 'A man named Irem Ol Thangiol gave it to me,' she began. 'He –' but at this, the priest leapt up and rushed from the room as if crazed, leaving her bewildered in mid-sentence.

An hour later, he returned with a second man who strode into the room with a strangely diffident air, frowning. He was about forty, thin and slightly stooped, with indifferent features and very grave, introspective eyes. He was clad in a wide-sleeved amber vestment, so Melkavesh took him for another priest. Without ceremony, Ol Melemen ordered her to remove the talisman and show it to the newcomer.

She obeyed and watched as he stared closely at it for several minutes, turning it this way and that, his eyes dark with a mixture of disbelief and wonder. Meanwhile, the priest bade her sit down and said, 'Now, you will explain yourself to both of us. Who are you?'

'I am a Sorceress,' she began, and proceeded to tell her

410

story straightforwardly, without any attempt at embellishment, just as she had once told Kharan. The words flowed naturally, and she was quite unaware that as she spoke the inherent power of her personality shone from her eyes and face without her willing it. Only when she came to the end, and saw that their eyes were riveted on her, did she realise that the intangible feeling of being in command – both of herself and others – had returned. 'I don't need to ask if you believe me,' she concluded softly. 'I offer you the secrets of sorcery. Freedom from Gorethria. At least, with all my heart I am going to try.'

The second man lowered his head. For a time, no one spoke. Then she noticed the convulsive shaking of his shoulders, but it still took her a moment to see that he was not laughing – but weeping.

'She has come at last,' he muttered. 'The enchantress has come at last.'

'And Irem Ol Thangiol,' said the priest. 'Is he alive?'

'I don't know. As I told you, he failed to escape, and I dared not hold out much hope for him,' she answered. 'What does your friend mean about the enchantress?'

'For centuries, the priesthood of Jaed and Fliya have predicted the coming of an enchantress who would bring the power of the moons into their own. It was never said that she would be Gorethrian. But it was said that she would arrive bearing the moon talisman of our land, entrusted to her by one of our brotherhood, and that was how we should know her.'

She looked at Ol Melemen in wonder. 'And you both knew Irem Ol Thangiol?'

There were tears in the priest's eyes, and he struggled for speech before replying, 'He was my brother.'

'And my friend. My friend,' said the second man. For a few moments, both men wept together, and although she felt almost embarrassed, excluded from their mutual grief, it moved her so deeply that she had to struggle not to weep with them.

Irem Ol Melemen recovered first, and said, 'I am sorry,

Lady Melkavesh, at the abrupt welcome you have received. We were not to know. You have shown great forbearance, when you might have wielded your power against us in anger. But by this, and by my brother's gift, and by your golden hair, we know that you speak truth.'

'And you can accept me – despite my face and my name?'

'Perhaps it is as it should be, that Ashurek's daughter, with the name of Melkavesh, should be the agent of the final destruction of the Empire.'

A shudder went through her at these words, but she suppressed it. 'There's a certain irony in it, I agree,' she said.

The other man raised his head and dried his eyes on the loose material of his sleeve. 'Believe me, Lady Melkavesh, if you knew the strength of this prophecy, you would know how very welcome you are to us now. Welcome, welcome.' And he suddenly jumped up and embraced her, leaving her rather startled. Standing back, he added, 'Naturally, you are no longer a prisoner. I will order your friends to be released at once, and the Mangorians to be housed in suitable barracks.'

'Thank you,' she replied, smiling with relief and elation. 'There's just one thing more.'

'Anything. Just ask.'

'Would you allow me to see the King now?'

'You are looking at him,' replied the man, with a grave bow of his head. 'I am King Afil Es Thendil, Sovereign Ruler of Kristillia.'

14

The Moonstone's Purpose

FALMERYN COULD not rest. The fire in his arm seemed to have spread right through his body, and he did not know whether it was due to amulin or fever, or both. From the caves he had been led up a series of staircases into an underground chamber, and thence into a hall inside a large monastic building. His arm had been bound, he had been given a nourishing drink and told to sleep – but until he saw Ferdanice again, he could not relax. Eventually the sages had tired of arguing with him, and one of them – a man called Cristanice – had taken him up to a small tower to talk to him until Ferdanice reappeared.

From the top of the tower he saw that he was now in the Circle of Spears. It was clear how it had got its name; it was a small, circular valley completely enclosed by brown cliffs that rose into points like spearheads. He could well believe that it was inaccessible except by the route through the caves. The valley glowed with rich colours in the sunlight, and there were black goats grazing and Kesfalian men and women working in the gardens below. The building itself, which stood in the centre, was two-storeyed with cloisters along each side and a russet-tiled roof. It might have seemed austere but for the stone of which it was built: a warm brown sandstone with tints of coral, silvery green and soft purple gleaming in its surface. As it was, the dwelling had a homely, peaceful atmosphere, which in normal circumstances Falmeryn would have welcomed.

The tower which stood at one end was circular, the top completely enclosed by a glass dome made of small panes ingeniously fitted together. It gave an unobstructed view of the whole sky, and the sages' interest in the heavens was obvious from the various optical instruments that were placed round the edges of the room. The floor was tessellated in subtle shades of umber, red and ivory, and the centre was dominated by a mechanism made of copper and dark blue metal; a complex arrangement of spheres and rings tilted at different angles to one another. It appeared ancient, grotesque, and utterly fascinating.

'Have you ever seen the like of this before?' Cristanice asked, patting one of the rings affectionately. He was a small, slightly plump man, dressed like Ferdanice in a plain brown robe, with two white orbs hanging one above the other round his neck. His face was round and small-featured, framed by braided black hair, and his eyes were tawny brown. He seemed friendly and talkative, but rather self-absorbed and indifferent to Falmeryn's anxiety. 'It is – I forget the word in Gorethrian. How ironic that we must communicate in the language of our enemies. Ah, I remember, it is an orrery. It shows the movement of the moons. Look, the small copper sphere in the centre represents the sun. The large globe is Earth, and the two small white ones are the moons, Jaed and Fliya. Now, watch . . .'

Cristanice began to turn a large handle, and the mechanism creaked into life. The Earth turned about the sun, the metal rings rotated and changed angles, and the twin moons orbited in graceful, precise phases. A rhythmic, penetrating vibration hummed in the bones of Falmeryn's skull, the same vibration he had noticed while in the maze with Raphon. The dance of the spheres was intriguing, but not enough to take his mind from thoughts of Ferdanice and the Lady of H'tebhmella.

Presently Cristanice stilled the handle, and let the orrery creak to a halt. 'Well, what think you?'

'It's fascinating. Did you build it yourself?'

'Heavens, no,' the sage chuckled. 'It is very old, and

414

demands constant attention to maintain it. Daily burnishing with seed-oil, adjustment of the gearing mechanisms, realignment . . .'

'It must be a lot of work.'

'It is, but I could not wish for a pleasanter duty. I pride myself on its accuracy, and it is dearer than a child to me. The precise phases of the moons mean everything to our studies. Now, are you sure you are well enough to endure my chatter? Won't you sit down, at least?'

'No, it's all right,' Falmeryn said, moving restlessly round the dome. 'I must see Ferdanice. There's a lot I need to ask him.'

'He'll be here in due course,' said the sage offhandedly. 'Ferdanice is the oldest and wisest of us, but he is a law unto himself, I'm afraid.'

Falmeryn turned to him and asked with a touch of desperation, 'Do you know what he wants with me and Raphon – and why he is fighting with the Lady of H'tebhmella?'

Cristanice raised his eyebrows. 'All I know is, you are Ferdanice's guest, and it is not for me to question his motives. As for the Lady, I did not see her. You are very feverish, and probably imagined it.'

Falmeryn felt angered at this glib reply, but forced himself to remain civil. He was certain that none of what had happened had been the fault of Cristanice or the other sages; Ferdanice alone was to blame, and it was only from him that he would get clear answers. Nevertheless, he must be able to learn something from Cristanice. He longed to know more about the stone from the moon Fliya which lay in the caves, but remembering that he had sworn not to speak of it, he tried a more oblique question. 'I've come here knowing very little about Kesfaline. What is the importance of the moons to you?'

The sage seemed pleased to talk about it. 'We believe that Jaed and Fliya govern our lives. It is a philosophy based not upon superstition but upon science. Do not the moons control the tides? Then how should they not influence us, who are tiny and more easily swayed than any ocean?'

'Do you mean you worship them?'

'No, no, we are not Kristillians, who see only the outside of things. We revere the moons, certainly, but we know they are not gods. We study them and they tell us everything – where to build, when to sow crops, when to harvest, and so forth. Perhaps this seems incomprehensible to you. But it is a gentle philosophy which brought peace and order to Kesfaline for centuries . . .' He moved to Falmeryn's side and gazed thoughtfully at the valley. 'Alas, as long as Gorethria rules, peace and order are lost. When they first conquered us – a thousand years ago or more – it was decided that our beliefs must be safeguarded, lest they be soured and destroyed by our oppressors. So, Kesfaline relinquished the philosophy by which she had lived, and this secret place was built, and the knowledge brought here to be preserved by a mere handful of us.'

'But you were free of Gorethria for a few years, weren't you?'

'Ah, but the moons told us it would not last and it's fortunate we heeded the signs. We must safeguard our philosophy a while longer yet . . .' He trailed off in thought for a few seconds, then said, 'Down in the caves, you know, there is some stone from Fliya itself.'

'How did it get there?' Falmeryn asked quietly.

'It was brought here out of idle curiosity by some irresponsible sage in a past millennium. While it remains on Earth, it is a danger. Truly, such things of power should be left well alone; the moons are to be revered, not violated. If only it could be returned whence it came, or at least taken to one of the Planes.'

'What is the danger?'

'It is connected with the birth of a power which I suppose could be called "sorcery". It was once predicted that a "Sorceress" would come here and ask the sages' advice about the power.' He smiled. 'If such a one exists, I doubt that she'd be bothered with us.'

'What would you have told her?'

'That although there may be a way for sorcerous power to

416

be born in the Earth, the price is far too great and she should leave things as they are. She would have understood.'

Just as Falmeryn was about to question him further, a new voice cut in, startling them both. 'You have said quite enough.'

Ferdanice was standing in the stairwell, his lemon eyes uncannily bright against his bronze skin. 'Cristanice, please leave us,' he said, climbing up into the room. 'I wish to speak to Falmeryn alone.'

'But we were having such an interesting conversation – oh very well, if you insist,' Cristanice exclaimed indignantly. He strode briskly round the orrery, pushed past the taller man, and vanished down the stairwell, leaving Falmeryn and Ferdanice staring gravely at each other.

'I am concerned for your health, Falmeryn, but as you insist on having this talk before you will rest, we had better get it over with.'

'I was on the point of trusting you,' he broke in angrily. 'But I can never put my faith in someone who is opposed to the Lady of H'tebhmella.'

'Don't be so hasty to condemn me.' The sage raised his hands in a placatory gesture. 'The Lady isn't right about everything.'

Falmeryn shook his head incredulously. 'You're not what you seem, Ferdanice. Cristanice said you're the oldest and wisest of the sages, but if he believes that, you've deluded them all. I don't think you're human at all. So what exactly are you?'

The sage looked skywards in exasperation, and exclaimed, 'I never thought, in choosing a pleasant, amenable Forluin-ishman, that I was going to have this trouble! Why did humans have to be cursed with brains?'

'I want an explanation,' Falmeryn persisted.

'Very well then,' he sighed. 'I am not a Kesfalian sage. I am a Guardian, and I have taken on this particular guise for convenience's sake. As you obviously realise, it was not Raphon who rescued you. It was I. Raphon was on Earth, and was just making his way to the Black Plane when I intercepted him. You happened to be nearby. The hounds had left you on the point of death, but I transported both you and the neman to the cave in the Guardians' domain where I healed you.'

In a sudden flash of memory, Falmeryn recalled waking in the cave and seeing a strange, gauzy grey figure seated by the bed. With a shiver, he realised that it must have been Ferdanice in his true form. Other things made sense now: the mysterious appearance of food and clothing, which only the Guardians could have effected. Estarinel had sometimes spoken of the Guardians, or Grey Ones – supernatural beings who strove to regulate the energies of the cosmos. They were neutral, capable of compassion but also of utter ruthlessness; to them, good and evil had little meaning except as disturbances of the energy flow through the Universe. His mouth dry, he asked, 'Why?'

'Raphon needed a companion to help him. You were in a particular place at a crucial time, which makes you a part of the events that are shaping themselves around Vardrav. Also, you are Forluinish, a race that proved its tenacity in the Quest of the Serpent. I thought if you did not know the Grey Ones were involved, it would avoid awkward questions.' He shrugged. 'I was wrong.'

'And you gave Raphon the lodestones by which to find our way here?'

'Yes. They should have delivered you straight here. Unfortunately, a miscalculation occurred, and you landed in Ungrem instead. There is always a risk of inaccuracy in these things.'

'Inaccuracy? Raphon almost died in that desert!'

'Ah, but he did not, because you were with him.'

'So, I was being used as kind of insurance against failure.' He folded his arms, nodding bitterly. 'And was it the Guardians who directed the janizons into danger, just so we could be brought to Kesfaline?'

'No harm was intended . . .'

'But it happened – whether through carelessness or deliber-

418

ate cruelty, it happened! People have died, I've been forced to kill someone, Raphon has suffered continuously –'

'Please, calm yourself. What you say may be true, but if it achieved its result – your arrival here, which incidentally I was able to effect by snatching you from those Gorethrian swords, you being within close range – then the means must be accepted and forgotten. You look horrified. I know we seem heartless to you, but the differences between good and evil are so vague, so subjective, that we can barely perceive them. The Grey Ones do not concern themselves with human morality; it is for humans to do that.'

'What Estarinel said about you is true,' Falmeryn said grimly. 'Cristanice was telling me about the stone you showed me in the caves. He said it was dangerous, and should be taken to one of the Planes. So is Raphon going to take it back to Hrunnesh?'

'Cristanice said too much. However, he and the other sages will be told that Raphon is taking the stone to the Black Plane, and that will keep them happy.'

'And what is the truth of the matter?'

'I can see there's no point in trying to hide anything from you, but again I ask you not to mention it to the others. The Sorceress of whom Cristanice spoke exists. The stone must be taken to her in Kristillia. You see, the death of the Serpent released energy which was essential for the Earth's survival, and for the balance of forces in the Universe to be re-established. I am speaking of the power which is oft-times described as "sorcery", although there is nothing "magic" about it: it is a very real energy that flows round and through the Earth. But the process is not yet complete. Something is obscuring the power, as if it is somehow . . . out of alignment with the Earth. The moonstone's purpose is to help the Sorceress balance the power and bring it to its full potential. There's nothing wrong in it, Falmeryn. On the contrary, it is essential for the natural evolution of the world.'

'If there's nothing wrong, why was the Lady of H'tebhmella trying to stop you?'

'Nothing more than fear of change. This vague "danger"

that Cristanice and the others predict is only that: the Lady, existing in a timeless domain, has more reason to fear it than most. It doesn't really matter, but it is annoying, and makes subterfuge necessary. And in case you are concerned for her, I can assure you I did not harm her, only requested her to return to H'tebhmella – which she did.'

'What is the change she fears?'

Ferdanice laughed. 'She doesn't even know. The Grey Ones themselves don't know. That is the whole point: the Guardians are outside the power. The Sorceress is within it, therefore it is up to her to discover what is wrong and how to put it right. The fabric of the moons will play an essential part. Which was why Raphon and I originally brought it to Earth some three thousand years ago. It lay dormant in the Earth until the Serpent died. Now power begins to stir within it, and it must be put to use. The stone of Jaed is already in Kristillia. The stone of Fliya is the missing key. Now, Falmeryn, does this still sound so terrible to you? Won't you help me, and take the moonstone to Kristillia?'

Falmeryn turned away and stared at the orrery, thinking. Eventually he said, 'I'm still sure it's wrong. The Lady is known for wisdom and compassion, the Guardians are not. It is her I trust. I'm sorry, I won't do it.'

'As you wish. I said we wouldn't force you,' said Ferdanice casually. Then, in a heavier tone, he added, 'Raphon shall go instead.'

'But you know perfectly well how much Raphon is suffering on Earth. If he stays here much longer he'll die!'

'He'll survive long enough for the purpose,' Ferdanice replied levelly, fixing Falmeryn with his pale, disturbing eyes. 'The task must be completed, and Raphon expects to do it.'

'That's sheer cruelty. It's wicked.'

'Well, if that's how you feel, Falmeryn, there is one simple answer. Agree to go yourself, and I'll let Raphon return to the Black Plane immediately.'

At once Falmeryn saw how he had let himself be manoeuvred into this. All along, he and Raphon – and other innocent people – had been manipulated by the Grey Ones,

420

but there was no escape from it just in arguing. He felt trapped, and still the amulin lurched in him like a wild sea in which it was impossible to judge right from wrong. Eventually he let out a slow, bitter sigh and said, 'This is what you wanted all along, isn't it? All right. I'll take the stone – in exchange for Raphon's safety.'

'Excellent,' Ferdanice said brightly. 'I knew we'd reach an understanding. By the way, if you consider betraying my trust en route, don't, because the Grey Ones will be watching you.' Falmeryn did not answer, but leaned his forehead against the dome and stared down at the peaceful valley. The glass was painfully cold against his burning skin. The Guardian went on, 'One small thing to console you: as I said, we do not concern ourselves with good and evil. However, we are not indifferent to the powerful feelings in Vardrav against Emperor Xaedrek of Gorethria. He has discovered a false method of theurgy which corrupts the power, but the Guardians themselves can do nothing to prevent it. However, once armed with the moonstone, the Sorceress may discover a way to defeat him.'

Falmeryn looked up sharply, more questions thronging into his mind. If that was true, it changed everything, and again he felt the sliding away of conscience he had experienced when fighting Oromek. Did anything else matter, when there was a chance of stopping Xaedrek doing to others what he had done to Kharan? But the fever was overcoming him, and he lost the strength to speak. He swayed, and Ferdanice caught his arm in a fatherly way, and smiled. 'Now, come down to the sleeping quarters and rest. It will be many days before you begin the journey, so until then I want you to feel completely at home in the Circle of Spears.'

In a cell deep in Shalekahh's dungeons, Xaedrek withstood the repulsive pale glow emanating from the deformed humans for as long as he could. Then, with perfect outward calm, he beckoned to Amnek and Ah'garith and said, 'A word with you both, outside.'

Once in the corridor, he pulled the door of the cell shut, but it did not quite obscure the sickly pinkish glare that continued to flicker round its edges. 'Well, Ah'garith, that was interesting, to say the least,' said Xaedrek. 'Perhaps you would now explain what it is.'

'Of course, Sire,' Ah'garith hissed, grinning. Her silvery, luminescent quality was more marked than ever; the ghostly demon-form overlaid on her human body was quite distinct, and Xaedrek's unease would have turned to outright fear, had he not kept himself severely in check. 'The amulin increased my perception and power, enabling me to create a lens on a huge scale. It draws the power directly from the Earth, without need of a machine. However, the power needs a focus, and that is provided by a link of three humans lying on the lens. The energy they absorb can be used in two ways: an ichor can be extracted from them to make a substance similar to amulin, but with far greater powers. Or the humans themselves can be unleashed in battle. Imagine it, Sire – an army not of men, but of human weapons!'

'An army of monsters,' said Xaedrek abruptly. Amnek and the woman-demon both sensed his disapproval and looked at him, startled. 'An army of monsters, instead of decent Gorethrian soldiers? Can you see it, Amnek? What would our friend Baramek say?' His tone was acidic, and Ah'garith began to look flustered.

'Sire – Sire, the intention is not to replace the army, merely to supplement it,' she said quickly. 'Once you see how powerful they can be in battle, you will understand –'

'No,' the Emperor interrupted. 'I don't care how powerful they are. We are not a weak nation, Ah'garith. We do not need to descend to such a level of depravity to maintain our strength. The day we do, I think we should admit defeat.'

Amnek had never heard Xaedrek say such a thing before, and stared at him in astonishment. 'Your Majesty, may I suggest that you do not come to a hasty judgement over this. Every source of power we can call on is to our advantage –'

'Not this one, Amnek,' Xaedrek replied, quietly but adamantly. 'I believe in giving my soldiers a degree of their own hyperphysical power in battle. I do not believe in sending out pitiful abominations to fight for me. It is un-Gorethrian.'

'I just do not understand you,' Amnek exclaimed. 'You do not scruple to use any number of humans in the amulin process, or to experiment on Irem Ol Thangiol. How is this different?'

'Yes, Sire. Why choose this moment to become so squeamish?'

'It is not squeamishness.' Xaedrek rubbed his chin, and his eyes were very thoughtful, as dark as garnets. 'How can I explain it? There is a certain dignity in simple suffering. When I see an enemy staring at me from defiant eyes, and I look back, we understand each other. However much pain he is in, we both know that if the positions were reversed he would deal with me in a similar way, and so we are equal. But this is different. This deformation of mind and body is an utter corruption of everything I have set out to make Gorethria, and I will not tolerate it. Do you understand me, Ah'garith?'

'To be honest, Sire, no, I don't,' she replied sulkily.

'It's all very well you condemning this out of hand,' Amnek added, 'but you have nothing to offer in its place. We must conquer Kristillia by any means we can. As long as she remains free, she is a threat to the very stability of the Empire –'

'You do not need to tell me that, Amnek.' Xaedrek raised a hand to quiet him. 'As it happens, I do have something to offer. I told you earlier that I had a new idea in mind.'

'And can you tell us what it is?'

'Machines, Amnek. Great battle machines which will crush our enemies as cleanly and swiftly as a man crushing a fly. I do not know exactly what form they will take, but that is secondary. The important thing is to prove the theory. If hyperphysical energy can be instilled into humans, surely it can also be used to power mechanical devices, and on a much greater scale? Then what need would we have of your monsters, Ah'garith?'

'I've nothing to say against your theory, Sire,' she replied.

'Good. Then you will not object to ceasing this experiment at once and killing those three wretched humans.'

Ah'garith did not reply, only rubbed her hands together and looked up at him with silvery, malevolent eyes. Then she went back into the cell and emerged a moment later, holding a phial of whitish liquid. 'But there is this, Sire.'

Xaedrek took the phial from her and inspected it. The ichor was as thick as cream, shot through with pinkish veins which writhed as if they had a life of their own. When turned to the light, it showed an unpleasant fluorescence. 'You say this has been extracted from their veins?'

'Yes, and it has greater power than amulin. Take it, Sire, and you will see what I mean at once.'

The demon sounded altogether too eager, and Xaedrek had no intention of doing as she said. He closed his fingers around the phial and asked, 'What power does it bestow?'

Ah'garith paused to give emphasis to her answer, a gleam of triumph in her eyes. Then she said, 'Far-sight.'

Xaedrek was careful not to react openly, but inside he felt that what he had thought was solid stone under his feet was about to split into a yawning black hole. 'Indeed?'

'Far-sight, Sire,' the demon went on eagerly. 'Have you not said to me, many, many times, how much you need the gift of far-sight? Drink the ichor in place of amulin, and you will become as powerful as Melkavesh. You will have no need to spy through second-hand, inefficient mediums such as the eagle. Your percipience will become as great as hers, if not greater. You will be a true Sorcerer –'

'That's enough. You've made your point.'

'In that case, Sire, do not tell me to cease my experiments. Do not tell me you don't need the substance, that you would rather show mercy to a few miserable humans than receive the gift you have craved for years. You asked for far-sight; I have delivered it. Do you still condemn my "monsters"?'

For once, Xaedrek could not find an answer. He looked at the ghostly, argent figure of Ah'garith, the tall, stooped shadow that was Amnek, and suddenly he felt sickened by the way they were leaning towards him, anticipating his reaction and trying to draw it from him like two vampires. He became aware of the glare from the cell pulsing like a heartbeat, outlining their forms with a blood-tinged aureole. The slick grey walls of the corridor seemed to be leaning at strange angles, and the combination of stenches became so overwhelming that his head swam. He had to escape. Still clutching the phial of ichor, he turned abruptly and strode away without a word, leaving his companions startled and aggrieved behind him.

Ah'garith and Amnek looked at each other. Then Amnek said, 'I blame Melkavesh for this foolish caprice that has possessed him. He will soon come out of it. Meanwhile, don't worry. If he will not help you, Ah'garith – I will.'

'I am so sorry, Ol Thangiol,' said Anixa. 'I was mad to think we could escape. Yes – yes, I *was* mad. With fear.'

'There is no reason for you to be sorry, dear Anixa,' the Kristillian replied softly. 'Nothing can make my situation worse than it is. It is I who should apologise to you. If not for me, this would never have happened, you would still be safe –'

'Hush,' she said, putting a finger on his lips. 'I am afraid, but I can be strong. I feel that we have met for a reason. There are things in this world that even Xaedrek does not understand, and I believe our being together will bring him grief in the end. Not triumph.'

They were sitting close together on the edge of the bed in Meshurek's chamber, talking in low voices as they did their best to allay each other's fears. Irem Ol Thangiol's arm encircled Anixa's slight shoulders, her dark head was nestled against his chest, and their hands were clasped together. Next to him, she looked as small as a child. Indeed, they were both like children; a brother and sister, perhaps, being unjustly punished by callous parents. Xaedrek, watching them from an adjoining chamber through what they took to be a mirror, was not so much moved by their conversation as nauseated.

He had now watched them intermittently for a couple of days, but so far they had said nothing that was of any value to him. Nevertheless, the heightened intuition that amulin provided kept hinting to him that Anixa knew something about Melkavesh. His only recourse was to interrogate her directly.

As when he had first questioned her, she began by maintaining a stubborn silence. But he had not underestimated her feelings for Irem Ol Thangiol. A simple threat to inflict some unspeakable torture on him was all it took to force the truth from her reluctant lips. Presently, the remaining mysteries about Melkavesh had been cleared up: how she had first infiltrated Shalekahh, and who had sheltered her. But in discovering these things, Xaedrek felt no sense of satisfaction whatsoever, only greater unease.

'You realise that you have committed an act of gross treason,' he told her offhandedly, already preoccupied with his own thoughts. 'I will have to decide how to punish you.'

'I may have been wrong to shelter her, Your Majesty, but not for the reasons you think,' was Anixa's disconcerting reply. 'The Kristillians say she will defeat you. My own people say she is a danger to us all. I have many reasons for hating you, Emperor Xaedrek, but I cannot be sure that the one I have sheltered is any better.'

Later, Xaedrek sat alone in his private office, brooding. The phial of white liquid stood on the desk before him, and he stared fixedly at it, finding it the focus of his dark considerations.

He had no doubt that it would bestow him with witch-sight, as Ah'garith had promised, but he also perceived that it was a trap. If he took the ichor, it would put him in the Shanin's power. His own will would be lost, and Ah'garith would have what she had desired ever since she had first come to him. Yet the temptation was still hard to resist . . . He had planned to send Anixa – whom Melkavesh knew and trusted – to spy for him in Kristillia, relaying what she learned through Ol Thangiol's mind as the eagle had done. If he simply gave in and drank the liquid, all that trouble could be avoided, and

nothing would be hidden from him. He had dreamed of such omniscience; never thinking it might have too high a price. After all his care, must he end up like Meshurek – a wretched instrument of the demon?

With these unpleasant thoughts vied another, a revelation from Anixa that he had never foreseen.

Kharan was still alive.

Objectively, he could only think of her and Melkavesh as enemies, plotting Gorethria's downfall as they travelled to Kristillia. Yet overlaid on that vision was another, more persistent image; Kharan as she used to be – warm, affectionate, unafraid of him. But when Varian had opened her eyes to what she saw as Xaedrek's barbarity, the Kharan of old had ceased to exist, and Xaedrek had felt that what was left was only a shell which must be destroyed. And yet, impossibly, she had evaded him and survived. He could not put a name to the feelings this knowledge stirred. Had he believed in such things, he would have said it was an immeasurably bad omen.

Then there was Melkavesh herself. He could not forget the time she had captured the eagle, and he had seen her eyes shining eerily from Irem Ol Thangiol's sockets. With that disturbing memory came others; Melkavesh moving through the halls of the palace at his side as if she belonged there. Dreams of flying with her through a void, while two spheres of rock drifted overhead, heavy with unrevealed meaning. Her hair . . . Perhaps he had made a misjudgement. If he had not been so obdurate with her, she might not have fled to Kristillia; it might have been worth sacrificing a few principles to keep her on his side, but now it was too late.

Between Melkavesh, Kharan's escape and the treacherous ichor, his confidence in himself had been badly shaken. He had never thought himself invulnerable, but more had gone wrong or escaped his notice than he could tolerate. Despite everything, he refused to be daunted; at least he was aware of the danger, and by pausing to reflect on it, he would grow wiser and stronger.

It all came back to one thing; what mattered most was Gorethria. On one side was Ah'garith, lusting for its destruction out of sheer malice; on the other was Melkavesh, misguided by ridiculous ideas of what she thought was 'right'. Xaedrek could not allow anyone to threaten the most precious and noble country on Earth. Great sorcerous battle machines would be created and would roll towards Kristillia, Melkavesh would be defeated, and Gorethria's future safeguarded.

But for the present, the demon Ah'garith was his greatest concern. The problem was not just that he needed her power. Even if he could have practised sorcery without her, he did not know how to destroy her; and as long as she existed, neither he nor Gorethria would ever be truly safe. Once he had been convinced that no problem was too great for him to solve, but now he was not so sure. This one remained stubbornly beyond him.

There was, however, one matter he could deal with. *Detained on the Emperor's orders* was a phrase that even the highest in Gorethria dreaded to hear, because the recipient could expect to vanish into Shalekahh's dungeons without trace. The Emperor was accountable to no one; no questions would be asked. Moving to a side-table, Xaedrek opened a large volume of records and looked up the names of the four incompetents who had failed to deliver Kharan to her intended execution. Then he went to summon a chamberlain and arrange for them to be duly detained.

Melkavesh, in contrast to Xaedrek, had never been more confident.

News of her arrival had spread swiftly through Charhn, and there was an electric current of excitement in the city. Everyone wanted to see the strange blue-skinned army, everyone craved a glimpse of the golden-haired enchantress who had come to their aid against Gorethria. The sun shone on Charhn's pastel towers, and they reflected the light joyously back at the sky, like a visible distillation of the optimism

that gripped the city. Melkavesh sailed on the feeling like a hawk on the wing, euphoric.

On the third day after their arrival, King Afil Es Thendil took Melkavesh and Kharan up to the Inner City. They left the Royal House – a rose-red mansion surrounded by gardens and trees – and climbed up towards the white wall that enclosed the ancient towers. With them went the priest, Irem Ol Melemen, several courtiers, and the Queen, Afil An Mora. The clothes they wore would not have been considered fit for a servant in Shalekahh; simple robes and tabards of cotton, dyed in dull shades of orange, blue and green. But they were clean and comfortable, and elegant enough in appearance even for royalty. The party were accompanied by a number of guards, bearded men wearing leather breeches, cloaks, and a profusion of heavy bronze ornaments.

The guards kept a respectful distance as they walked through the open gateway into the Inner City. The street changed from rough, glittering quartz to marble, so highly polished that its surface was mirror-like. Close to, the build-ings were no less impressive than from a distance; if anything, they were more beautiful, because all the subtleties of shading and veining could be seen in their softly coloured walls. So cleverly had they been built that the seams between individual blocks of stone could not be seen. Each house, hall, tower and spire appeared to have been carved from one giant semi-precious stone.

The city had an aura that was timeless, soothing, yet weird. It took Kharan a while to realise that this strangeness was due to the fact that there was not so much as a grass blade growing anywhere. The slabs underfoot were so tightly fitted together that even weeds could not force their way between them. Yet time and neglect had made some inroads into its perfection; as the initial impact wore off, she began to notice that the marble paving was cracked in places, and most of the buildings had doors missing. Underlying the transcendent beauty was an air of emptiness and dereliction that made her feel rather sad. Whenever they walked over a crack, the King would poke at it with his foot and shake his head regretfully.

'What a country this once was,' he said. The Queen was on his right, her arm linked through his, Melkavesh on his left and Kharan next to her, carrying Filmoriel. 'I dream of it, the glory of a thousand years ago. Imagine the hands and minds that built this city. How did they do it?' He scratched thoughtfully at his beard, then walked over to a pale silvery-mauve tower and ran his hand along the ledge of an arched window. A piece of stone came away and he crumbled it between his fingers. 'Look at this! It will fall down unless something is done to save it. This is what I want to restore to Kristillia, the wisdom that enabled us to create such beauty. I have spent the whole of my reign trying to preserve the Inner City. It was in a worse mess than this – birds nesting in the towers, cats and wild animals roaming about, markets held in the streets as if this were no different from any other part of Charhn. I put a stop to that, tidied it up and began restoration work upon it. But it is difficult. All able-bodied citizens are needed in the army, and we have lost the tech-nology to make effective repairs.'

'What happened to that wisdom?' Melkavesh asked.

'Gorethria, of course,' the King replied bitterly. 'The Empress Melkavesh. Our knowledge made us dangerous, therefore they had to strip it all away. The Inner City was once a treasure-house of learning. It was looted, everything taken, all our remaining wisdom suppressed until it was lost entirely. The architecture of the Outer City is the best we've managed since then. All they left us was our religion. Most generous of them. Yes, they left us that.'

They were strolling past a temple, its doorway guarded by the graceful statue of a woman on one side, a man on the other. Each held a large, white globe of rock.

'The temple of Jaed and Fliya,' said the Queen. It was the first time Melkavesh and Kharan had actually heard her speak, and they both looked at her in surprise. She was extremely beautiful, with a long mane of dark bronze hair, yet her beauty was of a strangely cold, unattractive kind. She was half-Kesfalian, the result of a royal alliance between Kesfaline and Kristillia, which accounted for her darker

colouring and quiet nature.' The male figure represents Jaed, whom we think of as ''our'' moon. Fliya belongs more to the Kesfalians.'

'Therefore you can lay claim to them both,' said Afil Es Thendil, patting her hand and giving her a fleeting smile.

'You must not think we worship the moons in a super-stitious way,' An Mora continued. 'Rather, we revere them. We see the Earth as their child. As the King says, this belief was all the Gorethrians left us.' Her tone was emotionless and formal, yet Melkavesh sensed in it the deep-seated hatred of Gorethria that pervaded everything the Kristillians said and did. While she understood it perfectly, she still found it unnerving.

'We first managed to throw Gorethria off some twenty-five years ago,' said the King. 'You know all about it, of course. Things became chaotic under Meshurek's rule, his army lost its strength, and we drove them out. If only we had crushed them totally while we had the chance! But a strange time of darkness came upon us, and we thought the end of the world had come. We prayed to the moons, and eventually it passed.'

'That was the time of the Serpent's death,' Melkavesh put in.

'Yes, of course, you told us about that yesterday.' He frowned, as he did habitually. He seemed a rather nervous, introspective man who took his responsibilities extremely seriously and never stopped worrying about whether he would prove equal to them. 'Kristillia had been allowed to keep its monarchy over the centuries – though in a much weakened form – but my father had proved too rebellious for Emperor Ordek, who had him slain.'

Ordek XIV had been Melkavesh's grandfather, and if the King had stopped to dwell on this, it could have made their relationship very uncomfortable. Fortunately it seemed to have slipped his mind for the time being, and he went on, 'Since then, I had been kept in hiding, but as soon as Gorethria was defeated, I was crowned. I was only a boy, but I already knew my duty – to ensure that my country never falls to Gorethria again. Never.'

'But Xaedrek is so strong, no one else has managed to resist him. How have you held out?'

'Xaedrek?' Es Thendil spat out the word like a mouthful of venom. 'To be honest, I am not sure. Desperation, determination, faith, what you will. All I know is that a great strength has possessed us, against us which even his wickedness cannot prevail.'

All this time Melkavesh had been gently probing the City with her higher senses, trying to unlock its secrets. But like the colossus and the moon leopards, it seemed veiled to her. Nothing was clearly perceptible; she saw empty interiors, libraries stripped of books, statues crumbled to dust on rose-red or beryl-green floors. The truth was there some-where, but always sliding out of the edge of her vision like countless pale grey shadows jostling and whispering just below the level of hearing. Charin kept its secrets.

Irem Ol Melemen, walking just behind them, said, 'We believe it is Jaed's blessing. We have a rather doubtful legend that there is actually some rock from the moon Jaed itself within the Inner City, and that is what protects us. No doubt if it was ever here, the Gorethrians took it along with everything else! At any rate, it has never been found. I do not believe it, but it is a pleasant story.'

'The problem is that it is not enough just to keep Gorethria at bay,' said the King. 'Unless we destroy Xaedrek totally, he is bound to win in the end.'

'I agree,' said Melkavesh.

'But how are we to defeat him? It seems impossible.'

'That's why I am here. You're right, Your Majesty, Kristil-lia can't do it alone. What I need to do is establish a head-quarters from which we can summon other nations to our flag. It may be inconceivable for them to form armies within their own countries, but it won't be so difficult for them to sneak out under Gorethria's nose and join us. A vast army, drawn from the whole of Vardrav, is what will defeat Xae-drek.' Her eyes shone as she spoke, and her conviction filled the party with a feverish excitement and hope.

But Kharan again felt a knot in her stomach. She under-

stood why Melkavesh had been so adamant about preserving the colour of her hair; it was symbolic, something that proved that she was first and foremost a Sorceress, not a Gorethrian, a standard to rally and inspire all of Vardrav. The whirlwind was gaining momentum, and while Kharan felt caught up in the excitement, she also felt herself to be outside it, an observer who saw what the others could not.

In a quiet voice, she said, 'What about your School of Sorcery, Mel?'

'There will be a School of Sorcery one day,' Melkavesh replied, smiling. 'But it can't exist until the threat of Gorethria is removed. One thing at a time. Besides, I've only got one pupil at present.' She made to touch Filmoriel on the forehead, but Kharan stepped out of her reach and turned away, angry.

It was not the first time she had sensed that possessiveness in Melkavesh, as if she thought Filmoriel as much her own as Kharan's. She tried not to show her resentment, because she would never forget that her daughter owed her very life to Melkavesh. All the same, neither that nor Filmoriel's supposed sorcerous power made her Melkavesh's property – or anyone's.

It was strange, Kharan thought as she walked slowly along-side the others, that she had not anticipated the repercussions of a return to civilisation. All through the journey – even after she had grown hardened to it – she had dreamed of having clean clothes, hot water and decent food. Now she had it all, plus a bed so soft that she could not even get to sleep in it. Physically it was blissful; emotionally, it meant nothing. The material comforts served only to remind her of Shalekahh, and that inevitably brought back memories of Falmeryn. Severed from the day-to-day difficulty of simply surviving, the pain she had suppressed for months was flooding back.

She had never imagined that she had got over him. There were some things, she thought, that were impossible to get over. Someone like Falmeryn would never be found again; indeed, there was no one else like him. If he had been with

433

her in the midst of these strange events, he alone would have made everything seem sane and tolerable. But he was gone, gone, and she missed him desperately and knew she would go on missing him for the rest of her life. She had to stay alive for Filmoriel's sake, and the ache of loss had to be endured.

Lost in these thoughts, she found she had wandered ahead of the others, so she turned and waited for them to catch her up. As she did so, she was astonished to find the King gazing at her with a lingering, unmistakable look. She was taken aback and avoided his eyes, embarrassed. Once she had relished such appreciation and taken full advantage of it, but those days had ended the moment she had met Falmeryn. She could not even understand it; she was thin from the journey, her face drawn and her hair chaotically untidy, yet he seemed to sense a warmth about her that the beautiful Queen Afil An Mora did not possess.

Hugging Filmoriel to her, she fell into step beside Melkavesh and tried to make herself as inconspicuous as possible. But throughout the visit to the Crystal City the King's eyes followed her so often that it seemed impossible that the Queen had not noticed.

That evening, Melkavesh sat in her room in the rose-coloured royal mansion, leaning on a windowsill but not really seeing the trees and rooftops of the Outer City below her. She was thinking of the vision she had seen in the swamp, the three malformed victims of Ah'garith's necromancy. Presently she would far-see and discern what was happening in Shalekahh; but that took energy, and at the moment she was too tired to do more than sit and let images wash over her.

Almost at once, an involuntary and unwelcome picture came into her mind; an infinite black marsh where lost souls wandered, trapped in pale bodies which were a mockery of human forms. Hideous birds flapped overhead, uttering soul-destroying screams. The atmosphere was of distilled evil, bleak and sterile, swallowing every emotion until only

despair and self-loathing were left. It was a vision of hell, and in it she wandered her mother, Silvren, thin and pale as death but reaching out to touch the deformed humans with nothing but compassion on her face. . . .

Melkavesh gasped, and shook the vision off. She had seen a nightmarish place that had been destroyed with the Serpent: the Dark Regions, home of the Shana, where Silvren had once been imprisoned. She wanted to forget what she had seen, but she forced herself to reflect upon it for a few minutes. The vision had had a purpose. . . Again she heard Ashurek's voice, as if in a dream, saying, *It cannot be suffered to live.* The demon should have died with its comrades, and as long as it lived it would strive to reduce the world to desolation and all humans to the same pitiful state. Its warping of those three men was just the beginning.

But to fight it, she needed more power, and she was still no closer to discovering what was restricting her use of sorcery. The centre of the sun remained dark. On Ikonus, everything had seemed so straightforward, limpid as glass. Here, all seemed shadowy and multi-layered, her Oath too easy to break and sorcery itself full of paradox and pain. Outwardly, she was confident – but inwardly, she wondered if she would ever find the answer.

There had been other visions; Ashurek, Silvren, Xaedrek and all her Gorethrian ancestors, wrenching her first one way, then another, as if they were trying to tear her apart between them. Whatever she felt for Gorethria, it was too late to withdraw from the path she had set herself on, and she knew she must use her faith in herself to rise above such conflicts. Her purpose in Kristillia was not in doubt. What really perplexed her was the unrelenting image of the two moons, gentle orbs that had lit the world for millennia with their benevolent light, impassive and unremarkable. Yet there was nothing impassive about the vast spheres of rock that haunted her dreams, emanating a heavy radiance that thrust her painfully towards oblivion in a dark ocean. The vision of the cold waves swallowing her made her shiver.

And after that, there was always the child with plum-red hair and the little bird perched on her hand . . .

She knew now that the child was Filmoriel.

It was all for a reason. There was a puzzle to be solved which would unlock the secret of sorcery, and she was in the mood to face the task with joy, not dread. It was her destiny, the reason she had come to this world. Everything had its part to play in shaping the nature of the Earth, the Serpent, the three Planes, the blackbird Miril herself. Now it was the turn of Jaed and Fiya.

'Melkavesh?' The voice interrupted her trance, making her jump. 'Can I come in?'

'Of course, you don't have to ask,' she replied, smiling.

Kharan, carrying the tiny infant in her arms, walked over to her and leaned on the windowsill, looking out at the white roofs of Charhn below them. 'You seemed so lost in thought, I didn't want to interrupt.'

'No, I don't mind. Actually, I'd rather talk.' She pushed her golden hair back from her dark face and stretched languidly. 'Well, how do you like Krisillia? Did I not promise I'd get you here in one piece? Two, counting the baby.'

Kharan smiled half-heartedly. 'It's a lovely country and I'm very impressed at the way you've won everyone over to your side. Not that I didn't believe you could do it. It's just that I never expected the reality of it to be so breathtaking. There's no stopping you, is there? I feel quite sorry for Xaedrek.'

'Well, false sorcery cannot hope to compete with true sorcery, and I think I'm very close to discovering what is wrong with the power and setting it free . . .' She continued to talk elatedly for several minutes while Kharan listened in silence, picking bits of loose stone from the windowsill and crushing them to powder with her fingernails.

Eventually she turned to Melkavesh and said, 'Mel, can't you see the reality of what you're doing? You make it sound so noble and exciting, like a rebirth.'

'That's what it is, in a way. That's why I'm here, to aid the birth of sorcery. Filmoriel is just the beginning.'